TRIAL AND ERROR

DI FRANK MILLER TITLES

CRASH POINT

SILENT MARKER

RAIN TOWN

WATCH ME BLEED

BROKEN WHEELS

SUDDEN DEATH

UNDER THE KNIFE

TRIAL AND ERROR

OLD SCHOOL – short story

TRIAL AND ERROR

John Carson

Copyright © 2017 John Carson

John Carson has asserted his rights under the Copyright, Designs and
Patents Act 1988, to be identified as the author of this work.

All characters in this publication are fictitious and any resemblance to real persons, living or dead, is purely coincidental.

All rights reserved.

This one is for the real Jeni Bridge

TRIAL AND ERROR

PROLOGUE

The twin barrels of the shotgun slammed against Hazel Carter's forehead.

'Welcome to the party, bitch,' the man said. He was dressed smartly, not somebody you would look twice at in the street. Unless you looked into the hard eyes.

'They'll storm this place if you shoot me. If I die, you're next.' Brave words, but Hazel didn't feel brave. The armoured vest she was wearing wouldn't do much good when the shotgun was going to blow her head off.

'Shut up and get in here,' the man said, lowering the gun and grabbing her.

'Please just tell me where the children are,' Hazel said, wincing as she was manhandled into the hallway. She flinched as he kicked the door shut.

'Shut your mouth and get through the back.'

Stay calm, they had told her. *No matter what he says or does, keep calm.*

The house was dim, like night had come early and Hazel noticed all the curtains had been drawn. She was roughly shoved towards the back of the house.

Her body was drenched in sweat and her legs were shaking as she entered the large living room.

The female uniform was sitting in a corner, a gag tied round her face. Her handcuffs had been used to keep her hands behind her back. She was making sounds behind the gag and wriggling.

The man smiled. Hazel knew he was mad; there was nothing in his eyes but pure hatred.

'Where are the children?' she asked, keeping her voice steady. God, she felt sick, like she was going to heave.

'What children?' he smiled at her, then pointed the gun at her face. 'Take off the wire you're wearing. Earpiece, microphone, everything.'

John Carson

Hazel stood and looked at him.

'Now!' he screamed at her and she closed her eyes for a moment, trying to stay calm.

'Okay, okay,' she said, pulling the wire from under her shirt and throwing it on the floor. Same with her earpiece. The man stomped on them, destroying them. Then he stepped forward and roughly patted her down.

'Where's the children?' Hazel asked again.

He ignored her and grabbed a hold of the uniformed girl and hauled her to her feet, causing her to whimper. Her eyes went wide at Hazel and she was violently shaking her head, as if trying to spit the gag out.

He stepped back from Hazel, keeping the gun trained on her.

She watched in horror as he roughly grabbed a hold of the uniform by the hair. 'Say goodnight, sweetheart,' he said.

He let her hair go and stepped back, putting the shotgun against the side of the girl's head and pulled the trigger.

For a moment, Hazel couldn't breathe as the noise in the room deafened her. The girl's body was thrown across the room with the force of the blast.

'Jesus Christ, he killed her,' she managed to say, as if the microphone was still attached to her.

She started sobbing when he grabbed a hold of her hair and put the shotgun under her chin.

'Why?' She looked him in the eyes, although his face was in shadow. 'Why are you doing this?'

'I think you know the answer, Hazel.'

She shook her head. This couldn't be happening. 'What do you want?'

'It's not about me anymore. It's all about Frank Miller now. Him and I have a score to settle.'

TRIAL AND ERROR

CHAPTER 1

A week earlier

Anybody noticing them in the muted ambience of the private club might mistake them for bankers, not ruthless killers.

Mr Black and Mr Blue. Dressed smartly in lightweight suits. Expensive, befitting of their surroundings. Mr Black was drinking Glenmorangie Signet and encouraged his friend to accompany him.

A roaring fire staved off the chill Edinburgh night. Summer in Scotland was a cruel mistress, taunting and teasing by day, punishing and mocking by night.

'Is everything in place?' Mr Black asked. His hair was cut short, in a fashionable style, spikes sweeping back from his forehead. The money he paid ensured that his look was contemporary. There was nothing anybody could do to reduce the ferocity in his eyes as he stared at somebody.

'It is indeed. Just like we talked about. Everything's going like clockwork.' Mr Blue was equally contemporarily dressed. He hadn't always dressed like this, but Mr Black had been quite specific about dress code for the club. It wasn't debatable. And since Mr Blue was earning a lot of money now, it wasn't as if he couldn't afford it.

Mr Black smiled and raised his glass. His friend clinked his own glass, the expensive crystal giving out a light chime.

The air in the club was kept at a steady sixty-eight degrees. Patrons were either comfortable with that, or sat near one of the open fires. The club was in a townhouse in the New Town and was on several floors. On the second floor where they were, there were several private rooms, each serviced by its own butler. Each room was booked in advance, with an additional fee. This not only assured anonymity but room service.

'Have you had dinner yet?' Mr Black asked, picking up a menu from the table between them.

'I haven't had time to eat. I've been too busy.'

John Carson

'Good. You can order anything from the menu, as much as you like. It comes with the room. They do a good sirloin.'

'I'm partial to sea fish.'

Mr Black laughed. 'That figures, considering what your line of work was.'

Mr Blue smiled back. 'You make me sound like a pirate.'

'Oh, you were much more dangerous than a pirate, my friend.'

'We both were. That's why we're here today, celebrating.'

'Not celebrating; planning. It's not celebrating until it's over. Until all our plans have come together.'

'I'll drink to that.' He raised his glass once more and looked through the menu. When they were both ready, Mr Black called for their butler. He appeared through the door like a ghost, moving silently.

'Ready to order, sir?' The man was former Scots Guards and was paid handsomely not only for his work but his ability to be deaf when the need arose.

'Yes, indeed. I'll start with the hand-dived Dingwall scallop, followed by roast lamb.'

'Very good, sir. And you, sir?'

'I'll have smoked salmon followed by wild halibut. And can we have some beer to wash it down?'

'Certainly, sir.'

The butler left the room to put their order in.

'He didn't ask if we wanted any wine,' Mr Blue said. 'I might have to knock this place down to four stars.'

'Tsk, tsk, Mr Blue. He knows you don't mix the grapes with the hops. You're obviously more a philistine than he is.'

'Good point, Mr Black. If there were such a place where one would leave a review for such an establishment, I would bring the review back up to five stars.'

'This place doesn't exist except to people who know it exists. Word of mouth only, old chap.' He took a sip of the whisky, savouring the liquid, before looking over at his friend. 'Do you foresee any problems with our friend?'

Mr Blue smiled, a shark swimming in ever decreasing circles. 'Absolutely not.'

'I don't want to come across anything that we didn't plan for,' Mr Black said.

TRIAL AND ERROR

'Of course. I agree. This was just like planning one of our previous operations.'

Mr Black nodded and leaned back in the chair, holding his glass in his lap for a moment before speaking.

'Are you prepared to go to whatever level it takes?'

'Without a doubt. I know the risks as well as the rewards.'

'Which leaves me one more question before we eat; are you prepared to kill a police officer?'

Mr Blue smiled again, but there was a hardness in his face that Mr Black liked. It was a look that showed ruthlessness. 'I assure you that if the detective gets in the way, he will be despatched just like the rest of them.'

'His own life depends entirely on how he himself reacts.'

'Precisely. His life is in his own hands.'

'Then let's hope he makes the right decision for his own sake.'

Mr Blue lifted his glass in salute. 'To Frank Miller.'

CHAPTER 2

'Do you want to know who my first victim was?'

Silence on the other end of the phone as the man waited for an answer.

Detective Inspector Frank Miller stood at his living room window, looking at the festival performers below in the high street. The light was dying outside, heading for full dark. Despite the summer warmth, Miller felt a shiver run through him as he listened to the serial killer on the other end of the phone.

'We arrested you. I know who your first victim was.'

'You *think* know, Frank. That's the difference.'

Miller turned around as he heard somebody enter the room, thinking it was the killer in the room with him. It was only his father. Jack Miller tapped his watch: *pub time.*

The Surgeon, Miller mouthed back. He turned back to the window.

'You remember what I told you last you called me at home?'

'Something about doing me bodily harm. I do remember your words, I just choose to ignore them.'

'I wouldn't allow you to use a packet of crayons in there, never mind a phone.'

'This is a hospital for the criminally insane, Inspector, not a concentration camp. Even prisoners like me have rights.'

'I'm going away now, so you enjoy the rest of your evening.'

'Don't you want to know about the other female I killed?'

Miller drew in a breath and let it out slowly. 'Not really.'

A faint laugh at the other end. 'Come on now. How long have we been playing this game?'

Jack stood still, listening as Emma capered in her room with her pregnant mother, Kim, who was trying to get her to settle to read her a bedtime story.

'What girl are we talking about?'

More laughter. 'Who do you think we're talking about, Frank?'

TRIAL AND ERROR

Miller gripped the cordless phone and imagined smashing it into the man's face. Over and over again.

'Marilyn Monroe,' he said, sighing.

'You don't sound as enthusiastic as the last time.'

'Because I listened to your pish the last time too, and that's twenty minutes of my life I won't get back again.'

'Is your father still enjoying retirement? No longer a Detective Chief Inspector. How are the fine lads faring without him?'

'We're managing.'

'What about you, Frank? Will you get the promotion you deserve?'

'Maybe one day.'

'Big shoes to fill.' Silence for a moment. 'I've decided to give Jack a long-overdue retirement present. Put him on the phone.'

Miller handed over the phone. 'The prick wants to talk to you.'

'I'm here,' Jack said, taking the receiver from his son.

'Tell Frank I heard that.'

Jack looked at his son. 'He heard that.'

'Tell him to go fuck himself. See if he heard that, too.'

'Let's talk about Marilyn Monroe, Jack,' the killer said, showing no signs he had heard Miller.

'Tell me where she is. This so-called first victim of yours.'

'Am I still detecting scepticism in your voice?'

'Look, I'm busy, being out here in the real world, so either tell me what you have to say, or sod off back to your cage.'

'Do you have the recorder running?'

The recorder Miller had bought to record the conversations. Maybe he'd write a book about this bastard one day. The tapes would come in handy.

'Yes, it's taping now.'

'Good. Marilyn was a pretty girl. Very friendly and outgoing. It was a shame she had to die.'

'I'm sure you thought otherwise when you were about to kill her.'

'No need to be pedantic.'

Jack remembered The Surgeon's victims, opened up and organs removed. Then stitched back up again.

John Carson

The two men turned round as another figure entered the room. Emma, Kim's daughter, having escaped the clutches of her mother.

'Grandpa! Grandpa!'

Jack bent over while the little girl gave him a hug. He kissed her on the cheek before his son took her back out of the room.

'Ah, little Emma!' the killer said. 'How's her schoolwork these days? Is she enjoying Primary 3?'

Jack gripped the phone harder, wanting to smash it against the wall. He wanted to go to the hospital and rip this bastard's throat out.

'Fuck off.' It was important not to let him have too much power.

'Now, now, that's not being very sociable.' There was an edge to his voice, annoyed at the change of conversation, but not ready to let it go yet.

There was silence for a moment. Stalemate. Broken by the Surgeon.

'As I was saying, Marilyn was a very nice person. Young, sweet, innocent.'

'Where is she?' Jack asked. *If she actually exists.* Miller came back into the room.

'She looked like she was sleeping. Her skin was soft and warm, to begin with. Her face was pink and rosy, at least until the life was sucked out of her. She was left like that.'

'I'm still listening but hearing nothing. If she exists, tell me where she is.'

'I think that's enough for one night, Jack. I'm tired. Put Frank back on.'

Jack shook his head and handed the phone back to his son.

'Do you have anything worth talking about?' Miller said.

'How's Kim pregnancy coming along? Being pregnant plays havoc with their hormones. You'll be pleased about that, won't you? Considering that Carol died before giving birth.'

'How about I come down to that hospital and rip your tongue out, you little fuck?' Miller said, then felt the phone being taken out of his hand and the call disconnected.

'Don't let him get to you,' Jack said, putting the unit back onto the base.

'He mentioned Carol being pregnant,' Miller said, his eyes on fire and his heart beating fast enough to explode.

Jack put a hand on Miller's shoulder. 'He's trying to get under your skin. And he's succeeding. You put him away and that's pissing him off. He's in a cell and you're out here. You won.'

'I know you're right.'

Kim came into the room and Jack took his hand off Miller's shoulder.

'I'm so sorry. I don't have the energy to deal with Emma just now.'

'Don't worry about it,' Miller said.

'Was that *him* again?' The Surgeon was before Kim worked in Edinburgh, but Miller had told her all about the man.

'It was. It's a pity we can't do anything about him.'

'I wish we could. I'll run it past the PF again, but he's already in the asylum, and what he tells you is just the ramblings of a lunatic. Even if he told us where to find another body, he's been judged mentally unfit to stand trial and he's going to spend the rest of his life there. He's got nothing to lose. But he just likes playing games with you, and he has the right to a phone call. His lawyer said so. How long is it since he started calling you?'

'About a month or so.'

'I wonder why he started now?'

'I have no idea,' Miller said, 'but it's going to wear thin, very quickly.'

'We can have a beer here,' Jack said to Kim, slipping his jacket off. 'We don't have to go to the pub. In fact, Samantha's in. Go along and have a cup of tea with her, if you like. She'll be pleased to see you,'

'She wouldn't mind?'

'Not at all. We'll watch the bairn.'

'Thank you, Jack.'

She left the apartment to go along to Samantha's, just along the corridor. Jack had moved in with her to give Miller and Kim the space they needed.

'I don't want to ruin your Sunday night,' Miller said.

Jack smiled. 'When you're retired, every night is like Sunday night. Come on, I know you have beer in the fridge.'

'I'll just let Emma know her mum is out.' He left the living room.

The phone rang again.

John Carson

It was the Surgeon. 'I think we got disconnected,' he said when Jack answered it.

'I'll fucking disconnect you if you bring up my dead grandson again, you little fuck.'

The Surgeon laughed. 'Easy there, Jack. You want to live long enough to see this new one, don't you? Put Frank on again.'

'What is this, pass the fucking parcel?'

'Please, Jack.'

Miller took the phone. 'Now what?'

'Marilyn wasn't who you would expect her to be. When you discover who she was, it will be obvious to you. Things will be different from then on. See you soon, Frank.'

'Wait…'

The line was dead.

CHAPTER 3

The infirmary in the hospital wasn't big. Just big enough for two sick patients at a time, and even then, if they were so sick they needed round the clock care, they would be taken to the Royal.

That's why Peter Mackay was quite happy to play babysitter to the patient who was lying on the bed, a drip feeding into one arm and a pair of restraints on each wrist. He wasn't going anywhere. It was a stomach virus the doc had said, and she should know. This one was no problem anyway. He never caused any trouble and always did what he was asked. Only now and again did he sit and stare at the wall.

He'd gotten worse over the last month. *Regression* the doc had said. The psychiatrist who oversaw the man's case told her that's what it was. A lot of them were like that, poor bastards. His old grandad had gone doolally at the end. Didn't even know who he, Peter, was.

He stood up from his chair in the observation room and stretched his muscles. His wife didn't like it when he was on night shift, but she was a nagging cow anyway, so it didn't bother him. He worked at night and slept during the day. The only interaction they had was a couple of hours in the evening and even then, she had her eyes glued to the TV.

Life's big dream.

This new doc was a bit of alright though. His wife would have a fit if she knew he thought that way. *Degrading to women* she would say. *Objectifying* she would call it if she had her teeth in straight.

There was no harm in having a bit of eye candy around. It wasn't as if he was ogling her, or any of the other female psychiatric nurses for that matter. But he was a red-blooded male. It didn't matter if you batted for the other team, but he himself appreciated a good-looking woman. Not that he was going to get any action in here, but it was nice to dream.

Some of them even had a decent bit of conversation in them. Like Lin, for example. His other half for the shift. They were on overnights, and had the same days off. So they wouldn't need to keep each other up to speed at work.

'Cup of tea?' he asked. Lin had her face in a magazine.

John Carson

'Thanks, love.' She smiled up at him. He didn't want to ask her age in case she thought he was an old perv, even though at forty-five, he didn't consider himself *old*. Still, she looked like she was in her thirties, so he was quite happy to give her his spiel and see if she ever came on to him. If she did, then he wouldn't fight her off, but you had to watch what you said to a co-worker nowadays. One little bit of innuendo and it was all over.

Lin was okay though. They told each other dirty jokes and they were good friends. Over the past couple of months, he had gotten to know that she was married, had two cats, no kids, liked her job but would leave if she won the lottery.

He walked along to the break room, switched the kettle on and looked out the door, through the windows of the nurse's station. It was like a little guard tower, with reinforced windows and door. Not like a regular station, which was open.

He wished they had a TV in there, instead of just a radio. Still, knowing there was life outside these walls eased the night away. At least they would get a heads up if the Zombie Apocalypse kicked off.

The kettle clicked off and he added the bags to the cups and finished them off with milk and sugar. 'There we are–' he started to say when he came out of the room into the corridor.

Lin wasn't in the station.

Oh fuck. One of them was supposed to be there at all times, unless it was an emergency.

Which he guessed this was when he saw Lin further down the corridor with the doctor, Tamara something. The woman had gone upstairs to the main level. He thought she'd gone away for a gas with some of her pals since everything was okay down here. Just as well he hadn't had his trousers round his ankles giving Lin a good seeing to when she came back.

He put the cups back down and quickly walked over to the entrance to the infirmary as the doctor wheeled a gurney in, helped by two orderlies from upstairs. Men who ignored him. Pair of steroid gorillas, men who couldn't start a crossword puzzle designed for children, but who could pull your testicles out through your ears.

'I've been treating this man for a few days now,' Tamara said as the orderlies departed.

TRIAL AND ERROR

Jesus, she looked fucking beautiful. He blinked his eyes. *Concentrate you twat.*

'What's wrong with him?' The man was in the foetal position, clutching his stomach and writhing around in pain.

'I think he has a burst ulcer. Call for an ambulance. He needs to go to the Royal.'

'Christ, we won't have more staff until the changeover at seven.' He looked at the wall clock: 5.26.

'This man needs to go to the hospital now. If he dies, it's all on you.'

His expression went from *I've just won the lottery!* to *What fucking iceberg?* in a second. 'I'll make the call,' he said, rushing to the nurse's station. They were supposed to call in back-up in situations like this, but there were few bodies on the floors as it was, what with all the cut-backs. And now that snitch and snatch had fucked off back upstairs, they had no choice but to deal with this themselves. Mackay looked at him. The state he was in, he couldn't fight his way out of a wet paper bag.

After the call was put through, he came back into the infirmary.

Fifteen minutes later, the ambulance was reversing through the main door, into the secure area. Once the outside door was down, the inner door was unlocked. The paramedics, a man and a woman, brought their wheeled stretcher out of the back of the ambulance. They came into an ante-room. The door from the loading area was locked and then the doors into the hospital were unlocked.

They came through.

'Morning,' the man said. 'Where's the patient?'

'Through here,' Tamara said. She led the way through to the infirmary.

The patient was lying prone on his back.

'What's the symptoms?' he asked, bending over to have a closer look. He didn't see his partner already slumping to the floor as he felt the needle going into his neck and tried to spin round, but his eyes rolled in his head and then nothing.

Before the ambulance crew got there, Tamara and Miles had taken care of the two nurses, Miles had quickly stripped Mackay and

13

shoved his unconscious form into the nurse's station, stripping off his uniform. When the crew got there, all they saw was the male nurse with the doctor, nothing to arouse their suspicions.

'I think I rather suit these nurse's duds,' Miles Laing said, smiling at Tamara.

'Well, now you're going to have to do another quick turnaround and get into these paramedic uniforms. We fooled the paramedics but now we still have to get out of here.'

'You're right. They're a bit tight round the waist.' He looked over to the nurse's station. 'I think young Peter over there was a little bit too fond of the custard creams.'

'Hurry, Miles,' Tamara said, 'we're against the clock here.'

Miles quickly took Mackay's uniform back off and slipped into a paramedic uniform. It was snug, but he would only need it for the next few minutes. He took the nurse's jacket and went into the station, putting it back on Mackay. He didn't bother with the trousers as he hauled Mackay off the floor and onto one of the chairs. Lin was still in her uniform, as they hadn't needed hers. She was hauled from the floor onto the other chair.

Miles placed them so that if anybody had a quick glance, it would look like they were sitting. Not that anybody would be coming in here for another hour or so.

'Help me get the paramedics onto the beds,' Tamara said.

'I'll deal with him.' He pointed to the form still lying unconscious on the bed. The drugs would keep him out of it for a little while longer.

'Get him onto the stretcher then we'll get him hooked up after we get those two onto the beds.'

Miles and Tamara worked like a well-oiled machine. The two paramedics were put under the sheets, an oxygen mask put on them both. They were hooked up to heart monitors, and a saline drip was put into the man's left arm. All designed to make it look like they were patients who weren't going anywhere.

The restraints were put on their wrists.

The patient who had been in the bed was on the stretcher.

'Will I pass as a paramedic?' Miles asked.

'He's a young guy. Besides, we just have to wait for another five minutes. Unlike the nurses, the guards at the gate change shifts at six, not seven.'

'I remember.'

There weren't any cameras in this part, all to do with patient rights, but there were cameras in the loading bay, but that was okay. All they would see was the paramedics taking the patient out.

He looked at the wall clock. 6.05 am. 'Let's go. If it's still the same guy, I'll resort to Plan B.'

Tamara knew that meant Miles would have to kill the guard.

For security, all the door locks had to be manually locked and unlocked from a panel. Tamara unlocked all the doors leading into the loading bay. Miles pulled the stretcher out. The patient had an oxygen mask on with a heart monitor by his side.

He pulled the stretcher up to the open back doors, keeping his face low. Not that it would matter. Tamara walked out a few minutes later, as if the duty nurse had been unlocking the doors and locking them behind her. That's what they would see when they checked the CCTV.

She helped Miles put the patient into the ambulance and she stepped inside. Miles opened the driver's door after hitting the button to open the roller door. When it was all the way up, he switched on the blues and drove the ambulance out and along the service road until he joined the main road leading out.

'This is it,' Miles said, feeling a bit shaky. It had been eight years since he had seen the outside.

He pulled up to the gatehouse, having no idea if this was the same man who had let the ambulance in a half hour previously, but if the shift change had gone ahead, it should be somebody different.

The man was dressed in a fluorescent jacket and a peaked cap. Probably an ex-cop.

'My colleague told me you were down there. Everything okay?' he said.

'Looks like a burst ulcer. We're taking him to the Royal. My partner's in the back checking his vitals.'

'Is he restrained?'

Fuck. 'Of course he is. I mean, we see a lot of shit, but we're not taking any chances.' No going back now. That was a blatant lie.

'Can you open the back door? I just need to check.'

'Sure. No problem.' Miles opened the driver's door and slipped out behind the guard, the syringe already in his hand as the guard opened the door. The meds would put him to sleep and leave him with a wicked headache, but he'd still be alive.

He had it partway open when Tamara shouted, 'What's the holdup, Charlie? We have a bleeder here!' She held up her gloved hands with blood on them.

'Christ, okay,' the guard said and closed the door. 'I'll get the gate. Do you need an escort called for?'

'We have outriders waiting by the bypass. Everything's arranged.' *Nearly your funeral too, lucky bastard.*

'Right, buddy. On you go.'

The guard practically ran back into the guardhouse and opened the first gate to let the ambulance into the holding pen while the gate shut. Miles sat and stared at the gate in front of him, not believing this was happening.

Then the gate slid sideways in front of him. The big, mesh gate on wheels just glided out of his way. He drove through slowly, making the ambulance jump a bit. It had been a while since he had driven anything, and the clutch on this machine was a bit stiff.

They had gone over the controls in the ambulance with Tamara a few times, until he could picture them in his head. He smiled as he looked over. They were exactly where he thought they would be.

He wasn't going to switch the siren on this early in the morning, but it would be fun to give it a blast. He resisted as he stopped before the main road. It would be getting busier by the minute as traffic started to come into Edinburgh.

It was getting light now and he turned onto the road and drove away at a steady pace.

He wasn't familiar with this place, but the hand-drawn map that Tamara had left in the library book was pretty accurate.

He drove along the country road until he saw the turn-off straight ahead. He killed the blue lights. If anybody saw that, they would think that an emergency call had just been cancelled.

Miles turned onto the track that led to an abandoned farm. He drove into the old barn and parked next to the car that had been left here for them. It was a nondescript Vauxhall.

TRIAL AND ERROR

Tamara climbed out of the ambulance and opened the boot of the car. Miles went into the back. He wanted to make sure that Bruce Hagan was at least still alive.

He was more than alive; he was sitting up and smiling.

Hagan put a finger to his lips. 'You still got the keys for this thing?' he asked.

'What?'

'Simple question. Hurry up. We haven't got long.'

'They're in the ignition.'

Just then, Tamara reached in and took the keys, quickly closing the driver's door again. They both heard her lock the door.

'Too late,' Hagan said, getting up. 'Get back in the front. She won't expect that.'

He moved through just as the back door opened. He turned to see Tamara come in, holding a gun. The doctor was surprised to see that Hagan wasn't on the gurney, but standing up. It saved his life. The oxygen tank he'd grabbed connected with her wrist, knocking the gun sideways, and the backwards swing caught her on the chin, knocking her out before she could fire the gun.

'Nice swing,' Miles said, coming back into the rear of the ambulance.

'I want to get out of here.'

'She said we were going to get out and then she would call about them coming to pick her up.'

'Somebody's expecting a call then, and when she doesn't call, I'm guessing that whoever was waiting will come looking. Or call the authorities.'

'Let's not waste any time.'

Miles felt his eyes going to where one of Hagan's ears used to be.

'Yeah, it hurt,' Hagan said. 'So did taking my fingers off.'

'Sorry, I didn't mean to stare. I know it hurts. I used to be a surgeon.'

'Don't you mean you were *The Surgeon*?'

'Yes. But that is a whole different story my friend. Let's get out of here. I owe you one.'

Hagan picked up the gun and Laing looked at it. 'Don't worry, it's just so that they can't get it. Take the ambulance keys back off her, too.'

They picked up Tamara and strapped her to the gurney after making sure she was still alive.

Then they got in the car and drove off into the morning light.

CHAPTER 4

'My hair's dry. My skin's dry. I have a blinding headache and my back feels like it's been jumped on. Thanks for asking.' Kim Smith took the glass of orange juice that Frank Miller was holding out to her.

'Apart from that, everything's okay?' he said with a grin. He felt it would be easier trying to take apart a hand grenade with the pin pulled.

'You know you're never getting to touch me again, don't you?' She washed down two painkillers.

'I had a rough idea that was on the cards.' He popped the toast he'd been making and poured a bowl of cereal for Emma, who was sitting in the living room watching cartoons.

Kim sat down at the table.

'You want some toast?' Miller asked.

'Dry please. Like our love life.'

'Just think, if it's a boy, you'll have two males in the flat. Both wanting your undivided attention.'

'God, I don't think I could handle two of you.'

Miller laughed. 'Twice the fun.' He cut a slice of toast in half and gave her it on a plate. 'Emma. Cereal's ready!' he shouted, and Kim winced.

'Good God, I swear if you shout like that again, I am going to do something dangerous to a certain body part.'

He laughed and ruffled her hair on the way out of the kitchen to spur on his soon to be step-daughter.

'Sod off, Miller.'

'Love you too, honey.'

Emma was eight years old and Kim's only child, until the new arrival came. She was sitting on the couch, a soft toy tucked under one arm, with Charlie, their cat, sleeping next to her.

'Frank?' she said, a serious expression on her face.

'Yes?' He knew it was going to be a deep and meaningful question by the look on her face.

'Do cats like babies?'

John Carson

'Yes, they do. Charlie will be curious about the baby when he or she comes home. And then when he realises the baby is here to stay, he won't be curious so much anymore.'

'Good.' She looked at Miller. 'I want to help with the baby, Frank, and I was worried Charlie might get jealous.'

He smiled. 'Charlie will be just fine.'

They went through to the kitchen where Kim was resting her head on the table.

'Are you tired, mum?' Emma asked.

Kim lifted her head. 'I am, sweetheart.'

'Is the baby making you tired?'

She nodded her head and got up from the table. 'Yes. It's what babies do. It's their job. I wish I still had a job to go to.'

Kim was an investigator and police liaison officer with the Procurator Fiscal's office, but more desk bound in their offices in the Sheriff Court building than being in the field.

'Doctor's orders. You're to rest now. Your job will still be there when you go back.'

'Ah, yes, the inimitable Sharon. I bet she's not as fat and ugly as me.'

'Well, she's not pregnant, if that's what you mean.'

'You would think already having one child would have prepared me more,' she said.

'Emma's not that old that you can't remember,' Miller said.

'I was talking about you. I'm off for a shower.'

'It all makes sense now, Frank,' Emma said.

'What does?'

'When you always say, *see what I have to put up with?*' The little girl sat at the table with her soft toy and started eating her cereal.

Miller's phone rang and he answered it. 'I'll be there in ten,' he said hanging up.

'What's wrong?' Kim asked him in the living room.

'All hell's broke lose. Or should I say, Miles Laing broke lose.'

'What? The killer you and Carol captured?'

'The very same.'

'How in God's name did that happen?'

'There's an emergency team meeting in ten minutes. We're getting briefed. Meantime, just be careful.'

TRIAL AND ERROR

'Why would you say that?' Kim looked worried.

'He's a lunatic and he's escaped from a psychiatric hospital, so he's dangerous. I caught him, remember. I saw first-hand what he's capable of. And he's been calling here, remember?'

'Okay. I'll be careful. But you be careful too.'

'I will.'

'I'm knackered,' Lou Purcell said, coming into the kitchen. His son was there, Detective Superintendent Percy Purcell. And Percy's new wife, Suzy Campbell. She was using her maiden name for professional purposes.

Bear, their German Shepherd, came across and nuzzled Lou.

'How are you knackered?' Percy said, pouring himself another cup of coffee. 'You just got back from holiday yesterday.'

'You know what they say – you come back home for a rest. I was out partying every night.' Lou rubbed the dog's ear.

'What are you like?'

Lou smiled. 'The old dog still has some life left in him yet.'

'I hope you were using protection.'

Lou walked across to the coffee machine and popped in a coffee pod. 'You have to take the conversation down to a lower level. It's an illness with you, you know that?'

'I meant sun screen protection, you wrinkly old sod.'

'Percy! Don't talk to him like that,' Suzy said, buttering some toast. 'He's just jealous, dad,'

'I know he is. He wishes he had the stamina that I still have.'

'The blue pills make you keep on dancing, do they?'

'I don't need any chemicals to keep this well-oiled machine ticking along smoothly,' said Lou.

'Listen to yourself. At your age, you should be looking forward to watching *Countdown* in your slippers and remembering to put your teeth back in after drinking your tea.'

'What? Pish. I feel like a twenty-year-old.'

'Me too,' Percy said, grabbing Suzy.

'I left twenty behind a long time ago, Percy,' she said, slapping him off.

'God. You would think you're a teenager,' Lou said.

John Carson

'We're newlyweds.'

'Well, you'll be needing to keep an eye on *your* ticker at your age.' Lou said, adding milk to his coffee.

'Your solicitor called yesterday. He sounded happy. I think I'll change careers,' said Percy.

'You wouldn't be able to sell houses for a living. You wouldn't get to shout at the clients and give them a good belting like you do now.'

'We're not the Gestapo. But anyway, give him a call. I think the people who recorded a note of interest made an offer. Two grand over the asking price.'

'You weren't discussing my private business I hope.'

'Of course I was. I told him you're senile and I have your power-of-attorney,'

'Christ, giving you power-of-attorney has gone to your head.'

'It's only so I can switch the machine off.'

'Try not to smile when you're doing it. And don't have a pillow in your hands beforehand.'

'Dad, don't be talking like that,' Suzy said, pouring herself more coffee.

'Don't worry, Suzy, if I get to the stage where I need my arse wiped, I'm sure *son of the year* will have found a way to starve me of oxygen.'

'Seeing all those half-naked women on the Spanish beach has obviously gone to your head. Made you delirious. I wouldn't even think about using a pillow on you.'

'Don't get all sentimental on me, now.' Lou popped two slices of bread into the toaster.

'I'm not. I know people who would do it for me.'

'I knew it was too good to be true. I should have given you a belting when you were a teenager. Too much letting you go out with your pals and staying out late.'

'Too late now, feeble old man.'

'Shut up. Tell me more about my house.'

'He wants you to sign some papers. He'll have them couriered to you.'

'Never mind that bollocks, I'll go up there. I still have stuff in storage. Me and Elizabeth are talking about moving in.'

TRIAL AND ERROR

'I don't know how you do it. First you come here to see an old friend from work, but she's not interested in dropping her drawers for you.'

'For God's sake–'

Percy held up a hand. 'Then Elizabeth kicks you into touch because she thinks that said friend *is* dropping her drawers for you, then you convince her that it was just a wee hooly down to Edinburgh to visit your favourite son–'

'My only son, thank God.'

'And you somehow convince her to bounce over to Spain with you for a week so you could no doubt take advantage of the poor woman. And now she's going to move in with you. I hope she's not up the duff.'

'Listen to yourself. Are you sure you're a copper? I sometimes think you're the janny, but you just wear a suit to work to impress people.'

'Just watch what you're doing, old man. And don't let her put her name on the title deed.'

'You think my head's buttoned up the back?'

'Women have a way of manipulating men, that's all I'm saying.'

Suzie looked at Percy.

'Some women. Suzie and I both contribute to the mortgage. Just make sure Elizabeth isn't a Black Widow.'

'Hello. I'm not twelve. I know what I'm doing.'

'Some men think with their small brain, and I hope that trip to Benidorm didn't shrivel yours. Any more. You need to think with your big brain when it comes to money.'

'I know. I *have* bought houses before. That's why I ended up in Aberdeen, remember? *Come to Aberdeen, dad* they said. *You'll love it there* they said. And I did until you got divorced. But now that I decided to move again, I've been house hunting. And I think I found a nice wee place.'

'Where abouts? Shetland?'

'Sod off. Henderson Row. Opposite Edinburgh Academy. One of those retirement flats there. It's the top floor and the living room window looks right onto the flats here. So I can wave to you.'

'Two-fingered wave, knowing you. And don't be walking around starkers. The last thing I need when I'm having my sausages is to look over and see Wee Willie Winkie bobbing about. Put me right off my breakfast, that would.'

'Walking about in your vest and skids gives you a sense of freedom.'

'Try telling that to the judge. See how much sense of freedom you have after that.'

'I'm not talking about in the communal area. I mean in the privacy of my own home.'

'As long as half of the New Town can't see you parading the catwalk with your curtains open.'

'None of your neighbours complain when I do it here.'

'You better be kidding, old man.'

'Of course I am. But be nice to me or I'll tell them you beat me.'

'Don't think I'm not tempted.' Percy drank some coffee. 'When is this happening? You moving?'

'I'll call the guy this afternoon and tell him I'll be up there tomorrow. Then I'll sign the papers. I've already had the offer accepted on the flat I'm buying, so maybe in the next couple of weeks.'

Purcell looked at his father for a moment. 'Please don't go, dad. I'll miss you. I don't know what it will be like around here without you.'

'Piss off.'

'No, seriously, I've forgotten what it's like to be in here without your manky old skids about the place. I wish you'd just put them in the machine with everything else instead of washing them in the bathroom sink.'

'Hey, that lassie has enough to do around here without washing my underwear.'

'I suppose she's thankful she doesn't have to touch them.'

'You could always do my laundry. It's not an exclusive thing for women.'

'I'd launder your Y's with a blowtorch.'

'Anyway, it's not too far away so I can come round and take Bear out. And close enough so I can still keep my eye on you.'

'Good idea for taking out Bear. I appreciate you doing that, dad,' Suzy said.

'It's not a problem. I'm going to catch up with some old friends now I'm living here, but I'll still be around.'

'Don't get into any mischief.'

TRIAL AND ERROR

'Just make sure those patrol uniforms know who I am. That will save me money on using taxis.'

'You wish. Don't be telling them you're related to me.'

Lou laughed and left the room.

Then Percy's phone rang. After he took the call, he looked at Suzy.

'It's going to be a long day.'

CHAPTER 5

No phone call meant trouble. Mr Blue drove past the opening to the farm twice before slowing down. Third time, he entered, driving slowly along the track, ready with his excuse of *getting caught short* and looking for somewhere to relieve himself. They wouldn't believe him of course, but he would deal with them on the spot.

Nobody was there. No other vehicles, especially not ones with flashing blue lights. Not yet, anyway.

The ambulance would have GPS on it, and as soon as they knew it was gone, they'd be all over it. He didn't know if they tracked them when they were transporting a patient, but he knew they would be looking for it and short of burning it to the ground to destroy the GPS, they would find it.

It was already light and apart from the noise of distant traffic, it was near silent. Birds were awake but there was no sound of any human activity. The farmhouse was boarded up, long ago abandoned by its owner. Mr Blue drove past the house and round the back to where the barn was. He'd been here before, scoping the place out.

The barn was old but not quite dilapidated. The door was open but he couldn't see inside. Driving slowly, he thought about the shotgun in the boot of the car. He drove in slowly. Switched the headlights on and the light picked out the ambulance sitting further in.

There was no sign of the other car that they'd left here. Something wasn't right. His senses were heightened now, honed by years of working in the military. Back then, he'd had to do things the man in the street couldn't even begin to imagine.

He didn't take the shotgun out. He could easily take anybody who was there to do him harm. His military training had made him supremely confident. He approached the back of the ambulance, pulled on a pair of latex gloves he had in his pocket and grabbed the handle, opening the door in one swift movement.

Nobody inside waiting to try and attack him. There *was* somebody on the gurney though.

TRIAL AND ERROR

'Jesus, Tamara,' he said, stepping up into the back of the vehicle. The doctor wasn't dead. She was unconscious, but she had been hit with something across her head. She'd have a hell of a headache, that was for sure. He looked around at the medical kits. Raked about until he found what he was looking for. Ammonia inhalants. More commonly known as smelling salts. He took the bottle and opened it, holding it under Tamara's nose.

She stirred and groaned, confusion in her eyes at first. Then she winced as the pain in her head kicked in. Her arms were restrained on the gurney.

'Are you able to tell me what happened?' he said.

Tamara groaned. 'I came round into the back to shoot them, but one of them hit me with something hard. I don't know which one.'

'It doesn't matter,' Mr Blue said. 'They'll both die. I'll see to that. But did they ask you anything?'

'No.'

'They didn't wonder why you tried to kill them?'

'If they did, they didn't say anything to me. Just hit me.'

Mr Blue stood up and took out the silenced gun and touched the tip of it to her forehead. Her eyes went wide as she realised what he was doing. Then he pulled the trigger.

He left the ambulance and got back into his car.

Then drove away.

The station was buzzing when Miller got upstairs. Everybody on the MIT A-team was present. He had promised to keep Kim informed, but her mother, the Procurator Fiscal, Norma Banks, was already there.

Percy Purcell was at the front with Detective Chief Inspector Paddy Gibb, who had a pen in his mouth and was no doubt pretending it was a cigarette.

'Ladies and gentlemen, can I have your attention, please?' Purcell said, and stood waiting for the noise of chatter to subside.

'As you all know, the killer known to us as The Surgeon, escaped from the psychiatric hospital early this morning. On my right is Detective Superintendent Leach, my counterpart from the Glasgow Division. The hospital is in their area. He and his team will be working with us to establish how and why Miles Laing escaped.

John Carson

'I also have Detective Inspector McNeil from Professional Standards.'

'Aw, here we fucking go,' Detective Sergeant Andy Watt whispered to Miller. All the team members looked at McNeil like he was the Antichrist.

'Detective Leach?' Purcell stood aside.

'I will be leading this investigation, along with members from my team. We will be working here for as long as it takes. We will be going through all of the files from eight years ago. For those of you not familiar with the case of The Surgeon, he was captured by DI Miller and his team, exactly eight years ago today. We'll be looking to see if this has any significance or not. Any questions?'

Watt looked at the Glaswegian detective. 'Can I ask why you're through here investigating instead of back in Glasgow? I mean, I know we have the old files here, but isn't it usual to have the files transferred and work at your home base?'

'Normally that would be the protocol, but we have intel that Laing will be coming back to Edinburgh. We want our team on the ground here, just in case. That way we kill two birds, going through the files and being on the ground here.'

Watt nodded his *total shite* nod.

'I have members of CID coming in to help go through the files. MIT A-team will go through and assist us, unless you get called out on a shout. Any other questions?'

There were none.

'Right. I don't want any rumours spread, so here's what we know so far; Laing had been complaining of stomach pains for days. In the wee hours of this morning, the duty doctor who is on nights, took him down to the infirmary. An ambulance was called. It left half an hour or so later, with Miles Laing at the wheel. The two paramedics had been given a drug through hypodermic needle, same with the male nurse on duty. All three were found safe and well but unconscious.

'We are working on the basis that the female doctor helped Laing escape. They also took another prisoner with them. One who was already in the infirmary. Former detective Bruce Hagan. The ambulance was traced by GPS to a place three miles from the hospital. We're assuming that they had another vehicle waiting for them. They haven't been seen since.'

'Why would they take Hagan?' Watt asked.

'We don't know that yet. Hagan was in a worse condition mentally than Laing, and we're going to be looking at his psychiatric reports later today, but we hope to find out more. We're not ruling out the possibility of him working with Laing and his partner.

'Anything else?'

Nobody said anything.

Miller noticed McNeil hadn't said a word but had kept his eyes on him the whole time.

'Right, let's get to it.'

As the team broke up, McNeil and Leach stood talking with Purcell, then the three men came over to him.

'Inspector Miller?' McNeil said. 'We'd like to have a word with you in one of the interview rooms. Do you want a rep to be present?'

'Am I going to need one?' Miller said.

'This is just an informal talk,' Purcell said, looking at McNeil.

'It will be recorded,' McNeil said back, unfazed by Purcell's look.

'I don't think I need a rep.'

'Then let's go,' Leach said. He was a heavily-built man with a thick Glaswegian accent. And a nose that had been on the receiving end of a smack or two.

They walked along the corridor and went downstairs to one of the interview rooms. Miller knew what this was going to be about; Miles Laing calling him at home.

After they set up the recorder, Miller sat on one side of the table with Purcell, while Leach and McNeil sat on the interviewing side.

'I just want to set the story straight here,' Leach said. He had brought a notebook along which he was now looking at. 'Eight years ago, you were a detective constable, and you hadn't been with CID long. Is that correct?'

'It is.'

'You excelled on that case, along with your now-deceased wife, Carol Davidson. You caught not only Miles Laing, but his partner-in-crime, Sherri Hilton.' He looked at Miller. 'Although it was later established that this was a fake name, and her real identity was never discovered, as it was presumed she died in the Firth of Forth.'

John Carson

'I saw her one night a couple of weeks later when I was in my girlfriend's hospital room.'

McNeil looked at some papers. 'Ah yes. You reported that you saw a nurse waving at you as she got into her car. It was raining that night and it was dark. You saw a nurse waving. Could it be that it was a nurse waving to one of her friends?'

'It could have been, but it was a nurse that shouldn't have been on the ward.'

'That exact nurse? You could tell through a window that was getting battered by rain?' Leach said.

'What is this? I made a report at the time, indicating what I saw. I clearly stated that it could have been.'

'It could have been your imagination hard at work, Miller.'

'Maybe. But I erred on the side of caution.' He could feel his face starting to go red, like he was a schoolboy in front of the headmaster.

'Let's move on to Miles Laing,' McNeil said. 'Why do you think he called you at home?'

'Well, it's not like I invited him to, and it seems that Scottish law has to be tweaked a little to prevent that sort of thing happening in the future. If there wasn't so much of this Human Rights nonsense, then he wouldn't have been able to.'

'Why do you think he chose to contact you?' Leach said.

'I don't know. I caught him. He wanted to play games.'

'We've got the tapes we want to listen to. All his calls were recorded. We'll have somebody listen to them and take notes, but we wanted to give you the chance to tell us what he spoke to you about.'

Miller shrugged. 'Mundane stuff. Then he started talking about the killings.'

'How many times has he called you?' McNeil said.

'It's all there in the file,' Purcell said, feeling his own hackles rise.

'I just want Detective Miller's perspective on it.'

'About a dozen times over the last month.'

'Including the call you received three days ago. Sunday night.'

'That's correct.'

'Can you tell us what that one was about?'

Why? Did the fucking tape recorder break down or something?
'He told me there was another victim before the ones that we found.'

'A victim we don't know about?'

'Yes.'

'What's your opinion on that?' said Leach.

'He's a lunatic. He's rambling, making stuff up.'

'Did you check up on his claims?'

Miller looked at Purcell before answering. 'Yes.'

'And did you find anything in the system?'

'No. There were no victims of a murder, with the same MO that he had used.'

McNeil was scribbling some notes down.

'Why do you think he started calling you after being in the psychiatric hospital for almost eight years?'

'I can't answer for his actions.'

'Now, I want you to explain something to me,' Leach said.

'Okay.'

'Why would Laing end the call last Sunday with *See you soon, Frank*?'

'I have no idea. Again, he's not got any lights on upstairs. Maybe he thinks we're going for afternoon tea.'

Leach smiled but there was no humour. 'And now he's out running about, that might not seem as far-fetched as we thought. Where were you in the early hours of this morning, Miller?'

'You're not serious,' Purcell said.

'We're deadly serious, Superintendent.' McNeil said it like he was trying to spit out a midgie at the same time.

'I was in bed with my girlfriend.'

'You don't think Frank had anything to do with this, do you?' Purcell said.

'We're not ruling–' McNeil started saying before Purcell glared at him.

'You might think you're the big cock in here, McNeil, but I was talking to Detective Leach. I know your powers stretch far and wide and you can overrule decisions and go anywhere to investigate, but Miller is one of my officers, and if you're going to accuse him of anything, you fucking well better have solid evidence.'

John Carson

'Take it easy, Percy,' Leach said. 'You know we have to establish what went on, considering he called Miller at home.'

'As Frank said, Laing was the one who called *him*. And you, McNeil, were the one who had a word with him for threatening Laing. I notice nobody had a word with Looney Tunes in the hospital. Well, maybe it's a good thing he's on the outside now, as that means we might have a chance of getting to talk to him face-to-face.'

'We all have rules to follow, Superintendent.'

'Agreed. And Frank didn't break any.'

Leach held up a hand. 'We just wanted to hear Miller's side of things. We don't think he had anything to do with this, but we just needed a chat, that's all. You can go now, Inspector.'

'But–' McNeil protested.

'There's no buts. The interview has been terminated.' He looked at Miller. 'If there's anything else we need to talk to you about, then we'll talk again. But let's concentrate on getting him back into that hospital.'

'Hazel Carter wasn't at the meeting,' Miller said. 'She's on leave. She's coming back tomorrow. Has anybody told her about Hagan?'

'No, not yet. I was told about her leave. We have a patrol car parked near her house in Baberton Mains, keeping an eye on her. And one near Tanner's Bar in Juniper Green where his wife still lives. No sighting.'

'I'd like to be the one who tells Hazel.'

'Fine.'

All four men got up and left the room, McNeil and Miller walking towards the end of the corridor and through a set of doors.

'I hope Miller doesn't put McNeil's lights out.'

'Frank's not stupid.'

'My instinct says he didn't have anything to do with it, but McNeil thinks everybody is guilty until proven otherwise.'

'Obviously the doctor helped him escape, Willie,' Purcell said, 'but what we have to establish is whether it was his accomplice from eight years ago. Nobody believed Frank back then, but he was convinced that she had survived that plunge into the sea.'

TRIAL AND ERROR

'I know that. I wonder why they would take Hagan? But we're going through everything we know about that doctor. Every interaction she had with Laing.'

'She was very clever, whoever she is. No alarms bells went off in anybody's head. Then they waltz out of there in an ambulance.'

'Aye, son, it was a cunning plan they had, and they pulled it off. They knew about the shift changes for the guards at the gate, and the nurses.'

'Why was Hagan in the infirmary to begin with?' Miller said.

'That's why we're having somebody go down to the hospital. I have some of my men there.'

'I'd like to go,' Purcell said.

'That's fine, Percy. I think Miller better take a couple of team members with him when he goes to see Carter.'

'He will.'

In the stairwell, McNeil turned to Miller. 'Christ, I hate this department, Frank. It alienates everybody. For what's it's worth, I have to seem to be tough with you, but I don't think for one minute you had anything to do with Laing escaping. What reason would you have?'

'I appreciate it, Harry.'

Harry McNeil had been friends with Miller for many years. He had been friends with Carol, too, and after they bought the flat on the North Bridge, McNeil had rented Carol's flat. He still lived in it.

'When are you coming back to CID?' Miller asked.

'They won't welcome me back with open arms. No, Frank, I think it will be somewhere else for me.'

'Not leaving the force, I hope? You're too good a detective for that.'

'No, not leaving, but maybe moving sideways. You know, I messed up one case, and then they stuck me in here. I know other people volunteer for it, but not me. And now they're going to spit me out the other end. But if they think I'm going to go digging up dirt on a friend when there's no dirt to be dug up, they can sod off.'

'I appreciate it, my friend.' Miller slapped him on the arm and they went their separate ways.

John Carson

Upstairs, Miller grabbed a hold of Andy Watt and Detective Constable Steffi Walker.

'I need you both to come with me.'

'Yes, sir,' Steffi said.

'I could do with a coffee break,' Watt said.

'We're going to tell Hazel that the man she had two children with was taken along for the ride when Miles Laing and his female friend took leave of absence from the hospital.'

'Christ, she's going to be gutted,' Steffi said.

'Not to mention the wife that nobody knew about,' Watt said, grabbing his jacket. 'What's her name again?' he snapped his fingers. 'Amanda Cameron, the one who lives above the pub.'

Paddy Gibb came up to them. 'Before you go anywhere, Jeni Bridge wants to see you,' he said to Miller.

'In her office?'

'In her outside office.' The car park at the side of the station, the designated smoking area.

'You two get the car keys and I'll go and see the chief super,' Miller said, leaving the incident room.

Outside, the car park was still in shadow, stuck in the stone canyon created by the buildings on either side of it.

'You should try these,' Jeni Bridge said, taking a puff of her cigarette and blowing the smoke out like a dragon that had lost its fire.

'Is that an offer or an observation, ma'am?'

'I'm not crashing my packet of fags, Frank, let's be serious. I get enough of that with Paddy Gibb when he comes out foaming at the mouth when he's run out of fags. A smoker who smokes the last fag in the packet and who doesn't have another packet waiting. I ask you.'

'You wanted to talk to me?'

'I do, Frank. Officially, I want to ask you one question: did you have anything to do with Miles Laing's escape?'

'No, I didn't!' Miller answered with conviction.

'Okay, don't get your string vest in a knot. I just wanted to hear it with my own ears. Mind you, if I thought you had, I'd have had you strung up by the balls with piano wire by now.' More sucking on the paper stick, tilting the head back and blowing smoke up to the sky.

'I think Superintendent Leach was disappointed. I think he'll take a lot more convincing than you.'

TRIAL AND ERROR

'Leachy the weedgie? He doesn't know you like I do, Frank. And McNeil? He's just been told to creep about with a raincoat on and spy on people. He's just doing his job, but what a job.' She held the cigarette between two fingers and used them to point at Miller. 'When he's done his time with the window-licking brigade, he can whistle if he thinks he's coming to work anywhere near me. I'll have him polishing the inside of a toilet if that happens, but it won't. Not while I'm the commander of Edinburgh Division. He can bugger off back to CID. He's not coming to MIT.'

Not for the first time, Miller thought he never wanted to get on the wrong side of Jeni Bridge. 'I've known him a long time. He's not too bad, to be honest. There's worse than him.'

Jeni looked sceptical. 'Sharks always look better when they're behind three feet of glass in an aquarium.'

'We're off to tell Hazel Carter about Bruce Hagan being on the lam,' he said when he saw Watt and Steffi come out the back door.

'Jesus Christ. She has two kids by him too. And he didn't even have the decency to marry her.'

'He wasn't right after being buried alive in a coffin.' Bruce Hagan had been a colleague of Miller's and had suffered what no man should ever suffer. Now, for some reason, Miles Laing had taken him out of the hospital. He hoped to God Laing hadn't done anything to him. He nodded for the other two detectives to wait for him in the car.

Jeni paced, taking a drag and then tapping the ash onto the ground. 'Let me ask you, Frank; do you think Laing did kill another other woman before you found your first victim?'

'I think he was capable of doing it. But there are no similar killings, unless he killed her in a different way.'

'Usually *coincidence* means that it's true, but I'm not sure about this one. He could have been trying to get under your skin.'

'And my father's too. He also worked the case. He and Harry Davidson were the lead detectives back then.'

'Harry was your wife's father? DCI Davidson?'

'Yes. They're both gone now.'

Jeni stopped pacing. 'I heard she was a good detective, your wife.'

'Better than me.'

'It was a tragedy, the way she died. I'll bet you miss her.'

John Carson

'I do. It was eight years ago today we caught the bastard. The day my wife nearly died.'

'Sherri Hilton, driving the car. I read the file.' One more draw from a cigarette that was at the end of its life. Miller was sure it would be joined by its brothers and sisters on the ground very shortly. 'Tell me though, Frank; do you think Hilton's still alive?'

'I've always thought so. When I looked out through that window in the hospital, even through the pouring rain, I *knew* it was her. She looked right up at me, not across to a friend or a colleague, but right at *me*.' Miller poked himself in the chest.

'Why do you think she was on the ward that night? Do you think she went into the room where your wife was?'

'I don't know if she intended to harm Carol, but she was certainly sending me a message; I can get to you anytime I want.'

'But you never heard from her again?'

'No. I never saw her again after that night.'

'And now, on the eighth anniversary of getting caught, her boyfriend escapes. I think she's sending you a message again; look what I did. I got my boyfriend out of the hospital. I'll bet when we rip that doctor's life apart, we'll find it full of red herrings.'

'I think you're right, ma'am. I haven't seen her in all that time, but I have a feeling it won't be long before we hear from Miles Laing again.'

CHAPTER 6

Mr Black and Mr Blue were in the drawing room, drinking coffee. Blue was watching the news on the TV while Black was reading that morning's edition of *The Caledonian*, already out for circulation before the story broke about the escape.

Another man in a suit was sitting drinking coffee, looking at the muted TV. News channels were reporting the escape.

The TV had no such deadlines.

'The good people of Edinburgh think they have to be worried,' the suit said.

Mr Black smiled and folded his newspaper, putting it on the side table next to him. 'And they might well be worried. Miles Laing being on the loose wasn't in the plan. Tell me in great detail what happened.' He looked at Mr Blue.

Mr Blue felt the adrenaline kicking in. *Battle juice* one of his fellow soldiers had called it, a man whose lift didn't go all the way to the penthouse. Maybe being off his nut got him through the war as he wasn't one of the casualties. He'd have given anything to have the man here with him now.

He explained to Mr Black what had gone wrong. He gave him the edited version, that Laing must have overpowered Tamara and executed her. He didn't explain that he, Mr Blue, had executed her. He would have done it with Tamara's gun, but he'd been unable to find it, assuming the two prisoners had taken it with them.

'A casualty of war.'

'Indeed.'

'Now we need to figure out where Miles Laing will run to.' Mr Black sat and steepled his fingers. 'You'll have to ask the woman who knows him, before they make any connection. I know it's unlikely, but now Laing is a wild card.'

'Do you think he'll go there?' the suit said.

'Probably not, but she might be able to help us with our enquiries.'

John Carson

'I'll get onto it. And we're going to need a solution, a Plan B, which I already had; Mr Red.'

'Who's that?'

'It's a name we've given him and which you shall refer to him by. You don't need to know his real name. However, he can get the job done, but before we invite him, you have to understand one thing; the man is unhinged. He works with a partner, and they're both very good at what they do, but they're ruthless.'

'Ruthless is good.'

'Ruthless is expensive.'

'Money is no object. Considering what a cock-up the last plan was.' The suit stood up and walked over to the drinks cabinet and poured himself a drink. A small measure, not big enough to make him fail a breathalyser but big enough to take the edge off.

'From what you told us, Laing should have been taken out a long time ago.'

Suit drank some of the whisky. Looked out the window at the building opposite. All of them expensive flats, in the New Town. He wondered what they would think if they knew what was being planned in this flat. He turned back to the two men in the room.

'That was a mistake, but it had to be made to look like he was ill. They would have been found out of course, but sticking a knife in him would have brought the gates down. It was attack and retreat, but they got wind of it and somebody had him removed. The next time, we won't be so subtle.'

'When you say *we,* I'm assuming you won't be getting your hands dirty?'

The suit smiled. 'That's your game, your expertise. I don't mind you overseeing the operation, so long as it gets done.'

'I have my suspicions where Laing might have run to, and if they prove correct, then it won't be easy getting to him,' Mr Black said. 'That's why I've drawn up Plan B. If we can't get to him, then he will have to come to us.'

'How do you propose we achieve that?' Mr Blue said.

'By utilising the amenities we have at hand, shall we say? Retreat and regroup, isn't that the mantra we lived by? The leadership courses? Not going into battle when your troops are down, but regrouping and going on the offensive using stealth and cunning? David

TRIAL AND ERROR

and Goliath, my friend. Just when Miles Laing thinks it's safe, we'll haul him back into reality.'

'What about the others?'

'Listen, we're going to use them all. Especially Frank Miller. Whether he likes it or not, he's been dragged into this. He thinks he's investigating the escape.' Suit drank more of the whisky and stared off into space.

'Little does he know just how far he's going to be involved in all of this. And it's not something he's going to come back from.' Mr Blue stood thinking for a moment.

'Does Mr Red know about your attempt to get rid of Laing in the hospital?' Mr Black said.

'Need to know. And right now, he doesn't need to know about Miles Laing. All he needs to know is the name of his target. Mr Red will be with us not long from now.'

'I hope he's discreet.'

Mr Black looked at Mr Blue before answering. 'I don't think he knows how to spell *discretion* but he gets the job done. He's ruthless. Nobody will stand in his way. You want the job done, he'll get it done. But we'll be there controlling him. From a distance. But we'll liaise with him at all times.'

'Christ, I don't want this backfiring.'

Mr Black smiled. 'Mr Red is a professional. This next part has to go like clockwork. Or else we'll all die.' He stood looking at the two other men. 'I have to go now. I have a busy day ahead of me.'

'What about the police? Do they even know the woman exists?'

'Not yet. And they won't make a connection.' He left the room.

"I don't like this one little bit,' the suit said. 'It's already gone pear-shaped.'

'A minor glitch.'

'Have you looked closely at your friend there? He's mental. How can we even trust him?'

'We have no choice. Unless you have an assassin on speed dial, we have to work with him. He's a mercenary. As long as he gets paid, he'll get the job done.'

'And now he has another nutter on board. God help us all.'

Mr Black smiled. 'That's why we have to make sure Miles Laing dies as soon as possible.'

CHAPTER 7

Mr Blue didn't like the suit at all. He wasn't expecting to meet the man, but he had shown up at the house uninvited. He understood he and Mr Black went back a long way, but there was something creepy about him. The man had never seen military duty, that was obvious.

He drove the Transit van through Fairmilehead and onto the Biggar Road, heading south out of the city. The country road wasn't too busy and he arrived at his destination a few minutes after passing the Hillend Snowsports Centre, with the ski slope on his right.

Easter Howgate, more of an area rather than a village, where Mr Blue thought he could quite happily live, away from the hustle and bustle. He had plans to live somewhere quiet, probably in the Highlands, after he was done working. Which was away in the future, but it didn't do any harm to plan ahead.

Like he was doing now.

Planning ahead.

This job was going to net him a lot of money. Sure, he and Mr Black went way back, but this wasn't the sort of job you did for a hobby. How would he be able to afford a little house in the middle of nowhere if he didn't make money?

He turned off the main road, past a small house that was set back a little bit and drove up the single lane road.

The house he wanted was tucked away on the other side of a hill, and if you didn't know it was there, you would think it was just the Pentlands in front of you. He could understand why the woman wanted to live in isolation.

He pulled the van in front of her house and went to the back, and took out the cardboard box he had for her. There was an address label stuck on the front with her name on it. Everything looked official. He carried a clipboard with a list of fake names on it, hers being in the middle.

He closed the van door then walked up to the front door of the house, holding the bottom of the box with one hand and the clipboard with the other. He rang the doorbell, looking around to see if there was anybody watching, but there were no houses that overlooked this property.

That made his job easier. If she'd lived in a tenement in the middle of Marchmont, it would have been more difficult. Not impossible, but he would have used a different tactic.

He heard the clack of a chain sliding across and then the door opened a crack. 'Yes? Can I help you?' the woman said.

'Delivery for Rena Joseph.' He held up the box, the size chosen so that it couldn't be slipped through a small gap like this. It was chosen so the recipient would have to open the door.

'I didn't order anything,' she said. 'Who is it from?'

Shit. 'It doesn't have a return address on here. Maybe there's a packing slip inside.' Now he was getting antsy but he made sure this wasn't transferred to his face.

'Take it back,' she said and slammed the door shut. There was glass in the front door and he could see the woman running down the hallway. Not just walking away in a pissed off type of way, the way a person who has been disturbed might do, but she took off running.

She knows!

Mr Blue was used to kicking down doors. He'd done it many times in Kandahar. There had to be no hesitation, or else the next thing you knew, there was a bullet through your eyeball. This was no different. This woman could be away to call the police. Or worse. She might have a shotgun.

He dropped the box and kicked the door hard and it flew inwards. There was no scream like he thought there might be. He didn't run through the doorway the woman had run through. He'd seen too many men die that way.

He approached slowly and low. Moved quickly through when he didn't detect a threat. The living room was empty, but the threat was in the kitchen, holding a large knife.

'Did that fucker Miles send you? Afraid to stand up to me?'

'Put the knife down, Rena,' Mr Blue said.

'Nobody's called me that in years.' Her voice shook but she wasn't holding the knife where she would bring it down in an arc. No, she was holding it away from herself, but close to her body, like she would jab at him, but keeping it out of his reach. She'd obviously been

John Carson

watching YouTube videos on *how to defend yourself with a potato peeler,* but she'd opted for the carving knife instead.

But what was that all about, not going by Rena for years? Bad intel again. Mr Black had some explaining to do.

'Put the knife down, Rena.'

'Is that what he told you to call me?'

'Nobody told me anything. I just need to talk to you. Come on, put the knife down.' The last thing he wanted to do was take his gun out. Her death would hardly look like she had kicked over a paraffin lamp if she had a bullet in her skull.

She snorted, her eyes wide, her unkempt hair falling over her face. She swept it out of the way, jabbing with the knife. 'You just want to talk? Is that why you tried to con your way in here?'

She's got a good point, old son. He had to draw her towards him. He took a quick step forward, and she reacted just like he'd hoped she would – she thrust the knife towards him. He grabbed her wrist with his right hand, swiftly moving his left hand up to her face and then he twisted her, sticking one of his legs behind her and taking her down.

She screamed and he took the knife from her. It would have been easy to ram it into her throat, but he didn't want that. Too easy for them to figure out. Better to knock her out before he started the fire.

But Rena Joseph wasn't having that. She screamed loudly, getting on her hands and knees. Mr Blue reached round the back of her head, grabbed her hair and with his hand on her chin, snapped her neck. The end result was the same, just a different manner. He placed one of the dining chairs away from her, on its side. It might be reduced to a pile of ashes, but if not, it might divert their attention long enough.

And they might not connect Miles Laing with her right away, but they would eventually.

Mr Blue went back out to get the box he'd brought and took it inside. He opened it and took out the paraffin lamp with the can of paraffin. He put the can on its side with the cap off, on the carpet. The contents ran out in a puddle. He placed the lamp on the counter, lit it, then brushed it off with his arm, stepping quickly away. The lamp fell and ignited the paraffin in a bright explosion as he grabbed the box and ran out of the room.

Woman falls, breaks her neck and knocks over lamp on the way down, setting the house on fire. He smiled at the thought as he ran along the hall. Of course, the fire investigators weren't stupid. Nor the pathologists. This was merely a message to Miles Laing.

As he drove away, he could see smoke starting to rise, in his mirrors.

CHAPTER 8

Miller told the other two detectives he wanted to swing by somewhere first. He rang the doorbell and stood back. It was a nice, old property. Five bedrooms, built solidly, back in the day when they knew how to build houses.

The door opened, and a big man stood looking out at him. 'Frank! Good to see you. Dawn called and told me she'd bumped into you.'

Vince Rutherford smiled and stood back to let him in.

'I had to go to the cemetery to see Carol's grave. What with it being eight years to the day since we caught him, and the fact he's now on the loose.'

They went through to the kitchen where Vince put the kettle on.

'Did Dawn give you the book?'

'Yes, thanks. That was very good of you, Vince.'

'It's a small gesture. Carol was my biggest fan. Everybody I knew said I would make it one day, and I'm glad I kept at it.'

'I read Dawn's stuff, too. She's an excellent thriller writer.'

Vince poured two coffees. 'I don't know why she hasn't been picked up, but self-publishing is such a big hit nowadays, she doesn't really need to.'

They sat at the kitchen table. 'Is she here now?'

'No. She's out shopping. She likes to do it by herself. I just hold her back, she says. I can never understand a woman who reads the label on every bottle and jar before throwing it into the trolley.'

'I'm the same. In, bung all the junk into the trolley, back out again. But Kim is particular about what we eat.'

'How's the pregnancy coming along?'

'She's over five months now, and starting to change, physically. Pain and all that. I don't know what pain she means. A woman doesn't know pain like a man knows pain after he's been kicked in the balls.'

'Jesus, don't go telling her that.'

Miller laughed. 'I'm kidding. We've had this discussion many times, but just as a joke.'

TRIAL AND ERROR

'I'm not as brave as you, mate. I wouldn't joke like that with Dawn.'

'How's Beckett doing? Dawn said he and Michelle are engaged?'

'Yes. He wanted to ask her out for the longest time, and then he plucked up the courage. Now they've got engaged.'

Miller drank more of the coffee. 'I was sorry to hear about your mother.'

'Thanks. She wasted away at the end. It was very quick. She was taken into the hospital, then the hospice and died two days later. Start to finish, less than two weeks.'

'Dawn said you were worried about Laing coming back for her.'

Vince looked at him. 'I'm not worried about what he would try and do to me. I'd knock the bastard out. But it's what he and that psycho bitch might do to her that worries me.'

'All I can recommend you do if you see him is give us a call.'

'I'll set Beckett about him. It's when Dawn is out on her own that I worry, but she says she's not going to live her life avoiding Laing.'

'For all we know, he might be on his way to London by now, or trying to leave the country.'

'You don't believe that for one moment. Do you? Be honest with me.'

Miller shook his head. 'You know I once told you he'dcall me and talk to me on the phone?'

'Yes.'

'He's been calling me for the past month. He called the other day. His last words to me were *See you soon, Frank.*'

'Do you think he's coming after you?'

'I'm not sure. He tried to tell me there was another victim before the first one we found.'

'Do you believe him?'

'No. I think he just wanted to rattle me before he escaped. I don't think he'll waste his time coming after us.'

'I'm not going to promise that I wouldn't take the law into my own hands if he came near us, but that would be the last line of defence.'

They were silent for a moment, the only sound a fan whirring in the next room.

'You still miss her, Frank? Carol.'

45

John Carson

Miller nodded. Took a quick breath before answering. 'I do, Vince. Every day. I'm with Kim now, of course, but Carol and I had something special. I think working together helped us bond.'

'Kim is an investigator too, just with the fiscal's office, but you still work with her. Do you feel that helps you bond with her?'

'I do. Every relationship is different. Carol was the first woman I ever fell in love with. If she hadn't been taken away from me, we would still be together. Some guys go out messing about with other women, but I never had a hankering for that.'

'I know I had been out with other women, but not one of them compared to Dawn. I couldn't believe it when she came back into my life. I thank God every day for that. And now we have two little boys. One I didn't know about at first, but they are all my life. If anybody comes close to touching them, it will be all over for them.'

'I know, pal. I have little Emma, who I look on as my own daughter, and now we're going to have another child. Being a dad changes everything, doesn't it?'

'It does. Miles Laing better stay away if he knows what's good for him.'

'I feel the same way.' He finished his coffee and stood up. 'I'd better get going. If Laing isn't planning on coming near me, it doesn't mean I don't have to go after *him.*

'Let me know if you catch him, Frank.'

'You'll be my first call.'

CHAPTER 9

Miller headed out to Tanner's Bar in Juniper Green, on the west of the city.

'How's things with Jean?' he asked Watt.

'Pretty good, to be honest. Her house is down the road from Tanner's, and I feel at home there.'

'You ever come up to the pub?'

'Nah. I drink in Colinton Village now. It's an old man's pub, which is good as there are no young tossers in there looking for a fight.'

'I thought your attitude was, you hadn't had a good night out unless you had skelped somebody?'

'That's slander. Me being an officer of the law, I would never say such stuff.' Watt looked out the passenger window as they drove up Clovenstone Road. 'Mind you, I've had my fair share down there.' He nodded to the flats down below. 'I lived there when you first joined CID. When they found out I was a copper, they tried their pish on, but they soon learned a lesson.'

'What about your own place in Oxgangs?'

'I rent it out now. I use the money to pay my way at Jean's.'

'It sounds serious with her.'

'We're good for each other just now. I never look past tomorrow. You don't know what's round the corner.'

Don't I know it? Miller thought about Carol going out to do the ransom drop and then watching her die before his eyes in Accident and Emergency.

He shuddered for a moment and then stopped at the traffic lights, waiting to turn right.

'It must affect you, knowing it was eight years ago that we caught that bastard. If you ever need to talk, Frank, I'm only a phone call away. If I'm not washing my skids or giving Jean one, then we can get a pint.'

'There's a lady in the car,' Steffi Walker said from the back seat.

'Where?' Watt said, grinning.

'Very funny, sarge.'

'I try to be.'

Tanner's Bar was on the left. A smart-looking pub, set back from the main road. A vennel led to a car park and the entrance to the restaurant.

There were a few customers in, and they saw through the front window that Amanda Cameron was behind the bar.

Bruce Hagan's wife.

'He must have literally been mental to give up Hazel for this woman,' Watt said, getting out of the car. They were parked next to the owner's Jaguar.

'Sometimes we make decisions in the heat of the moment, Andy.'

'I wonder if that's what it was when Hagan decided he was leaving the hospital?' Steffi said.

Inside, there was the low hum of chatter competing with the news of the escape on TV. They were only mentioning Miles Laing's name, and *another suspect* whose name hadn't been released yet. Amanda Cameron looked up as the three detectives walked in. She whispered something to the bar manager, who glared across at the two suits. Watt was pretty sure he'd lifted the man before, or maybe he was a resident of Clovenstone.

'What's wrong now?' Amanda Cameron said to them as she came round the bar.

'Can we talk in private?' Miller said.

Amanda had a worried look on her face and both detectives were watching her closely.

'Sure. We can talk up in the flat.' She took her keys out as she walked along the short corridor where the entrance door to her flat was.

Upstairs, the smell of stale cigarette hadn't quite managed to dissipate. A few dishes were in the sink in the open-plan kitchen area. 'Sorry, I wasn't expecting guests,' she said.

'This is not a social visit. We're here to talk about Bruce,' Miller said.

'You want a coffee? Something stronger?' she said, as if she hadn't heard them.

'No thanks. You want to sit down?'

TRIAL AND ERROR

'I'm on my feet until five o'clock. If I sit down now, I'll just crash out. Late night last night.' She looked at the them for a moment. 'Is he dead?'

'No, far from it. At least, that's what we think.'

'What do you mean?'

'You heard about Miles Laing escaping from the hospital this morning?'

'I did. Creepy bastard. What's this got to do with Bruce?'

Miller hesitated before answering. 'They took Bruce with them.'

'What do you mean?' The puzzlement showed on her face.

'Laing had an accomplice. When they left, and I can't reveal any details, they took Bruce with them. Three of them left the hospital this morning.'

'Jesus Christ.'

'Has he been in touch?' Watt asked, looking around the flat to see if there was any sign of a man having been there.

'No, of course not.'

'Don't sound so surprised, Amanda. Most escapees come looking for a loved one. You mind if Sergeant Watt has a look around?'

'No, not at all. Check out everywhere. He's not here.'

Watt left the room and headed down a short corridor, disappearing from view. Steffi stood by the window, looking out. 'Has he contacted you recently?' she asked.

'No, he hasn't.' Amanda walked over to a cupboard and took a packet of cigarettes out. Opened it and lit one, offering the packet to Miller. He waved a hand at her.

'I'm asking you to keep this under wraps. If word gets out, you won't be able to leave here for reporters. They'll be camped out here.'

'Fuck them. I won't say a word to those scum-sucking savages.' She puffed furiously.

'There's a fifty-fifty chance that Bruce will come here, but if he does, you have to be careful. We know his mental state is in-and-out. Sometimes he will seem lucid, other times he will stare right through you. We had reports faxed over to the station. Bruce is far from being well.'

'That's all I need, him coming knocking on my door.'

John Carson

'If it's any consolation, we think he was taken. He was ill in the infirmary in the psychiatric hospital. We think they took him because it needed to look like they were taking a patient to the Royal.'

'I wanted him to do it the right way.'

Watt came back into the room, shaking his head at Miller.

'What do you mean?' Miller asked Amanda.

'I got a lawyer and we were putting in an appeal on his sentence. Bruce was fucked up because of all those drugs they pumped into him at that clinic. He didn't know what he was doing. I want him out so he can get proper attention, not shoved in a room to sit and twiddle his thumbs all day.'

'It's hardly a Victorian establishment,' Steffi said.

'You ever been in there as a patient?'

Steffi shook her head.

'He shouldn't be there. He needs real help. What he did wasn't his fault. He's being punished for something somebody did to him, a person who's rich and wasn't made to pay for his crime.'

Miller couldn't argue with that. He took out a business card. 'Call us if he comes here. We don't know what mental state he's in.'

'I'll call my lawyer.'

'You might want to reconsider if it's Miles Laing who turns up at your door.'

'Well, I'll tell you what, that bastard better come for me in my sleep, because if he comes for me when I'm awake, I'll fucking knife him. I have family who live just down the road. A van load of them will be up here in five minutes and they'll throw that bastard off the bridge just outside, right down onto the bypass.'

'Don't be saying this to us,' Miller said, but without much conviction. 'Call us if he comes near you. We have some hard men down in Wester Hailes who can also be up here in a van in a few minutes.'

'Aye, don't be doing anything daft,' Watt said.

'You're not from around here, are you?'

'I am actually.'

More sucking the life out of the cigarette. 'Well, you'll know what I'm talking about. We look after our own. In fact, I think I might move back in with my mother. Fuck this place. If Laing the bampot

TRIAL AND ERROR

wants to come look me up, he can come knocking on my mother's door. My brother will show him what mental is really all about.'

Miller handed her a card. 'Miles Laing is extremely dangerous. Please call us if he comes round. We're better equipped to deal with him.'

Amanda smiled at him, but there was no humour. 'You think so? I know *you're* definitely not from around here.'

CHAPTER 10

'Personally, I don't think he'll show his face round here,' Watt said as they got back in the car.

Miller shook his head. 'I wish I wasn't on duty. I could murder a pint right now.'

'You and me both, squire.'

'I'll just have an orange juice, if you're buying,' Steffi said.

'I'm not,' Watt said.

'Tightwad.'

'You know him too well,' Miller said.

'Don't encourage her.'

Miller joined the traffic on Lanark Road, turning left onto Wester Hailes Road. Left at the Clovenstone roundabout, into Baberton Mains. Then round The Drive and off into Hazel Carter's cul-de-sac.

There was a patrol car parked outside her house. Miller approached the driver's window. 'I'm assuming since you're still sitting here that there's been no sign of him?'

'Correct, sir. DS Carter didn't want anybody to sit in with her.'

'Thanks.' They were greeted at the door by a dishevelled Hazel Carter. Her eyes were red.

'I can't fucking believe this,' she said, stepping aside. The detectives followed her into the living room, Watt closing the front door behind him.

'No contact at all, then?' Miller said, but he knew Hazel would have called it in if there had been.

'Yes. He popped round and he's sitting in the dining room eating lunch. Of course he's not fucking turned up.' She stopped on the threshold between the dining area and the kitchen and turned round. 'I'm sorry, sir. I just feel like there's electricity running through my veins.'

Miller put a hand on her shoulder. 'It's fine, Hazel. I can't even begin to imagine the stress you're going through.'

Miller and Watt sat at the dining table. Steffi stood at the window. 'I wish you would let one of the uniforms sit in here with you,'

TRIAL AND ERROR

Miller said. The small room was a continuation of the kitchen, which itself wasn't overly large. The window to the rear overlooked the small garden. Surrounded by a fence on three sides and the side wall of the detached garage. He couldn't help thinking that if Bruce Hagan decided to jump the fence, there wasn't much Hazel could do about it.

'If he comes in here, this time he'll get it, Frank.' Hazel turned round from the kitchen counter with a knife in her hand. A knife used for stripping meat off the bone, which would no doubt strip Hagan's flesh.

Miller stood up. 'Listen, you need to go somewhere else, somewhere Bruce doesn't know about.'

'Oh, really?' She slammed the knife down. 'Where do you suggest, sir? Holyrood Palace? The Balmoral Hotel has probably got a vacant suite available. Maybe I should book myself in! Or I've got an even better idea; why don't me and that fucker's wife club in together and we can find a place!' She was starting to shout at the top of her voice until Steffi went over and put her arms round her and held her tight.

Hazel cried hysterically, holding onto her until the anger subsided. She pulled away from her and looked Miller in the eyes, tears streaming down her face. 'Why? Why did he go behind my back and marry her? Especially when I'd just had his second child.'

'He was suffering from PTSD, Hazel,' Watt said, standing up. 'I don't even think he knew what he was doing.'

'Then maybe their marriage should be void,' Hazel said, finally letting go of Steffi. She turned and switched the kettle on. Leaned on her hands on the counter, head bent over.

'Let me do that,' Watt said. Hazel turned without looking at him and sat down at the dining table. Miller followed her.

'I know it's hard, but we're all here to help you.'

'You won't be here, twenty-four seven though, will you? And I wouldn't expect you to be.' She wiped her eyes and looked at him as Watt busied himself with the mugs. 'You know the thing that's most fucked-up about this? If that bastard came in here and I stuck that knife right through his heart, I'd be the bad one. You know the Crown Office would have me up on charges for unlawfully killing him. But I don't care. If he comes near the kids, I'll kill the bastard.'

'Where are they now?'

John Carson

'Upstairs. Jane is playing and Daniel's sleeping.' Watt came over with the mugs. Collected his own and sat down.

'You know, I still have nightmares,' Hazel said, wrapping her hands round her mug. 'Bruce used to have dreams about being in the coffin, but I have dreams about him throwing Daniel off the bridge. What if you missed? What if you reached out and you hadn't grabbed him? What if this, what if that? They should have hanged the bastard, instead of putting him in a nice wee cell in a psychiatric hospital. Or at least given him a lobotomy and regular electric-shock treatment. He's the one who got away from it all, and I live the nightmare every day. Who got the life sentence, Frank? Me or him? I'll give him a fucking lobotomy with a hammer if he comes near me.'

Miller looked across at the older sergeant. 'Listen, Hazel, I think we should get you somewhere secure. You and the kids. I can talk to Neil McGovern and see if we can get you into the safe house up in Juniper Green. He won't know you're there. You'll be safe. They have twenty-four-hour guards.'

She shook her head. 'He's not going to let us do that.'

'Would you go there if he gives it the green light?'

'I don't know.'

'You have to think about the kids, Haze,' Watt said. He reached over and took her hand. 'Plus, I'm at Jean's house just down the road in Colinton Village. We can go to the village pub and shake our stuff on their wee dance floor.' He let go of her hand and moved his hands about.

Hazel laughed and sniffed back some more tears. 'You're a mad sod. But you're the best friends I have, and if my best friends say I should move, then I'll do it. But I know it's not a guarantee.'

'Listen, if any man can persuade Neil McGovern to have you as a house guest, it's this man.'

'He means me,' Miller said.

'Duh.' Hazel smiled.

'But I'll not make the call personally,' Miller said. 'I'll have Kim talk to her dad. She has more clout than I do.'

Miller called Kim. Ten minutes later, Miller got the call from Neil McGovern.

'I was going to give you a call later,' McGovern said. 'I'll call round tonight, if that's okay?'

'No problem.'

TRIAL AND ERROR

'Good. The Range Rover will be there in five minutes. Tell Hazel to make herself at home. There's people waiting for her in the house.'

Miller looked at Watt. 'It's a go.'

CHAPTER 11

'I'm telling you, that place gives me the heebie jeebies,' Paddy Gibb said as they pulled up behind the line of police vehicles leading up to the barn. He held his packet of cigarettes in one hand, the lighter in the other. He flicked the lighter constantly, like he wanted to ignite a can of petrol.

'Relax, man,' Percy Purcell said. 'They're all locked up.'

'So was Miles Laing,' DS Julie Stott said from the back seat.

'True. I tell you what though, if there's a mass breakout, I'm running like fuck.' He looked at Gibb and then Julie in the mirror. 'No offence, people, but it's every man for himself.'

Gibb nodded his head. 'Agreed. If you think I'm one of those blokes who say, *Go! Save yourself!* then you don't know me at all.'

'You'd take the whole platoon down with you?'

'Of course I would.'

'That's bad patter, Paddy. I would expect you to form an indomitable wall with Julie while I make good my escape.'

'Well, sir, as much as it pains me to admit it, it's a matter of who can run the fastest when the zombie apocalypse hits.'

'And I can run faster than you both,' Julie said, grinning.

'You can't leave senior officers behind. It's against the law,' Purcell said. 'You'd have to stay behind and fight.'

'The name's crafty, not dafty.'

They got out of the car and showed ID to a uniform.

Inside the barn, it was lit up with arc lights. The ambulance sat near some old, rusting farm equipment. Jake Dagger, one of the city pathologists, appeared at the back of the ambulance.

'Who's the life extinct?' Purcell said.

'Doctor Tamara Child.'

'The one who helped them escape,' Julie said.

'I don't know why they didn't take her with them, but she was restrained on the gurney and then shot in the head. One bullet it looks like, right through her frontal lobe.'

'Where would they get a gun?' Julie said.

TRIAL AND ERROR

Purcell climbed up into the ambulance after pulling on gloves. 'I don't think they walked away from here, so they must have either carjacked somebody, or else they had one waiting for them.' He looked at the corpse of Tamara Child before turning to look back out of the ambulance. 'My guess is, she had left a car here, ready to transfer into, but that raises another question; how would she leave here if she was dumping a car?'

'She had help,' Gibb said.

'I would say so. That would be the obvious answer. But why kill her? And where was the help?'

'She wouldn't need the help if she was just planning on them bringing the ambulance here. The car would be waiting so there would be no need.'

'Correct,' Purcell said. 'But again, why kill her?'

'She was just an added ingredient that they didn't need,' Julie said.

'If they do indeed have another partner, won't that person be suspicious? And why did they restrain her before shooting her? Why not just shoot her?'

Purcell climbed back out. 'Unless they tied her up and she was executed by her friend, if she does indeed have one.'

'We'll run through all the possibilities back at the station. Meantime, we have to go to the hospital.' They said goodbye to Dagger and got back in the car.

Ten minutes later, Purcell stopped the car at the gatehouse. There were armed officers standing next to it, their car parked inside the gate.

'The boys from Glasgow,' he said, winding the window down.

'Can I help you?' the guard said, looking at the three detectives with suspicion.

'Superintendent Purcell,' he said, showing his warrant card. 'DCI Gibb. DS Stott.' He looked at Gibb as the other detectives held up their own warrant cards.

'The Edinburgh contingent,' the guard said, making it sound like they were a bunch of beasts hanging about outside a primary school.

'Just open the gate, pal.'

'What's your business here?'

John Carson

Purcell gave Gibb a *You're fucking kidding me* look, before answering the guard. 'Some numpty let three nut jobs waltz out of here in an ambulance, so take a guess why we're here.'

The guard made a face and popped back inside the guardhouse. The gate slid open to let them into the pen.

'And it was only two nut jobs,' Purcell heard the man say as he started driving forward. 'One was a doctor, smart-arse.'

The gate slid closed behind them and then the other one opened to let them into the grounds. It was like entering another world.

'I'm getting a shiver running up and down my spine,' Gibb said, looking out the window as if he was expecting to be rushed at from the woods. 'Why do you suppose they have so many trees? To keep the nosy bastards from gawping in, or to prevent the inmates from seeing out?'

'God knows, Paddy. But you could drive yourself mental thinking about it. If you'll pardon the pun.'

Julie laughed from the back seat.

Gibb looked over his shoulder at her. 'I'm not chivalrous, either. I'll be fucked if I'm staying behind to fight for you when it all goes down.'

'You're letting your imagination run away with you again, Paddy. Relax.'

'It's hard to relax knowing that the dafties weren't that daft they couldn't form a plan to get out of here.'

Purcell took the road that went down on the right, the same road the ambulance came up. More armed officers were down here. Purcell held up his warrant card for it to be inspected.

They parked the car and approached the loading bay door. Inside, it was cooler, a relief from the August sun beating down on them.

'Superintendent Percy Purcell,' he said to the suit who was hovering about inside the infirmary. 'Edinburgh Division.'

'Super Harry Cole. Glasgow. Why are you boys through here? Standards? Oh, it's yourself, Perce.'

'No, we're not from that department. We're here because one of our officers escaped along with Miles Laing,' Gibb said. 'And we think Laing might be hiding out in Edinburgh.'

'It's been a long time, Harry,' Purcell said.

'It certainly has,' Cole said. 'The wife wants to come through to do some shopping in your fair city, so maybe we could have a pint?'

'Count on it.' Purcell took out a business card and scribbled his mobile number on the back. 'Give me a bell.'

Cole smiled and put the card away in his jacket. 'Aberdeen too hot for you?'

'There was a certain ex-wife who wanted to make it too hot for me, Harry, but that got sorted.'

'Good man. I hear that your love life took a turn for the better though.'

'I lost your address or I would have sent you an invite to the wedding.'

'Who needs to go to a wedding to get pished?' Cole laughed.

'The numpties from Edinburgh are here,' a young suit said as he walked round the corner.

Cole's smile dropped. 'This is Detective Superintendent Purcell from Edinburgh, if that's what you meant.'

'Oh, yes. Sorry. No offence, sir.'

'Offence taken. Just give us a rundown on what happened here, son. We're trying to get a location on our guy and the killer,' Purcell said, his eyes boring into the younger man.

Cole shook his head. 'Sorry, Perce.'

'The nurses and the medics are still here. We're wanting them kept on-site for the time being, before we take them away to question them separately.'

They walked along the corridor to the infirmary. Cole indicated with his head that the younger sergeant should make himself scarce.

'I'll catch you before you go, Perce,' Cole said, heading upstairs.

'Paramedics, eh?' Purcell said to Peter Mackay as they stopped at the nurse's station.

'I've already told this to a detective from Glasgow,' he complained. 'I'm fucked. I was on all night and it's past lunchtime. I can barely stay awake.'

'Try harder. A can of Red Bull does the trick.'

'I've had so much coffee my back teeth are floating.'

'Miles Laing gave no indication that he was faking being ill?' Paddy Gibb said.

John Carson

'I told them this already. That doctor brought him down. Tamara. They had him on a gurney. Her and a couple of knuckle-draggers they call orderlies. He was clutching his guts like he was about to have the shits or something. Then she gave us some spiel about him having an ulcer. Isn't that right, Lin? You were with them first.'

Lin gave Mackay a look, thinking he was trying to cover his own arse. 'Yes. She brought him down on a gurney with two orderlies. They left, she stayed.'

'Why didn't the men stay with her?' Gibb asked.

She sneered at him. 'Because the suits who don't have to come in here and actually work, think we have enough staff as it is. We're spread thin on the ground. That's why they couldn't stay down here.'

'Did you see him restrained with your own eyes?' Julie asked.

All the detectives saw the hesitation for a moment, the briefest indecision, that if you weren't looking closely, you would have missed.

'Well, he was under the sheets. Writhing about. And if the doctor herself was bringing him down, then he must have been restrained. Mustn't he?' She walked away, angry.

Purcell turned to Gibb. 'Find out how long that nurse has been here.' He turned to Julie. 'See what the others have to say about her. See what kind of relationship she had with Laing.'

The two detectives left the infirmary and headed upstairs.

'Do you think this will harm my chances of promotion?' Mackay said, shaking his head.

'I think you'll be lucky to get a job cleaning toilets after this,' Purcell said. But his mind was on a nurse who had helped a serial killer escape from a psychiatric hospital.

And how long she had known him beforehand.

CHAPTER 12

Jeni Bridge's office was stuffy when she opened her door. Det Sup Leach followed her in, with DI Harry McNeil bringing up the rear.

'It's one of those rare Edinburgh days where the sun's shining and there's no forecast for rain. We should mark it on the calendar,' Jeni Bridge said as she ushered him into her office. The corridor was stuffy, even with the windows open.

'Well, it *is* Edinburgh, ma'am, so let's give it time.'

'Where's Miller just now?' Leach said. 'He's with some of his team speaking with Hazel Carter.'

'How is she doing?' he asked, when they were seated.

'Not good at all. I arranged for her to be taken to a safe house run by Neil McGovern's office.'

'He's Kim's father, isn't that right?' McNeil said.

'Yes. His department deals in witness protection and they have several safe houses throughout the city.'

'That girl has been through the wringer. I'm assuming that Hagan hasn't been near her?' Leach said.

'No. But she's angry and in shock. It was bad enough that the father of her children was locked in a coffin, then had drugs pumped into him and now he's been taken from a secure hospital.'

'That's what's puzzling me, ma'am. Why would they take him?'

'We're thinking it would make it look better that they had a patient in the back of the ambulance, when they were dressed as paramedics.'

'True. But knowing Miles Laing, I don't think he would have left a guard alive if he were cornered. But it just seems odd to me that a former detective connected to Miller would AWOL at the same time. We've asked for Hagan's medical file from the hospital. We want to know why he was in there, what drugs he was on and what his behaviour has been like leading up to today.'

'Good. I want to see that file when they get it through to us.' She sat back in her chair.

'Do you think he'll make contact?' Leach said.

'I really don't know. It's hard to tell. We're going to just have to wait and see. But we've had officers out all morning up Lanark Road, looking at premises that have CCTV.'

'That's a busy section of road in the morning,' McNeil said.

'The ambulance left the hospital just after six, so we've narrowed the time down. We're taking a note of the cars that drove along.'

'There are other roads they could have taken though, isn't there?'

'Yes, there is. But this is worth giving it a shot. I don't know if anything will come of it.'

'Yes, a small chance is better than no chance.'

Just then, there was a knock at the door. 'Come!'

Andy Watt popped his head round the door. 'Sorry to interrupt you, ma'am, but I thought you might want to see this.'

'Come in, Andy. Close the door.'

Watt was holding a DVD and a brown envelope in one hand. 'The uniforms hit pay dirt from the CCTV trawl.' He handed it to her and left the room.

'Thank you.'

Jeni put the DVD into her laptop on her desk. She played it, staring at the screen intently. 'Jesus Christ.' She hit a couple of buttons and played the image again, this time swinging the laptop round so the other detectives could see the images as well.

The time stamp was 6.17 am. That morning. A nondescript car pulled up outside a newsagent's and the passenger door opened. They could see the partial outline of somebody sitting in the back, but they couldn't make out the features.

But Leach and McNeil looked at the man who got out of the car and stood in front of the camera. He looked up at it, smiled and waved.

Miles Laing. Wearing a paramedic's uniform.

He brought a sheet of paper out from behind his back. Jeni paused the scene to read the writing on the paper. They stared at it.

See you soon, Frank!

'I wouldn't mind staying in a house like that, under different circumstances,' Hazel said, keeping a tight hold of Daniel, her little boy and Jane, her daughter. 'If it was a country hotel or something. I'm sorry, but I've changed my mind. Sorry for messing you about, but I'm not going to be shoved out of my own home because of him.'

Miller and McGovern were sitting on Hazel's couch.

'Please think about this, Hazel,' Miller said. 'Your safety would be guaranteed up there.'

'Sir, I appreciate the offer, but you have to understand that if Bruce comes here and tries to touch the kids, I will knife him. And I don't mean, scratch him with a nail file. I mean, ram a fucking carving knife into his heart.'

'You have to think of the children,' McGovern said.

'Didn't you hear what I just said? Sorry to be blunt, but I'm not running or living in fear. I'll take care of the children. Bruce will never grab my kids again and put them in danger.'

McGovern stood up, followed by Miller. 'I respect your decision. It doesn't mean we're not here to help, if you need us. We're only a phone call away. I mean that. If you change your mind, Hazel, the offer is open twenty-four seven. One phone call and I'll have two men come pick you up.'

'Thank you, I appreciate the offer, but we'll be fine.'

'I'll talk to Jeni Bridge about getting a patrol car from Wester Hailes to swing by regularly,' Miller said.

'Look, I really appreciate your help, both of you, but I don't think Bruce will come anywhere near us. He's probably long gone by now, messing about with his pal, Laing. And the tart who got them out.'

'You sure we can't twist your arm?' Miller said.

'I'm sure.'

Miller sighed. 'Just watch your back at all times, Hazel.' He and McGovern left her house.

'This is a right balls-up,' McGovern said when they were outside the house.

Miller turned from the driveway. The sun was high in the sky but the room was cool. 'Christ, it's that alright.'

'Sometimes I wish I could just get blootered and when I wake up, all this would be finished.'

'The sentiments of many a policeman, I'm sure,' McGovern answered. The driver was waiting outside the car for him.

'You going back to the office?' Miller said.

John Carson

'I'm going up to the safe house.' He looked at Miller. 'Do you think he's coming after her?'

'I certainly fucking hope not.' He looked at the older man for a second. 'I worked with Bruce a long time ago. Hazel fell in love with him. They had kids together. He was a good laugh, always went the extra mile. He was a bloody good police officer, yet I find it hard to think about him as a normal man. Before the incident. Before going off his head. Know what I mean?'

McGovern looked at the detective. 'Yes, I do. My old man was a great influence in my life. Always had time for me and my sister. He would play football with me and then when my pals came out, he would stay and still kick the ball around. He was my best friend growing up and we went drinking together. Once a week, we went for a pint. But now he's gone, I can't for the life of me remember what his voice sounded like. He died alone in a hospital bed and I cried when I saw him like that, and every time I think about him now, the image of him wired up to a machine in a hospital bed is what comes to mind first, not the good times we had when I was a boy.'

'It wasn't Bruce's fault, but he was treated like a pariah. Shoved away in a rubber room where he couldn't do himself or anybody else harm. I wish to Christ I had known what he was going to do that night. The night when he ended up being put into a coffin.'

'You can't blame yourself for that, Frank.'

Miller looked down at his shoes for a moment, feeling heat creep into his body, the product of stress, not the weather. Then he looked back at the civil servant, the man who would shortly be his father-in-law. 'I do though. Every senior officer likes to think they're looking after the people below them, and although I'm not that senior, I want to take care of my team. I let one of them down, and now he's out there, running about with a couple of nutters.'

'I've asked Jeni Bridge for a copy of the report on Hagan, just so I know what we're dealing with. God knows, we don't want to harm him, but we have to know what level of restraint we're looking at.'

'The last thing I want is for him to be harmed, especially since he doesn't know what he's doing.'

'If he comes for Hazel, we'll make sure he's sent back to the hospital.'

TRIAL AND ERROR

'You know that Miles Laing stopped their getaway car at Tanner's Bar across the road and held up a sign that said, *See you soon, Frank!*?'

'I did know. Jeni Bridge told me.'

'He called me the other night and said the same thing. They think I'm involved with him.'

McGovern smiled. 'Some of the suits upstairs take their jobs far too seriously. But they have to look into it I suppose. So long as they don't give it any credence.'

'I hope not. There's always somebody with a grudge though, isn't there?'

'I'd better not find out there's any shenanigans going on.' He looked at Miller. 'How's my daughter doing? Bending your brain yet?'

'Hardly.'

'Their hormones are all over the place. Give it time, she'll be picking up a carving knife one minute then showering you with kisses the next.'

'I'll buy a crash helmet.'

'Seriously though, I'm glad you two are making a go of it.' He looked at Miller for a moment. 'Can I ask you something personal?'

'Of course you can.'

'Are you going to marry my daughter soon?'

Miller looked away for a moment. 'We were supposed to be married already, but Percy Purcell was getting married and we thought it would clash. So we've just put it off for a while.'

'She wants to be married before she's thirty. That little event will happen in November. Is that something you're prepared for?'

'I am. We just have to find the right time now. What with the baby coming.'

'And the due date is not long after her birthday. She's already five months, and trust me, nine months will be here before you know it. And my wife is champing at the bit. She is looking forward to having another grandchild, but an unmarried daughter who drops a baby isn't going to go down too well.'

'I'm thirty, turning thirty-one next month. Maybe we should do it before that. You know we're just having a quiet affair. Kim and I have both been through the big wedding before, so neither of us want a big do. It won't be hard to organise.'

John Carson

'If I was you, I would give it some serious consideration.'

'I'll get right onto it.'

McGovern looked at him. 'I know you arrested Miles Laing eight years ago today, and that must be weighing heavily on your mind, considering you were with Carol at the time, but all I ask is that you make my daughter happy.'

Miller looked at him for a moment before answering. 'I will. Her and the baby. And little Emma too. I would do anything to protect them all.'

'Let's hope you're never in a position to put that to the test.'

If he only knew.

CHAPTER 13

'You drinking on your own?' Jack Miller said as Frank showed him into the living room. 'That's a slippery slope, son.'

'Why don't you join me in one. That way I won't be on my own.'

'You've twisted my arm. A short before we go over the road.'

Miller poured his father a whisky from the decanter into one of the crystal glasses from the wall unit. Jack stroked Charlie the cat, who had run over to him. He accepted the glass and they clinked.

'Cheers, son.'

'Cheers. Grab a seat.' Jack sat down on the new leather recliner that Kim had bought so she could rest with her legs up. Charlie had already made his mark on it with tiny pinprick claw marks.

'You look like you've lost a pound and found a penny.'

Miller drank some more of the whisky. 'All I'm saying is, I'm glad Kim is away to her folks' house with Emma.'

'Why? What happened.'

'Miles Laing called me a little while ago.'

'Jesus. Did you call it in to the station?'

'Of course I did. Bill Leach wanted to come round tonight but I told him I have it recorded and I'll let him hear it in the morning. Laing didn't give any clue as to his whereabouts.'

'Do you trust Leach?'

'I have no choice in the matter. Him and McNeil will be all over me if they think I'm trying to keep something from them.'

Jack made a face. 'McNeil is a weasel. Nobody ever liked him and that was before he went to the snooping squad.'

'I don't think either of them are convinced I'm not in this with Laing. Christ, they might well think I was driving the getaway car.'

'If you only had a clue where he was, you could send round some of the armed boys.'

'He's not that stupid.'

'What did he want?'

John Carson

Miller looked at his father before answering. 'I'll let you hear for yourself.'

He stood up and walked over to the little table where the phone lived and picked up the voice recorder. A recording unit had been brought round by a tech and attached to his house phone, but Miller had put the cordless phone unit on speaker and recorded it as well. He put the little Sony machine on the coffee table between them and hit play.

'Frank! Glad I caught you in. Such a splendid day for a psychopath like me to be walking about loose in the streets of Edinburgh, don't you think?'

'I think you shouldn't be calling me.'

'Now, I can see why you might be a little bit tetchy, what with Kim almost at the end of her second trimester. It must be getting on your nerves.'

'Why don't you do us all a favour and hand yourself in?'

'Where's the fun in that?'

'You know I'm going to catch you again.'

'I never got that feeling from you, Frank. Not the first time round, and not this time.'

'What do you want?'

'I did tell you that I would see you soon, didn't I?'

'I have to tell you that coming up to my flat wouldn't be a good idea.'

'I know you have to say that on the phone, Frank, but trust me, you and I will have a nice long chat. First though, I want to be able to help you.'

'With what?'

'Helping find my other victim of course! Have you forgotten already?'

'I'm not playing any of your stupid games.'

'It's not a game. It's a chance for you to put some poor soul to rest.'

'Listen, Miles, why don't you just meet me at the station. I'll take care of you. Make sure they know you came in on your own. What do you say?'

TRIAL AND ERROR

'I say that wouldn't be any fun. It would be like handing you the combination to the safe without making you try and work it out. No, that won't do at all, Frank. But if you do your homework, it will be easy for you to figure out who I killed.'

'I need something more to go on,' Miller said.

'The key to solving this is right in front of your face, Frank.'

'What do you mean? Hello? Hello?'

Frank took another sip of whisky. 'He hung up.' He walked over to the window, which was open. Festival crowds were in the High Street below. People dressed up as clowns started playing instruments.

'He's away with the fairies,' Jack said.

'He didn't seem that way when I first met him eight years ago.'

'True. But who knows what goes on in the minds of the insane?'

Miller spun round to look at his father.

'I was just saying,' Jack said, taken by surprise.

'No, it's not that. It's that band downstairs.' Miller turned back to the window and closed it. He picked up the recorder again and rewound it a bit.

'The key to solving this is right in front of your face, Frank.'
Then the sound of a band starting, just a split second. Miller put his glass down and looked out of the window again. At the three red phone boxes that stood on the High Street, a little bit further up and across from his apartment.

'Fuck me, I think he was calling from across the road. In the phone box. That sounds like the band starting up, on the tape. I closed the window when he called.'

'What?' Jack put his glass on the table and jumped up. 'Do you think he's still there?'

'Not a chance. He'll be long gone, but you heard what he said. The key is right in front of my face. He meant in the phone box!'

He ran for the door, his father right behind him. A neighbour was coming out of the lift so they both ran in and hit the button for the ground floor. Outside on the North Bridge, there were a lot of people. It was early evening and the fun was just starting for some of them. It

John Carson

was cooler in the shadow of the building, but Frank felt nothing as the adrenaline was setting him on fire from the inside.

He and Jack ran to the corner of the street, barging past pedestrians, Miller pushing his way past the tourists. They crossed the road at the top of Cockburn Street, narrowly being missed by a taxi as it weaved through the crowds and turned down the side street.

The phone boxes were empty. They were a fixture on the street now, a tourist novelty rather than a necessity. Miller swung the first door open, figuring Miles Laing would have been in this one which was the only one he could see out the side of to look up at Miller's window.

There was a metal shelf in the phone box, and Miller felt underneath it.

Jack was standing outside, holding the door open and trying not to breath in the smell of stale urine. These phone boxes obviously doubled as toilets in the wee hours of the morning.

'Got it,' Miller said, holding up the envelope by one corner. He shook it side to side. He felt something move inside.

'Right in front of my face. The key.'

'Better get it to the lab,' Jack said as they crossed back over, Miller scanning the crowd. He was trying to see Miles Laing, but had a better chance of picking out one grain of sand on the beach.

Back upstairs, he took the envelope through to the kitchen where he put it on the counter. He put on a pair of rubber gloves and took a sharp knife out of the kitchen drawer. He slid the knife under the flap and cut it along the seam.

A key was inside. It fell onto the counter top. Miller looked inside. There was an accompanying note. Miller opened it up and read it:

Frank! I knew you would find this. The key opens a door. Not hard to find, but it's more than physical. It's symbolic. Follow the clue and you'll be on your way. "Take a step. Or 143 steps. On the other side of the lights to Heaven, you'll see the home fires burning."

Time is against you, Frank. Good luck. See you soon.

'What the fuck does that mean?' Jack said.

TRIAL AND ERROR

Miller read it again. Looked at his father. 'God knows. What's the significance of 143 steps?'

'Kim helped you solve a puzzle before by asking her cronies at GCHQ. Maybe you could ask her again.'

'No. This is for me. This is a personal thing for me and Laing. He wouldn't have written a puzzle for me if he didn't think I could work it out.'

'Lights to Heaven. That's what that fucker will be seeing if he comes near me.'

'I don't think he intends to come near you.' Miller looked at the key, knowing he would have to hand it over. But he didn't want to do that.

Not yet.

This key was going to help him track down Laing. Then the bastard would get what he hadn't got eight years ago.

He called Harry McNeil.

CHAPTER 14

Kim Smith felt like shit. It was a beautiful morning, the sun sitting in a blue sky, the air was warm, her daughter hadn't tried to watch more cartoons before school, Frank had mentioned the *M* word last night in bed. Mentally, she was happy, but physically, she felt like shit.

'The green man's on, mummy,' Emma said, tugging her mum's hand.

'Don't pull me, Emma.' The little girl let go her hand and ran across the road. They fought against the crowds of Germans, Italians and God knows how many other foreigners who just had to be up at the crack of fucking dawn to go and rub Greyfriar's Bobby.

Jesus, Kim, listen to yourself. You were never this grumpy in the morning. Yes, you're pregnant, but you've been pregnant before. Yes, but I was married the last time! And that was the crux of the situation. Frank could talk the talk, but he sure was looking like he couldn't walk the walk. Yes, they'd talked last night, after he'd been talking to her father in the afternoon, but would he have talked about it otherwise? She didn't think so.

Christ, where the hell was Emma? Her heartbeat started to increase, and God knows she didn't need her blood pressure getting any higher. She looked through the throng of people coming towards her. 'Emma!' she shouted, starting to shove past the crowd, the large bag she was holding almost acting like a weapon. She couldn't see her daughter.

Then there was a break in the crowd and she saw her. A man was hunched over slightly, talking to her. 'Emma!' she screamed. People turned to look at her. She felt like it was a hundred degrees outside.

Her daughter waved at her. A group of teenagers stopped in the road, right in the middle of the fucking road, blocking her way with their backpacks, stopping to take photos of the Royal Mile, snapping away both north and south, standing in her way, laughing as she tried to push past them. They giggled and laughed and sniggered at her. At the pregnant fat cow she'd become.

'Get out the fucking way!' she snarled at one lanky teenager. He dropped his smile and stepped aside, clutching at his camera like she was about to steal it.

When she got to the other side, she couldn't see her daughter. She looked all around her and then she saw her, sitting on the steps of the Bank Hotel.

'Emma!' she said, rushing over to her, as fast as she could move. 'What did I tell you about leaving my side?'

'Sorry, mum,' the little girl said.

'Who was that man?'

'He picked up Charlie. I dropped him and he picked him up for me.' She held up her soft toy cat, named after their real cat.

'What did he say to you?'

'Nothing. He just picked my cat up. Did I do something wrong?'

Kim looked around to see if she could see the man, but he wasn't lingering about. *Ease up, Kim. A tourist picked her toy up.* She tried to convince herself, and it was probably fine, but all this business with Miles Laing was getting to her.

'No, honey, but remember what we spoke about. No talking to strangers.'

She took Emma's hand and they made their way down the high street, the little girl skipping as they weaved through the crowds. She was used to big crowds having lived in London, but sometimes this place seemed too small to hold all the visitors. She wished she didn't have to carry her bag. Most days, before she was pregnant, she would carry a wallet and her ID. Now this huge bloody thing went with her.

Her mind wandered back to Frank and his talk of marriage. She loved him, she knew that, and hadn't wanted to pressure him into a wedding, but she wanted to be married before she turned thirty, and that was coming up soon. And if they left it any longer, the photographer would have to put a wide-angle lens on his camera.

With Emma's hand firmly ensconced in hers, they started on down the high street. Past the Christmas shop that was open year-round. She loved Christmas time. Especially with Emma, and this year there would be another child there on Christmas Day.

John Carson

Emma's school was down almost at the bottom of the hill, but she would get the bus back up. Thank God the new babysitter was picking her up from school and taking her to her house for a couple of hours. Each day was getting harder and harder, and she wasn't even working. She felt so tired these days. Her moods were swinging as well. Sometimes she loved Frank so much, other days she would happily knife him.

'Bye, mummy!' Emma said, tugging at her hand.

'Oh, bye, honey.' She kissed her daughter on the cheek and waved to her, but the little girl was already running across the playground to join her friends.

Kim walked to the bus stop and waited with the others. She wondered if she would have already had another child with Eric, her former husband, if they'd stayed together. She liked to think they would have. He already had another child with his new wife, so she thought that they probably would have. If he hadn't cheated on her.

The bus came up the hill. She shuffled forward and got on in front of an elderly-looking man with a walking stick. There weren't many seats left, so he sat down beside her.

'How far along?' he said to her, one hand still gripping his stick.

'Excuse me?'

'My daughter's six months pregnant.'

'Oh, right. Five months.' She gripped the bag on her lap, not feeling like a conversation but not wanting to be rude to the old man.

'My daughter has two already,' he carried on, as the bus glided up the High Street. 'Two boys. She's hoping for a little girl this time.'

Kim tried not to look at his unkempt beard and the glasses that were so old they were coming back into fashion. She didn't dislike elderly people, far from it, but she had a headache and felt so uncomfortable that the last thing she wanted to do was strike up a conversation.

Unless it was with Frank about setting a date.

She was tuning the man out as he went on about his grandchildren. She felt bad. Maybe this was the only time the old man got a conversation.

'…children?'

'I'm sorry?' she said again.

TRIAL AND ERROR

'Do you have any other children?'

'I have a little girl.'

'Nice.' He smiled at her, the smile of the aged innocents.

'Excuse me, this is my stop,' she said as the bus pulled into her stop on George IV Bridge.

'Oh, yes,' he said, standing up. He was a bit unsteady on his feet and overbalanced slightly before stopping himself from falling over with his stick. 'Enjoy the rest of your day,' he said, smiling at her.

'You too, thank you,' she said, standing behind the other passengers who were waiting to get off.

The sun was baking Edinburgh as she walked along the pavement towards Chambers Street and the fiscal offices. God, she felt like she had no energy these days, but then she smiled to herself. It was going to be worth it. A mother to two children.

Upstairs in the office, she was ushered into the office by the Procurator Fiscal, Norma Banks.

'Jesus, Kim, you look tired.'

'Thanks, mum. Good to see you too.'

'I'm your concerned mother as well as your boss.'

'You only saw me last night.' Kim eased herself into the chair on the opposite side of Norma.

'I know, and maybe we should restrict your visits to the weekend.'

'You make me sound like a prisoner.'

'Oh, hi, Kim,' Sharon Hardy said, coming into the office.

'Hi, Sharon.'

'I didn't realise you were coming in today. We're just going over some files, but I can wait outside.'

'Thank you,' Norma said. 'She's a good worker.'

Sharon Hardy was Kim's temporary replacement, taking over the role of investigator while she was off.

Norma smiled. 'How about a bottle of water before you start?' The question was more rhetorical as she opened the bottle that sat beside her coffee machine. 'I had my secretary bring one in.'

'Thanks, but I could murder a cup of tea right now.'

John Carson

Norma plugged the Keurig in and waited for the water to heat before making her daughter a cup of tea. The tea in the K cups wasn't quite the same but it was a good second best.

'Milk and one?'

'Just milk. I have a little packet of fake sugar in my bag.'

Kim opened her bag and reached in. 'Jesus Christ,' she said, taking out a strip of paper that had been put inside. She held it up and read it.

Tell Frank I'll see him soon!

'Where the hell did that come from?' Norma asked.

The old man on the bus who fell against her as she got up from her seat. The old man who wasn't an old man.

'I think I just met Miles Laing.'

CHAPTER 15

'What makes them do it, boss?' Andy Watt said, steering the car round into a little side street in Stockbridge. 'The women who fall in love with the nutters in hospital.'

'Your guess is as good as mine, Andy. Some people see past the evil and then see something there that the rest of us don't.'

'Tamara Child obviously saw something in Miles Laing. And being a nurse, she was able to get close to him. She was taking a risk.'

'I don't think they see it that way,' Miller said, getting out of the car. He hadn't been down here in ages. Carol's local had been this hotel and they had been patrons of it many times.

The hotel that had been owned by Miles Laing's parents.

Dean Park Terrace. The row of townhouses hadn't changed much in the last eight years, including the Wellness Clinic that had been owned by a near-victim of Laing's. Miller wanted to talk to Perry MacKinnon even though the doctor had already been visited.

The previous day, they had raided the last known address of Tamara Child, but the doctor's house had been empty, cleared of everything, like she had been well prepared for the escape. But everything about Tamara Child had been fake.

'She certainly did a number,' Miller said, standing in the shade of the trees on the Water of Leith side of the street while he looked up at the building. 'Bank accounts cleared out. Nothing left behind.'

'And she doesn't exist beyond three months,' Watt said. 'This has been in the planning for a long time.'

Despite a raid on her house – which was a rented property – there had been no sign of Tamara Child. There was a patrol car sitting outside the house, just in case she returned, but nobody expected her to.

Miller spoke to the crew in the patrol car, the uniforms sitting outside the hotel. Like with Tamara Child, they didn't expect Laing to show up.

John Carson

'Remember this place when we came here with Carol?' Miller said.

'How could I forget, boss? Christ, I still miss her too.'

For a moment, Miller was transported back eight years, to a time when he and Carol would come to the hotel for a drink. Where they'd met Miles Laing.

He shuddered for a moment, feeling chilled despite the August heat.

'Come on, Andy, let's get inside.'

They climbed the steps up into the hotel, going through another door into reception.

'Can I help you?' the receptionist said.

They both showed their warrant cards. 'Is the owner in?'

'It's the manager. He's through the back. I'll go and get him.'

A big man came back through, sweat lining his forehead. 'Shifting those bloody barrels at my age. It should be a crime. Jacob Hunt. What can I do for you gentlemen?'

'Can we talk in private?' Miller said after introducing himself and Watt again.

'Of course. Through here.'

He led them to a back office, a place that Miller had never been in before, despite knowing Laing. 'Sit down. Take the weight off your feet. It's what the wife is always saying to me.'

'It's about Miles Laing,' Miller said, getting straight to the point.

Hunt looked at him for a moment. 'The psycho who escaped this morning?'

'Yes, him.'

'What about him?'

'We want to know if you've heard from him at all. Or anything suspicious happened lately?'

Hunt shook his head. 'Nothing. As I told the other bloke, I haven't heard anything. I have a few big lads who work behind the bar, so I think we could handle him if he turns up.'

'Don't underestimate him,' Watt said. 'He's extremely dangerous, and he's nothing to lose.'

'I worked a few doors in my time.'

'But still,' Miller said.

TRIAL AND ERROR

'Just because he lived and worked here doesn't necessarily mean he'll come back.'

'His family owned it, so it was his home. He might feel an attraction to the place,' Watt said, starting to feel irritated by the man's nonchalance.

Hunt looked puzzled. 'I don't think he owned the place.'

'It belonged to his father,' Miller said. 'Miles was going to buy it from his father so the old man could retire.'

'And the father's name was Laing, too?'

'Yes, why?'

'That isn't the name of the owners. It's a corporation.'

Miller sat up a bit straighter. 'Can you tell us the name?'

'Thor Industries. Laing and his family ran the place but after what happened, his mother and father left, I assume. I put in for the manager's position with the company, and I got the job. Been here ever since. However, there are photos he left behind, in the filing cabinet.'

'Can we look at them?'

'Sure. I have two rooms downstairs. One of them is my bedroom. The other is what I call the *junk room*. It's where all the crap goes that I don't know what to do with.' He got up and the two detectives followed him out of the office. They went back to the reception and took the staircase behind it. Miller remembered it well.

It was where Sherri Hilton had stayed, when they thought she was the victim of a crime. Nobody knew then what she was really like.

'My wife calls this place the dungeon, and thank God we have a couple of lassies who clean the place because she doesn't come down here with a Hoover.'

They made their way downstairs. The walls were covered in a dark wallpaper, and it was like they were on the set of a Gothic horror movie. The wall lights were adequate and they made their way along to the end of the corridor. On the left was a door, with its twin on the right.

'That one in there is my bedroom.' He unlocked the other door and they went into the room, which wasn't large but you could still swing a proverbial cat.

John Carson

Odds and ends of furniture were stacked. Old toys. Detritus from moving house that was on a list for going through but the enthusiasm was always going to be more than reality.

'The cabinet's over in the corner,' Hunt said. He squeezed past a few boxes, knocking one over in the process. 'Jesus. Time for that diet I think.' He reached the black cabinet and pulled open a drawer and took out a small box.

He handed it to Miller, who opened it. Inside were some toy cars. A photo of a little girl, sitting on top of a couple of old packets of photos with the name of the store that had developed them, probably now defunct.

Miller looked at the little toy cars. Chipped, and obviously well played with. He took out the photo and looked at the girl. She might have been three or four with blonde hair and a smiling face that any father would have been proud of. Miller wondered if his own child would be a girl, and if she would have her mother's looks.

He fished for the first packet of photos and handed the box to Watt to hold.

He opened it and saw the little girl again. She was standing next to a little boy. They were holding hands at a funfair. The first few photos were of the pair, smiling, coming off a ride, standing at an amusement stall. It was clearly summer. The sun was shining but it looked like it was late afternoon or early evening.

Then Miller recognised the place – the *Pleasure Beach*. Blackpool, a British resort on the west coast of England, looking out onto the Irish Sea. He himself had been there with his parents when he was a boy. It was almost like a rite of passage. Take the kids, let them experience it, ride a donkey on the beach, dip a toe in the sea, take a ride up Blackpool Tower (if the parents could afford it). Walk the promenade. Visit Louis Tussauds, now Madame Tussauds wax museum. Ride the trams, sometimes taking one all the way to Fleetwood. See a show on one of the piers. He remembered seeing a show on the north pier with his mum and dad One time Miller had been taken over to the Isle of Man on the ferry..

It was almost as if the photos belonged to Miller. The feelings he had rush through him made him feel happy and sad all at the same time. His mum was gone now, but she had loved Blackpool. He remembered her laugh when she had won a prize at one of the many

TRIAL AND ERROR

bingo places dotted along the promenade. She had dragged him in while his dad had nipped in to the pub next door for a pint.

He recognised the cable car ride that you sat in and surveyed the park below. The log flume, now long gone to be replaced by another ride.

Miller kept flipping through the photos, getting a peek behind the curtains of somebody else's life.

Another photo with a man and woman in it. The woman was planting a kiss on the man's cheek as he smiled into the camera. Next, he was standing beside another woman, both of them smiling. Then one with the first couple, the boy standing between them. The second woman standing beside the little girl. Different poses with the man and women with the kids, always with one of the adults missing, presumably standing behind the camera taking the photo. Then there was one of the five of them, the man's head almost cut off in the photo. Miller guessed that a stranger had been shanghaied into taking the photo, somebody with holiday-photo camera skills.

Candy floss. Miller remembered eating the treat that was like eating hair that fizzled in his mouth. He had special memories of Blackpool, just like the people in these photos.

He wondered who they were. But, he knew who they were.

Miles Laing and his family.

When he got to the end, he flipped them over to see if anything was written on the back.

His mother had liked to write the names of people on the back of her photos, and a date. *You might know who they are,* she used to say, *but people looking at them years from now might not.*

There were a few that had names written in pencil on the back.

He was wrong. It wasn't Miles Laing but another family entirely. He looked puzzled.

'Who are these people?' he asked Hunt.

'I have no idea. I assumed that box was meant to be taken away when the hotel was sold and the last owners moved out, and it slipped past somebody. I didn't even think they'd come back for them. I think I'm a bit of a hoarder.'

Miller looked at the names on the back. *Leif, Patricia and Doreen.* He turned it over and saw the little boy, the girl and the woman who looked to be older.

John Carson

Another one: *Lance and Doreen.* Then: *Me and Patricia.* A photo of the younger woman and the little girl.

Who were these people? All of them were dated August 4, 1982.

There were no more names. He put them back in the packet and handed it to Watt, who put it back in the box. 'Give me the other packet, Andy,' he said.

Watt handed it to him.

'Cheers.' He opened it up, expecting to find more holiday snaps, but what he found made him shiver.

The first one had the same little boy in it. But this one had been defiled. The boy was on the beach, with Blackpool Tower in the background. Miller turned it over and saw the date – August 6, 1982. *The last day of the holiday!* Horns had been drawn on the boy's head.

Another one of the boy, sitting with who Miller assumed was the father. This time a red pen had been taken to the boy's face, a crude drawing of the devil scrawled over it. And the rest. All of them with the boy's face obliterated, with more ferocity as he got through the photos, until the last one, where dots from the tip of a pen surrounded the centre where the boy's face used to be, but where a hole had been stabbed through with the same pen.

On the back, the writing got worse as if the words were written in haste with extreme anger.

Little devil!
How can he be allowed to breathe God's air?
Little bastard!
I fucking hate the little fuck!
I am going to kill the bastard!!

Miller looked at the manager. 'Any idea who the boy is?'

The man shook his head. 'I've seen those, years ago. I have no idea who it is. Somebody started hating him though. Maybe his mother went off the deep end. I've read about things like that.'

'I'd like to take these, if you don't mind.'

'Go ahead. They're no good to me.'

Miller thanked Hunt and he left with Watt. They got back in the car.

'We're going to pay a visit to Perry MacKinnon, but look at those photos first.' Miller handed the packets to Watt.

'Fuck me. *Little bastard*? Which one of the adults do you suppose did that?'

'Your guess is as good as mine. But there's a name on the front. *Rena Joseph.* I'm assuming she's the one who's listed as *me* on the back of some of them.'

'We can run the name through the system, but if she hasn't done anything to get herself a record, then we might never find out who she is.' Watt looked at Miller. 'But it's hardly a crime to draw stuff on a photo.'

'No, but she might be connected to Miles Laing in some way.'

'True. I'll run her when we get back.'

'Right. First let's go and see MacKinnon.'

They got out of the car into the sunshine. 'I never liked that man,' Watt said as they closed their doors. 'Let's go and put the shitters up him. Tell him Laing's been seen lurking about outside with a knife.'

'As much as I'd like to, Andy…'

CHAPTER 16

Matthew Webb refreshed the browser, just in case. But after a few moments, he saw there was nothing there. He drank his coffee. He knew he shouldn't. His doctor had told him that he needed to watch his caffeine intake, but what did he know? Gin-tottering old fuck. One time he'd suggested to Matthew that maybe he should bend over the examination table so he, Dr Death, could shove a gloved finger up his arse.

He tried shutting the computer down. Switched it back on. It was taking ages to reboot. Christ, it wasn't as if the thing was powered by coal. He'd bought it just two months ago. Squirreled money away so he could pay cash. Oh yes, only cash for this kind of stuff. Mother didn't need to know about any of his purchases.

How about the fact you're sitting at the dining table, powering up the old wank box? Thursday was her day at the club. God knows why women in their seventies needed to do yoga, or have a disco. He wondered if any of the old sods got horny? He didn't give a toss, as long as the old boot was out of the house every Thursday afternoon.

This was *his* time. His time to talk to the lovely ladies. This was his *private* time. Or his *shag bag* time, according to his friend, Mark, who, let's face it, couldn't pull a woman if she was wrapped in a polythene sheet and had been in the water for two weeks.

'Is she on yet?' Mark said, coming out of the kitchen.

'Does it look like she's fucking on?'

Mark looked at his Rolex, the fake one he'd got somebody to get for him on a trip to Hong Kong. Most of the slappers round here wouldn't know the difference between this and the real thing, and this piece of fake crap looked good. It made his wrist turn green when he was sweating but nothing a nail brush and a bar of soap didn't take care of. He wore it when they were out and about. A bit of flash, a bit of cash and Bob's your uncle, you were away with the first prize.

'You said she has a friend, right? And I don't mean an imaginary one.'

TRIAL AND ERROR

'Relax, Markie. She said she's twenty, she has a pal who's twenty-one, and they're both looking for a good time.'

'How old did you say I was?'

'Oh, I can't remember. Fifty or something.'

'Fifty? Fuck off.'

'Okay, maybe fifteen, I can't remember.'

'Thirty-one, you said.'

'Well, why are you fucking asking me?'

'I'm just going over the details. We want to make an impression.'

'I'm sure when you wipe yourself on her pal's curtains, that'll make an impression.'

Mark drank more coffee. *His* doctor wasn't concerned about his caffeine intake, more about his obsession with taking enlargement pills. 'When's that new pal of yours coming back round?'

'He didn't say. He had to meet up with another friend of his.'

'They're not a couple of arse bandits, are they?'

'What if they are? It's no concern of ours. Besides, he's the one who put me onto this site. We've already been out with a couple of tarts, so what are you complaining about?'

'First of all, that was a different site you were on, not one he told you about. *Date a scabby old boot dot com.* Christ, I don't think I've ever seen so much hair, and that was just her fucking armpits. *She's beautiful* you said. *Plays a fucking tune on it* you said. I swear to God I thought it was a trucker in tights.'

'There *are* women truckers, you know,' Matthew said, wishing he didn't have to piss so much after drinking coffee. It was why he drank whisky in the afternoon normally, something old Dr Rubber Hands didn't know about. He got enough lecturing about his bladder without telling the old wank that he had a drink problem as well.

'That may be so, but those truckers are lookers. This one looked like she would rip your nuts off and wear them for earrings. And the fucking mouth on it. Smoked like a chimney and her breath stank.' Mark pointed at him. 'And that was the only thing she smoked. Thank God, I suppose. We dodged a bullet with those two, let me tell you.'

'I told my friend about that. That's why he gave me this site. It's by invitation only, and he kindly invited me to join.'

'What does he want in return?'

'Nothing. He's a good friend.'

'A good friend? What, he just follow you home one night? You going to adopt him?'

'He bought me a drink. We got chatting. He's a good guy. Should have seen the bird who came and picked him up.'

'You told me; only wears knickers to keep her ankles warm.'

'For fuck's sake, will you get a grip? He said he met her on a site where younger women look for older blokes. Women who still have their own teeth.'

'Me, I couldn't care less about her teeth,' Mark said. 'I want a woman who will satisfy me and leave me for dead.'

'You'll get your wish if she stabs you and fucks off with your wallet afterwards.'

'Aw come on, man. I thought you were into this? It's you who told *me* about it! You got my engine revved up.'

'It's this fucking computer. I'm telling you, I'm going to take it back to the store and shove it right up the salesman's jacksy.'

'It'll be fine. Are you sure you put the right password in?'

'Thanks for that, Bill Gates. Of course I did.'

'Oh wait!' Mark looked at the screen as the site came on.

'About fucking time,' Matthew said.

'Easy, Tiger. Get in the mood. Let's just get this going and see where it goes. And remember and ask her about her sister. Or her friend.'

'Or her granny?' Matthew said, looking at his friend and laughing.

'Funny man. Just get typing.'

'Slow and steady, Markie my boy. We don't want her to think we're a couple of deviants.'

'That shipped sailed a long time ago. Who does she think comes on here? Carol singers from the Salvation Army? No, she knows exactly what she's getting into. Young women looking for old men.'

'Sugar daddies, Mark.'

'Well here's a fucking news flash; I've not got two pennies to rub together until I get paid at the end of the week.'

'What? Tight arse. What if she says, meet me in the boozer? How are you going to get your rock 'n' roll if you stand about with your

TRIAL AND ERROR

hands in your pockets, looking like you can't string a sentence together, never mind pay for a round.'

'You're right. I'll just nick it out of my mum's tea caddy. She keeps extra in there, for Christmas and stuff. My nephew's birthday's coming up. Two years old, but fuck 'im, me getting a piece of the action is more important. Besides, I can always put it back.'

'Or tell her the milkman must have dipped it the last time he was round shagging her.'

'What? Fuck off! Milkman.'

'Don't you call him *dad*?'

'Smart-arse. No, that's the postie.'

They both laughed as the girl came online.

'There she is!' Mark shouted and almost dropped the mug Matthew had given him.

'Watch out, man. That mug says *World's Best Son,* not *Clumsy Bastard.*'

'Sorry, mate. I'm just getting excited.'

'Well, put the tea down before you spill it. The last thing I want is my mother coming home and thinking there's a pish stain on the carpet. Which wouldn't be so bad if we had a dog.' Matthew looked at the name. *Honeygirl.* 'Just her name gets my bell ringing.'

'Well, give her a fucking bell now, or else she might invite some old tossbag to chat with her.'

Matthew started typing a message.

- Hi Honeygirl! It's Big Matt here! How's things?

'Why didn't you write some funky pish that the young ones use nowadays? You know, all that shite they tap out in a text message?' Mark said.

'First of all, numb nuts, we're older blokes. When was the last time you sent a text to a bit of fanny? And, please God, don't tell me he sends texts to schoolies.'

'Bollocks. You're right, I don't do text messages. And if I did, I wouldn't be sending one to Barbie or Tulip or whatever other fancy fucking name lassies go by nowadays.' Mark finished his coffee. 'And thanks for thinking I'm a fucking beast.'

Matthew laughed. 'Relax. We're a couple of rich divorcees who're looking for a bit of fun. The hootenanny like that sort of stuff.

John Carson

Take them for a meal, a dance, get them pished, back home for a bit of *Kenny G* on the CD player, then–'

'*Kenny G?*'

'Yes. Why, what would you have on? *The Sex Pistols*? That would go down well, I'm sure. Trying to get your end away to *Anarchy in the UK*. We're trying to woo them not make them think we're serial killers.'

-*Hi Big Matt! I've missed you! Where have you been?*

Mark grinned and nudged Matthew's shoulder. 'Eh? Fucking missed you. Her knickers are probably in her handbag already.'

'Sit down, fucking clown. I'll end up typing some shite to her.'

Mark, still grinning, sat down. Stared at the screen, at the words that were sitting there.

-Missed you too, Honeygirl. I was doing some business this morning. What have you been up to?'

Mark nudged Matthew again. 'Haha. Fucking business. Having a ham shank is the only thing you've been doing this morning.'

'Shut up. Try and take this seriously, or else the only girlfriend you'll be doing is the one who has a plaster over her arse to stop her deflating.'

'Hey, Pam wouldn't like to hear you talking about her like that.'

'Why did you call her Pam? After your hand?'

'No, after that lassie on Baywatch.'

'Jesus. First of all, that thing you call Pam looks like a corpse with lipstick on. And it's fucking creepy seeing it sitting on the couch when I come round to your place. Next time, make sure the air's out of it before I come in.'

'What? No chance. By the time I blow her up, I'm out of fucking breath. It's not like she's the size of a beachball.'

'Right, pay attention, she's back.'

-*You make everything exciting!*

'See that!' Mark said. 'Exciting!'

'Let's hope her pal has the same attitude when she sees the size of your nob.'

-*I want to make you excited soon, Honeygirl.*

'That's it, don't be farting about with niceties. Time for the nitty gritty. Ask her about her pal, and tell her to bog off if she says she hasn't asked her yet.'

TRIAL AND ERROR

'Just *bog off*? Not fuck off, or piss off? Just ease into the obscenities. Jesus, you have a lot to learn my son.'

-My friend *Big Mark* and I would like to see you both soon. I'm assuming you spoke to your friend?

'I like it. *Big Mark.*' Mark was grinning like a schoolboy.

'Cool your jets there, I mean that you have a big nose.'

-*She's excited about it. She wants to meet for a liquid lunch. Is that okay for you?*

Matthew felt his stomach lurch. He'd thought he would have to work a bit harder than this, but she was far more eager than he'd anticipated.

'Fuck, yeah,' Mark said, standing up and grabbing the back of Matthew's chair. 'I'm more than ready. Pam hasn't been given an outing in ages. Now here's the chance of the real thing.'

'Okay, Clark Gable, keep it together. Remember, this is a real woman, and she might object to you storming around only wearing a condom and a pair of socks. Ease into this, don't make her think you're related to Fred West.'

'Just answer her. And tell her we've plenty of money. Make them think they've hit the motherlode.'

'Didn't you just say you were skint?'

'They don't have to know that. My mother has money stuffed in her wardrobe as well as her tea caddy.'

'I'd worry if you said her money was in her knicker drawer.'

-That's perfect! Where do you want to meet?

'We don't know what she looks like,' Mark said, his smile gone. 'What if they're a couple of pigs?'

'Again – Pam the air hostess is hardly competition.'

'Ask if she can show us a photo.'

'That'll look good. She'll think we want to send her a photo of us in our Y-fronts.'

'That might not be such a bad idea.'

'Behave for God's sake. I don't know about you, but I don't want to spend all my spare time trying not to get nobbed in the showers up in Saughton.'

'Just ask her for a photo of her face then. At least we can get a squint at her. Then if she looks like the *Elephant Man* we can just tell her we were having a laugh.'

John Carson

'Listen, you know I don't know all this technical shite. I'm messaging her, but fuck knows how to add a photo to it. Why don't we just wing it? Ask her what they'll be wearing, then we stay back, have a spy and if they turn out to be a couple of dogs, then we bail.'

'Good man. Brilliant. Tell her that pish you just told me.'

'What, you mean tell her we'll be spying on them?'

'No, I mean ask them what they'll be wearing. Fuck's sake, Matt, keep up.'

'Says Stephen Hawking.'

'Get her to send you a text with her photo in it. Surely a bawbag like you can work that out?'

'Cheeky sod. Of course I know how to do that, but then she'll have my phone number.'

'Oh, yeah, I never thought of that.'

Matthew shook his head.

-We could meet at the Haymarket Bar if you like? My friend is excited about coming along. A nice wee cosy foursome.'

'Jesus. Do you see that? A cosy foursome, she says. By Christ, this is going to be magic. But wait; where are we going to bring them back to? My mother will be in. We'll have to bring them here,' Mark said.

'Here? I don't think so. Bring some bint back to my place? What if she turns out to be a nutter? Or a squatter? She might come here and never leave.'

'Listen, when she sees your Y-fronts sticking to the wallpaper, she'll want to leave as soon as she's sobered up.'

'Naw, fuck that, Mark. A mate of mine took a hoor home one night, and when he woke up in the morning, she was gone and she'd taken his *Best Man* tankard. He had felt her rummaging about under the covers, and he'd thought she was trying to give him a tug, but he reckoned later on that she was trying to take his watch. She couldn't undo the clasp. He got off lightly. He was ex-army, and always sleeps with his wallet in his pillowcase otherwise she would have been off with that too.'

'It would just be my luck, *Honeygirl's* pal would be a fucking tea leaf.'

'Aye, my mother would have a fit if I brought a dame home and she fucked off with her carriage clock or something.'

TRIAL AND ERROR

'How about we go to one of those dodgy hotels that rent a room by the hour?'

'Know any in particular? The Balmoral, perhaps?' Matt said.

'Let's just play it by ear. Make sure they know what we look like.'

'I can always have somebody photoshop you.'

'Just get on with it, Matt, before she leaves and finds some real rich bastard.'

-Great. What will you be wearing?

-*Something light and summery. I'll wear a rose. What about you?*

'Christ, what will we be wearing? I don't want to wear a suit.'

'Of course you won't be wearing a suit. We're picking up two women, not going to a funeral,' Matt said. 'We'll wear casual shirt and trousers. Something that looks good for a couple of old farts but doesn't look like we inherited them from dead grandfathers.'

-Casual shirt and trousers. We'll find you. How about 12 o'clock?

-*That sounds brilliant! And bring some flavoured ones. My pal likes a cocktail now and again!*

-Haha. Your wish is my command. See you at 12!

-*Bye, lover boy!*

The connection was cut and Matthew leaned back in the dining chair, grinning. 'Lover boy. Didn't I tell you my pal was a good guy?'

'You did indeed. That's magic. I'll need to buy him a pint. You won't mind introducing me to him, will you?'

'Not at all. But go home and get ready, and by that, I mean shower, not pull the head off it.'

'You're a good guy, Matt. One of the best. Did I ever tell you that?'

'No, you did not, my friend. But just leave it to Matt and you'll always have a good time with the ladies.'

Matthew closed the laptop. Maybe he wouldn't insert the computer into the salesman after all.

CHAPTER 17

Lothian Buses central garage was an old, red-brick building in Annandale Street, just off the top of Leith Walk. It was originally built for the Edinburgh Exhibition Association in 1922. Its centrepiece was a huge glass dome in the middle of the roof.

'Christ, this place has changed so much,' DS Steffi Walker said as she backed the unmarked car into a space outside the garage. 'My dad used to be a bus driver and I would stay on the bus sometimes and he would take me in with him when he was finishing a shift.'

'It seems they're throwing up flats everywhere,' Kim said from the passenger seat. 'Somebody's getting rich, and I don't mean legally.'

'You'll get on well with Percy Purcell,' Steffi said, laughing. 'He thinks everybody's corrupt.'

'Tram money. That's all I'm saying.'

Steffi came round and opened the passenger door.

'Christ, I feel like a whale and I'm only five months gone. God knows what I'll be like when I'm nine months,' said Kim. Steffi grabbed a hold of her arm and hauled.

'You okay there?' a bus driver said, coming over to them. 'Oh, let me help you,' he said when he saw Kim struggling.

They managed to get her upright. 'Thanks,' Steffi said.

The driver held up his hands. 'Not that I'm suggesting you wouldn't have managed, but my old man brought me up to be a gentleman.' He smiled at Steffi, showing a perfect set of teeth.

'I'm not too proud to ask for help.'

He gave her another smile before walking away.

'See? Not all bus drivers are bastards,' Steffi whispered to Kim. Kim laughed and held her belly.

'I never said they were.'

'Somebody I knew thought all they did was sit on their arse all day. My dad worked bloody hard for his money. Not only dealing with

TRIAL AND ERROR

passengers but drivers too. And almost everybody he met wanted to slap him.'

It was sunny and warm. The sky was clear and Kim felt like she was carrying a bowling ball under her dress. They walked into the front car park of the garage, which was marked as no entry for buses and employees' cars.

'Times change,' Steffi said. 'They tore down Shrub Hill.'

Kim looked puzzled. 'What's that? I lived in London for the longest time.'

'It was the old tram depot. They had maintenance workshops there. The tailor's where the drivers would get fitted for their uniforms. Offices. It was a big place, but like every other spare inch in Edinburgh, it was knocked down to make way for flats.'

'Fuck me,' Kim said, bending over for a moment.

The bus driver stopped and turned to look at them. 'You ladies okay?'

'I'm pregnant,' Kim said, straightening back up. 'It was just a twinge.'

He smiled again. 'I don't want to put you off, but you might have trouble squeezing behind the wheel.'

'What?'

'If you've come looking for a job. Maybe better leave it until you've had the wee one.'

'I'm not here for a–'

The driver laughed. 'I'm kidding! I can tell your condition. But seriously, where do you need to go?'

'I'm a police officer,' Steffi said. 'DC Walker. This is Kim Smith with the Procurator Fiscal's office.'

The driver put his hands up and laughed again. 'It wasn't me. I was on a back shift.'

Despite herself, Steffi smiled. 'We're here to talk to Dot Lynch, operations manager.'

'Allow me to escort you there,' he said, coming back towards them. 'My name's Peter Hanson. Driver of the year. That's not an official title, mind, but bear that in mind if you ever get on my bus.'

Kim took his arm, like they were lovers out for a stroll, and put her other arm through Steffi's. 'I don't know why I'm feeling like this. I wasn't this bad with the first one.'

John Carson

'How far along?' Hanson asked.

'Five months. This is not normal but I get cramps now and again.'

'Well, just think, five months from now, you'll be able to think of the day you met Peter Hanson and laugh about it.'

'I'm sure you'll be at the forefront of my thoughts. The driver who walked slowly towards the inside of the garage where the cool shadows were, keeping me out in the heat. Just before I ripped his nuts off.'

'Well, why didn't you say that, madam?' he said, smiling and walking faster.

Inside, the cavernous building was almost devoid of buses. Hanson took them through a swing door on their left and into the office area where the drivers signed in. The office was behind glass windows on top of a counter, as if they were expecting bandits to come storming in.

'There are two police officers here,' Hanson said to one of the office staff. The man was on the phone and held up a finger indicating to give him a minute. Hanson smiled at Steffi again. 'I'll be through in the muster room if you need me. Good meeting you, DC Walker.'

She smiled back at him. You too, driver Hanson.'

'Keep away from him or else you'll end up like this,' Kim said, patting her belly.

'I want to be a mother one day, Kim. But I need to find a husband first.'

'I don't have a husband and I'm this way. My mother isn't happy, always bending my ear about us not being married. I'm surprised she hasn't used the term *with child* by now.'

'I thought Frank wanted to get married?'

'He does, but we just haven't had the time to sit down and thrash out the finer details. At least, that's what we're telling ourselves.'

Steffi put a hand on her shoulder. 'Make the time, Kim. Frank's a keeper. I love working with him and I'm learning a lot. Just don't tell him I said that. I don't want him to think I'm crawling to his fiancée behind his back.'

Kim smiled. 'Your secret's safe with me.'

'Ladies, how can I help you?' the manager said.

TRIAL AND ERROR

'I'm DC Walker with Police Scotland. This is Investigator Smith with the Procurator Fiscal's office. We're here to see Dot Lynch.'

'Right. I'll have somebody take you up to the control room.' He called over a young man and told him where to take the two women.

Upstairs, the control room was like the flight deck of the *USS Enterprise*. Men and women sat at consoles while huge monitors lined the walls, showing different street scenes around Edinburgh.

'I'm Dot Lynch. We spoke on the phone,' one of the women said. 'You wanted to look at the CCTV from one of our buses. I had it taken off the road and we have the footage from the time frame you gave us. 'Are you looking for anything in particular?'

'A man who was sitting beside me.'

Kim was sweating from the heat inside the room.

'Would you like to sit down?' Dot said.

'Yes, please.'

Dot brought one of the computer operator chairs over and Kim sat on it, feeling like her face was going to explode.

'Right, let's run this and see what we have.' She tapped a few keys at a console and they watched as the bus drove up the Royal Mile, from the driver's perspective. The door opened and the view was of the passengers getting on and they clearly saw Kim coming on, ahead of an old man. The interior view showed her sitting down and the man sitting down beside her.

'That's him,' she said.

She watched as the man chatted to her as the bus moved up the hill. Then when she stood up and he stood to get out of her way, he fell against her.

'Stop! Right there!'

Dot stopped the frame and they could see the man slipping something white into her bag.

'That's it, the piece of paper. That *is* him.'

'Who?' Dot asked, but Kim just shook her head slightly. 'Sorry, I can't say. But that's the man we're looking for. Can you show me where he got off?'

'Yes, I can.' The video showed the bus moving after Kim alighted. 'There. The next stop. Teviot Place.'

John Carson

Miles Laing got off the bus and walked back the way they had come.

'Thank you. Can I get a copy of that?'

'Of course. I'll get a DVD made up.'

Five minutes later, they were heading downstairs again. Kim went in search of a bathroom. Steffi went in search of a coffee. She was aware of the men watching her as she walked through the canteen area of the muster room. Peter Hanson looked over at her and got up from the table.

'Are you looking for a coffee or a cold drink?'

'I was going to get a Coke while I'm waiting for my colleague.'

'Let me get it for you.'

'Wow. Last of the big spenders.'

He laughed. 'I could buy you a real drink one night, if you like.'

She smiled at him. 'Why not? Give me your number and I might call you.'

'Might? How could you resist my charm?'

'You're next in line, Romeo.'

He bought her a bottle of Coke. Then gave her his number.

'Maybe tonight?' he asked her.

'We're working a big case, so maybe later in the week.'

'I'll be in.'

She walked away, glad that there were no wolf whistles, even though there were women drivers there too.

'I feel better already,' Kim said as they left the garage.

'Thursday lunchtime, shouldn't be too hard to spot a couple of hoors having a good scoop,' Mark said as he rang the bell on the bus.

'Jesus, we're not going to a fucking sauna. They're probably a couple of nice office workers or something.'

'Or a pair of scamming tarts who've got their pimp waiting in the toilets.'

The bus swung round into Morrison Street and made the green light. The city was bustling with visitors. It was warm but a cool wind was waiting to be invited in.

TRIAL AND ERROR

'I wish I'd put on a warmer shirt,' Mark complained as they crossed the road towards the *Haymarket* bar.

''It's a bit nippy. I don't know how those young twats walk about the streets with only a T-shirt on.'

'In the fucking winter, too.'

'Aye, there's nothing like a pair of long johns and a set of flannel pyjamas.'

'Too right–'

'I was being facetious, big fanny. Next you'll be telling me you're wearing sheepskin Ys.'

The bar was quiet, unlike the weekend nights when it was full of hooligans getting juiced up before going into the city centre proper, where a club and a fight was waiting for them.

'Right, let's get our stories straight again,' Matt said as the barman handed them their bottles of lager.

'I'm a British spy up from London, looking to recruit a couple of young women,' Mark said.

'We discounted that one, remember? On account of it sounding like you're talking pish.'

'Sounds pretty good to me.'

'If you're fucking twelve. And let's face it, if those lassies look like they're twelve, I'm off. I want to be sure they're not a couple of schoolies playing grown-ups.'

'Right, right. If they look legit, we tell them we're video game developers. We're freelancers who sell our stuff to big companies. That way if they were to check up, they won't find anything.'

'Now you've got it, Mark.'

'There's only one flaw in your plan.'

'What's that?'

'Aren't those kind of blokes loaded?'

'That's the whole point! They're looking for rich older blokes, remember? We buy them a few drinks and then take them back to their place. Promise them a trip to Florida or something.'

'Or the fucking moon. I can afford that as much as I can afford Florida.'

'Jesus, Mark, we're not really going on a trip. Let them think that. We only want a good time with them, not to whisk them away to an arranged marriage in Disneyworld.'

John Carson

'Good point.'

'Can you see them?'

'Not yet, but we're early.'

'Are you sure *Honeygirl* didn't send you a photo of herself?' Mark asked.

'I would have said so.'

'I'm getting a bad feeling about this.'

'Relax. They'll be here.' Matt tried to sound confident but couldn't pull it off. Then the barman came over.

'You two Mark and Matthew?'

'Yeah. Why?'

'Your girlfriend called and said she can't make it.'

'Pair of fucking boots. They probably live in Nigeria. I wouldn't be surprised if they've wiped out our bank accounts by now,' Mark said.

'Let's not be hasty. Maybe they can meet us tonight.'

'Or they're round tanning your fucking house.'

'For fuck's sake. I knew we should just have gone to a singles club.' Matt looked at his friend.

Mark nodded in agreement. Now he'd have to try and sneak his mother's money back into her drawer.

CHAPTER 18

'I swear to God.' Doctor Perry MacKinnon paced around his office, shaking his head. His clinic was a couple of doors down from the hotel Miller and Watt had just been in. The townhouse that the clinic was in was now twice the size since the townhouse next door had been bought years ago and extended into.

'Has Laing had any contact with you at all? Either before or after his escape?' Miller said. The room was very plush. Miller wished his own office had carpet this thick.

'What?' MacKinnon stopped pacing. 'Of course not! I would have been right on the phone to you lot. Wait. You don't think he'll come after me, do you?'

'We're not suggesting that,' Watt said. 'We're just advising people to be cautious. He's dangerous.'

'Don't you think I know that? He wrapped cling film round my head. If you hadn't come in when you did, Miller, I would have died.'

'What about Sherri Hilton?'

'What about her? She hasn't been near me, not that I know of. Mind you, I haven't been a patient in a hospital. I wouldn't want the mad cow visiting *me* in the dark.'

'Has Miles Laing ever called you from the hospital?'

'No, thank God. Look, if it was up to me, I would have had him put in the electric chair by now. Lunatics like him don't deserve to live.'

'I see you went ahead with extending the clinic into the townhouse next door.'

MacKinnon sat down heavily in his office chair while the two detectives remained standing. 'Let me tell you, I very nearly upped sticks and went to live in America. But I thought, why should I run? Screw him. But now I wish I had done exactly that. Who knew he would be running about again one day?'

Miller took out a business card and handed it to him. 'If you need to call me.'

John Carson

MacKinnon looked at it and nodded. 'Do you really think he'll come after me?'

'We don't want anybody taking any chances.'

He and Watt left and went out into the fresh air again.

'You can just feel the money oozing out of him,' Watt said.

'You never did like him, did you, Andy?'

'I wouldn't have lost any sleep if *The Surgeon* had wrapped MacKinnon's head a few minutes earlier.'

They got in the car and drove up to the station.

The conference room in the High Street was warm, but a fan was sitting off to one side.

'This heat is killing me,' Kim said to Miller as he poured her a glass of water. 'I feel that if somebody says something to me the wrong way, I'll throw them out the window.'

'I'm here for you, honey.'

'Are you? That would be great if you were, Frank.'

Miller looked around the room at the others gathered in small groups. 'Look, if you want to talk to me about anything, I will always listen. We're in this together.'

'Are we?' Kim was struggling to keep her voice down. 'Now, you know I've been more than accommodating when it comes to Carol, but for fuck's sake, I'm here now. *I* need your attention. God bless her, Frank, but she's gone. You have to let go.'

Miller felt his face go red for a bit. 'I know that. It's just all this stuff with Miles Laing escaping-'

'Don't. Don't make excuses. Is that why you went to the cemetery? Or was that just another excuse?' She took the water from him and sat down next to Paddy Gibb, putting her bag on the chair next to her, sending a clear signal to Miller. He sat further down the table.

Jeni Bridge was talking with Percy Purcell and then moved to the front of the table. An overhead projector sat at one end, the lens facing a white screen on a roller that had been pulled down and set against the back wall behind Jeni.

Det Sup Leach was talking with Harry McNeil and everybody looked at Jeni as she cleared her throat. 'Ladies and gentlemen, I'd

TRIAL AND ERROR

like to get started as soon as possible. Norma Banks will be joining us shortly.' She looked up as the door opened and Norma walked in.

'Sorry I'm late,' she said, closing the door behind her. She put her bag on a seat next to the one at the bottom of the table.

'Can I get you anything to drink?' Miller asked his future mother-in-law.

'Any OJ?'

'There is,' Jeni answered, nodding across to the fridge in the corner.

Miller poured some for Norma and they all sat down.

The only one who remained standing was Jeni. 'I don't know if you know Detective Superintendent Bill Leach from Glasgow Division,' she said, indicating with her hand the man who was sitting a few chairs up from her.

'We haven't met before.'

'It's a pleasure,' Leach said, smiling. If not meaning it then giving a good impression that he did.

'Likewise.'

'How are you feeling, Kim?' she asked.

'Aching, light-headed, and sweating like a pig. But apart from that, I'm fine.'

Norma looked at Leach. 'She's my daughter. She's allowed to be sarky with me.'

'It's almost like a gathering of the clans then?' he smiled when he said it, but more than one person had commented how so many members of the family worked in law enforcement.

Norma ignored his remark and looked at Jeni. 'Carry on, Chief Super. I have another meeting to go to.'

'Thank you, ma'am.' She looked at the others in the room. 'Kim was on a bus this morning, and a man was behind her, who then sat beside her. We believe this man to be Miles Laing, in disguise.'

'How can you be sure?' Leach said.

'Kim found a note in her bag when she got to the PF offices. It wasn't there this morning, obviously, so she suspected it was dropped into her bag by this man. She liaised with Lothian Buses and they brought the bus in and checked through the CCTV footage. Every new bus has cameras on it. So when she looked at it, they could see he slipped the paper in.'

'What was on this paper?' Harry McNeil asked. 'Some kind of confession?'

'I don't believe we've been introduced,' Norma said.

'I'm DI Harry McNeil, Professional Standards.'

'I'll thank you to keep to what your department name implies – *Professional*.'

'I apologise if that came across as sounding facetious, but–'

'If you stop interrupting then maybe Chief Super Bridge will be able to enlighten us more.'

Miller couldn't look at his colleague, and since the chairs were leather, he managed to slide down another couple of inches without it being conspicuous.

Jeni Bridge drank some of the water she had in a glass in front of her. 'It said, *Tell Frank I'll see him soon!* We don't have it with us as it was taken away by forensics, but the DVD clearly shows him slipping it into her bag.'

McNeil looked across at Miller with raised eyebrows. 'He seems to be obsessed with you, Miller. Any thoughts on that?'

'He's a madman,' Miller said, sitting up straight again. 'He's obsessed with me because I caught him.'

'You and DS Watt.'

'Both of us, yes.'

'Has DS Watt had any such messages?'

Miller shook his head. 'No, just me.'

'Has he given you any messages that we don't know about?' Leach asked.

'No.'

'You sure about that?'

McNeil looked at his superior officer like he wanted to say something.

'Yes, Inspector?' Leach said.

'We're here to ascertain whether Miles Laing's messages have any real meaning and whether Inspector Miller's life is indeed in any way in danger.'

'And to make sure there's no shenanigans,' Leach said, all traces of a smile gone.

'I'll determine that.'

'*Sir.*'

TRIAL AND ERROR

'Lest you forget, *sir*, in my position, I rise above any rank, and while I'm happy to acknowledge the fact that you are of a higher rank, I will carry out my duties as an investigator. I've seen nothing so far to indicate that Inspector Miller had anything to do with Laing's escape, so let's try and keep this on track. We need to find out *why* Laing is sending him messages, not whether Miller was driving the getaway car or not.'

'I–' Leach started to say but Norma cut him off.

'Unless you have anything constructive to add, Superintendent, please allow the Chief Super to carry on.'

Leach gritted his teeth with his mouth closed and Miller could see the knot of muscle in his jaw tighten. He was probably literally biting his tongue.

'Inspector Miller had a call from Laing, which he recorded, and if I'm not mistaken, a copy was handed over to Standards?' Jeni said.

McNeil nodded.

She carried on. 'It was when he noticed a noise on the tape that Inspector Miller later figured out that Laing had been in a call box across the road from his flat. When he went over to the phone box, there was an envelope with a key and a note in it.'

She switched the projector on. The note had been copied onto a sheet of transparency film and they all looked at it and read the words:

Frank! I knew you would find this. The key opens a door. Not hard to find out, but it's more than physical. It's symbolic. Follow the clue and you'll be on your way. Take a step. Or 143 steps. On the other side of the lights to Heaven, you'll see the home fires burning."
Time is against you, Frank. Good luck. See you soon.

'Has anybody any idea what it means?' Norma said, fanning herself with a piece of paper.

'Lights to Heaven, 143 steps, home fires burning,' Jeni said, looking around the room. 'Don't be shy. Any ideas, fire them out. Nobody will laugh, and you won't have to stay behind and write your name out a hundred times as a punishment.'

That brought a small round of laughter.

Then a knock on the door.

John Carson

'Come in!' Jeni shouted.

Steffi Walker came in holding a sheet of paper. 'Sorry to interrupt.' She looked at Norma. 'There was a message for you. They were told you would have your phone off but they asked me to give you this.'

She handed Norma a note and she stood looking at the white screen at the end of the room.

'Any ideas?' Jeni said again.

Steffi put her hand up, like she was in school, and then put it down again.

'Yes?' Jeni said.

'Sorry, ma'am, but I couldn't help notice the writing on the screen.'

Jeni stood up straighter. 'Anything spring to mind?'

'The bit about the 143 steps.'

'What about it?'

'I was at school with a girl who said her granny used to live in the Nelson Monument on Calton Hill, when her granny was a little girl.' She saw everybody looking at her, like she was a magician who was on the verge of telling everybody how the last trick was done.

'And the Nelson Monument has 143 steps inside it.'

CHAPTER 19

'He's a fly bastard,' Percy Purcell said. He looked at Miller who was in the front of the car. They were being driven by Steffi Walker. 'Did you hear what I said?'

Miller turned to face him. 'Yes, I did.'

'Well I'm not a mind reader, Miller. Grunt or something.'

Miller faced the front again. 'I was miles away, sir.' He looked out the window. 'All of this doesn't make sense,' he said, as the car turned left off Regent Road and headed up Calton Hill.

'It sounds like you two are going to meet up for a pint, the way he talks.' Purcell got out after Steffi parked the car. A wind was whipping across the grass area, blowing through the Nelson Monument that was modelled on the Parthenon. Edinburgh's disgrace, as it was better known.

The Nelson Monument sat on top of a small hill. They climbed the steps to the entrance. The monument was a small stone building with the monument itself built in the shape of a telescope standing on top of it. It was a museum now.

'Are these part of the 143 steps?' Purcell asked Steffi.

She turned to answer him. 'No. They're inside.'

A curator was inside. Purcell showed his warrant card and introduced the other two detectives. 'We'd like to look up the monument itself,' he said. 'It's part of an ongoing investigation.'

'Okay. Help yourself.' The woman was old and eyed them with suspicion, as if they had just conned her into getting a free tour of the place.

Purcell looked at Steffi. 'Stay here and ask her about anybody acting suspiciously. Show her the still that was taken from the bus CCTV.'

'Yes, sir.'

Purcell and Miller climbed the stairs to the top, going round in circles. They stepped out onto the viewing area. 'I think this trip up here might have a different ending if you were with Miles Laing,' Purcell said.

John Carson

It was windy but worth facing the cool breeze for the views afforded. They could see over the Firth of Forth to Fife, the contrast of the hills diminishing the further away they got. The sea shimmered, light bouncing off it. Small boats traversed the water. Some sort of tanker was moored. A gas carrying ship, Miller guessed, if such a vessel existed. The sea and its users weren't his forte.

They walked round and looked over to the Pentland Hills. It reminded Miller of the view he'd had when he was on the roof of Robert Molloy's club just a few months back, when a deranged killer had leapt to his death.

It had been windy then, too. It seemed that the wind was waiting above a certain level, waiting to jump out and tackle the unwary. 'You don't wear a toupee, sir, do you?'

'Sod off, Miller.' Purcell absent-mindedly ran a hand across his short cut hair. He looked at the hills in the distance. 'Do you think Laing is trying to lead you into a trap so he can get his revenge?'

'That occurred to me more than once.'

'You can't go into something alone, you know that, right? If he leads you to some abandoned warehouse or something, you're not going alone.'

Miller nodded. He knew Purcell had been in a fight for his life recently, attacked by a man who would have killed him and left him in the deserted warehouse without a second thought.

'You don't just have yourself to think of,' Purcell continued, as Miller had been daydreaming again.

'I know, but maybe not for much longer.'

'Christ, man, you know how women's hormones change. I wasn't listening to what Kim said, but I'm not deaf either. She's pissed off with you. She just wants to know that you're supporting her and that you're there when she needs you.'

Miller turned to face him. 'I am there.'

'Not when you're down visiting Carol's grave, you're not.' He held up a hand as Miller started to protest. 'That's her viewpoint, not mine. I'm just saying.'

'Jesus, Percy, this whole thing with Laing is doing my head in. If it was just some nutter that I'd put away, it would be a different story, but seeing that it's the man who Carol helped put away, it's getting to me.'

TRIAL AND ERROR

'I understand. Lots of memories dredged up, good and bad. I can't imagine how you're feeling, so I won't bother telling you that I do. But Kim's a good woman. My advice to you? Don't fuck it up.'

'I don't wake up in the morning thinking that's my daily goal.'

'I know that, but sometimes we can't see the wood for the trees.'

'This might sound strange, but there seems to have been a shift in our dynamic as a family.'

'You mean the honeymoon period is over and now you're getting down to real life? She baulks at the idea of washing your Ys now?'

'Something like that.'

'Or is it maybe because you're putting off setting a date? Correct me if I'm wrong, but shouldn't you have exchanged vows by now?'

Miller looked at his boss for a moment. 'Yes. She wanted to name a date, but I keep coming up with some shite about how we have to wait a bit longer.'

'At this rate, she won't be able to fit into a wedding dress.'

'We're not going for the big do, Percy. We've both been there.'

'So, it's a quick get-it-over-and-done-with at the register's office, round to Greggs for a Scotch pie then back home for a bit of how's your father? Oh wait, I don't think Kim will be in the mood for that. And she might be put off having a pie.'

'Your wisdom knows no bounds.'

'That's why they pay me the big bucks.'

'Let me ask you though; how is it with Suzy, now that you're married to her.'

'It's great. Now that we're not dancing round the *when will we get married* thing, we can get down to the business of getting on with our lives. She's not even giving me any grief about my old man kipping at our place while he's selling his house.'

'I don't know what the fuck is wrong with me. That's the honest truth.'

'You love Kim, don't you?'

'Of course.'

John Carson

'Then there's something in your head that's stopping you from actually marrying her. Maybe you should go and talk to Doc Levitt over at the uni. He's still the force therapist.'

'Maybe I will.' He turned and looked at the hills again. Then he had a thought. Looked back at Purcell. 'You're on Facebook, aren't you?'

'I don't know anybody who isn't. Even Lou dabbles on there. It wouldn't surprise me if the old sod isn't on Tinder or something. Maybe he's even got a photo of himself on *Willies-Are-Us*.'

Miller looked at him.

'What? I just made that last bit up, Miller. Don't look at me like I've got a photo on there too. It's not even a real site. I don't think.'

'Anyway, can we just move on before it gets even more depraved?'

'You started it.'

'Okay, listen; I follow a site called *Edinburgh Framed*. This guy takes photos of Edinburgh and posts them online. He makes up merchandise and stuff.'

'And this has to do with Miles Laing how?'

Miller turned back to the Pentland Hills. 'There. I just remembered a few photos the guy put up, taken from Calton Hill. Maybe not from up here, but you can still get a good view from the hill. Anyway, he took photos of the Pentland Hills at night. The ski slope is lit up. It looks like there's lights in the sky, as you can't see the hills in the dark. *On the other side of the lights to Heaven, you'll see the home fires burning.* We've come up the 143 steps, and if it was dark, the ski slope would look like lights going to Heaven.'

'Jesus, maybe you're right. But what does he mean about the home fires burning?'

'That we don't know yet.'

CHAPTER 20

Mr Blue carried himself well. After years of training in the military, he walked with a confidence that spoke to a potential mugger: *you're welcome to try*. He hadn't ever been mugged. Which is not to say somebody wouldn't try, but that person would go home empty-handed and with a very sore part of their body.

There wasn't much chance of him being mugged in the Gyle shopping centre, on the west of the city. He sat reading a paper in the food court upstairs and looked at his watch again. Mr Red was on his way. He'd sent a text from his burner phone to Mr Blue's burner. The directions had been simple yet detailed: stay on the Aberdeen train to Haymarket. Get off and take a tram out to the Gyle Centre. He knew the man would be tired from travelling from London, but he had been in first class, not in the cattle cars.

If somebody in the street looked at Mr Red, they wouldn't give him a second glance. He wasn't overly tall, didn't have the physique of a body builder, but he did have one thing going for him; he knew how to kill.

Mr Black still had connections in the *dark world*, as he liked to call it. A world where the last resort was to step outside the law in the name of national security. He had made a call to a man in London, who had apparently said, *leave it to me*. And now this man, who was given the moniker Mr Red, was on his way up. With a partner in tow. They worked as a pair, which didn't bother Mr Blue either way.

From his vantage point, Mr Blue could see over the car park to the tram stop. He watched as Mr Red walked down the pathway, carrying a holdall. An unassuming man, he also carried himself well. He was wearing dark slacks, and a dark coloured lightweight blazer, with his shirt fashionably untucked.

Just a man going shopping. Carrying a holdall to put his bought goods in. Mr Blue knew there would be something in the bag that would be doing the business later and that Mr Red would be armed to the teeth.

John Carson

Mr Red walked out of view and five minutes later was up in the food court. He sat down at the next table to Mr Blue, close enough to talk.

'How was your trip?' Mr Blue asked.

'Very relaxing,' Mr Red answered.

'You want a coffee or anything?'

'No.'

Mr Blue hadn't expected him to drink anything. He knew the effects caffeine could have on the body, and Mr Red wouldn't want his hand shaking.

'Did you get the email about Aunt Nellie's funeral?'

'I did. It was unexpected but I'm looking on the bright side; a little trip to Edinburgh. Catch some sights while I'm here.'

Aunt Nellie: codename for the operation.

'Is your sister travelling with you?' *Sister*. Mr Red's partner. She was his wife and the second half of his team. Both nutters together.

'She's coming up shortly. She's not far behind me. She'll meet me later.'

'Good. We should get going,' Mr Blue said.

Mr Red nodded and they went to the front exit and across to the taxi rank, neither of them saying anything else. The place was covered in cameras, and although it was a very long shot that they would actually check here, they didn't want some forensic lip reader to see them talking.

They took two taxis, each of them being dropped off at a different street around the corner from the address they were going to.

Neither of them looked suspicious. Just somebody getting out of a taxi, heading home after a day out.

Mr Blue arrived first. Mr Black was in the study, sitting at a computer.

'Cup of tea?' he asked.

'Thank you.'

Mr Black stood up and walked over to a table where a tray sat with a pot on it. 'Do you think Mr Red will want anything?'

'Maybe water. Nothing with caffeine.'

'I'll leave him to help himself.' He poured the tea and gave the cup to Mr Blue, who nodded.

TRIAL AND ERROR

'I've been in touch with our client. Through a secure site as usual. More instructions,' Mr Black said, sitting back down. Mr Blue sat on a leather couch.

'Does he know Mr Red is arriving today?'

Mr Black looked at his colleague before answering. 'I didn't think it pertinent to mention that. All he has to know is that we have expenses and if we need to subcontract, that's an expense. He won't question anything we're doing. In fact, he wants to distance himself from this as much as possible.'

Mr Blue shrugged. 'If he gives us free reign to do the job, then that's all that matters.'

'It's best this way. At the end of the day, Mr Red is expendable.'

'Agreed. He'll prove useful though. As long as he stays professional, he'll be fine. It won't come back on us.'

'I hope not, Mr Blue. We have a good thing going, you and I, and it would be a shame for us to ruin it.'

'I'll keep a tight leash on him.'

'I want him put to work today. We have already started so he needs to do his part. He does know this, I assume?'

'He was given the instructions.'

'Excellent.' Mr Black sipped at his own tea. It was some herbal muck that Mr Blue wouldn't use to clean a toilet with, but he felt it gave him energy. No highs, no lows, just an even keel.

They heard a light knock on the door. 'Go and let him in, please. The less he's seen by the neighbours the better.'

'He's only going to be here for a little while then he'll be moving to the safe house.' He left the room to go and answer the door. Mr Black felt a buzz inside. He hated bringing Mr Red in, but needs must. This was just like the old days; planning, plotting, and then executing the plan. The only down side this time was, he wouldn't get to blow away a room full of terrorists.

Killing was the thing he missed most about his old life.

CHAPTER 21

The flat was quiet without Emma running about in it. The babysitter had said she would keep the little girl for dinner then drive her back afterwards.

Kim put her arms around Miller while he was rustling up their dinner in the kitchen. 'I'm sorry about earlier. What I said about Carol.'

He put the salad tongs into the bowl and turned to her. 'Don't worry about it. I know your hormones–'

She let him go and stood back. 'It's not my hormones, Frank. It's how I feel. I know I could have gone about it better, but they're my feelings. They just came out the wrong way.'

'Sit down at the table and we'll talk about it over dinner.'

'Look, I don't mean to be a cow, but–'

He smiled. 'Go sit. I'll bring the stuff over.' She sat down while he laid the cooked chicken pieces to one side on each plate and then put them on the table. When everything was set, he sat down opposite her.

'Tell me the truth, Frank; do you still love me?'

'Of course I do. You don't have to ask.' He passed her the tongs and she scooped some salad onto her plate.

'I just think you've been distant since you found out that I was pregnant.'

He didn't answer her for a moment. He did love her, didn't he? Of course he did, it was just sometimes his thoughts were elsewhere. *Like down in the cemetery.* 'I wasn't aware. That's not an excuse, but I'll try harder. And yes, I was down at Carol's grave. She and I caught Miles Laing, and I… well, I don't know. It just seemed appropriate that I tell her. I know it sounds daft, and I can't really explain it.'

'I know that she was pregnant when she died, and I sometimes feel bad that now I'm the one who's here, carrying your child.'

'Christ, you don't have to feel bad.'

'We have our feelings, and sometimes we can't help them, and that's how I feel.'

He reached over and held her hand. 'I don't want you to feel this way. I want us to be happy, be a family, the four of us.'

She gently pulled her hand away. 'Then why don't you want to marry me?'

'I *do* want to marry you.'

'We haven't set a date.'

'Work just got in the way, that's all.'

'Jesus, you can't blame that on work.' She stabbed a leaf of lettuce with her fork without picking it up.

'I'm sorry, but things have just been so busy lately, you know that. And now this thing with Miles Laing on the loose, not to mention Bruce Hagan.'

'Fuck me, are you going to look for any excuse under the sun? I moved in here with you, changed my daughter's school, started to build a new life with you. Now I'm pregnant and wanting to get married. I thought we were in this for the long haul!' She suddenly scooted her chair back and threw her fork down, rushing out of the kitchen.

'Where are you going?'

She ignored him and he heard the bedroom door slamming shut. He knew he should get up and go in after her, to reassure her, tell her things were going to be alright, that they would get married, that weekend if she wanted, but he couldn't move. Couldn't force himself to go to her.

Would you go to Carol if she was hurting?

'Yes, I would,' he said out loud. He got up from the table, his own appetite leaving him. It was still light out and would be for hours yet. He walked over to the window, to look down on the crowds in the High Street below. He should be happy; no, *ecstatic*, at the prospect of a woman wanting to spend the rest of her life with him and having his child, but he felt only a deep sense of loss.

He looked down into the high street. There were crowds of festival-goers, with a few performers further up.

Then he saw her again.

Carol. Standing opposite, looking up at him.

Good God, no. Why was he manifesting her image now? Because he had been thinking about her a lot? No wonder he wasn't displaying his affection to Kim, when all the time, he was subconsciously wishing Carol was still alive.

Then something happened that jolted him.

Carol turned and bumped into somebody. She held up a hand, apologising, and the man smiled and waved, indicating it wasn't a problem. Then Carol looked back up at the window and smiled before she walked away.

He took off then, running for the door. A neighbour was coming out of the lift. They were on the fifth floor. He hit the ground floor button and the lift doors closed agonisingly slowly. Then it took him down in what felt like hours. When the doors opened, he ran out, along the hallway to the front door and out onto the North Bridge. Right and up to the lights. She was wearing a white shirt and jeans, so he was scanning the crowds.

Do you really expect to see somebody who clearly only exists in your mind?

Yes! Yes, I do! He looked around, his adrenaline pumping. The pavement was in shadow and the breeze that hit him made him shiver. Then he saw her. On South Bridge. She was on the other side of the road. She looked round and saw him.

The traffic was flowing. He couldn't get across. Then a bus came across the junction, blocking his view for a moment.

She was gone.

Then he saw her. In a taxi. She turned and looked out the back window as the cab pulled away, driving away from him. He couldn't make out the plate number, but he did see the red call-sign sticker on the back window: A39. Alpha three-nine. He and the other detectives had gone over the various colours of call-sign stickers on the front and back windows of cabs in the city, so they could easily identify a particular one should the need arise. Like now.

He reached into his pocket for his mobile phone and realised he had left it at home. He walked back to the entrance to the flats. Rode the lift back up to the flat. Found his phone and called the cab company. *Edinburgh Cabs.*

'My name is Detective Inspector Frank Miller, Police Scotland. I need to know where a passenger is going in one of your cabs. The call sign is Alpha three-nine.' He gave the despatcher his detective ID number, if she wanted to check him out with the station.

TRIAL AND ERROR

'Frank, this is Linda. We spoke before. I was at the meeting when you lot were doing training. Give me a minute.'

He held on and could hear her talking over the radio. Then she came back with an answer. 'Frank, the woman was dropped at Waverley station. The driver took her via Chambers Street, Infirmary Street, and across Jeffrey Street, because of the High Street being blocked at Cockburn Street.'

'Can you ask him if she said what train she was catching, or if she mentioned meeting anybody?'

'Hold on.'

Again, the voices in the background while she asked. Then she came back.

'She said she was going to Fife.'

'Thanks a lot. I owe you one.' He hung up and left the flat again, grabbing his phone and this time running for the stairs. He took them two at a time and hit the hallway running, his breath already laboured. He didn't feel the cool, evening chill at the side of the building as he ran down the North Bridge, hanging a left after the entrance to The Scotsman hotel.

The hotel was closed for refurbishment, but access to The Scotsman stairs wasn't. This was a stairwell with bars over open windows. The stone steps had been completely refurbished some years ago and they were still used as a shortcut to get from the North Bridge down to Waverley station. There were 104 steps, each of them clad in a different shade of marble. It was better than it used to be, when it was used as a big toilet.

Miller ran out of the entrance on Market Street. Across the road, dodging traffic, and into the lower entrance to the station.

It was busy. Commuters from all over who had poured into Edinburgh for work, were now busy funnelling their way into the station. He was slowed down by passengers walking along the bridge that traversed the railway tracks below. A train sat on the platform, ready to head off to London. He ran, sweating now, still dodging people, shoving his way through.

He made it to the stairs that led down onto a platform, where just a few short months ago, a woman had come crashing through the glass roof to land here, killing herself.

John Carson

Miller turned right, looking up at the display board. Where the hell were the Fife trains? Then he saw it; Dunfermline. Platform 14. He ran past the crowd and up to a ticket inspector at the barrier. Held his warrant card out.

'I'm pursuing somebody. I think she might be on that train.'

'Ticket dodger, is she?' the man asked sarcastically.

'No, she's a serial killer,' he lied. 'Rips men's nuts off and force feeds them. I'll give her your name if you like.'

The man made a face and opened the barrier for Miller.

The train doors were closing as Miller got to the last carriage and a few seconds later, it started moving off. The commuters were packed like sardines into every space available.

''This is a bloody disgrace,' he heard a woman complain. 'And we still have to stop at Haymarket.'

Miller tried to push his way through, but it was a struggle. He kept getting looks from people. The train roared and moved but not at a great pace. He was looking for the woman wearing a white shirt and jeans. Christ, there were lots of people wearing white; women *and* men. Businessmen with white shirts, ties taken off because of the heat. Female office workers with summer colours on, including white.

He struggled past the crowds. Easing his way agonisingly slowly. Looking left and right. Not seeing her. Looking ahead through to the next carriage, but only getting a glimpse. The sliding door opened. He walked through a group of people who were packed in like sardines, standing between the doors. He couldn't imagine how even more people would get on.

They were now in the tunnel that ran under Lothian Road, all the way to Haymarket. Christ, he was only in the second carriage. How many were there?

Listen to yourself! You don't even know if she's on here or not. You're chasing a ghost, Miller!

He suddenly felt more foolish than he'd ever felt in his life. What the fuck was wrong with him? He was seeing his dead wife, and what would he do when he caught up with her? Invite her back home?

Yet, didn't she bump into somebody? How could she have done that if she was a ghost? Or did he just imagine that?

He had nothing to lose now, so he kept pushing forward.

"Next stop, Haymarket," the conductor's voice said over the intercom.

Jesus, they were almost there. He moved faster, eyes scanning the crowds. He was given a dirty look on more than one occasion. Into the third carriage. Pushing harder now.

'Police!' he shouted, his voice loud and urgent. 'Out the way! Police!' That got their attention. He shoved his way past, pushing harder. 'Move!'

They turned to look at him. He took out his warrant card and held it up. 'Move!'

A youth was standing with huge red headphones on, and didn't see him coming. Miller pushed him. The man turned and grabbed a hold of Miller's shirt. Anger flared in Miller's eyes as he shoved his warrant card in the man's face. The man let go of his shirt.

Into the fourth carriage as the train smoothly came to a stop. It looked like a football match had just got out with the number of people who were standing on the platform. He kept looking further into the carriage, watching as people stood up to get off. More people flooding on, pushing, cajoling.

No woman in white.

Well, what did you expect?

He shoved past a few people and got onto the platform. He was going insane, that was the truth of the matter. All this nonsense with Miles Laing escaping was doing his head in.

Then he saw her. Getting off the first carriage. White shirt. Jeans. She looked quickly at him and pushed her way through the crowd.

How the hell did he miss her? The toilet. She'd been in there the whole time.

He tried to make his way through the crowds trying to get onto carriages that weren't built to take that many people. Carol ran for the stairs, fighting past the crowds coming down.

He got up onto the main concourse and looked around but couldn't see her. He saw a member of staff and grabbed the man's arm.

'I'm a police officer. Did you see a woman wearing a white shirt and jeans come up here?'

John Carson

The man looked like Miller was unhinged. 'Just one? You should try standing here all day mate and see how many women in a white shirt go by.'

'I'm asking you a serious fucking question.'

'No. No, okay?'

Miller walked out onto Haymarket Terrace. Carol was nowhere to be seen. *Of course she isn't! She's in your head!*

It seemed like all of the air left Miller. He felt like a deflated balloon. He walked towards Morrison Street and crossed the road into the Haymarket Bar. Bought a pint. Switched off his phone. Thought about drinking himself into oblivion.

CHAPTER 22

'Tea would be great,' Kim said to Samantha Willis. 'Although if I wasn't pregnant, I'd be getting blootered.'

'I'll have a word with him,' Jack Miller said as he went through to the kitchen to put the kettle on.

'No, Jack, it's fine,' she said to his back as he left the room.

'Where is he now?' Samantha asked.

'Your guess is as good as mine. He stormed out. Twice. I feel like he's slipping away.'

Samantha's flat looked down onto Cockburn Street. The windows were open, letting in cool air. The sounds of the festival were filtering in.

Jack came back through with the tea and a cold drink for Samantha. 'I don't know what's got into that laddie. He needs a bloody good talking to.'

Kim sipped at the tea. 'This thing with Miles Laing has really got under his skin.'

'That's no excuse,' Jack said, sitting down on the couch next to Samantha.

'He feels it, Jack. Carol dying hit him hard, from what I've heard.'

'It did, but this is the land of the living. My wife – his mother – died as well, but we have to move on. I loved Carol, but what happened is in the past.'

'But her father was murdered, too. There was a lot of death in Carol's family.'

'I'm going to boot him up the arse. He might be younger than me, but I'm still his father. He's lucky that I don't still live with you both.'

'You know I love him, but sometimes he drives me insane. All I want is for us to set a date so we can get married. I don't want to be standing at the alter looking like I have a beach ball under my dress.'

'I don't blame you, not one bit,' Samantha said.

John Carson

'It can't have been easy for you, having Laing sitting next to you on the bus.'

'I'm lucky he didn't try and kill me. Which still surprises me, to be honest. It makes me think he has bigger plans.'

'I don't think he's after you,' Jack said. 'If anything, he's after Frank. Which makes me even more worried now that we know he's out of the flat and we don't know where he is.'

'Jesus, I didn't think of that. I thought he was just pissed off and wanted to walk around. Christ, what if Laing's done something to him?'

Samantha shot Jack a look.

Jack realised he'd put his foot in it. 'Anyway, we invited you round here to talk to you about something.'

Kim looked at him but her mind was elsewhere. Miller was lying in a ditch somewhere, his throat slit open. Or his guts slit open, *The Surgeon* standing over him.

'Are you okay?' Samantha asked.

'I'm just feeling a bit flushed, that's all.'

Jack got up and went into the kitchen and came back with a glass of cold water. 'It's an old wives' tale that a hot drink cools you down. It just makes your body hotter and so your pores open up more.'

She thanked him and drank some of the cold liquid, feeling better right away.

'Listen, Jack and I were talking this over, and we'd like to pay for your wedding.'

Kim looked at her like she was talking Chinese. 'What?'

'We want to foot the bill. You both deserve it. I know you said you didn't want a big, fancy affair, but we can make your day special.'

'Oh, Sam, that's fantastic, but we couldn't.'

'Of course you can. I mean, we're not wanting to push you into anything of course, but Jack and I would love to. I don't want to put your dad out, or anything, but we'd like to ask is permission too.'

'I don't know what to say. But thank you. That's so kind.' She smiled sadly. 'If Frank ever gets round to setting a date with me, that is.'

Just then, Kim's phone rang. 'Hello?'

TRIAL AND ERROR

She listened to the voice on the other end. 'What? What do you fucking mean?!' she screamed, standing up fast. Then the pain hit her and she grabbed her stomach, letting her phone drop to the floor.

She screamed again as Jack picked up her phone. He spoke to the person on the other end then hung up and turned to Samantha.

'We have to go.'

CHAPTER 23

In the end, he sat and nursed one pint. Only had a sip of it. He was sitting in a corner, watching the TV. Christ, what was wrong with him, not even wanting a drink? He stood up, not knowing exactly how long he had been in the pub. But he had felt comfortable. He was ignoring the life he had and thinking about the life he *should* have been living. It was wrong, and he knew it.

He walked out into the cool evening. The sun had dipped below the buildings opposite and now he was feeling chilly.

He remembered he had switched his phone off and took it out of his pocket and switched it back on. There was a missed call from Jack. The old man probably wanted him to go for a pint, but he would put him off.

He listened to the voicemail.

Frank! Where the fuck are you? Emma's missing! When you decide to pull your finger out your fucking arse, get down to the babysitter's house!

Miller stood in shock for a moment. Emma? Missing? Jesus Christ. He listened to the message again, to his father's angry tone, and he barely caught the address. Then he flagged down a cab. 'Chancelotte Mill. Connaught Place. I'm a police officer. This is an emergency. There's a twenty in it if you can get me there as fast as.'

Miller sent his father a text message. He wasn't in the mood for a shouting match on the phone, not trusting himself to stay calm.

The driver moved the black cab like the expert he was. He skirted the city centre, driving through Stockbridge, along to Warriston, connecting with Ferry Road before getting as far as he could until the patrol car blocking the end of the road stopped him. Miller paid the fare and added the promised twenty before leaping out of the cab.

Jack was waiting for him. 'Where the fuck have you been?' he said.

'I'm not in the mood for this, dad. Where's Kim?'

TRIAL AND ERROR

'You're not in the fucking mood? Good for you, but while you've been off poncing about doing whatever the fuck it was you were doing, your girlfriend's little girl has gone missing.'

'I know that!' Miller shouted. 'Just take me to the fucking house!'

Jack was breathing heavily and he marched his son to where all the police vehicles were.

Miller was shaking, feeling like he had never felt in his life before. Police patrol cars were outside the house. The front door was wide open. Uniforms and suits were inside.

Andy Watt was the first detective he came to. A knowing look passed between them. It was something that both of them had experienced in their time, whether as beat coppers or as detectives: a child has gone missing and you think the worst has happened.

Both detectives had been at the scene where a young body had been found. It was so hard when you go to a house and the girl's boyfriend had shaken the baby because he wouldn't stop crying and now the wee life was gone. It was harder when a small body was found dumped, murdered or abandoned, left to die.

Then there were the kids who were taken, the younger ones. A man has lost his puppy and could little Johnny or Jenny come help him find it? The child takes the adult's hand and goes off to help find the poor dog. Some were never seen again.

These thoughts were running through Miller's head as he walked into the house. Kim was sitting on a couch, another woman sitting in a chair opposite. Percy Purcell was standing in front of the woman while Steffi Walker was sitting next to Kim.

'Kim!' he said, rushing over to her.

'Where were you?' she said to him, bursting out crying.

'I was out,' he said, holding her as she started sobbing uncontrollably into his shoulder. He couldn't even put into words what he had been doing: *following a woman I thought was my dead wife.* The words sounded so unreal, he didn't want to voice them.

She pulled back from him. 'Out where?'

He looked her in the eyes. 'I just went for a pint. I wanted to give you space. I'm sorry I pissed you off. I just wanted to get out of your hair for a wee while.'

Purcell came over to him. 'Frank. A word in the kitchen.'

John Carson

Miller followed him.

'I'm sorry, pal. We've got everybody in on this. A dog handler is on his way.'

'Sir, how do we know the babysitter hasn't just taken Emma to the pictures or something?'

'Because that's her sitting through there. Don't you recognise her?'

'No, I've never met the woman. She's new. She came highly recommended.'

'Right. Well, the woman – Lisa Sterling's her name – says her daughter was home and she asked her to stay with Emma. Apparently, one of her other clients had an emergency and Miss Sterling rushed out to go get the other kid. She was just going to be looking after him for an hour or so. Extra money she said, as it's been hard after the divorce. Anyway, she nips out, and when she comes back, her daughter is gone and so is Emma.'

'Did she try calling her daughter?'

'Of course she did. There's no reply. We're working with the phone company now to try and see if they can get a ping from it.'

'Okay, so how do we know the daughter didn't just take Emma somewhere. A friend's house or something?'

'We've called all her friends' houses. Nobody has seen her. Nobody talked to her. She hasn't been in touch.'

'Come on, Percy, there has to be an innocent explanation for this. Please tell me there is.' Miller's voice broke for a second before he composed himself again.

'Frank, I promise you we're going to do everything we can. You know the procedure.'

'Nobody's making any sense. Tell me why you think something bad has happened.'

Purcell took a deep breath and let it out. 'Ms Sterling went out into the street looking for her daughter – Lynne – and she bumped into a neighbour who cycles along the pathways that run along the back of here. There's a warren of them, the Water of Leith Walkway, Chancelot Path. Anyway, this guy had finished his cycle, when he saw the girl walking with Emma. He didn't think much of it. He knows Ms Sterling is a babysitter. But when he turned and looked, he saw Lynne stopped, talking to an older man.'

'Please tell me he got a description.'

Purcell shook his head. 'Dark hair. Only saw his back. He was wearing a lightweight jacket. Average build and height.'

'Fuck me.' He looked at Purcell. 'It might still be innocent.'

Purcell put a hand on Miller's shoulder. 'You need to come and see this.' He led Miller out of the kitchen and they went back through the living room and into the hallway. Upstairs to the girl's bedroom.

There was a man inside, with his shirt sleeves up, like he had been asking somebody to step outside for a fight.

'This is Stan from the computer crimes department,' Purcell said.

'Hello, sir,' Stan said. He was a young man, younger than Miller.

'Show him what you found, Stan.'

'They called me in because the mother saw something on the screen.' Stan sat down in the chair and pulled on a pair of nitrile gloves he'd had in his pocket. He played around with the mouse as the two detectives watched, mesmerised, as if the magician was about to go for the big reveal.

It was a tower computer, attached to a monitor. They could hear the fan whirring away to itself from its space below the desk top. A chat room came up on the screen. Words typed between two people.

'Who the hell is *Honeygirl*?' Miller asked.

'We're assuming it was Lynne,' Purcell said.

'And she was chatting to… *Big Matt*.' Miller straightened up, a chill running through him. 'The guy she met on the pathway?'

'We're working on that theory.'

Miller read the seemingly innocent banter, but then he saw it was a site where young girls logged on to meet older men. 'Christ, how old is this girl?'

'Seventeen. Nearly eighteen.'

'There's nothing perverted in here,' Stan said, directing his conversation to Miller. 'But just the fact that she seems to be chatting to an older man is cause for concern. And the fact that she had the wee girl with her when she went to meet him.'

They all turned at the sound of somebody knocking on the door. Andy Watt. 'Sorry to disturb you, sir, but the dog handler is here.'

'Right, Andy,' Miller said. Then to Stan: 'Can you get the ISP address for whoever she was talking to?'

'Working on that now, sir. It won't be long.'

'Get it to somebody whenever you get it, Stan, then get them to give it to me.'

'Listen, you'll not be going round knocking on anybody's door,' Purcell said when they were out in the corridor.

'Like fuck I won't.'

'I'll be doing the knocking. I mean it. You're too involved to be doing anything like that. You're taking a back seat.'

Miller went downstairs and outside, looking for the dog handler. He was bringing the German Shepherd out of the back of the van. 'Will we need any clothing or something?' he asked the officer.

'An unwashed article of clothing would be good,' the man said.

Miller went back and had Lisa Sterling fetch a piece of her daughter's laundry. Miller took it back out to the officer. He was starting to shiver now, a combination of the chill and nerves.

More uniforms gathered and Paddy Gibb came back with a group of uniforms. 'We've been round all the doors. Nobody saw anything out of the ordinary. Not even the guy Lynn was supposedly seen with.'

'Right, we're going to let the dog sniff that shirt then we'll see if he picks up on anything.'

Miller watched as the handler put the shirt over the dog's snout, letting him sniff it again and again. Then the dog picked up on a scent and the handler gave the shirt to another uniform.

'I'm coming with you,' Miller said. 'I don't care what you say.'

'For fuck's sake, Frank.' Purcell shook his head. 'There's no way you're coming.'

Miller walked away.

They moved round the garage block as the dog darted back and forth, keeping his nose low to the ground. Purcell, Gibb, Watt, and Julie Stott. At the end, there were bushes. He led them all through, and they were led onto Chancelot Path, which had once been a railway line until the tracks were pulled up.

Many years ago, back in the 1970s, two trains had collided head on at this intersection. It was a long stretch in each direction, but they still hit head on.

The dog picked up speed and took them in a westerly direction, towards Warriston Road. Council allotments were on one side, bordered by a small wall. A quarter-mile along, the dog changed direction and went to the wall. It wasn't a high climb to get over it.

The pathway was a long one, ending after it went under the Rodney Street tunnel at Broughton Road and stopped at King George V park.

They wouldn't be going that far.

The handler was up and over the wall, followed by Purcell, Watt, Gibb, and Julie, who were trailed by uniforms.

'If I find some bastard in a hut with Emma and his trousers round his ankles, I'll rip his fucking nuts off,' Watt said.

'That's why you'll be letting me deal with him. We'll all be picking straws to see who gets to kick his head in first, but it won't be you,' Purcell said.

The dog started getting agitated and was barking.

'Has he got something?' Purcell asked.

'He's got the scent of something, sir.'

The dog led the handler to a gate. A rickety fence surrounded the allotment. Purcell wasn't green-fingered so he couldn't understand why people would want to rent one of the little gardens that belonged to the council. It was a fair bit of land, divided into hundreds of little gardens, each one individually tended to.

There was a small hut at the back of the garden. Painted light blue, it had seen better days, with paint flaking off all around it.

'Right, get your dog in there,' Purcell said, drawing his extendable baton. The others did the same.

The handler opened the gate, and uniforms moved to surround the hut, some of them taking up position at the back. The dog handler shouted: 'Police. I have a dog. If there's anybody in there, come out and show us your hands!'

John Carson

The dog was getting more agitated as they approached the door. Purcell took a flashlight out of his pocket and had Gibb grab hold of the handle. 'Get it open, Paddy!'

Gibb turned and pulled but it was locked. Andy Watt stepped past him and kicked it hard.

The door exploded inwards.

The handler let the dog go inside.

Purcell was right behind him, shining his light around.

'Jesus fucking Christ,' he said. 'Get the dog out! Get it out right now!'

The handler got in and got a hold of the dog.

'What's in there?' Gibb shouted at Purcell.

Purcell came out, his flashlight still on. They still couldn't see in.

'What's in there, sir? Julie said. 'Is it Emma?'

'Nobody can go in there.' Purcell looked at the others. 'It's a crime scene now.'

CHAPTER 24

It was full dark by the time the chief pathologist got to the allotments, along with pathologist Kate Murphy.

'We've been up to our eyes in it, Percy,' Professor Leo Chester said.

'You and me both, doc. Hi, Kate.'

'Hello, Superintendent. I heard what happened. I'm so sorry.'

'We're pulling out all the stops on this one. We have to find that wee girl.'

Arc lights lit up the hut from the outside and a forensic screen covered the doorway, should any nosy journo manage to get hold of the story. No doubt they would, in time, but right now, Purcell wanted things to be kept quiet.

'Maggie Parks is in there now. Her and her motley crew,' Paddy Gibb said.

'I heard that,' Maggie said, coming out of the hut.

'You were meant to.'

'What have you got?' Chester said.

'The older girl. The babysitter's daughter, Lynn Sterling. Aged seventeen. She's been opened up in front, but you're the medical expert so we'll get out of your way.'

'Thanks, Inspector.'

The head of forensics nodded. She intended to go home and give her own daughter a big hug later on, whether her daughter liked it or not.

'You okay?' Paddy Gibb said. Despite their banter, they liked each other a lot.

'I'm fine, Paddy. I hate it when kids get done like this.' Despite being in the job for years, she still couldn't use the words *murdered* and *children* in the same sentence. 'I'm going to have a bloody good drink later.'

'Me too.'

'Still with your girlfriend?'

John Carson

'No, that went tits up a wee while ago. Excuse the expression. We were planning on going to Spain to live, but then I told her I was staying on a bit longer, and she decided to go by herself. So now I'm still young and fiancée free.'

'Never mind, Paddy. I'm sure there's somebody out there for both of us. My ex certainly moved on quickly enough. Bloody young waitress. I hope she grows up and tells him to sod off.'

'Let's hit a bar later, Maggie,' Paddy said. 'I'm feeling gutted for Frank and Kim, and I need to blow off some steam. It's going to be a late night working, but–'

'Let's do that. But I have a sixteen-year-old at home and tonight, I don't want to be boozed up. I have a few bottles in the fridge. We can have a beer and a chat. Talk shop, if you like.'

'I'll text you when we eventually get done.'

She patted his arm and walked back to the van with her crew, Fukuto and her photographer.

Kate Murphy and Leo Chester had finished suiting up and stepped into the hut. It smelled of gardening chemicals and old soil. Smaller versions of the arc lights outside were set up in here, the low hum of a generator nearby breaking the silence. It was cold in here. A grimy window that hadn't seen water in years was on the back wall with crude, homemade wooden security bars nailed across it.

The wooden floor had ground-in dirt on it. Cobwebs hung from the ceiling in the corners. Some old, worthless garden tools leaned against a side wall; a spade, a fork with dirt still on it.

'I've never seen the attraction myself,' Chester said, pointing to an array of hand tools sitting on a dirty work bench.

'Me neither. I don't mind eating vegetables, I just don't want to grow them.'

Chester pulled up his face mask, Kate following suit. He stepped forward, closer to the lifeless form lying slumped in the corner. Blood had spilled from the deep incision in the girl's abdomen, pooling on the floor and seeping through the joins in the wood. Without the lights, it would have looked like spilled oil, but the lights showed it for what it was; the girl's life force had left her.

'She was probably dead before all that blood left her,' Chester said, crouching down. The girl's face was waxy and had a death pallor about it. Her eyes were open, staring back at him.

'Poor little thing,' Kate said, her London accent thick. 'Nobody deserves to die like this. Especially a young girl.' She looked at her boss. 'I just hope to God that whoever took Emma has a conscience and does the right thing. I mean, the bastard doesn't need to harm her. He can drop her outside a fire station or something.'

Chester stood up and pulled down his face mask. 'I fear that we're dealing with somebody who isn't of a sound mind, Kate. I don't think a fire station is on his agenda right now.'

'I don't think getting a fucking warrant is going to be a problem, do you?' Purcell said, ending the call on his mobile.

'I have the B Team drafted in too. They're going to get going on looking through all the pervs who were released in the last six months,' Gibb said. 'Then twelve months if nothing shows up.' He took out his packet of cigarettes and got as far as taking one out before shaking his head and putting it back. *Just a stay of execution, you little bastard* he thought.

'Right, let's get back to the house.' Purcell turned to a DS who was standing with a detective constable. 'Keep in touch with my sergeant. You have his number.'

'Yes, sir.'

'Are they giving us a hard time about getting a name for the ISP from the internet?' Gibb asked.

'Of course they are. Shower of bastards. All this privacy pish. They're shitting themselves in case some axe-murdering bastard gets caught and decides to sue them for giving us his name.' They walked up the pathway to the garden gate. 'It's PC gone off its fucking head.'

More arc lights were illuminating the gardens surrounding the crime scene, but when they got to the old railway line, the path was lit by headlights from police vehicles; headlights competing with blue strobe lights.

'How's Frank?' Gibb asked as he and Purcell walked back the way they had come, towards Lisa Sterling's house.

'He's trying to keep it together for Kim's sake. She's a basket case right now. And who can blame her. I don't have kids but if somebody took mine, I'd be clawing the wallpaper off.' Or if somebody took Bear, he was going to say, but it wouldn't have

John Carson

sounded appropriate. It didn't lessen the sentiment though; if somebody took his dog, he'd rip the bastard's kneecaps out with a claw hammer.

There was a police car sitting on the pathway at the intersection. A few onlookers had gathered, more than likely neighbours, but Purcell pulled one of the uniforms aside. 'Take photos of these people. Just in case.'

'Right away, sir.' The uniform stepped aside from his colleagues as Purcell and Gibb walked through the bushes to the garage block and back round to the Sterling house.

Miller was standing in the living room, pacing back and forward, his mobile phone in his hand.

'Jack,' Purcell said.

Jack walked over to him, an imposing man of 6'5", taller than Purcell. 'Jesus, what a fucking mess this is,' he said. 'Anything that can give us a lead to where Emma is?'

'Listen, Jack,' he said, steering Jack back into the hall, 'I hate to say this, but there's no *we* here. You and Frank have to go home and wait.'

Jack straightened up even more. 'I don't think so, son.'

'I thought you would say that. However, I have officially warned you.'

'Right, you've done your job. Let me do mine.' He went to walk away when Purcell grabbed a hold of his arm.

'What do you mean, *your job*? You're retired, Jack.'

'Semi-retired. I still do some work for Neil McGovern.'

'You're retired from the force. I know this is your family, but for God's sake, I can't have you trampling all over this. The Crown Office would have a fucking field day if they knew. Imagine we get the guy and his lawyer said, oh yeah, they had civilians working for them and we didn't get a Miranda Right read to us.'

'For fuck's sake, Percy, I haven't been out of the job so long that I don't remember that stuff, but listen to me; civilians don't give Miranda Rights.'

'Civilians don't do police work! For Christ's sake, Jack, you and Frank are on the back bench for this one. I won't have some murdering pervy bastard walk free on a technicality.'

TRIAL AND ERROR

'You do it your way, I'll do it mine. I already have my buddies talking to a network of people, in case somebody's heard something.' Jack turned and walked away. Purcell shook his head, seeing the whole case go up in smoke.

Miller ended his call and put his phone in his pocket.

'Frank, how's Kim?'

'They've taken her to the Royal, just as a precaution.'

'Lisa Sterling?'

'She's through in the kitchen.'

'Right, come with me, Paddy,' he said, and Gibb followed him while Miller stayed in the living room.

Lisa Sterling was being comforted by a female uniform. Despite all the PC tosh these days, Purcell still preferred to see a female comfort a woman. Lisa Sterling looked up when the two detectives entered the room.

'Did you find them? Are they okay?'

Purcell didn't answer for a moment. Lisa started sobbing.

'Oh God, no, please.'

'I'm sorry, Ms Sterling, but we found the body of a young woman we believe to be your daughter, Lynn. There's no sign of Emma.'

Lisa started crying uncontrollably. Purcell turned to Gibb and ushered him back out. 'We'll have to get a formal ID later, at the mortuary. We also need to ask Sterling whether she remembers seeing any strangers here the past few days. Not right now, but wait until she calms down a bit. Get the police doctor over here. She's going to need some medication to calm her down a bit.'

'I'll get on it.'

Purcell turned round to see a short man standing in the doorway. A man he hadn't seen in a long time.

One of the most dangerous men he'd ever met in his life.

CHAPTER 25

'Why don't you be adventurous and try something different,' Norma banks said to her husband as they sat in the Chinese restaurant, Cool Jade, in Downie Grove, which was part of the main road leading into Corstorphine, opposite Edinburgh Zoo.

Neil McGovern looked at her. 'Do I look like the sort of bloke who takes a risk when it comes to food?'

She smiled and shook her head. He ordered the usual and waited until the waiter walked away. 'Tell me about your conversation with Frank.'

McGovern rubbed the stem of his wineglass between his finger and thumb, staring at the glass of red. 'He seems fine, Norma. By all accounts, life's just been getting in the way.'

'God, if we let life get in the way of everything, nothing would get done.'

'True, but we don't want to rush him. He's a good guy and I like him a lot. And he likes Kim.'

'I hope he loves her, after getting her in the family way.'

He looked at his wife. 'Of course he does. Maybe there's something mentally blocking him. I personally think that he's holding back after what happened to his first wife.'

'Well, if he doesn't get a move on, the baby will be born out of wedlock, and I won't be a happy mother-in-law.'

'Listen to you,' McGovern said. '*Wedlock*. Life isn't an Emily Bronte novel.'

'Don't mock me, dear husband.'

'I'm allowed to. I'm picking up the tab for this.'

'We're married. You're supposed to.'

He laughed. 'But just ease up and for God's sake, don't get on to Kim. She wants to be married just as much as you want her to be.'

'Looks like Aunty Norma will have to have a little word with DI Miller.'

'What are you like? Are you going to be one of those nagging in-laws who can't keep her nose out?'

TRIAL AND ERROR

'I didn't hold back on Eric after Kim found out he was cheating on her and I most certainly won't hold back on Frank Miller. If the SAS don't scare me, there's little hope for Police Scotland.'

Just then, McGovern's mobile phone rang. His face fell when he heard the person on the other end and he jumped up so suddenly, his wife thought for a second he'd had an electric shock. McGovern's chair fell over.

'What do you mean, *missing*?'

Norma Banks felt an icy chill run up her neck. 'Neil, what's wrong?'

He held up a finger to quieten his wife. A waiter came over to see what the fuss was. McGovern reached into his pocket and threw enough bills onto the table to cover the cost of the meal they weren't going to eat.

'Right. I'll be there right away. Text me the address.' He hung up. 'We have to go.'

'Tell me what the fuck's going on!' Norma said, feeling panic rise up, and she wasn't a woman who was susceptible to panicking.

'It's Emma, Norma; she's gone missing.'

'Oh God, no. How? Where from?'

He nodded to the waiter as he ushered his wife outside. It was dark now with a chill in the air. 'Listen, Kim's been taken to the Royal. Emma disappeared from the babysitter's house. I'll get the driver to take me down to the house now. You get a taxi to the Royal. I might not be able to pick you up later but get a taxi.'

The black Range Rover was sitting at the kerb. McGovern was on twenty-four-hour stand-by as head of the Scottish branch of the witness protection department.

'God Almighty, Neil, what's happened to her? How did she go missing? Where was Kim?'

He grabbed his wife by the shoulders. 'Listen, Norma, our daughter needs you now. I'm going down to the scene of where Emma was taken.'

'Wait! What do you mean, *taken*? You said she went missing. How do they know she was taken?'

McGovern took a deep breath before letting it out. 'That was Jeni Bridge on the phone. The babysitter's seventeen-year-old

John Carson

daughter was looking after Emma, and she was found murdered in a hut on the allotments next to the estate where they live.'

Norma put a hand to her mouth. 'Oh my God, no, Neil, please don't tell me—'

'There's no sign of Emma. Everybody's on it.'

'What about Frank?'

'He's down there with Percy Purcell but they have to keep him out of it. He can't be part of the investigation, love.'

She nodded. 'I know.'

He flagged a passing cab and saw her into it. Gave her money. 'Call me and let me know how my daughter is.' He turned to the taxi driver. 'Royal Infirmary. Quick as you can.'

He watched as the cab pulled away and got into the back of the Range Rover, looking at the text he'd been sent with the address. He told the driver where they were going.

Then he sat back and dialled a number. Credenhill. South of England. Home of the Special Air Service.

'This is Neil McGovern, Special Ops.' He gave the operator his number for her to check. She came back on the secure line a few moments later.

'Go ahead, sir.'

'Colonel Berkley. I need to speak with him immediately.'

'Putting you through to his personal line now, sir.'

A few clicks and the phone was picked up on the other end. 'Neil, you old dog! How's things up in Scotch Land?'

'Oliver, I have bad news. My granddaughter's been abducted. I need to know if there's been anything on the wire. If not, I have a suspect, but first of all, I need you to release Operator Eric Smith, the little girl's father.'

'Good God, Neil. That's awful! Of course, I'll get one of the team onto it right away. How about your own department?'

'I'm working on that. I don't think it's anybody after me or my ex son-in-law, but we have to cover all bases. More than likely it's something to do with my future son-in-law.'

'Whatever you need, Neil. I can have a team ready in twenty minutes if the need arises. It will take them an hour to get there, fully rehearsed, you know that.'

TRIAL AND ERROR

'I appreciate that, Oliver, but Eric will do just now. He should be here.'

'Right, but if I hear any whispers on the wire, I'll be sending a four-man right up there. I'll alert the barracks in Edinburgh Castle on the off-chance. I'll tell them I have a man coming up to stay. I'll recall Smith right now. He's training right now, thankfully, and not out in the field. He's going to be devastated by this.'

'I know. I already had it confirmed that Miller can't be on the case. The head of Edinburgh's CID assured me Miller would be kept back from this.'

There was a small laugh on the other end, but not an ounce of humour in it. 'I know, Neil, in case the bastard gets off on a technicality. But here in the SAS, we don't do technicalities.'

'I know, but let's not get ahead of ourselves. Let's just get Eric up here.'

'I'll have him flown up. But tell me, how sure are you that the little girl isn't just somewhere and hasn't been abducted?'

'Because her babysitter was murdered. The girl who was last seen with her, and she was seen talking to a strange man. So I'm pretty sure.'

Silence for a moment. 'Bastard. Do what it takes to get her back, Neil. And remember, one phone is all it takes for me to get a team up there for back-up. No warrants, no lawyers, no Miranda Rights.'

'Thanks, my friend. I'll be waiting for Eric when he hits Edinburgh. He has my number.'

He hung up, knowing in his heart that it wasn't somebody out to get back at him, but rather Frank Miller was the target.

Miles Laing was playing games and now he'd just taken it to a new level. Well, he, Neil McGovern would show him what real games were all about. Miles Laing had just entered into a battle that he would never win.

137

CHAPTER 26

'Neil, long time no see,' Percy Purcell said as McGovern stepped into the room. He was a small man, but carried a big, proverbial stick.

McGovern shook the Superintendent's hand. 'I wish it was under better circumstances. Where's Frank.'

'He's upstairs. Let me take you to him.' He led him up to where Stan and Miller were standing over the computer. Miller turned around when he saw McGovern walk into the room.

He couldn't even form words. His eyes were red. McGovern stepped forward and gripped his hand, putting a hand on his arm.

'Frank, we both have to stay strong,' he said when he saw Miller couldn't speak. Miller merely nodded. 'None of this is your fault. Miles Laing is a nutcase. We need to concentrate on getting Emma back.'

Miller sniffed and composed himself, forcing himself to speak. 'I've been distant with Kim, Neil. I should have been there for her, and I don't mean physically.'

'Time for that later, son. Eric's on his way.' He looked at Purcell. 'Eric Smith, Kim's ex and Emma's dad. Sergeant Smith, SAS.'

'I'm sure Jeni Bridge would have told you that we can't have any family involvement,' Purcell said, his cheeks a little red.

McGovern held up a hand. 'I get that, Percy. But he's Emma's dad, so he has to be here. He's being flown up. Meanwhile, what do we have?'

'We have Lynn Sterling's computer,' Stan said. 'She was chatting to a man on here, an older guy called *Matt*. We're trying to get a warrant for the cable company just now so we can get his ISP address.'

'Is there a problem with the warrant?'

'No, not a problem,' Purcell said, 'but it takes time.'

'Really now? My wife knows Sheriff Wilson. He'll issue one in five minutes.'

TRIAL AND ERROR

'Call her now, then. We could do with this being fast-tracked.'

McGovern pulled out his phone and called his wife and told her what he needed. 'She's going to call him now. Wilson lives in Heriot Row. He'll be waiting for you. I'll be going out to the airport to pick up Eric.' He looked at Purcell. 'Make sure you get the bastard. I'm relying on you to find out where Emma is. If I have to get involved, then I will. I'm not in the mood for this PC crap. Do whatever it takes.'

Miller came through. 'I'll kill the bastard when I get a hold of him. Fucking Miles Laing playing games. First killing his aunt, now taking Emma. They won't need to keep a room for him at the hospital.'

McGovern led Miller outside. 'Don't be talking like that in front of your colleagues. When push comes to shove, they'll throw you under the bus. But trust me, if that fucker's hurt Emma, you're right; he'll never need that room again. But let's get the warrant issue sorted first. Purcell is taking the troops over to the sheriff's house and then they'll execute the warrant.'

'What about a warrant for murder?'

'Already taken care of. Wilson's a good guy. He knows what needs to be done.'

'Christ, I just can't sit around and do nothing, knowing that Laing is behind this.'

'You're coming with me to the airport. Percy will deal with this. He's experienced.'

'Okay.' Miller felt the rage taking a hold of him and felt he wanted to harm Laing more than anything. 'I feel guilty though, Neil. Kim told me about Laing being on the bus with her and putting a note in her bag. I should have picked Emma up and brought her home.'

McGovern put a hand on his shoulder. 'Listen, son, I sent a car to the school. Emma was picked up by members of my team and driven to the babysitter. Kim wanted normalcy for her daughter. My team weren't followed, certainly not by Laing.'

'Are you saying this is not connected? I don't believe in co-incidences.'

'That's what we're going to find out.'

CHAPTER 27

The building was, in Purcell's opinion, a monstrosity. Situated on Lothian Road, it was a modern building that didn't fit in with the old splendour of the Waldorf Caledonian hotel next door.

This was the headquarters of *Thor Industries*, and housed several companies under the *Thor* umbrella. One of them being ScotNet, a cable TV and internet provider.

'I'm getting a bad feeling about this, sir. Miller said that *Thor* owned the hotel where Miles Laing worked. Back then, Laing told Miller that his folks owned it. His folks just ran the place.'

'Laing was probably boosting himself up. Look at me, I'm the big man, my folks own the place.'

Gibb parked in the inside lane on Lothian Road, blocking the traffic, two patrol cars behind them, lights spinning in the dark. A van load of uniforms was behind them with instructions to come in with the detectives. A show of force would have a bigger impact.

Purcell and Gibb went up the wide front stairs, followed by six uniforms being tracked by the ever-watchful eye of the security camera, and they approached the front doors, seeing their reflections in them. They were locked, operated only by one of the security men at night.

Purcell could see a man behind a console just inside the main foyer and he was watching the two detectives. He didn't make a move to get out of his seat. Purcell rapped lightly on the door and held up his ID. Still no joy. He took out his mobile phone and dialled the company's number. It rang and he watched as the security guard picked it up inside.

'ScotNet, how can I help?'

'You can open the bloody door for a start,' Purcell said to him. 'We're police officers.'

The guard looked across at the two men, the uniforms behind them, then he wandered across, peering through the glass, taking his time deciding whether he trusted them or not.

'Fuck me, open the door man!' Purcell yelled, slapping the

glass.

The guard unlocked the door and opened it, looking at the warrant cards.

'I need to speak to somebody that's in charge,' Purcell said to him.

'We're closed.'

'Call somebody. This is important.'

'I'll phone one of the managers upstairs.' Purcell heard him talking to somebody before putting the phone down.

'Mr Edwards will be down shortly. He's the night-shift manager.'

'Fine. Try and stay out of trouble now, eh?' The detectives and the other officers stood in the foyer. A few minutes later, one of the lift doors opened with a chime and a young man stepped out, all smiles, wondering what the police could possibly want at this time of night.

'My name's Bill Edwards. How can I help?' He held out his hand, practising the PR he'd learnt at whatever sort of class those guys go to to learn how to become greasy and smarmy.

Purcell dismissed his hand and looked into his eyes. 'I'm Superintendent Purcell, Police Scotland. We need to connect a name with an ISP address. We have a warrant.' Purcell held out the piece of paper and Edwards read through it.

'Sure thing. Come upstairs and I'll get you what you need.'

They stepped inside the lift. It too was plush. If it were just a bit bigger, they would have mistaken it for a room in a five-star hotel. Or at least a bathroom, what with all the mirrors. Purcell caught Edwards sneaking a glance in one of the mirrors, no doubt checking there was no hair out of place, although he thought it would probably take a blow-torch to interfere with the coiffure.

'This office block is certainly something else just for an Internet Service Provider,' Purcell said to him.

'Oh it's more than that; this is *Thor Industries* new HQ. It was an insurance company HQ before they moved out.'

The lift glided to a halt on the fourth floor. The doors opened silently, and they stepped out into what Purcell thought was the control room of a spacecraft. Everything was modern, almost too modern, although it was very impressive. An empty reception desk stood before them.

John Carson

'My office is just down the way,' Edwards said to the detectives, leading the way. They followed him into his office after he opened it with a swipe card. High security was top of the list, that was for sure. The uniforms stayed in reception.

Purcell and Gibb sat down on a leather settee while Edwards sat himself on his chair behind the desk. Purcell couldn't help noticing they were seated lower than he was and thought that this was probably deliberate so that he could intimidate the lower echelons. A trap-door probably opened beneath the seats so that interviews could be terminated early

'Now, gentlemen, what can I do for you?'

Didn't I just fucking tell you downstairs why we were here? Purcell kept the thought to himself. 'Here's the ISP address we got from the computer. We need to know the name and address that goes with it.'

'Okay, I'll see what I can do. I'll have to have a word with the duty supervisor and he'll be able to retrieve it.' He got up out of his chair and left the office.

Purcell stood up and paced the office. 'Fuck me, this is turning into a pile of shite, Paddy.'

'Too right it has. As if Miller hasn't been through enough, what with Carol dying while she was pregnant. And now he's settled down with Kim, and she's expecting their first child together, Kim's daughter gets taken by a fucking pervert.'

'When we get this name, Paddy, I want you on your radio and get every man and his dog to the address. I want the fucker's street closed off. Dog handler there, so the Alsatian can be hanging off his nuts if need be. The bastard will tell us where the wee girl is, or by Christ–'

'Mark Hamilton,' Edwards said, coming back into the room. 'Forty-six–'

Purcell snatched the piece of paper out of the manager's hand. 'Thanks for your help, son.'

He marched back to the lifts and showed Gibb the paper. 'Give it a green light, Paddy. Every man and his fucking dog. Now.'

Back out on the street, as Purcell opened the door of his car, a pair of eyes watched him, studying his features. They kept on watching as he and Gibb got into the car and the convoy drove away.

CHAPTER 28

There were two emergency vehicle entrances to the airport. The one on Turnhouse Road was used for escorting VIPs to and from the airport. It was this gate that Neil McGovern used. Chief Superintendent Jeni Bridge had been in contact with the airport manager and airport vehicles were waiting for the police convoy as it sped towards the gates. They were opened for the lead police car, which was followed by a Range Rover.

They sped across to a hangar, and then the airport escort vehicle sat off to one side while the black SUV entered the hangar. The police vehicles waited outside.

The private jet landed and taxied into the hanger. McGovern waited for the aircraft to spool down and then the door opened and the stairs were lowered. Eric Smith came down. He was an unimpressive man, not too tall, not too bulky, but he had a look about him. Something that somebody in a pub would not be stupid enough to tackle.

'Eric,' McGovern said, holding out his hand.

Smith shook it. 'All they told me was that my little girl was taken,' he said.

'We'll get to that. I have Frank with me.'

Smith walked over and nodded to Miller. 'Good to see you again. I wish it was under better circumstances.'

'Me too, Eric. But all the MIT teams are working on this.'

'Any suspects?'

'There was a prisoner escaped the psychiatric hospital–' McGovern began, but Miller interrupted him.

'He's after me. He's been calling me at home. He left a message for me in a call box. He even slipped a note into Kim's bag when she was on the bus. He wants me, Eric, and I think he's going to use Emma to get to me.'

'What's his name?'

'Miles Laing. I caught him eight years ago, and he hasn't been happy about that since.' Miller looked him in the eyes. 'If you need to vent, vent to me. This is all my fault.'

'It's not your fault. But if this is a roundabout way of getting to us, then he's playing a dangerous game.'

'I don't think it's you he wants. He wants to get to me through your daughter.'

'*Our* daughter, now. We'll get her back.'

'He's right,' McGovern said. 'If we have to use unorthodox methods, then so be it. Don't worry, your team will get credit if Laing gets arrested and we'll slip away, but if he thinks he's going to get one over on us, then he made a mistake.'

Smith was dressed casually in black jeans and a black shirt. He put on a lightweight windcheater.

'I have you billeted in the Edinburgh Castle barracks,' McGovern said.

'I'd like to see Kim,' Smith said.

McGovern nodded. 'She was taken to the Royal, just for a check-up. She's almost six months now.'

Smith turned to Miller. 'I'm glad for you both, Frank. I mean that.'

'Thanks, Eric.'

'Right, let's get up to the Royal,' McGovern said.

They pulled out onto Turnhouse Road again, the cars moving fast, the traffic patrol car once again taking the lead. A few minutes later, they were on the Edinburgh bypass. Miller looked out of the window at the lights of the city, and wondered where his little girl was.

Smith had been right about one thing; Emma *was* his now too. And he missed his little girl more than anything.

CHAPTER 29

Marie Anders paced around the living room, holding a cup of coffee in one hand.

'Why don't you relax?' Anders said. 'Maybe drink decaff.'

'Aren't alarm bells ringing in your head?'

'You think I'm worried about Mr Blue? Please.'

'He looks like he's not all there. He calls you Mr Red.'

'He's just a go-between. It's how they operate. We should just think ourselves lucky we got the intel on the target. What's got you so worried anyway?'

'When he came early, in that dirty little van of his, he opened the back to take out the box of groceries.'

'Did he forget the fat-free milk?'

'Jesus, Brett, can you take me seriously for a minute?'

He looked at his wife. 'I'm sorry, honey. Go ahead.'

She stopped pacing. 'I saw in the back of that van. There was a little girl sitting in there. She smiled at me and waved.'

'I wonder who she is? And bringing her here?' Anders stood up. 'I'm going to call him.'

Marie put a hand on his arm. 'Don't. Not yet. I may be over reacting, but now that we have our own little girls, it jarred with me. I just heard a news report that there's a little girl missing. She fits the description.'

'Christ, if I find out he's touching kids, I'll have more than a word with him. I'll go visit the Consulate tomorrow. I know somebody there.'

'Won't he wonder why you're up here?'

'Trust me, this guy won't ask any questions.'

'Okay. But I think I'll have a soak in the tub and have an early night. Mr Blue's coming back with the details, right?'

'No. He'll text me on a burner phone.'

'Oh God.' She held her husband for a second. 'I'll see you upstairs. I'm going to call the nanny. Make sure our little princesses are okay.'

John Carson

Anders shivered. Surely this guy Mr Blue, wouldn't be touching little girls? He knew what he would do to anybody who even went near his daughters. If he found out that this British asshole had taken a little girl, he'd get what was coming to him.

He lay back with his feet on the couch, and absent-mindedly flipped through the TV channels with the remote thinking about the time he had first met Marie.

He had played the part of her boyfriend, somebody she had met in a nightclub. She was working as a nanny for a family, the Robinsons. He was a scientist, his wife worked in the UN and one of the kids went to Columbia University while the younger one went to a good high school. All-American family. They would move out of the city when the boy and girl graduated and buy a house in Westchester County. Maybe a little town like Somers. Not a city like White Plains. No, something small.

Anders had been sitting in the living room of the rented brownstone in Cobble Hill in Brooklyn. It wasn't too far from where he stayed in Cadman Plaza, and they would walk along the promenade down by Jane's Carousel, a children's ride, housed in a steel and glass enclosure. They would stare over to the illuminated Manhattan skyline, just two lovers enjoying being in each other's company.

The truth was, they were out in the open and nobody could hear them talk. Marie would give him a daily report on the family. The all-American family, the do-no-harm family, who were in fact Russian sleepers. It was only a careless little slip that had given the game away one day and the authorities had picked up on it. Then housekeeper Marie had taken up a job with them, looking after them, after the present one suddenly quit.

Nobody ever suspected Anders was her handler, and it might have stayed that way if Marie hadn't got caught.

One afternoon, before the schools got out, Marie was alone in the house. Or so she thought. She was in Mr Robinson's study, trying to open the desk drawer for a little poke around, when she felt the presence behind her.

She had stood up, ready to come out with some bullshit story and saw the wife advancing on her. Marie had gone into self-protection mode, ready to fight, but the wife had a gun in her hand. As

TRIAL AND ERROR

Marie put her hands up, she had been pistol whipped.

When she came round fifteen minutes later, she was tied to a dining chair and the wife was on the phone. Talking in her native Russian, and although Marie wasn't fluent, she'd picked up enough of the conversation to know the husband was being informed of the situation and he was on his way home.

'Who are you working for, you little bitch?' the wife said.

'The housekeeping agency. You know that.'

The wife had back-handed her, the slap hard and sore.

'Who are you working for?' the wife repeated.

'Fuck you.' Marie felt her own anger accelerating, but Mrs Robinson wasn't angry. She was very professional. And Marie knew then that she had made a mistake as the wife smiled at her.

'You have just confirmed my suspicions. Now you will tell me what department you work for. CIA? No, they don't operate on American soil. NSA? Defence Department?'

When Marie didn't answer, she got another slap.

'I told you, I'm a nanny.'

'Good grief, woman, you're a disgrace to your country.'

'Untie me, then, and we'll fucking see.'

Mrs Robinson rammed the gun against Marie's forehead. 'Your government will never find your body. I hope you know that.'

Marie stared ahead and thought of Brett Anders. Wishing he was here now.

Brett Anders was close by. In an apartment further down the block. The Robinson's were experts in terrorism and regularly swept the house for bugs. They didn't find any. They were well hidden. Anders had had a tech take Robinson's computer apart. It was a 27" iMac. Unlike the old ones, where the glass screen was held in by magnets, this one was glued on. The tech knew there were hidden cameras in the house, and they'd intercepted the Wi-Fi and played the images on a loop, so if Robinson or his family looked, they would see the same image, but the sun coming in the windows would change position, which gave the tech a limited time window. He had got to work. Anders had stood guard, a silenced gun in his hand, ready to take down anybody who came in. This job was covert, but needs must and protecting their identity was a priority.

The tech had fiddled with some wires and added a microphone to the two the machine already had. This third microphone would capture any conversation in the office where Robinson regularly contacted his superior officers. The recording would then be sent via Wi-Fi to the apartment along the road where it would be analysed.

It was this microphone that saved Marie's life. The software was programmed to send an alert at a key phrase.

'Are you a fan of Simon and Garfunkel?' Marie asked, setting in motion the red flag that would alert Anders.

The job was supposed to last three weeks. If she didn't find something in that time, they would have a Plan B, but Marie had only been with the family eight days.

Anders was sitting in a coffee house just along from the apartment when he got a call.

'The package won't be arriving as usual tonight. It got broken in transit.' *Marie was in trouble. As bad as it would get.*

Anders calmly got up from his table and left a bill to cover the coffee then walked round the corner to where the brownstone was. He took out his phone and dialled a number. 'Tell me,' he said to the operator.

'The key phrase was just uttered. There was some kind of questioning going on, and we ran it again. The wife caught Marie at the husband's desk. She doesn't believe she's a nanny and she has a gun. Life in immediate threat.'

'I'm going in. Time it for three minutes and then make the call. Cut the feed now and after it's copied, erase it all. Make it look like there was a fault from two hours ago.'

Anders walked casually along the street, a warm, summer afternoon in June. People were going about their business, not paying attention to what anybody else was doing. He took the steps up to the front door of the brownstone, and took out the key he'd had copied, and slipped inside like he belonged there, quietly closing the door behind him.

There was a coat closet just inside the front door and he quietly opened it. He'd come in here one day and taped a loaded pump action Mossberg to the wall above the opening. You couldn't see it if you didn't go right in and look.

TRIAL AND ERROR

He took the gun down and peeled off the tape. There was already a round in the chamber. A lot of householders in America didn't like to keep one in the pipe, preferring to chamber a round so any intruder could hear the universal chit-chit sound of one being loaded. It was usually enough to scare somebody off, but if you were foolish enough to ignore it, you knew what was coming.

And Mrs Robinson would definitely know what was coming. But by the time he chambered a round, she could be spinning round and putting a bullet in his head. So now all he had to do was pull the trigger.

He stepped into the office, silently approaching Mrs Robinson. She didn't hear or see him.

'Drop the gun,' he said, knowing she wouldn't. She was an enemy combatant, plain and simple. She turned, her finger on the trigger, but Anders fired the shotgun after stepping to one side, making sure Marie wasn't in the line of fire.

He had loaded the gun with buckshot – bigger diameter shot but more deadly. It took the side of Mrs Robinson's head off. He laid the gun on the desk and turned to Marie.

'Christ, I thought she was going to kill me,' she said.

'Now, would I let that happen to you?'

'We better get out of here. Somebody might call the police if they heard the shot.'

'Relax, Marie. They had this house soundproofed. We looked at the contractors' worksheets after the job was completed. You could let off a nuclear bomb in here and nobody would hear it.'

'I lived in a neighbourhood like that once. Nobody wanted to get involved.'

'I bet your neighbours weren't KGB.'

Both of them turned round when the front door slammed shut. Anders knew it couldn't be Mr Robinson. The man couldn't have gotten home in such a short time. He was at least another ten minutes out at this time of the day.

Anders looked at Marie as the two boys walked into the office.

Half day, Marie mouthed at him.

There was nothing Anders could say to the kids. He wasn't sure why the older one was home, but what was in the front of his mind right now was the boy charging at him. Marie side-stepped the

149

older boy as he crashed into Anders. They went rolling onto the floor, but then Anders kept on rolling and ended up on top of the boy.

'You bastard!' the older boy screamed.

The younger boy screamed and turned to run at Anders but Marie caught him.

The older boy was athletic, strong, and kneed Anders in the side. Anders could fight, but something held him back for a second. Hitting a boy? Then he was knocked off balance and the boy was up.

Anders was always taught to never underestimate an opponent. If he had he might have just thought the boy was trying to escape when he got free. He might not have thought he was going for the shotgun. But the college boy was indeed going for the gun. His father had taught him well. All Ruskies together, obviously.

Marie's reflexes were much sharper than they used to be and while she fought off the high-schooler, she saw college boy making for the desk. She slapped the high-schooler, knocking him off balance. Then she grabbed the shotgun just before college boy's hand hit the desk.

She turned the shotgun towards him and pulled the trigger.

College boy flew backwards, a gaping hole in his chest, his heart disintegrated before he hit the carpet.

Anders turned to the schoolboy and saw a mask of pure hatred. The boy was obviously being groomed to spy for the motherland, as he swore at them in Russian, just before he bent down and picked up the hand gun.

Marie didn't hesitate. She racked the shotgun and let the schoolboy have it. The seventeen-year-old was blown off his feet.

Anders looked at Marie. She was panting hard, but there was a slight smile on her lips, a feral look that only somebody who has killed another human being can possess.

They both turned when the front door opened. 'Put the shotgun down,' Anders said in a whisper. 'I have to leave. Backup's on the way. They won't be long. The next few minutes count. Don't move and whatever you do, don't go for the shotgun. There are no shells left in it anyway.'

He took the hand gun and rushed through the back way to the kitchen and down the basement steps, knowing he could get out the back way.

TRIAL AND ERROR

Marie put the gun down on the floor. It didn't feel right but she had to trust Anders' judgement.

Mr Robinson walked along the hallway and stopped outside the office. Saw the gun on the carpet. Saw his son lying dead. His eyes were wide and then he saw his other son and wife lying dead on the floor.

'What have you done?' Mr Robinson said, a hint of Russian accent slipping out.

Marie stood and looked at him.

He picked up the shotgun. They were oblivious to the front door opening.

'I will fucking kill you!' he said, pointing the gun at Marie. She tensed and prepared to die, but in a strange way, she knew she wasn't going to. *Don't go for the shotgun* Anders had said. He must have had a reason to say that.

The reason was coming in through the door, two of them, their guns drawn.

'I will fucking kill you!' Mr Robinson screamed louder, then he caught movement out of the corner of his eye.

'Police! Drop the gun!'

But Mr Robinson was angry, the blood rushing through his ears. He didn't hear what they said. Wasn't listening to them. All he could see were the dead bodies of his family lying on the office floor.

He turned to the sound of the shouting again, swinging the shotgun.

The first officer's bullets tore into his chest, followed by the second officers.

Marie screamed. She heard them perfectly well.

'Come out with your hands up!' the first officer shouted.

She came out, holding her hands up, and started to cry. 'He killed them,' she said. Over and over.

They asked her who she was and she told them. They called for an ambulance but even she could see Mr Robinson was dead.

She told detectives he had come in and started shouting at his wife. Then his sons came in but he shot her, then shot his sons. She had been in the kitchen and tried to run but he was waiting for her.

They didn't know why Mr Robinson had killed his family and was going to kill the housekeeper. It happened more frequently than

151

John Carson

they liked. Murder-suicide. First the head of the house kills the wife, and then the kids, before killing himself.

Marie was just unlucky enough to be in the house at the same time. The officers clearly heard him shouting that he was going to kill Marie, just before he tried to turn the gun on them.

Anders caught up with Marie that night, at the little apartment she had in a quiet neighbourhood.

'He could have killed me,' she said, pouring them both a glass of wine.

He had smiled at her as he sat down with his glass.

'No, he couldn't. I only put three shells into that shotgun. The police didn't know it was empty. They do now, of course, but they'll think he just miscounted or something.'

'I messed up.' She sat down beside him.

'No, you didn't. It happens. It was taken care of. The Russians will think he snapped under the pressure. We got him, that's the main thing. But he has been sending them false information. *That* we did make sure of. And we put his computer back as we found it. Without the added microphone.'

She drank some more wine. 'I thought the Cold War was over?'

He shook his head. 'It never stopped, Marie. It just took a different direction. It'll never stop.'

'What's going to happen to us now?'

'The bosses were impressed. They want you to carry on with your training, but we're not supposed to work on American soil. They're sending us to London. I'm going to be mentoring you still.'

'I've always wanted to visit London.' She reached across to him and kissed him. 'My handler. My lover.'

'We're going to achieve great things, my love.'

And they did. Including meeting Mr Black, a former army officer and Intelligence Chief. A man who was in the same game as they were.

CHAPTER 30

Matthew Webb sat in the interview with his head in his hands. 'I've told you, I don't know what you're talking about.'

His lawyer sat beside him taking notes.

Percy Purcell sat opposite him, Paddy Gibb by his side.

'We traced the ISP address to your house. The very modem sitting in your living room. Your laptop is being pulled apart by our forensic techs right now, but we thought you'd like to give us your account.'

'Look, how many fucking times do I have to say this? I didn't do anything wrong!'

'Do you know a girl who goes by the name of *Honeygirl*?'

Matthew sat up and looked at him. 'Yes. But I never met her.'

'You were planning to though.'

'Yes. I was given a site by a friend of mine, where you could chat to young women who were into older men.'

'Before the techs strip down your hard drive, they'd found a copy of a conversation between you and *Honeygirl*.'

'So what? It's not illegal.'

'Abducting an eight-year-old girl is,' Gibb said. He threw that in to rattle Matt.

'Wait, what? What the hell are you talking about? I never touched a little girl.'

'Do you know *Honeygirl's* real identity?'

'No. She never told me. That was the exciting thing. And her being younger, that made it all the more fun.'

'You like young girls?' Gibb asked.

'What? Yes. I mean, no. Not the sort of young girls you mean.'

'How old are you?'

'You know how old I am.'

'I'm asking you.'

'Thirty-seven.'

'And you think it's okay to go out with a sixteen-year-old?'

Matt's lawyer cleared his throat. 'My client is being forthright with you, detectives. As you are well aware, the age of consent in Scotland is sixteen. My client isn't breaking any laws.'

'Abducting a child is very much against the law,' Gibb said.

'Do you have any proof my client took this child?'

'We're working on it. That's why he's here and we have technical staff going through his laptop and a whole team of people stripping your client's flat.'

'You won't find anything because I haven't done anything,' Matt said. 'It's not illegal to date a young woman.'

'Girl,' Purcell corrected him.

'Girl. Young woman. Same thing. As long as she's legal. I could marry her here in Scotland and there's nothing you could do about it.'

'So why don't you enlighten your lawyer about where you were going to meet this girl.'

Matt looked at his lawyer. 'In the pub.'

'Correct me if I'm wrong, but the legal age to start drinking in Scotland is still eighteen,' Purcell said. 'So that's not exactly true when you said you were doing nothing wrong.'

'She didn't turn up.'

'Not the point,' Gibb said. 'What were you going to do? Meet her in the pub with your pervy pal and get the lassie pished so you could take her home and have sex with her?'

'No, we were just going to go and have a laugh.'

'Have a laugh with a sixteen-year-old and her friend. You did write to her and ask her to bring a friend along for your own friend, what's his name again?' Purcell looked at his notes. 'Mark Valentine.' He looked at Matt. 'He like little girls as well, does he?'

'Look, for fuck's sake, they said they were twenty and they liked going out with older men. I'm thirty-seven, Mark's thirty-six. We met at work, got talking and found that we were kindred spirits. Both divorced, back home living with the folks, just 'til we got on our feet, so we were just looking for a good time.'

Gibb was looking at a notepad in front of him. 'How well do you know the Bonnington area of the city? Trinity, Warriston, round about there.'

'I don't know it at all.'

'It's not that far from where you live.'

'I have no reason to go there.'

'Not even to meet your girlfriend?'

'She's not my girlfriend. I've only ever spoken to her online. I've never met her, spoke to her on the phone, nothing. Only typed messages to her.'

'Ever suggest you meet up for sex?' Purcell said.

'That was the point, yes, but as I said, she said she was twenty. If she looked like she was skipping high school for the day, we would have fucked off. Neither one of us is into that sort of stuff. We go to the singles club in Stockbridge and we've picked up some women. My mother goes to visit a friend down in Carlisle sometimes, so I have the flat to myself. Me and Mark have picked up some women and taken them back to my place and had a good time. We thought this would be the same.'

'Know what I think?' Gibb said. 'You met this girl online, agreed to meet up with her and she said she'd bring a pal. But you found out she was having you on. You found out she was only sixteen but you wanted to meet up with her anyway. So, you went down to where she lives, and thought you were onto something, but then you see she'd got a kid with her. You try to get her to come with you for sex somewhere, but she starts to back out. But you kill her and take the little girl. Did you kill her as well? Did you? Answer me you little bastard!'

'What? Fucking kill her? I didn't kill anybody.'

'We'll soon find out,' Purcell said, staying calm. 'We have a warrant for your DNA and blood samples.'

'I'm giving you fuck all.'

'Listen son, I don't think you know how it's going to go down; if you refuse, I'll have six uniforms in here holding you down while we pluck your hair out and before we get one of them to ram a cotton bud down your throat. One way or the other, you'll be giving us a sample. The easy way or the hard way, your choice.'

Matt looked at his lawyer. "He can't do that, can he?'

'He has a warrant. You have to comply.'

'Christ, alright, I'll give you the samples.'

'Tell us again what happened when you met the girl in the pub.'

'She didn't turn up.'

'Is that when you decided to go down to where she lives?'

'I don't know where she lives. She never told me where she lives when we were chatting.'

'Did you ever send her naked pictures of yourself?' Gibb asked.

'Of course I didn't. What the hell do you think I am? Some kind of pervert?'

'That's exactly what I think you are. Talking to wee fucking lassies on the computer.'

'Where's the little girl?' Purcell asked. 'Did she scream? Shout for her mummy after she saw what you did to her babysitter?'

'I don't know anything about a little girl. I didn't touch *Honeygirl*. Fuck, I don't even know her name.'

'If she's alive, that will make it a lot better with the jury. It can make the difference between you going into solitary right away, or being put in general population for a few hours. You do know what they do to kiddie fiddlers in prison, don't you?'

'Detective, I really must protest strongly–'

'Merely trying to establish if your client was involved.'

'I'm not involved in anything,' Matt said. 'I didn't meet her, didn't touch her, didn't kill her. Why won't you believe me?'

'So, you met up with her?' Gibb said, trying to trip the man up. 'Where was this again?'

'I told you, she didn't turn up. It was at the Haymarket Bar. She was bringing a friend with her, but she didn't show. And you can beat me to a pulp now trying to get me to change my story, but I can't because it's the truth.'

The uniforms were sent into the room while Purcell and Gibb went upstairs to the conference room. Jeni Bridge was there with Andy Watt.

'Frank's going off his fucking head,' Watt said. 'Sorry, ma'am.'

Jeni waved his apology away. 'Coffee anybody? If I wasn't still on duty, I'd be getting wired into a bottle of wine.'

They all agreed coffee would be good. When they were settled, Jeni sat back in her chair. 'Tell me he confessed, Percy.'

'I wish I could, ma'am. He denies it every step of the way. He admits he and his friend were chatting with Lynn Sterling – although he never once mentioned her by her proper name – but he says the last thing they knew, they were supposed to meet in a bar but she didn't show up.'

'None of this is making any sense. And we're still no further forward to knowing who took little Emma.' Jeni sipped more coffee. 'Do you think this Matt and his friend took her and killed her? Or worse, are keeping her for nefarious purposes?'

Purcell shook his head. 'I don't think they did. I don't think he's in the frame for Lynn's murder either.'

'What's your take on it then?'

'I think Matthew Webb's new friend, who he said he just met, introduced him to Lynn, aka *Honeygirl*.'

'Why?'

'So he could kill Lynne. Get into Matthew Webb's house and use his computer. Make it look like Webb's the killer. Have us chase our own arse in circles. We're looking at Webb and his friend while he's away with Emma. We're looking in the wrong place. That would be my guess.'

'If that's the case, then we might never find out who he really is.'

'That's a possibility.'

'Has anybody heard how Kim is doing?'

'I'll call Miller and see,' Watt said.

'You can't give him any details about the men we picked up,' Jeni said. 'You can keep him updated, but no names or addresses.'

'I know, ma'am.' He left the room.

'What's happening with our two suspects?' Jeni asked Purcell.

'They're being held overnight. We have them for twenty-four hours, then we can get an extension if we need to. We'll have the lab run the blood samples, but the DNA isn't going to come back for a little while. We also pulled prints so we'll run them too. I don't think we're going to find anything incriminating.'

'Which leaves us to wonder, where exactly is little Emma?'

CHAPTER 31

Kim had been given something for the stress. It was important that they keep her calm. She was in a side room when they came in; a detective, a government official, and an SAS soldier.

'Did you find my little girl?' she asked Miller when he came into the room.

He hesitated for a moment. 'Sorry, love.'

She started crying. 'Where were you tonight?' she asked him for the second time that evening.

He didn't know what to say. Visions of Carol were in his head again. He couldn't voice what he had been doing. Chasing a ghost would have been his answer, if pressed.

'We'll find her,' Neil McGovern said, brushing past Miller.

'Oh, dad.' She held onto her father for a moment.

'We'll get her back, Kim,' Eric said. He took the place of her father. She held onto him.

Miller had never felt so unsure of himself at that moment. He wanted to hold her, to tell her things would be okay, that they would get married, he'd be a good father to Emma, but none of those words came out.

'Oh, you're here then,' Norma Banks said, coming into the room. Miller knew she was addressing him. 'Give me an update.'

Miller saw her eyes were red with crying. 'They traced an ISP address and lifted two men. One of them had been talking to Lynn Sterling, Emma's babysitter's daughter. One of them said he had been given the name of that site by a man.'

'What man?'

Miller hesitated for a moment. 'He doesn't know him that well. He had just met him.'

'I'm going to have the Solicitor General throw the book at him. They have charged him haven't they?'

Again, Miller was thinking before answering. 'They're keeping them overnight, but no charges have been pressed yet. They're technically holding them for questioning.'

TRIAL AND ERROR

'Christ Almighty. And tomorrow they walk.'

'We're having the Sterling house dusted for prints and we'll compare tomorrow. CCTV in the area of the housing estate where they live is being checked. Everybody who was on Lynn's friends list on Facebook is being contacted. We're checking everything, including her Twitter feed, to see if there is anything from the man who was talking to her. So far, it seems to be some messaging thing.'

'Does he have any prior arrests?' Eric asked.

Great; the Spanish Inquisition is well and truly up and running.

'Nothing. He's not on the sex offender's list, he isn't a known perv and so far, his laptop is clean. They found the messages between him and Lynn, but there was nothing filthy on there between them. She's sixteen and he's thirty-seven, but there's nothing illegal there.'

'Did he mention Emma at all?' Norma said.

'No. Purcell said the suspect didn't know who Emma was.'

'You said there was a man who was seen talking to Lynn when she was with Emma. Have you traced him?'

'No. We have no positive ID on him. The witness said he didn't get a good look. Average build with dark hair, which is probably half the men in Edinburgh.'

'And that being a walkway and cycle route, he could have come to her on foot or on a bike.'

'He could have. It's a big network.'

'Did this witness say if she was standing talking to him like he was a friend or like she was just asking for the time?'

'Talking to him. It appears that maybe she thought she was meeting the suspect, who goes by the moniker *Big Matt*. There is a message on her computer, but not one on the suspect's laptop. That's why we think whoever sent the message, gained entry into the man's house and plugged the modem into another laptop, making it look like it was the suspect's laptop.'

'He must have known you'd find out,' Eric said.

'It's just a diversion tactic. Designed to waste our time.'

'We're talking about Miles Laing here, right?'

'That's what we're working on just now.'

'So, he had this planned all the time he was in the hospital. And the bastard knew a lot about you, Frank. Where you live, your number, the fact you live with Kim and her daughter. Emma's name and what grade she was in school,' Norma said.

'He certainly didn't get that from me.'

The muscles in the side of her jaw were tightening and her cheeks were going red. 'I'm going to tell you to your face, Frank; I've been in touch with Jeni Bridge, and she'll be giving you the official news tomorrow morning. You've been suspended from duty.'

'What? Why?'

'Why? Are you fucking daft? All those cosy chats you've been having with Miles Laing. Him saying that he'll be seeing you soon. Now Kim's daughter has been abducted. Why do you think?'

'Now, listen here, Norma,' Miller said, his own face flushed with anger. 'I've done nothing wrong. He's playing games. Always has done. That's all in his mind. He's pissed off because I caught him and put him away. And now he's trying to get back at me.'

'You couldn't work this case anyway, but it's better you're kept well away from things.'

'Norma, it's not his fault,' Neil said. 'Frank loves Emma almost as much as her own father.'

'He's right, Norma,' Eric said. 'I wouldn't let Emma live with somebody I didn't trust.'

She turned on them both. 'That may be the case, but something's not right with this case, and until we get to the bottom of it, Miller's suspended.' She turned back to Miller. 'Report to the station tomorrow morning with your warrant card. Nine o'clock sharp. If you don't, I'll have the sheriff issue a warrant for your arrest.'

Miller stood in silence for a moment, then the doctor came in. 'I'd like you to keep the noise down in here,' he said.

'That's my daughter there!' Norma said.

'And she's my patient. She's heavily pregnant, in case you weren't aware,' he said, his voice filled with sarcasm. 'She needs rest and support. I've been informed of the situation, so we need to make sure Ms Smith is kept comfortable, for both her and the baby's sake.'

'Sorry, doctor,' McGovern said. 'I'll make sure my wife is quiet.'

Norma turned to him but he gave her a look that wasn't meant to be argued with.

'Is she well enough to come home?' Miller said.

TRIAL AND ERROR

'I'd rather she stay in here for a couple of days.'

'Frank, promise me you'll let me know as soon as you hear anything,' Kim said.

'I will.' He walked past the others and bent over to give her a kiss. 'I love you.'

She didn't say the words back but kissed him. He turned and walked out of the hospital room.

Outside, the darkness had brought the chill with it. He was waiting at the taxi rank when his mobile rang. His heart started racing, which he guessed would happen every time it rang from now until they got Emma back.

'Hello?'

'Frank, it's me.'

Miller had to think for a moment before he recognised the voice; Robert Molloy.

'I'm a bit busy at the moment, Molloy.'

'Yeah, I heard about the wee girl. You have my sympathies. However, I'm calling to invite you down to the club for a drink.'

'Thanks, but I have drink at home.'

'We need to talk.'

'Can't it wait?'

'No, it can't.'

'What's it about?'

'My daughter. Your wife. Your dead wife.'

CHAPTER 32

Robert Molloy's club in George Street was simply called *The Club*. An old banking building, back in the days when banks were bricks and mortar, he had bought it and converted it into what it was now.

Miller stepped out of the taxi and one of Molloy's doormen approached him as he walked up the stairs to the front door.

'Inspector Miller, we've been expecting you. Follow me, sir.'

Miller didn't know this man but he followed him in through the club to the back. 'I know where I'm going from here,' he said.

He went up the stairs to Molloy's office and opened the door without knocking.

'Jesus, Frank, I might have had a filly in here with no clothes on and you come bursting in without knocking.'

'You were tracking me on your cameras. Any *filly* would be spirited away by now.'

'Come in and get yourself a drink. You won't have to worry about drinking on the job now that you've been suspended.'

'How did you…?'

Molloy stood up from behind the desk and walked over to his drinks cabinet. 'It can mean the difference between life and death, Frank. Me finding things out. Sit, sit. We can have a whisky.'

Miller sat down on a couch, facing a large screen TV. Accepted the drink from Molloy.

Molloy sat down on a chair and took a sip of his own whisky before looking at Miller. 'You know something? When I told you I wanted to speak to you about Carol, you didn't ask why.'

'So?'

'You know, don't you?'

'Know what?'

'Come on, don't be coy. I want to know what the hell is going on.'

'I don't know what you mean.'

Molloy picked up a remote control, changed the picture on the muted TV and then hit a play button. The DVD player kicked into life and then there she was.

Miller kept the glass up to his mouth for a second, his eyes staring at the image on the screen. 'So, I'm not going mental,' he said after he put the glass down.

'You've seen her, haven't you?'

'Yes.'

'Who the hell is she?'

'I have no idea. I followed her onto a Fife train but she got off at Haymarket and gave me the slip.'

'She gave my men the slip too. The thing is, I can understand if it was maybe somebody who looked similar, but she's the spitting image.'

'So, what are you saying?'

Molloy stared into space for a moment before answering. 'I know Kim's father is in charge of the Scottish branch of the witness protection programme. I want to throw something out there, Miller, and give it some thought. What if she never died? What if McGovern had her put into the programme for some reason?'

'What? That doesn't even make sense.' He looked more closely at the TV. 'It has to be somebody who looks like her.'

'Then why is she here in my club?'

'Coincidence?'

'Pish. Where did you see her?'

'Looking up at my flat from the High Street.'

'You've just answered your own question there, son. I want to see her face-to-face, to see how closely she resembles my daughter.'

'There has to be some plausible explanation. I mean, she hasn't come back from the dead.'

'No, I don't think she has.'

They drank in silence for a moment. 'Do you think your suspects are the ones who took Emma?' Molloy said.

'No. Somebody's making it look like that though.' He explained about Matt Webb's laptop.

'I've put some feelers out. I'll let you know if I hear anything. Or I can have some of my people interview them, and this time the little fuckers won't have a lawyer with them.'

'You don't have to. We have a lot of people working on it.'

'Bunch of fannies who have to go by the rule book. The only rules that apply to me are, there are no rules. I don't have to wait for a sheriff to see if he wants to sign a warrant or not.'

'Christ, we don't want anything jeopardising the case.'

'Relax, Frank. I would never compromise anything. And trust me, if I catch the bastard first, you'll have a full confession if he knows what's best for him.'

Miller finished his drink and stood up. 'I'll let you know if I see... *her* again.'

'Likewise.' Molloy stood up. 'I really do hope you get your wee girl back, Frank. I'll do everything I can.'

'Thanks.'

The same doorman who'd been waiting for him, led Miller outside.

The air had a smell about it. Diesel fumes, outside cooking, and a million other odours. He didn't know what to do with himself now. Kim wasn't coming home. Emma wasn't tucked up in bed. He didn't have a job just now.

For the first time in his life, Frank Miller was lost.

He started heading for St Andrew Square, swept along in the throng of visitors. Edinburgh was becoming busier every day, and not just at festival time. Then he heard his phone ringing. Thinking it might be Kim or somebody with news about Emma, he snatched it out of his pocket.

'Hello, boss.' It was Andy Watt. 'Time for a beer?'

Miller looked at his watch. 'Sure. It's not like I've anything else to do.'

'Logie's?'

'I'll be there in ten, Andy.'

Miller stepped out across St Andrew Square and up the North Bridge. For the second time in his life, he could feel things slipping away from him. Getting blootered with Andy Watt sounded just the ticket.

There were the usual punters in the bar, chatting, watching a game on the TV. Watt was standing with two pints of lager, one of them started.

'Let's get a seat, boss,' he said, handing Miller a pint.

'Cheers, Andy.'

TRIAL AND ERROR

They found a table up on the gallery, looking down on the customers below.

'You heard about me getting suspended tomorrow?' Miller said, supping at the cold liquid.

'I did. Bastards. That nutter calls you and you're the one they drop in it. The whole force has gone to fuck.'

'They're just covering their own arses. In case I turn out to be some head case who had a regular chat with a convicted killer and we had planned his escape together. But fuck them. They'll find out soon enough that I wasn't doing any such thing.'

'Nobody believes that you did anything wrong, boss.'

'I appreciate that. But unless we get the bastard soon, then they're going to take it further.'

'You know, as much as I enjoy having a pint with you, I called you here to go over something with you. As far as I'm concerned, you're still my boss and if they don't like it, well, what you just said. But I wanted to talk to you about something.'

Miller leaned forward. 'Go on.'

'There was a fire in a house in Easter Howgate, on the Biggar Road. They saw pretty quickly that it had been started deliberately and there was a woman in the house, so it's been classed a murder.'

'Okay.'

'I didn't think much about it until I saw the name of the victim; Rena Joseph.'

Miller sat back, a thoughtful look on his face. Then he shook his head. 'Andy, it doesn't ring a bell.'

'The name on the packet of photographs you took from the hotel manager, the place where Miles Laing used to work. It's the same name.'

CHAPTER 33

'A foursome?'

The way Peter Hanson had answered her made Steffi Walker's heart sink. It was wrong calling him. Why would a bus driver want to go out with a cop? He probably saw enough fights on the buses and had to deal with his fair share of drunks without wanting to spend time with her.

He gave you his number, didn't he?

'You're not interested. I'm sorry, Peter. Maybe some other time.'

'No, no, wait. All I meant was, will your police officer friends be interested in talking to a bus driver?'

'For goodness sake, don't put yourself down like that! Of course they would. It's the person you are, not the uniform they're talking to.'

'In that case, I'd love to.'

'Great! My friend and her boyfriend can meet you up town. How about at *The Club* in George Street?'

'That's not too far from me. I live down Leith Walk.'

'Fabulous.' They had discussed a time and after she had disconnected, she called Julie Stott.

'Christ, Steffi, didn't you hear?'

'Hear what?'

'It's already on the news. Frank Miller's stepdaughter is missing. Her babysitter was murdered and somebody abducted her.'

'Jesus Christ, no.' Steffi was stunned. 'Julie, I didn't know. I haven't had the news on. God Almighty, what must Peter think of me? I just made the arrangements.'

'He probably doesn't know who Emma is. They haven't released the connection.'

'Julie, I'll call him back and cancel. Where are you just now?'

'Still at the scene at Bonnington. I'm sorry, Steffi. We can do it some other night, yes?'

'Oh, yes, no problem. I'm sure Peter will understand. If not, tough shit.'

'I better go. Forensics are crawling all over the place. It's like a fair down here and now the TV news crews are starting to turn up. God knows how they hear about these things.'

'Call me later, Julie. We can talk.'

'I will. Later hun.'

Steffi hung up. She had formed a close bond with Julie after an operation they had worked on together. Now they socialised all the time, and Julie had gotten herself a boyfriend, a sergeant who worked in the drugs squad.

She tried calling Peter again, but there was no answer. Maybe he had gone for a shower. She sat and watched the TV reports of a murder in Edinburgh and a little girl who had gone missing. She felt anger inside now. Somebody fucking with the team. They all stood together when push came to shove, and she had been proud to work with Frank Miller and knew she was lucky to be in MIT.

She called Peter again. No answer.

He might have left already. She hated to stand him up and then call him with a *Sorry I got caught up at work* excuse.

She pulled on a light jacket and decided she would go and meet him herself. What was the harm? He was a nice guy, and if he turned out to be a not-quite-so-nice guy, well, she had spent four years in the army as a combat medic, and knew how to handle herself. He'd find out what it was like not only to fuck with a police officer, but a former soldier at that.

She left the TV on, closed the curtains and put a light on. Some habits died hard. The place looked like a laundry basket had exploded, but she would fix it in the morning. It wasn't as if Peter was coming back here on the first date.

Is that what this is? A date?

It was. Sort of.

She closed her door and walked downstairs. Her Mini was parked in a space near the door. The small car was fine for doing her grocery shopping, but she didn't like taking it to work or when she was going into town, especially when she would be drinking.

Her father hated her walking along to the bus stop. North Werber Park was just off Crewe Road South, with plenty of buses passing, but after she turned right from her flat, it was almost like

167

being on a country road. Bushes and trees blocked the view to the flats, and on the other side were playing fields with trees and a large hedge affording privacy. There were three parking bays at the side of the pavement, cut into the grass verge. Cars were reversed in.

Nobody was about, except the man at the very end parking space trying to change a tyre on a van. While he was leaning on a walking stick. He let out a gasp as the tyre iron slipped off the lug nut.

'Do you need a hand?' she said, not wanting to get filthy, but she always carried a packet of paper hankies and a bottle of hand sanitizer in her bag, so she could wipe her hands if she got them a bit dirty. Or she could run back and wash her hands properly.

The man smiled at her. 'Oh, my goodness, I couldn't possibly ask you. Could I? If I could only balance myself and put weight down on the tyre iron, then I could get the wheel off.'

'Here, let me help you.' She took her bag off her shoulder, and placed it in front of her. The panel van was dirty but at least it was dry. The wheel was the passenger side, rear wheel. The back doors were open and she could see a spare wheel sitting waiting to come out.

'That's awfully good of you,' he said in an upper crust English accent.

'It's no problem,' she said. 'I'm a police officer.' She bent over and grabbed the tyre iron.

'I know you are, Miss Walker,' he said, and she realised in that moment in time that she had royally messed things up. Several things happened at once; she started to get up just as the wooden walking stick fell beside her, and one arm snaked round her throat and tightened.

Despite her training, he was strong and knew what he was doing, slowing down the flow of blood through her neck, just enough to subdue her, but not enough to kill her. Then something was pressed over her face. It was enough to render her unconscious in under a minute.

Nobody was nearby. And even if there were, his tactic of getting her to help him with the tyre meant that she could have been there for a few minutes, and all they would see is her helping a man change a wheel.

She didn't feel herself being put into the back of the van. Or being tied up. Or gagged.

TRIAL AND ERROR

She didn't hear Mr Blue go through her bag and throw her phone away, or close the back doors of the van and drive away.

When she woke up, she was cold. They were in a place underground. The stone walls were cold and were made of large stones. A dim light shone above her. There was a small window in the steel door that faced her. There was another door opposite the mattress and she could see it was a small bathroom.

Christ, I'm in a jail cell.

'Hey! Let me out of here!' The gag had been taken out of her mouth but her hands were still tied behind her back. Her feet were tied together at the ankles. She noticed she was sitting on a camp bed with a mattress on top. There was another mattress on the floor.

She was about to scream again when she heard the door unlock and the man who had been at the van was standing in front of her, smiling. He didn't have a walking stick.

'I'm glad you're awake. Sorry about the choking part, and I had to give you something to keep you asleep for a little while, but there are no side effects. Would you like something to drink?'

'I'd like to get out of here, so if you wouldn't mind untying me.'

He walked forward and took something out from behind his back, something she couldn't see but was about to feel.

The shock ripped through her, making her spasm. She flopped about on the bed, having no control of her muscles. Then it stopped and she gasped. She knew she'd been tasered.

'That's just a taste of what you'll get if you mess me about, Miss Walker.' He turned and left the cell, locking the door.

After a few minutes, she recovered. Then he was back, unlocking the door. This time there was somebody with him. A little girl.

'This is Emma. You're going to be looking after her for a little while.' He shoved the girl into the room and followed her. 'She was waiting for you in another room. She doesn't like it in there, do you, petal?'

Emma shook her head. She'd been crying.

'Miss Walker is going to be looking after you. You'll be fine as long as you do as you're told. Now, Miss Walker, turn around and I'll cut the ropes off your hands.'

She scooted round on the bed.

'If there's any funny business, the little girl will get a taste of what you just got. But for longer. Do you understand?'

'Yes.'

He took out a knife and cut the ropes. Then the ones at her ankles.

'I'll be back in the morning. You're in an old locker room. There's toilet paper in the bag by the sink in there. The light will stay on. I'll bring you food. If you try anything funny, I'll kill you both. Understand?'

Steffi nodded.

Mr Blue left the room and locked the door. Emma threw herself into Steffi's arms and she held onto her as Emma started crying.

'I want my mummy.'

'You'll be fine, Emma. I work with your daddy, Frank. I'll keep you safe.'

Steffi hoped her words sounded a lot more confident to the little girl than they sounded to her. But first she had other things to work out.

Like, where the hell were they?

TRIAL AND ERROR

CHAPTER 34

Fredrik Torgersen felt every one of his seventy-nine years. Usually in the morning, he would walk a mile on the treadmill and have a light breakfast whilst watching the morning news. Up at seven every morning, every day without fail. Fit as a fiddle, as the English liked to say. The Scottish too, he supposed.

This morning, he felt more tired than he'd ever felt in his life.

He was sitting in his penthouse apartment on top of the ScotNet building in Lothian Road, the triple-glazed windows keeping out the noise and the fumes. He turned when the figure entered the living room.

Fredrik turned to his butler. 'Can you rustle up some more scrambled eggs, please, Roger?'

'Right away, sir,' the butler said, heading off to the kitchen.

'I'm not hungry,' Miles Laing said, as he sat down at the table, pouring himself a coffee. He was already showered and dressed.

'They're not for you.'

'Morning, squire,' Bruce Hagan said, coming out of the kitchen, eating a piece of toast. He sat at the table with the other two men.

'Have you seen the headlines?' Miles asked.

Fredrik nodded. 'Good God, I am always amazed at how human beings can treat each other.' His Norwegian accent got thicker when he became angry. 'Two little girls. One dead, one missing. It is an atrocity.'

'I agree,' Hagan said. 'And I've seen some of the worst. *Experienced* the worst.' He held up a hand to show his missing fingers.

'I think you have. And experienced them the other day. If it wasn't for you, Miles would be dead,' Fredrik said.

'I owe you one,' Miles said, looking at his new friend.

Hagan waved away the apology. 'I was just there at the right time.'

Fredrik drank some more coffee. 'Tell me again, why do you

think they decided to take you out of the hospital with them?'

'If you look at their plan, they needed a patient to be taken out in the ambulance. If I hadn't overheard Tamara, then I wouldn't have known what they were up to.'

'And you don't know who she was talking to?'

'No. I had to play dumb, or else me and Miles would both be dead.'

A few minutes later, the butler came through with the eggs. Put them in front of Hagan.

'Thank you.'

Frederik looked at the detective as he tucked into his food. 'I don't mean to sound impertinent, but I need to know what I'm dealing with here, so I'd like to talk about your illness.'

'I don't think that's any of our business,' Miles said.

Frederik held up a hand. 'This is a very unusual situation we find ourselves in here, so I would like to know so we can make plans. It's only going to get worse. They've taken Frank Miller's little girl. Where are they going to stop?'

'I don't know why they took her,' Miles said.

'I do. They want to get to you, obviously. It may not be clear just now, but trust me when I say they will stop at nothing to get you. They're desperate people, Miles, and desperate people do desperate things.'

Hagan finished the eggs and washed them down with coffee. 'Listen, I don't mind telling you about myself. I'm not some psycho who climbed over the wall. In fact, if they hadn't wanted to use somebody, I would still be in there, heading for what was, if not a cure, then at least a shot at normalcy.'

'That's good news.'

'Mostly. My doc says I have fifty per cent non-regressive syndrome.'

'Which means?'

'It means, I only have half of my awareness from my previous life.'

'When he wasn't mental,' Miles added.

'Yes, thanks Miles,' Frederik said.

'Exactly,' Hagan continued. 'But with the regulated drugs, I can give the appearance of normality and then my brain will retrain itself.'

TRIAL AND ERROR

'Do you know about your past life as a detective?' Frederik said. 'And do you remember the people in your former life?'

'Yes. I remember being with Hazel.'

'This is serious business,' Fredrik said, 'so I need to ask you a few questions before we go on.'

'Sounds better than talking about me behind my back.'

'Anything we have to say will be said to your face.'

'Fire away.'

'Do you know where you are?'

'I don't believe I've been in your fine-looking apartment before.'

'That's not what I meant.'

Hagan smiled. 'I think we have to talk about what is wrong with me. I'm assuming you know the basics of dementia. I have a form of this. Huntington's Disease is linked to dementia, and they were trying to find a cure when they pumped me full of that stuff they were making. Dementia is damaged nerve cells in the brain. They damaged mine by injecting me with their cocktail of drugs.'

'How does this affect your ability to do things?' Miles said.

Hagan sat silent for a moment before looking at him. 'Imagine sitting in a darkened movie theatre, and then suddenly getting up and running outside into the bright sunshine of a summer afternoon. You can't see everything right away because your eyes haven't adjusted to the light yet and it's painful. You put your hands up to shield your eyes. That's what I'm like; I sometimes can't make things out, and I have explosive anger, but when I get settled, I can see more clearly. Until I have to go back into the movie theatre. You know what it's like going into a darkened room after being out in bright sun. I flit between being out in the sun and being in the movie theatre, and it's during the transition periods that I can't see clearly.'

'Do the drugs help you focus?' Fredrik asked.

'Yes, they do. It would be like putting on sunglasses when you leave the movie theatre, to keep going with this analogy. The drugs stop me from being blinded, as it were. And turning the lights on when going into the theatre.'

'And if you don't take the drugs?'

'Then sometimes my eyes don't adjust to the bright sunshine, and if I go back into the movie theatre, then I can't see. I'm in limbo for a while.'

'You know I'll get you the medication you need. I know people.'

'I appreciate that.'

'I'll speak with the doctor I know later. But meantime, we'll keep you safe. If that woman tried to kill you both, then I have a feeling they're going to try again. After all, they poisoned you both in the hospital.'

Miles finished his coffee. 'We know why but we don't know who. Now all we need to do is find out who they are and put a stop to them.'

CHAPTER 35

It was a small window of opportunity. So far, her routine had been to get in the car, put the kids in the back and make the two-minute drive round to the primary school. From Baberton Mains Dell to Baberton Mains Wynd, took a couple of minutes by car.

The woman would come round onto the main road, and turn right. She wouldn't even have to leave the development to drop off her child. It was quicker than walking but now she had the baby to get in the car too.

Mr Blue sat in the van, eating a bacon roll and drinking coffee from a flask. He was sitting on the main road adjacent to the little footpath that ran from the Drive through to the Dell. He had a newspaper on his steering wheel. Just another workie waiting to start a job.

He wasn't staring down the pathway, but was more keeping an eye on the street with his peripheral vision. Then he saw her walking to her driveway. He casually tossed the unfinished roll onto the floor, threw the remaining coffee out the window and put the newspaper away. Started up the clanking diesel.

'Christ, where's my fucking phone,' Hazel Carter said to herself as she smacked aside a newspaper that was lying on the settee, not quite having made it to the recycling bin. *Come to that, neither had the takeaway containers, or the glass with the dregs of the wine in it.* She looked around the living room and knew that anybody coming in would think the place had been turned over.

She surveyed the small room, and then her eyes went through to the open-plan dining room. It wasn't much better. In fact, the whole house could do with a complete makeover, she thought, but when in God's name am I going to have time to do this? Painting and decorating wasn't solely a man's job, but help would have been appreciated. Why did Bruce have to go and marry that bitch?

John Carson

She was teetering on the edge of a huge, mental abyss, a place where if she just took one more step, she could be in the same place as Bruce. But the children came first. That's what kept her off the ledge.

'Jane! Are you ready?' she shouted.

'Yes, mummy!' her daughter shouted back from upstairs. Which meant that she wasn't. She had probably been reading a book, which wasn't a bad thing, but not before school. Her teeth wouldn't have been brushed. Hazel would be lucky if her daughter actually had clothes on.

'Have you brushed your teeth?' she shouted.

'Yes!'

'Go and do them now!'

'Yes, mummy.' The sound of feet running from the bedroom through to the bathroom could be interpreted as if a herd of elephants had escaped from the zoo and were now residing in her upstairs bedroom.

Daniel was already strapped into his baby seat. Thoughts of little Emma still being missing shot through her mind. She'd called Frank Miller earlier and there was still no word. Nobody thought it was anybody else other than Miles Laing, trying to get back at Frank for arresting him eight years ago. Yes, they had warned her about Bruce, but the last time she'd been to see him, he had sat staring at her, like some basket case. She knew it had been wrong to go and see him, but one half of her had to know, to see for herself, if he would recognise her. The mother of his children. The doctor said Bruce had just been given some meds, so it was understandable.

That had been a couple of months ago and she'd never been back. Miles and the female had taken Bruce and done God knows what with him. Or more to the point, Miles had done something to him. He'd already killed the doctor who helped him escape, so it was reasonable to assume that he had killed Bruce.

Miles Laing had no beef with her, so she wasn't worried. That's why she refused protection from Neil McGovern. She was more than capable of taking care of herself and her kids.

'Remember to spit!' she shouted again. Her son kicked in his car seat.

Then the lead elephant came running down the stairs, putting her school blazer on. 'Ready mummy!' Jane shouted, grabbing a hold of her school bag.

TRIAL AND ERROR

'Don't shout. Mummy's got a headache.'

'Is it the wine again?' the little girl said, tilting her head.

'Cheeky. And get the door open for me please.'

Jane opened the front door and stepped out. Hazel shut it behind her having already hit the key fob to unlock the car doors. Jane opened hers and climbed in the back, sitting on the booster seat and putting her seatbelt on. Hazel came round and put Daniel in the back, belting him in. He was facing backwards in his car seat and held out a hand to Jane.

'Oh damn! My phone. Stay there, don't touch anything I will be back in thirty seconds.' But the thirty seconds became two minutes. She eventually found her phone under some magazines on the dining table.

She rushed back out, locked the door and got in the driver's seat. 'What song are we going to sing today?' she said, reaching for her seatbelt.

No reply.

Hazel felt the panic rise up before she even turned round.

She screamed hard as she saw the empty place beside the car seat.

'Won't my mummy worry?' Jane said as the man made her sit on the old mattress in the back of the van.

'Not when she knows you're going to be with Frank. He'll come and see you later, but first we have to get you out of here.' Mr Blue didn't even look down the footpath as he put the van in gear and drove off. He drove round the main road, leaving the estate by the top exit, going straight over the roundabout into Clovenstone Road.

The van was a white Transit, just one of many thousands on the road. He kept to the speed limit and didn't draw attention to himself. Nobody would be looking for him. He didn't think the copper had even seen his van, she was too busy trying to get the kids settled.

He couldn't believe it when he saw her going back in. That had made his life much easier. He'd been going to knock her out and then grab the child, but this way was even better.

Twenty minutes later, he was at his destination.

CHAPTER 36

Kim was too busy to take Miller's call. 'What's she so busy doing? Putting marmalade on her toast?'

'Cut the lassie some slack,' Jack said, pouring himself another coffee. 'Her own wee lassie is missing, and she's pissed off at you for storming out. Do you want to tell me where you really were?'

Jack had come round for breakfast with his son. Miller looked rough, unshaven with bloodshot eyes.

'What makes you think I was lying?' He sat in the kitchen with his own coffee.

'I was a murder squad detective, remember? I know when people are talking pish.'

'Well, for your information-'

'Let me stop you right there. You don't seem to grasp the seriousness of the situation. Your stepdaughter is missing! Or your future stepdaughter, when you finally put a ring on your girlfriend's finger.'

'Is that what this is all about? Me not getting round to setting a date? Well, has it ever occurred to you that maybe I don't want to get fucking married?'

'I think it's occurred to everybody! Including Kim! So why don't you just admit you ran away and stuck your face in a pint glass?'

'If you must know, I was following Carol.'

Jack sat down at the little table in the kitchen, opposite his son. 'Look, Frank, you know Doctor Levitt can help you. I know it was hard losing Carol, but we're all here to help you.'

'You don't understand; I saw her. In the street. I chased after her. She got on a train and then off at Haymarket. I followed her but I lost her.'

'Christ, Frank, this is getting beyond a joke now. You need help, son.'

'I knew you would say that. And to be honest, I thought I was going off my head. But then Robert Molloy called me. He saw her too.'

Jack looked sceptical. 'Explain.'

TRIAL AND ERROR

'He called me to his club. He showed me Carol on the CCTV footage. She was in his club and he saw her.'

'Jesus, you are going to get help. I refuse to sit by and let this happen without anybody doing anything.'

'You have to believe me. You can ask Molloy.'

'Listen, I can call Levitt if you like.'

'Just fucking call Molloy!' Frank stood up and put his jacket on. 'I have to go before the Queen and have her lop my head off.'

'They have to formally suspend you.'

'No, they don't. They could have sidelined me, but oh no, they choose to put me on paid leave because they think Miles Laing and I were pen pals and I helped him escape.'

'They're covering their own arses. You can't blame them.'

'Well think on this; I spoke to the new manager of the hotel where Laing worked, you know, the *Savoy*. He showed me a box of stuff that Laing had left behind. It had a couple of packets of old photos in it, from '92. Family snaps, in Blackpool. The name on the front was Rena Joseph. I don't know who she is, or I didn't, and I didn't follow up on it. And you were with me when Laing left that clue in the phone box. Look over the lights to heaven. The ski slope. Over the Pentlands where the ski slope is lies a little place called Easter Howgate. A house went on fire there. There was a woman inside. The owner. Rena Joseph. Somebody set fire to her house and killed her. Not long after Miles Laing escaped. So, you tell me what the connection is.'

His father remained silent.

Miller grabbed his keys from the coffee table. 'Can you feed Charlie?' The cat sat on the end of the couch looking at Jack.

'Who do you think was in the photos?'

Miller stopped. 'Rena Joseph, another man and woman, a little boy and a little girl. I think the little boy is Miles Laing.'

'What is this place?' Steffi said.

'I told you what it is,' Mr Blue said. 'It's a locker room. Without the lockers.'

'I meant the building.'

'Never mind.' He put the carrier bag of food and drinks down.

Jane started crying when she saw Steffi.

John Carson

'Come here, honey.' The little girl ran into her arms. Emma sat on the bed, watching them.

'Here's breakfast. Meantime, you can look after Hazel Carter's offspring too.'

'Why are you doing this?'

Mr Blue took a step towards her but she didn't flinch. 'Your job is to entertain the kids. Nothing more, nothing less. You will be released unharmed, if you don't do anything stupid. I don't normally harm kids, but I can make an exception. Their safety is in your hands. If you try and tackle me, I'll shoot you all in the head.'

He turned and walked out of the cell, slamming the door behind him.

CHAPTER 37

Miller was starting to hate the crowds. It was the same every summer; the tourists would invade his city and take over and leave their mess behind.

It's a multi-cultural city, Frank, get used to it. His father would be appalled by the way he was thinking, and the truth of the matter was, Carol had loved the city and its vibrancy, soaking in the festival atmosphere. He knew he was just redirecting his anger.

He walked past the Starbucks on the High Street, not looking inside. Had he, he would have seen Carol sitting there, and she might have answered all his questions, but he didn't.

He walked uphill to the station and through the main entrance doors.

Upstairs to the incident room and into his office. Or what *had been* his office. He looked at the clock. No, it was still his office for another seven minutes.

There was a knock on the door and Andy Watt came in.

'Any news about Emma?' Miller asked.

'Nothing, boss. There were no other witnesses who saw the man Lynn Sterling was talking to before she was murdered. We're still canvassing and we'll put out a request to the public, but so far, nothing. And you look like shit, by the way.'

'Cheers for that, Andy.'

'No problem. If I can't be straight with you, boss, nobody can.'

'That's true. Tell me honestly, what are people saying? Do they think I helped Miles Laing escape?'

'There are whispers, but nobody's come out and said so. You know what a bunch of sweetie wives they can be though.'

'I'm going to tell you to your face, Andy; I didn't help him. In any way. And God knows why he sent me that cryptic message, but the house in Easter Howgate going on fire, belonging to the woman whose photos were left behind in the hotel, well, that's something I'm going to look into.' He looked at the clock. 'Well, time I was going upstairs.'

'Good luck, Frank. Don't let the bastards grind you down.'

John Carson

Miller left the incident room and walked upstairs. DCI Paddy Gibb was waiting for him in the corridor. 'Along this way, Frank. The conference room.'

'Not Jeni's office?'

He shook his head. 'No, son, there's a group of them.'

He knocked on the conference room door and ushered Miller in. They were all gathered round the top half of the table, and one chair at the opposite end was pulled out for him.

'DI Miller, please come in and take a seat,' Jeni Bridge said.

Miller looked at the faces in the room as he sat down. Two men he didn't know, but one of whom he recognised. And his future mother-in-law, her face like fizz. And the temporary investigator, Sharon Hardy.

'You may know Ewan Simmons, our Justice Minister. On his right is his assistant, Michael Kelly.'

Miller looked at them both, taking an instant dislike to Kelly, who looked like he was going to be an opinionated sod. Jeni Bridge of course, and Paddy Gibb, who at least had the decency to look embarrassed. Harry McNeil.

The door opened behind Miller but he didn't look round.

'Are you wanting to have a representative here?' Jeni asked.

'I'm his representative,' Percy Purcell said.

'This is highly irregular,' Simmons said.

'No, it's not,' Purcell said. 'In the maters of disciplinary hearings, the officer above the rank of Inspector can elect to have a senior officer represent him. Or her.'

'I've never been to a hearing where a senior officer has represented another officer. That's just ludicrous.'

'I'm not here as a federation representative of course, but to oversee the hearing to make sure my officer gets a fair trial.'

'For God's sake,' Kelly said. 'This isn't the Spanish Inquisition. We just have a few questions and then Miller will be on his way.'

'Like jumping into a pool filled with sharks.'

'What did you say?'

'I'm sorry, but have we been introduced?' Purcell said, staring at Kelly.

Simmons held up a hand. 'As Justice Minster, you all know I oversee the legal system in Scotland. I am particularly interested in this case since it involves a serving officer, and I want to make sure that the press don't think we're trying to pull the wool over the eyes of the public.'

Nobody spoke for a moment, then the silence was broken by Jeni.

'Detective Miller, first of all, you have our condolences. I know this is a bad time for you, with your future stepdaughter being abducted. And of course, Ms Banks' granddaughter.'

Miller and Norma looked at each other like duellists about to draw.

'It is with regret that I have to ask you these questions again. First of all, we want to know what, if any, relationship you had with Miles Laing.'

'He was a serial killer. I arrested him eight years ago. He's pestered me with phone calls, for the last month.'

'And you reported this?' Kelly said.

'Yes, I did. I even started to record the phone calls and handed them over to my superior officer.'

'That's me,' Purcell said, 'in case there's any ambiguity.' He looked at Simmons as he said it.

'And you had no idea why he was calling you?' Kelly asked.

'No idea.' Miller closed his eyes for a moment. 'We've been through all of this.'

'And you didn't help him escape?' Kelly said.

Miller wanted to answer sarcastically, but kept it in check. 'No.'

Silence again as Simmons looked at Jeni.

'Considering your position with Emma Smith, I am relieving you of your duty,' Jeni said. 'It's administrative leave. You will not contact any officer who is working on the case, and you may not enquire about the case to any serving officer working on the case. Do you understand?'

'Yes.'

'Please hand over your warrant card.'

Miller fished it out of his pocket and slid the black wallet over the table.

'You will return to duty after the investigation comes to a satisfactory conclusion. Any questions?'

'I have one; shouldn't Ms Banks be suspended from duty as a procurator fiscal, considering her personal involvement?'

'Ms Banks will not be working on this case,' Simmons said.

'Anything else?' Jeni said.

Miller shook his head.

'Then you're free to go.'

Miller slid the chair back and walked out of the conference room, followed by Purcell. He left the door open, hoping that he would hear somebody say something. *Eavesdropping* Lou would have called it.

'Christ, I'm taken off the case. That's exactly what Laing wants. Now he's free to try and get at me. You know he took Emma to get back at me?'

'I know that, Frank. But listen, we're all behind you. Call me at any hour if you hear something. Meanwhile, the techs are coming around to your flat to wire up your phone.'

'Jack will let them in.'

'What are you going to do now?'

'I want to go and see Kim in the Royal but somehow I think she'd rather get the plague than a visit from me.'

Purcell was silent for a moment. 'She's hurting, Frank. Go home.'

'And do what? Sit by the phone? Not my style, Percy.'

'Don't do anything stupid.'

'I don't intend to. I want to go and check out Rena Joseph's farmhouse.'

They stepped aside for Ewan Simmons and Michael Kelly. Sharon Hardy came out next. None of them looked at Miller.

'Just be careful what you're doing. And for God's sake, don't let anybody see you there.'

'I won't. Thanks for coming in there with me.' He patted Purcell on the arm and walked away.

Back out in the sunshine, he loosened his tie. Right now, his life was going down the toilet. His girlfriend was pissed off at him, somebody had taken Emma, he was on the verge of losing his job and every man and his dog thought he'd helped Miles Laing escape from the hospital. Of course, they weren't coming out and saying that, but they were all mentally pointing fingers.

TRIAL AND ERROR

His life couldn't get any worse.

Then he saw Carol. She had come out of Starbucks further down the road, and then she stopped and looked right at him. He started running after her. She turned and fled.

He dodged people, pushing past some, shoving others out of the way. Carol had turned into Hunter Square. He rounded the corner and looked around. Woman in a white shirt and jeans.

She was gone.

CHAPTER 38

The room smelled of decay and dampness, the wallpaper hanging off the walls like flesh hanging off a corpse. Drizzle fell in through the hole in the roof, soaking him through to the skin. They wanted to make sure he was thoroughly miserable before they killed him.

'So, mister SAS man, you're not so hard now, are ye?' the thick Belfast accent whispered to him. The bearded face came up close to his, getting covered in the rain but he seemed oblivious. Their eyes locked, each pair boring into the other, neither giving up until another voice in the room spoke up.

'Just do 'im, Dermot and get it over with. I don't like it in 'ere.' Seamus O'Connel was only nineteen and still wet behind the ears as far as kidnapping and torture were concerned, but he'd learn, Dermot Hagan thought.

'Take it easy there, laddie. We're going to have fun with this Sass man before we go home. Have ye ever wondered what the human body looks like after it's been cut open?'

'Not really. I'd prefer it if ye went straight for a head shot.' He'd really prefer it if Big Dermot would take the shotgun from him and blow the soldier away so's they could get home in time for tea.

'I make the decisions round here and I'll kill him when the time's right.' He turned his attention back to the soldier. 'Now, where's that mate of yours gone?'

Mr Black sat still and said nothing.

'I know youse bastards are trained to withstand pain, but not the kind of pain that we'll give ye if ye don't talk.'

He ran the knife he was holding lightly across Mr Black's right cheek, drawing blood.

'Right, that's it decided. If ye won't talk, I'm gonna start by shooting yer ankles and working my way up. You're gonna be one sorry soldier.' He punched Mr Black in the mouth for good measure and the soldier rocked back on the chair he was tied to, but Dermot caught it before it fell back.

TRIAL AND ERROR

Then Dermot started laughing loudly. After all, there was nobody around for miles to hear them.

Declan was another young soldier in the Republican Army, eager to please Dermot in any way he could. That's why he didn't mind when the big man told him to stay outside and keep watch. Then the boredom had set in. There was nothing to look at here except trees. The abandoned cottage had lain empty for a long time, ever since they had moved the owners out with the firebomb. That had been a laugh as well.

He laid his rifle down on the ground to try and get a better light for his cigarette. It was against Dermot's instructions but what the hell, there wasn't anybody around for miles and he was gasping on a fag.

Declan never even had time to take his cigarettes out of his pocket before the shadow slipped out from the side of the building and rammed the hunting knife into his ear.

The young Irishman died a martyr, a soldier that fell in the great war. That was what his family would be told. In reality, he was taken out by a highly-trained soldier fighting a war against terrorism.

As the cooling corpse lay in the rain, the camouflaged shadow slipped back behind the one-storey building.

Dermot chambered a round in the Browning 9mm and smiled at Mr Black. 'This is where we start our fun, soldier boy.'

'You got lucky, that's all,' Mr Black told him. It was true; they were reconnoitring the abandoned house, knowing it was being used as an ammunition dump, when he'd been surprised by Declan looking for somewhere to have a pee. He had thought he was lying unseen in the undergrowth but the boy had caught a glimpse of the prone figure and had pointed his gun at him, shouting for his friends.

'Yeah, we're better than you because we captured you. Now you're ours.'

Mr Black had thought he and his partner were goners but the other figure lay still, ready to start opening fire and he hadn't been caught.

John Carson

Now, the shadow slipped along the quiet hallway, listening to the men's voices in the living-room.

'On second thoughts,' Dermot said, laughing. 'Here Seamus, a chance to make a man of yourself. Take the gun and shoot the Sass man.'

Seamus didn't look sure of himself but he stepped forward and took the gun from Dermot.

'This is for all the boys that youse bastards have killed.' He levelled the gun at Mr Black's head.

'And this is for our boys,' Mr Blue said, stepping into the room and firing a split-second later. Seamus took the first bullet in the forehead and the second in his heart. A double tap. Dermot fumbled in his waistband for the second gun. It was to be the last thing that he ever did.

Mr Blue shot him twice.

'You took your time,' Mr Black, said.

'Thought I'd make you sweat a bit.'

'Well I'm sweating blood now,' he replied as Mr Blue cut the ropes that were binding him to the chair.

'You're worse than a woman,' he said, grinning, knowing he had just saved his best friend's life. And knowing Mr Black knew it.

After making sure that the cut on his face wasn't life threatening, Mr Blue wiped down the pistol he'd killed the two men with, and left it on the floor. They had taken it from a gunman who was on opposite sides and their lot would get the blame.

A crew would be right behind to take the ammo.

After a few minutes, the two camouflaged shadows slipped out by the kitchen, which had no door, and merged with the greenery, leaving no trace behind.

**

Mr Black stood next to Mr Blue now, just two ordinary men in the street, nobody giving them a second glance.

'Everything being taken care of?' Mr Black asked.

'Yes. I have somebody looking after the kids.'

'Not willingly?'

'No. She's been told they will be fine if she doesn't do

anything stupid.'

'Good. Move on with the next part of the plan. I don't want Mr Red getting antsy.'

'The antsier the better.' Mr Blue walked away, looking forward to shooting Brett Anders.

CHAPTER 39

Miller walked back round into the High Street, intending to go into Starbucks and ask them about the woman in the white shirt, when he saw patrol cars and unmarked cars come screaming out of the vennel from the station, turning left and heading up the hill, sirens and lights blazing.

No sooner had he stepped over the threshold of the coffee shop than his phone rang.

'Frank, have you heard?' It was Jack.

'Heard what?'

'Hazel's daughter was abducted from outside the house.'

'What? When?'

'Not so long ago. They sent a patrol car from Wester Hailes up to Hazel's house and they reported it. Now your team is going there. I just had Andy Watt on the phone.'

'Jesus Christ. I should be there!'

'Frank, you're no longer working there, remember?'

'She's my friend, Jack. If I want to go and see my friend, I will. Fucking Bruce Hagan. I said we shouldn't underestimate that bastard.'

There was silence for a moment. 'If he's got Jane, there's little chance–'

'Don't, Jack. I don't want you to voice that.'

'However, if they are both on the run together, and seeing what's happened, it's safe to assume they are, then maybe they've taken the kids just to get back at people to scare them. Maybe they will bring them back unharmed.'

'They shot the woman in the ambulance dead. They were literally taking no prisoners. They're ruthless.'

'Have you heard from Kim yet?'

'Not a thing.'

'You need to go and speak to her. Talk to her face-to-face.'

'I will, dad.'

'I'm assuming they've suspended you?'

'They did.'

'It's just a formality.'

'A fucking formality that will go on my record.'

'It's an administrative suspension. They do that all the time when a detective is personally involved in a case. It's not a disciplinary suspension. You have nothing to worry about.'

'I'm going to check out a dead woman's house. I think it might be connected to Miles Laing.'

'Don't be doing anything you shouldn't.'

'I know, but I can't just sit around and do nothing. I'll check this place out and then I'll go and see Kim.'

'Do you want me to come with you?'

'No. I'll be fine. I'll call you later.'

'And for God's sake, if you see Laing, you call for back-up. You do not tackle him yourself, do you understand?'

'I do.' He ended the call and walked out of the coffee shop with a black coffee and walked across the road to where his Audi A6 was parked. He drove down Cockburn Street and hooked a right into Market Street, doing a full one-eighty so that he was heading south. Up past St Leonard's police station, he was listening to the radio, when a song came on. A song that was one of Kim's favourites.

'What the hell are you doing, Miller?' he asked himself. 'You have a beautiful woman who's carrying your child, and here you are chasing after an imaginary woman who looks like your dead wife. You need to get a grip of yourself.'

He would talk to Dr Harvey Levitt, a charismatic American who was a Professor at Edinburgh University, and the force psychologist. He had told Miller before that thinking about Carol all the time had manifested an image of her that would become so real looking to him it would seem like she was really there.

And that's what he had done. Now he felt like a fool, chasing a ghost. 'It's about time you were bringing yourself back into the real world, Miller.'

He took the back road out, eventually connecting with the Straiton Road and drove past Bilston, turning right onto Bush Loan Road. Easter Howgate was a hop, skip, and a jump from there.

He found the farm no problem. Or the farmhouse. Records showed that the actual farm had been sold many years ago, and a new house built on the opposite side. Rena Joseph just kept the farmhouse, and Miller noticed the old farm buildings, looking rundown. He wondered why she would keep them.

He could see the blackened windows in the downstairs, where the fire had raced through. The detritus from the aftermath of the fire lay on the driveway; charred wood, charred belongings, burnt objects that once held the shapes of interior décor.

Beyond the farm buildings were nothing but fields bordered in the distance by a line of thick trees. Hills were in the distance. Anybody wanting to hide from the world could do a lot worse.

He pulled up at the front door. A temporary one had been fitted. Boards had been screwed over the windows where once glass had been. He got out of the car and walked round the back of the old, two-storey farmhouse. The back windows had been boarded up as well. He pulled on one until it shifted a bit and then climbed through the gap he had made.

He took out his phone and put the flashlight on, shining the little LED light around. He was standing in the kitchen. It looked like it had suffered smoke damage. He walked through to the hallway and up towards the living room where the fire had originated. A stairway was on his left. The living room was on the right. He shone the light around. Nothing but blackened walls remained. What furniture had been in here had been turned into ash and thrown out of the window by the fire fighters.

An experienced eye would be able to tell where the seat of the fire was. To Miller's untrained eye, there were just charred remnants of somebody's life.

He walked back out into the hall. A weak light was coming from upstairs where the windows hadn't been boarded up. He shone the light from his phone on the stairs to make sure he wasn't about to trip on anything.

Upstairs, there were three bedrooms and a bathroom. The first bedroom had been occupied. A bed was in what was the biggest of the three rooms. It looked relatively unscathed. A couple of drawer units sat against one wall. An old wardrobe sat against another wall.

Miller pulled on gloves and looked through the drawers. Nothing but clothes. He went into the next bedroom. It was filled with boxes. He opened a couple and found old clothes and books.

TRIAL AND ERROR

He opened the door to the third bedroom.

It was a shrine.

It was obvious from the pink colour scheme that a little girl had lived in this one. There were soft toys on the bed. Children's posters were on the walls. Bits and pieces that a little girl might collect. And it was spotless. The candles that had been arranged round the photo of a little girl had been recently lit. It had been a little girl's bedroom at one time, but he guessed that Rena Joseph had spent a lot of time in here.

He had a quick look around before picking up the photo in the frame. It was the face of the same little girl who had been in the Blackpool photos. He put it back. This was definitely the right house.

Back on the landing, he wondered if there might be something worth looking at in the attic. There was an airing cupboard, somewhere that he would keep the pole for grabbing the latch in the attic hatch. He was surprised to find it there but he grabbed it and put the hook into the latch and pulled. The hatch dropped down and he grabbed the ladder and slid it the rest of the way down.

He put the pole to one side and started climbing the ladder. He shone the light about, his head just poking above the floor level of the dark room. The light beam illuminated old cardboard boxes. A Christmas tree in its original box.

Miller was sweeping the light about when he smelled it. The first traces of smoke.

He was about to take a step down when a hand grabbed his leg and pulled.

CHAPTER 40

'I don't know, alright?' Hazel Carter said through sobs. She was sitting on the couch with Percy Purcell.

'I'm sorry, Hazel, I know you're going to be sick of being asked the same question over and over, but you more than anyone has to understand that.'

'I know, I know, I'm sorry, but I didn't see who took her. I can't tell you it was Bruce if I'm not a hundred per cent certain.'

'You didn't hear anything? No screams, shouting?'

'Nothing. I came in here to look for my phone and then when I went back out, only Daniel was in the car.'

'You don't think she could have just slipped out of the car and wandered off?'

'Do you?'

'I can't speculate, you know that.'

'I'm sorry. No, she didn't just get out of the car. She knows better. I've put the fear of God in her about all the weirdos out there.'

Purcell sat silent for a moment. 'You know we're working on the assumption that Laing and Bruce have taken the children. Laing we know wants to get back at Frank Miller, and Bruce might want to get back at you. Now they're working together, we can safely say that nobody else took Jane. Ninety-nine per cent sure. Nothing's ever a hundred per cent.'

'So, what now?'

'We're getting officers to go through CCTV. Even from Lothian Buses. There were two buses going round the Drive at the time, and they've contacted the drivers. They'll be met with replacement buses and those two buses will be taken down to Annandale Street where the footage will be analysed. It's going to take time, but we're on it, Hazel.'

'Thank you, sir.'

Purcell stood up and left Hazel with the two uniforms in her living room. He went outside and found Andy Watt.

'Get one of our team to stay with her. Steffi Walker. She's got a good head on her shoulders.'

'I'll get onto it right away, sir.'

Watt walked away from the noise of the chatter and stood across the other side of the road, away from the patrol cars, took out his mobile phone and called the station. After a few moments, he hung up and made another call.

'Julie? Andy. I'm trying to get hold of Steffi Walker and they said at the station that she didn't turn up for work this morning. Have you seen her?'

'No, Andy. We were supposed to go out on a foursome last night, but me and my boyfriend couldn't make it. She said she was going to call her date and tell him. I called her this morning but she didn't answer her phone. I went round to her place and there's no answer there either.'

'Do you know who this guy is?'

'He's a bus driver. Peter Hanson is his name.'

'Do you know if she went out with him regardless?'

'No, she just said she would call him.'

'Maybe he persuaded her to go out with him anyway. You got her phone number?' Julie rattled it off for him. 'Thanks, Julie.'

He hung up. Steffi had either got lucky or something was wrong. He called her number and it went right to voicemail. Then he called Lothian Buses, getting through to the control room. He identified himself. 'Can you check if a driver called Peter Hanson is on duty today?'

He waited for a few moments while they checked.

'Yes, he signed on at seven twenty-three this morning. He's out on a bus now.'

'Do you know which one?'

'Service 16.'

'Where will he be now?'

'Colinton. Westgarth Avenue. He'll be there in about ten minutes. That's the terminus, outside the lawn tennis club.'

'I'm going to meet him there. Get him to hold his position. It's important we speak to him.'

'Okay. I'll contact him now.'

Watt hung up and walked over to Paddy Gibb. 'Sir, we need to go and talk to a bus driver. Steffi Walker didn't show up for work and she was supposed to see this guy last night. He's going to be over at Colinton.'

'I'll come with you. I could do with a fag. Go and tell Purcell in case he thinks we've disappeared as well.'

'We could do with Frank here, let me tell you.' He walked over to Purcell and explained the situation.

Purcell flapped his arms up and down, once. 'That's all we need. Good God, this department is going to hell.'

'Do you want to drive?' Watt said.

'Are you taking the piss? How can I light one up and drive at the same time? You're the chauffeur, get your arse in the driver's seat.'

Watt booted it away, heading up and round to the Drive, heading for Wester Hailes Road.

'I'll tell you something for nothing,' Gibb said, 'if Walker is lying in her pit, pissed out of her skull, having spent the night with the tossbag, she'll be getting her jotters.'

'We can hardly afford to lose another member of the team. First Frank, then Hazel and now Steffi Walker. I hope to fuck she's not messed up.'

Gibb lit a cigarette and blew the smoke out of the open window. 'If anybody asks, you didn't see me smoking.'

'Buy me a pint in Logie's and I saw nothing.'

'Everything in life has a price. That's what I get for taking you under my wing.'

'Under your wing? Shouting your mouth off, you mean.'

'Tough love. You wouldn't have respected me if I hadn't shouted at you.'

Watt stuck the siren and lights on as he approached the junction of Wester Hailes Road and Lanark Road, navigating his way through. Down into Colinton village and up the other side.

'Christ, I haven't been here in a long time,' Gibb said. 'I remember there used to be a Porsche and Ferrari dealer there. Now it's more flats.'

'They'll be building flats on Arthur's Seat next.' Watt turned right into Westgarth Avenue. The double-decker was sitting where the bus controller said it would be, outside the lawn tennis club. Watt pulled up in front of it and the two detectives got out.

'You Peter Hanson?' Watt said, as the driver opened the door.
'I am. What's wrong?'
'Did you meet with Steffi Walker last night?'
'No. I was in the shower and I missed a call from her. So I called back and there was no answer. I thought she might have been running late. I went to the bar anyway. She didn't turn up and I didn't know her friend so it's not as if I could ask her. Not that they would turn up if Steffi called off. No point in having a foursome if there's only three of you.'
'Did you speak to her this morning?' Gibb said.
'I tried calling again, but only the once. I think she got cold feet, and that's okay. I just wanted to see if she wanted to go for a drink tonight, but if she's had a change of heart, that's okay. I don't want her to think I'm chasing her. If she wants to call me sometime, fine. If not, that's life and I'm a big boy. I'll get over it.'
'Give us your address, son,' Gibb said, and Watt wrote it down.
'What's this all about, anyway?' Hanson asked. 'Is Steffi okay?'
'We'll be in touch,' Gibb said, ignoring his question. They stepped off the bus and got back in the car.
'You know if that nutbag's touched her, we're going to punch his fucking ticket,' Gibb said, lighting up another cigarette.
Watt called Steffi's number again. Voicemail.
'Get to the back of the line, sir. We'll all be wanting a boot at him. But let's say for a moment, it panned out like he said. Steffi didn't show up or call him. Where the hell is she?'
Gibb took his phone out. 'I'm going to get a patrol to force entry into her flat. All this pish with Miles Laing has put me on edge.'

'This place might as well be a cell,' Steffi said under her breath.
'What, Aunt Steffi?' Emma said. The little girls were eating rolls that the man had brought them. There were also bottles of juice.
'Nothing, honey, I'm just talking out loud.' They were somewhere underground but God knew where. Old, thick walls. Edinburgh was built on top of the old city, so there were many places

underground.

She looked at her wrist, but realised that he had taken her watch. She didn't have her mobile phone obviously. The light was dim, so she didn't know what time of day it was. Then she turned to Jane.

'What time was it when your friend took you into his car? Can you remember?'

'School time.'

'Do you know when that is?'

'We start at nine o'clock.'

Steffi nodded as the girls carried on eating. If she didn't know where they were or the time, she wouldn't know how long it had taken him to get here. Ten minutes? Two hours? It had to be mid-morning, but not knowing the time was driving her crazy.

They had to get out of here.

She knew that it was only a matter of time before he killed them all, no matter what he said.

CHAPTER 41

Miller came crashing down the ladders, landing on his front, putting his hands out to save himself.

He felt a boot crash into his ribs. He rolled onto his side and saw a figure in motorbike leathers and wearing a crash helmet with the visor down. The man kicked him again. Miller had his back against the wall but managed to deflect the next kick.

The man leaned down and grabbed hold of him by the front of his jacket and hauled him to his feet. Miller punched him in the guts but it had little or no effect. The visor was darkened so he couldn't even see the man's face.

A gloved fist came towards his face but he blocked the move. Punching the helmet would have no effect so he tried slapping the side of it, trying to knock the man off balance. It only succeeded in moving his head sideways a little bit and he came back with a wicked punch, catching Miller high up on the cheek bone. His head snapped backwards, jolting his neck.

Smoke was starting to pour up the stairs now, and Miller could hear the crackling of fire below as it gripped what was left of the house.

The biker wasn't playing around. Miller felt a surge of anger and panic shoot through him. All the frustrations of the previous days came into sharp focus. He jumped, grabbed hold of the side of the ladder and pulled his legs up then shot them straight out, directly connecting with the biker's chest.

The biker fell backwards but merely rolled, his legs coming up and over and then he was back on his feet as if nothing had happened. Then he came back at Miller. He ran at him but he couldn't get up to speed with the ladder in the way. Miller shifted sideways so the full force of the run wouldn't knock the wind out of him. That would have been fatal.

As they collided, Miller got his hand round the back of the helmet and he tried pulling but the chance was only there for a fraction of a second before they went crashing into the bedroom that had been kept as a shrine. The biker landed on top of Miller and punched him in the face again, opening the cut wider. Miller blocked the next one and slipped his arm under the biker's and he pushed the man's head with his right hand, rolling sideways, twisting with his hip.

The biker rolled and punched Miller on the nose, causing it to explode with blood. Then he was on his feet. Miller kicked out, ignoring the pain and the tears blasting into his eyes, and his foot caught the biker behind one knee. He went down.

Miller rolled and got up again, kicking the biker in the ribs as hard as he could. The biker grunted and toppled sideways for a moment, before regaining his composure.

Miller's face was screaming in pain. His nose and his cheek on fire now, and blood was pouring down to his mouth. And yet this biker was up and on his feet like he was a machine.

He turned away from the biker as the man rushed at him. The biker snaked an arm around Miller's neck and the detective knew with certainty that he was going to die in the next few seconds. Blindly, Miller snatched at a small vase that sat on the drawer unit. It was made of clear, heavy glass. He gripped it by the base and smashed it on the pink, wooden surface where the top broke off in shards. Miller turned it in his hand like it was a knife and tried to stab it into the biker's leg. The biker knew he had a choice; have the vase implanted into his leg or let Miller go.

He let Miller go and deflected the hand with the weapon.

Which told Miller this man knew what he was doing.

The respite was brief, as he grabbed Miller again and dragged him backwards towards the bedroom door. Miller tried to stab him again, but the biker let him go. Miller was lying over the threshold of the room. The biker backed out, and stood looking at him.

'I'm going to fucking kill you, Miller,' he said, his voice muffled behind the protection of the helmet.

Suddenly, hands roughly grabbed the biker, one hand between his legs, the other on the collar of his jacket, and heaved him over the banister.

Miller saw the view upside down. He couldn't see who it was that was behind him now.

The biker landed on his feet on the stairs and let out another scream but he threw himself into a roll and tumbled down the stairs

TRIAL AND ERROR

safely. They heard him crashing out through the board that was over the front door.

Miller couldn't see who'd saved him for the tears streaming down his face, where they mixed with the blood. He felt he was losing his grip on consciousness. He wondered why the man hadn't killed him. Then he saw a figure standing looking down at him. He couldn't make out the features for the tears blurring his vision.

He heard a motorbike start up and come crashing into the house.

He struggled to clear his eyes, and then he saw him standing there.

'I told you I'd see you soon, Frank,' Miles Laing said.

Miller lost the fight and slipped into darkness.

CHAPTER 42

Brett Anders and his wife walked up Broughton Street then up Leith Street. The old St James Centre shopping mall was being torn down, an eyesore that had sprung up in the 70s. They walked hand-in-hand, just a couple of lovers out for a walk.

Nobody would have taken them for the pair of expert killers they were.

'I'm worried about that little girl,' Marie said to her husband.

'I wish to God we had just taken her now. I never knew that mad asshole would take a kid.'

Marie squeezed his hand tighter. 'If he does anything to her, you know I'm going to take him out, right?'

'I know, honey.' It never failed to amaze Anders how his wife could be a loving mother one minute and a ruthless assassin the next. 'Did you call our girls this morning?'

She jerked his arm a bit. 'Of course I did. I miss my girls but our faithful nanny is taking good care of them. But it got me thinking.'

'Uh oh. Don't be doing that too often!'

'Smart-arse.'

'Tell me what you're thinking.' They turned up into Calton Hill, the little street that ran up to Waterloo Place, named after the hill on top.

'I'm thinking I'd like to go home soon. I mean, not home to New York but maybe we could buy a horse ranch or something. Somewhere in the country.'

'You're a city girl at heart. How would you manage a horse ranch?'

'Oh, don't mock me.'

'I'm not mocking you. But Wyoming in the winter? New York is bad enough, and since we've been in the UK, we haven't had the same taste of snow.'

'What about the Hudson Valley? Somewhere it's not too far away from the city.'

'It might be an idea.'

TRIAL AND ERROR

'Aren't you fed up of London? This job? I really want the girls to grow up in America. Sure, London's fine, but sometimes I miss the skating in Central Park, the Rockefeller tree at Christmas time. Seeing the stores with their Christmas displays. We could live somewhere that's a short train ride away.'

He looked at her. 'You're serious about this, aren't you?'

'I am, Brett. I've never been so serious about anything. I want our girls to grow up in America.'

'You might have a good point. We'll talk about it later.'

Five minutes later, they were at the American Consulate General in Regent's Terrace. Black bollards were placed across the road on either side of the consulate to stop traffic approaching the townhouse. A large American flag hung outside.

Anders had called ahead and spoken to the member of staff he knew. Security was waiting for him inside and they were shown to an office in the back.

'Good God, it's been a long time,' Leonard Katz said, welcoming them into his office.

'This is my wife and colleague, Marie.'

'Pleased to meet you. I had heard you got married of course, and I'm sorry we haven't seen each other in a long time.'

Anders waved away his apology.

After coffee was served, they sat on leather couches facing each other, Marie by Anders' side. 'How you liking Edinburgh?'

'I thought it was going to be a lot quieter than London, but what with the flights landing at Prestwick, well, it keeps me busy.' Katz was a year younger than Anders, and a lot thinner, but he knew how to handle himself. 'So, what brings you in here today, Brett?'

'I'm looking for a favour, Len. We were given a directive from our boss, who was acting on information from a British counterpart. All well and good.' Anders hesitated for a moment.

'But you think there's something up,' Katz said.

'The associate of the British agent had a little girl with him last night, and long story short, we think she was a kidnap victim, the daughter of a police officer.'

Katz set his coffee cup down on the table in front of them. 'Where is she now?'

'That's the thing,' Marie said,' we don't know. I'm worried

203

he's hurt her.'

'Have you asked him directly?'

'We haven't seen him today. We have to sit tight and wait for his instructions again. But I can smell bullshit a mile away. I'm not happy with this situation.'

'I can make a call to London and see what's going on. I'll do it right now, if you want to wait.'

'I appreciate it, Len.'

Katz got up and left the room.

'How do you know him, exactly?' Marie asked.

'Len and I worked together before I met you. He's a great guy.' Anders sat back and told the story of how he and the big man had met when they were in Delta together.

After a little while, Len came back into the room. 'I made a few calls. You know the score; when there's an American citizen doing something on British soil, something that is a threat to our national security, we call you in and the Brits turn a blind eye. You get your orders in London from your handler, but this time, you got your orders from your Brit counterpart.'

'That's right.'

Len sat back down again. 'This isn't a US sanctioned job.' He put a sheet of paper on the table. Anders picked it up, looked at it and flipped it over. It was blank both sides.

'That's right,' Len said, 'the operation you're on right now isn't official. New York doesn't know about it. Whoever has hired you, is doing it privately.'

'What? We were told by our handler that it was a matter of national security, as always.'

'Looks like London was duped. The intel was genuine, coming from the UK side, but it seems they were duped too. Whoever is behind this is playing a dangerous game. They're trying to get you to take out a phantom target. I can have a team in here to deal with him, if you like?'

'Thanks, Len. You've been a great help, but no, we'll clean up our own mess.' They got up and shook hands.

'Why don't you come up to Edinburgh for a social visit soon?'

said Len.

'I'd like nothing more, my friend. We'll have dinner, with you and your good lady.'

Before he opened the door, Len stopped and looked at Anders. 'Just be careful out there. If you need my help, just holler.'

'I will.'

They left into the warmth of the Scottish summer.

'You want to get a coffee somewhere?' Marie asked.

'No, honey, I want to go back to the house. We need to deal with this problem. *Mr Blue.* Jesus.'

'I want to ask him about that little girl, Brett.'

'There's going to be no physical contact from now on. He gave us the target. The job's on. Except now that we know it's not official, there's no way I'm taking out the target.'

'He must think we're a couple of dummies.'

'Then he's going to get a surprise, isn't he?'

They walked down to the house, which was downhill all the way.

Back inside, Anders sat in front of his iPad, looking at the images. 'I told you,' he said to Marie. 'There he is.' The covert camera was facing the front door from the mantelpiece in the living room. It didn't open.

'Christ, how did you know he had been in here?'

'He's covering his back. He wants to leave something behind that can be traced to us.'

'He's setting us up?'

'I would say so.' He smiled at her. 'But I did what I always do; I changed the locks. I'll put the original back before we leave but he doesn't have a key. There was no forced entry. So he had to have got in here somehow.'

'By picking the lock?'

'No. I put a sliver of tape on the door and it was still there.'

'How the hell did he get in here, then?'

'These properties are old. Very old. Let's go and have a look around.'

Marie watched the video of Mr Blue walking about the living room. He had come in from the kitchen but hadn't entered through the front door. All the windows were secure. Then they found the

John Carson

basement door. The lightbulb afforded little light as they made their way down the stone stairs.

Marie took out her mobile phone and used the flashlight to see her way. The subterranean room was filled with old bits of furniture that were dirty and dusty and had obviously been here a long time.

They looked around, each of them with a flashlight shining now. There was a recess in the back corner. Cobwebs hung down from the wooden rafters.

The recess was darker. Ander shone his light into it and saw another door. He grabbed the handle and looked at his wife. It opened without any squeaky hinges. He shone the light in and saw more stone steps leading down.

'Now we know where he came in,' he said, and started down.

CHAPTER 43

Miller groaned and thought his face had been trampled by horses. He put a hand up and felt the blood still coming out of his nose.

Fire! He tried sitting up and felt the pain shoot through his ribs. His head exploded and he lay back down again. Opened his eyes again and moved more slowly, getting on his side.

Have to get out. House on fire.

He felt warmth, thinking that the flames were trying to burn him but then he realised that he was outside. He looked over to the house. The flames were gripping the structure, throwing smoke high into the air.

Miles Laing! Jesus, had he really been there or had it been a figment of his imagination? Hell, he couldn't even remember if he had actually been fighting a man in a biker outfit.

Was Laing still about? Miller struggled to his feet, but then he remembered that he had blacked out in the house. Laing must have brought him out. It didn't make sense. The house was well alight.

He heard sirens coming but he didn't want to be found there. He staggered over to his car, feeling like his face was twice the size, and his ribs felt shattered, although they were probably only bruised.

He took out his car keys, and felt in his pocket for his phone, feeling relief that it was still there. He looked around for his car and couldn't see it. The only other car was a little Renault hatchback. He looked at what he'd thought were his car keys and they belonged to the French car. He staggered his way over to it. Took his phone out but it wasn't his phone. It was a smartphone that *looked* like his phone, but it was a throwaway. What the hell was going on? He used the phone to call a number, one he had used so often, he didn't need to think about it.

'Hello?' the female voice on the other end answered.

'Kate? It's Frank Miller. I need your help.'

'Hi, Frank. Sure. What do you need help with?'

'I need fixing up. I got a beating and I need some cleaning up. I think my nose might be broken.'

'Oh my God! Where are you?'

'Just outside Edinburgh on the Biggar Road.'

'You need to go down to the A&E.'

'I can't, Kate. I don't have time for that. I just need a quick fix. Can you help me?'

'Of course I can. I'm at home. Get down here as fast as you can, but in one piece.'

'Thanks, Kate.' He hung up and as he was heading back into Edinburgh, the first of the fire engines zipped past him, followed by a patrol car.

He didn't want to be pulled over by a zealous patrol officer so he kept to the speed limit, or just over. Blood was running down from his nose. He looked in the rear-view mirror and didn't recognise the man looking back at him. His nose was swollen, the cut on his cheek was deep, and his eyes were already starting to blacken.

He felt like shit.

The little car had a manual gearbox, unlike the automatic of the Audi. It hurt like hell to change gear, but luckily the unmarked cars they drove on a daily basis were manuals, so he hadn't lost the touch.

He headed east on the city bypass, connecting to the A7. Twenty minutes later he was pulling up outside Kate Murphy's apartment complex. He couldn't remember the last time he'd felt so sore. It was difficult breathing through his nose, so he stopped trying. He was in Hutton Road at the side of the building off Holyrood Road. He called Kate and she came down and opened the garage door. Miller pulled in and parked in a visitor's space.

'Jesus Christ, Frank! I didn't think it was this bad,' she said when she opened the driver's door. 'Come on, let's get you upstairs.'

He climbed out and felt the power leave his legs. She held onto him and helped him over to the lift.

Upstairs in her apartment, she took him through to the bathroom and took his jacket and shirt off. She had a doctor's bag sitting on the floor near the shower.

She looked at his face, pushing and pulling his nose. A guttural noise of sheer pain was in his throat but he sat still.

'Good news; your nose isn't broken, and the cuts don't need permanent stitches. Butterflies should hold them together. You're going to have two cracking black eyes though. And there's bruising on your ribcage. You're lucky he didn't break any. The bruising will look bad for a week or so but it'll fade. You've also got bruising on your neck.'

'My looks are going to be spoiled for a little while, then?'

'A little while. Now sit still while I clean your wounds and patch up your nose.'

When that was done, she gave him a towel and told him to shower then she'd put the butterfly stitches on.

When he was clean, the blood was starting to run down his face again. As he was sitting with the towel round his waist, she stopped the bleeding and put the stitches on his face.

'You'll be fine. I don't think it will leave a permanent scar. You'll have to get those changed though. I can do it. Just come and see me.'

'I can't thank you enough, Kate.'

'You looked after me when I needed you, Frank. In this profession, we look after each other. I might be a pathologist, but I work closely with police officers. We're here for each other.'

'Jimmy won't be coming in anytime soon, I assume?' Jimmy Gilmour, a police firearms training officer and one of the detectives who used to be on Miller's team.

'You haven't heard?'

'No. Heard what?'

Kate stood up and looked away for a moment. 'Jimmy and I finished a few weeks ago. He went back to his wife. He put in for a transfer down to the Met. He's moving there shortly.'

'Oh, God, Kate, I'm sorry.'

'Don't be. It ran its course.'

'Do you have anybody special in your life now?'

She gave a brief laugh. 'Just you. My special detective friend.'

He gave her hand a brief squeeze.

'Now, you get that robe on. I've got your shirt and underwear going through my washer dryer. There's nothing I can do about your trousers, but I can run a damp cloth over them and dry them with a hairdryer. Then you can tell me what happened, if you like.'

He felt his face going red for a moment.

'You don't have to be embarrassed. I've washed a man's

underpants before.'

'Jesus, I didn't think my face could feel any more on fire.'

Five minutes later, he was in the robe and sitting in her living room, a cool glass of water sitting on the coffee table in front of him.

'Do you want to tell me who you were fighting?' Kate was sitting in a chair. Daytime TV had been muted.

'I don't know.' Miller recounted his story to her. 'Somebody stepped in and saved my life. The house was burning and I'm guessing it was the same person who set the first fire in that house, but this time he was going to do a better job of it.'

'You've no idea who this biker is?'

'None at all. But somebody didn't want me digging around Rena Joseph's house.' He took a sip of the water and sat looking at the images on the TV.

'Rena Joseph? The woman who was found in the house after it was set on fire?'

'Yes, that's her. I just wanted to check something out.'

'We did the PM on her. Frank, she was killed by having her neck snapped. And not just any way, either. Her neck was broken using a technique taught to special forces soldiers. Maybe he was trying to kill you too.'

Miller felt suddenly cold, icy fingers running down his neck. That would certainly make sense.

'This is going to sound daft, but you know who it was who came into the house?'

'Tell me anyway.'

'Miles Laing. Well, that's what he looked like. Mind you, I've been chasing the ghost of Carol for the past few days.' He told her about the images he'd seen.

'It sounds like you need a rest, Frank.'

'I know, but I clearly saw the biker being thrown over the banister in the house. And then when I came to outside, I found the keys to that Renault in my pocket and that phone I used to call you. My car was gone. I think he took it.'

'Have you checked the phone for any numbers or calls or anything?'

'It's probably a burner. But I'll have a look anyway.' He winced as he sat forward so Kate got it from the dining table where his wallet and car keys sat in a small pile. Miller looked through it.

There was one number under contacts.

'One number.'

'Call it.'

Miller hit the dial button. He didn't expect anybody to pick up but somebody did.

'I'm glad you called, Frank,' Miles Laing said.

'What the hell's going on?'

'You're going to have to figure this one out. I only know part of the story. The rest is up to you. I'll help you as much as I can, but you're on the right track. Together we can crack this.'

'What are you talking about?'

'About who took Emma and why.'

'Where is she, Miles? Please don't hurt her. She's just a little girl.'

'That's what I'm trying to say; I don't have her.'

'What about Bruce taking his little girl? Don't you know what damage you're both doing to those little girls?'

'Frank! You've clearly banged your head. We need to meet up and we will, but meantime I have work to do. Me and Bruce don't have the children. We didn't take them, I can promise you that. As you saw today, you're dealing with dangerous men and we're in just as much danger as you.'

'When are you going to give me my car back?'

'I don't have your car. Bruce drove me to the house. The biker put his bike in the house, right into the flames. He was the one who took your car.'

CHAPTER 44

Kim Smith felt sore but most of all empty inside. Except she wasn't empty inside. She was carrying Frank's baby and that was very much letting itself be known. She didn't want to know what the sex was, unlike a lot of mothers-to-be.

She looked out of the window of the Royal Infirmary. It was sunny now, and warm, a rare feat in Edinburgh. There were people out there going about their daily lives with not a worry. She looked up towards where the sun was and wondered if her little girl could see it now. Was Emma outside? No, of course not. She was inside. Not dead. No, she refused to believe that. Somebody had taken her and was keeping her safe. That's what she believed. The thought of somebody touching her was driving her insane.

She sat back down on the chair in the ward, taking the weight off her feet. Thought about Frank and how she loved him. She wished they were already married, but they had issues to work through.

She had been mad at him for not being there when she got the phone call, but all this wasn't his fault. He wasn't to blame.

Miles Laing is though, and he took her to get back at Frank. Don't forget that little nugget.

No, she couldn't blame Frank for this. Couldn't blame the actions of others on him. Now he was coming to pick her up and they would talk. The doctor had advised against it, but she'd told him she was going stir crazy in here and she would rather be out. She had sent the uniform away. Miles Laing wasn't going to come here and try anything with her. First of all, it was too busy. Second of all, he didn't want her.

Her case was packed. She had everything ready to go, so when Frank got here, she could just slip out. She heard the text message coming in. *I'm here. I'm parked right at the door so I can't leave the car.*

She smiled. Having him here made her feel better. Not the family liaison officer, or the protection officer, or the detectives. Just Frank. She didn't need those people milling around her. They could just as easily come round to the apartment and talk to her. It wasn't as if she was a civilian who needed those people.

I'm coming she replied. She took the painkillers the doctor had prescribed and carried her small case. Outside, the corridor was busy with people, all of them going about their lives, oblivious to her plight. All they saw was the newspaper headlines.

She took the lift downstairs and made her way out through reception and out to the black Audi. The boot popped open as she approached. Lazy sod couldn't be bothered getting out of the car to take her case, but never mind. The back door was ajar, waiting for her to get in. She slammed the boot shut and opened the back door. Frank had his arm out the driver's window, adjusting the mirror.

Later, when she was running this scene through her head, two questions would come to mind; why is he manually adjusting the mirror when it's electric? And, if he'd driven here, why would he need to adjust the mirror?

She found out when she closed the rear door and Mr Blue turned round to face her.

'Who are you?' she said.

'Frank sent me to pick you up,' Mr Blue said, smiling. He was wearing a casual shirt with a light casual jacket.

'No, he didn't. That text came from his phone.' She tried the handle to get back out of the car but the child locks were on.

'You're right. I lied. But you might not want to make a fuss. You see, I'm going to take you to see Emma.'

She stopped dead, right then. 'What?'

'You have a choice to make; you can either put on the eye mask when we leave the car park and sit and behave. Or I can let you out here. You can go back inside, unharmed and I will drive away. And then I'll call my colleague who will shoot your little girl in the head. You'll always wonder if you would have seen your daughter again, if you hadn't been so silly. So, go ahead, leave if you want.'

He was looking at her in the rear-view mirror. She knew she had little choice. If she was going to die then at least she would die knowing that she had made the right choice.

She picked up the mask.

'Good. When we get out onto the main road, put it on. Lean back as if you're just having a nap. If I see you've taken it off, I'll stop and make the call. Do you understand?'

'Yes.'

'Give me your phone.'

She reached into her bag, took it out and handed it to him.

He put the car in drive and drove off. As he approached the main road, he looked at her again. She put the sleeping mask over her eyes. Being a beige colour, it didn't stand out.

He opened a window and threw her phone out.

Kim was shaking. She didn't know who this man was, and he could easily be taking her somewhere to kill her, but she had to take the chance. She wanted to see her little girl again and would do anything, even trust this stranger.

If he killed her then so be it. She'd have died trying.

She sat back in the car, remembering the last time she had been in it with Frank and Emma. It was something mundane, like going to Tesco. In her mind's eye, she pictured him sitting in the driver's seat, her next to him, her daughter in the back, playing with a soft toy.

Christ, why did this have to happen to her?

Tears rolled down her cheeks, squeezing past the eye mask.

If she hadn't been pregnant, she would have taken this man on in a fist fight. But her condition got in the way. Maybe if Frank got a hold of him, he would kick his arse for him.

She sat back and thought of her family. How she might never see them again.

They had been driving for a while when the car slowed down and stopped and she heard the unmistakeable sound of a metal roller door rising up. Then they were inside a garage, away from the heat of the sun. The car stopped and the engine was turned off.

'You can take the mask off,' the man said. He got out of the car and walked round to open her door. He left her case in the boot. Her eyes were already adjusted to the dark with having the mask on. She took it off and as she was doing so, the gloved fist punched her right on the nose.

Kim screamed and put a hand up to her face as blood spattered out across the tan seats. 'What the fuck?'

He took a hanky out of his pocket and handed it to her. 'Just a taste of what you'll get if you try something funny.'

'Hit a fucking pregnant woman? You fucker.'

TRIAL AND ERROR

He smiled. He couldn't tell her he wanted to leave the car with blood on the seats. 'Get out.'

She held the hanky to her nose. Looked around the underground garage. It was a building site, tools, vehicles, and building detritus lying around. It was well lit. Obviously a business place.

'Where is this place?'

'Not your concern. However, you can still leave. I can have the garage door open and you can walk out. But by the time you get help, we'll be away and your daughter will be dead.' He held up a garage door opener, ready to press it.

Kim shook her head. 'Take me to my daughter.'

The man smiled, and she thought she would like nothing better than to wipe that smile of his face.

'Move to that door over there,' he said, putting the garage door opener away.

She walked across the dusty concrete floor, wondering what this building was, but it was obvious that it wasn't in use now, or was being refurbished.

They went through the door after the man unlocked it. He locked it behind him and told her to walk along the dimly lit corridor. It smelled dusty.

'Turn right,' he told her after unlocking another door.

She stepped through and turned right. Down another corridor. Through another door that he unlocked. Then they were in a short corridor with several doors.

'Clean your face up in that bathroom next door.'

She looked sceptical at first but when she looked in, it was a room with a toilet off it, with a sink and what looked like a fresh towel. She cleaned the blood off her face and dried it off. The blood had stopped flowing but her nose was throbbing.

He unlocked another door and then Kim saw her daughter. And another little girl and a woman.

Jane and Steffi Walker.

'Emma!' she said and her daughter ran into her arms.

'Kim, what's going on?' Steffi said.

'He's taken me, too,' Kim said.

'And I'm going to tell you both; if you do anything stupid, I'll kill the children. But I'll leave you both alive so you can think about your mistake for the rest of your lives. Do I make myself clear?'

'Yes,' Kim said. Steffi nodded.

'I'll bring you something to drink later. I'm going to keep this room door open so you can use both the toilets whenever you need to. You won't be able to get out, I can assure you, so don't even think about it. If I even think you tried to escape, well, you don't need me to finish that statement.'

He turned and walked away. Steffi stepped forward but Kim put up a hand.

They waited until they heard him walk down the corridor and go through the door, locking it behind him.

'Thank God, you're alright,' Kim said, hugging her daughter. She put an arm out for Jane to get a hug too. Steffi stepped in as well. Group hug.

'You know I'd die first defending these two,' Steffi whispered into Kim's ear.

'Me too.'

When they parted, Kim watched the little girls sit down then she took Steffi aside. 'How did you end up here?'

'He grabbed me near where I live.' She explained what had happened. 'Then he brought Jane here.' She looked at the front of Kim's dress. 'Is that blood?'

'It is, but it's nothing. A nose bleed. I didn't know she was missing.'

'He must have snatched her.'

Kim shook her head. 'You know they're going to be looking in the wrong direction, don't you?'

'What do you mean?'

'They're going to think it was Bruce who snatched Jane. They won't even be looking for a stranger.'

CHAPTER 45

'Frank. Where have you been?' Andy Watt said.

'I find it touching that you worry about me so much, Andy, but people will talk.'

'I've been trying to call you but your phone just went to voicemail. Where are you?'

'I'm with a friend, Andy.'

'Well, I just thought you'd want to know we have a positive ID for Tamara Child, the doctor who helped Laing escape.'

Miller was sitting on Kate Murphy's couch and leaned forward. 'Who is it?'

'Faith Hope.'

Miller couldn't process the name for a moment. Then it slammed into his head. He couldn't believe he was hearing right. 'Faith Hope? The nurse from eight years ago?'

'The very one. The woman who worked in the hotel behind the bar in her spare time.'

'Good God, Andy. I remember calling my dad from Fife and he said that Faith Hope was with him, and she had nothing to do with it. He said she was shaken and it was obvious she wasn't involved.'

'I don't know about back then, but she was certainly involved this time.'

Miller stood up and walked to the window. Looked down on the traffic below. The tour buses were going into the Our Dynamic Earth exhibition at the foot of Holyrood Road, next to the entrance to the Scottish Parliament building, andopposite the building which used to house *The Caledonian* and *Edinburgh Evening Post* newspapers, and which now housed a video games company.

'Listen, I'm going to throw this out there, right? So don't dismiss it out of hand.'

'Okay, I'm listening.'

'I don't think Laing or Hagan murdered Faith Hope.'

There was silence on the other end for a moment. 'Okay. What makes you say that?'

'I'd rather tell you face-to-face, Andy.'

'Right now, me and Gibb are going to an address we have for Faith Hope.'

'Don't tell me what it is. That way they can't say you did.'

'We're going there now.'

'I know where she lived. Thanks for letting me know.' He hung up, putting the burner phone in his pocket. Kate came out of the kitchen. 'I have to go, Kate.'

'I'll get your clothes. They should be dry.'

He sat down again. Kate sat opposite him, in a chair.

'Frank, did Jimmy ever say anything about his relationship with me?'

'No, I can honestly say he didn't.'

'His wife was involved in that case, and although she didn't serve jail time, she was put on probation. I can't understand why he would want to go back to her. He was with that mental girlfriend, and then he moved in with me. It was like he was reliving his youth before going back to the wife.'

'I wish I knew what was going through his head. I haven't heard from him for ages, now that he's working with Lloyd Masters up at the firing range.'

'I miss him, Frank. I have to be honest. I've accepted what it is, but sometimes I'm lonely.'

'Kim and Sam like going out on a girl's night with you.'

'Oh, don't get me wrong; we have a great time. But it's nice to have a man to come home to. To share my life with. I miss that.'

'Jesus, Kate, you're a gorgeous woman. There are many Jimmy Gilmour's out there. Better than Gilmour. He wasn't the man for you, but the right man is out there.'

He stood up, wincing at the pain in his side. 'As soon as I sit down and get comfortable, my side gets stiff.'

'It's going to get worse before it gets better.'

'Your bedside manner needs brushing up on, doctor.'

'Cheeky sod.' She laughed. 'I'll go and get your clothes.' She left the living room and went through to the kitchen. He heard her open the machine door and smiled to himself. Kate Murphy had been in witness protection, had moved from London to Edinburgh, and had taken up a position as one of the pathologists in the city mortuary, where she fitted in just fine.

Miller reckoned Jimmy Gilmour needed his head examined for dumping her.

She came back with his clothes, all dried. He got dressed in her bedroom.

He felt alive again, but his face still felt like a horse had kicked it.

'Take some painkillers,' she said, when they were at the door. 'Come back and see me and I'll change your stitches.'

'Thanks for everything, Kate. You're a real pal.'

That's just what I need, she thought as she shut the door. *Another male friend.*

He walked down to the parking garage. He had hesitated about telling Andy Watt his thoughts about why the biker had taken his car.

He hoped to God he was wrong.

He'd soon find out.

CHAPTER 46

Mr Black stood in the living room of the house, his back to the room, staring out of the window. 'You didn't kill Frank Miller?' Only after the words left his mouth did he turn and face Mr Blue.

'He fought hard, I have to admit, but unfortunately, his guardian angel turned up.'

'Explain.'

'Miles Laing. We fought, but the fire was raging. I had to get out of there and I escaped after smacking Laing,' he lied. 'I don't know if they got out. I took Miller's car and dealt with his girlfriend.'

'Tell me what you did.'

'I took her from the hospital. She's with the kids and the other copper.'

'I do hope you know what you're doing.'

'Of course I do. They're all expendable.'

'I don't want any children dying.'

'Then the women can be taken care of. It's no skin off my nose.'

'What about Miller's car?'

'In the street where he parks it. I left his phone in it too.'

'They're going to connect Tamara Child with Faith Hope.'

'I know. That's why it's better I go now and deal with the last piece of this particular puzzle. Then we'll deal with the others.'

Mr Black took a sip of the drink. He was pleased with the way things were going, but it was the final loose ends that had him worried. Miles Laing and Bruce Hagan.

'You'll make sure those other two are taken care of, won't you?'

'Of course I will. Leave it to me. I'm off now to deal with the other problem.'

Mr Blue left the house and got into the Transit van that was parked down the road. He was tempted to go round the corner and see that Brett Anders was ready, but with the bollards across the road cutting off the rat run, he couldn't be bothered driving round the long way. Besides, the American and his wife were annoying. If they weren't working for him, he would gladly dispose of them too.

He started the van up and wound the window down, relishing the cool air. God, how he missed the killing. Being at the top of the tree in the army was a rush he had never felt in civvie life, unless it was on jobs like these, but even then, nothing could compare to being on a mission. Even Mr Black, as one of the officers, couldn't fully grasp the feeling they got.

He drove away, feeling the old excitement grip him as he thought about tackling Miller again, and this time finishing the job.

'Kim, it's me. I know you're pissed off with me right now, but I need you to listen. Stay in the hospital whatever you do. When you get this, call me.'

He drove away from Kate's place in the French car.

Faith Hope had had a small flat in Stockbridge. He remembered the street and that it was above a wine bar. Surprisingly, the bar was still there with the same name.

The lunchtime crowd had gone back to work, and he saw the bar was quiet. He had sent Andy Watt a text, telling him he was going for a pint in Stockbridge.

Let me guess what bar came the reply.

So here he was, standing outside, lurking about like he was about to go in but was waiting for a pal.

The unmarked patrol car pulled into the side of the road. Watt was driving. Paddy Gibb got out the passenger side.

'I shite myself every time you drive,' he complained. 'You know, I have high hopes of collecting me pension one day.'

'Isn't it funny how the old ones always think you're speeding when you're only doing twenty? My old ma used to be like that, but she was seventy.'

Gibb looked at Miller, or rather he saw a man standing on the pavement, his face looking like it had been used for practise by Mike Tyson. He did a double-take when he saw who it was.

'Fuck me, Frank, what the hell happened?'

'Oh, you know, there I was, minding my own business when somebody tried to kill me.'

'What? Who was it? Did you see him?'

Miller looked around. 'Funny thing is, no I didn't. But who wants to stand about on the pavement gassing when we could be sitting down somewhere?'

Gibb looked at Watt. 'You told him.'

'Christ, sir, he's one of the team. Look at the state of him.'

Gibb looked between the two men for a moment. 'For God's sake, keep your hands in your pockets. I don't want your bloody fingerprints all over the flat.'

'Absolutely.'

Gibb led the way upstairs to Faith Hope's flat and took out a set of keys. 'They were in her uniform,' he said, sticking a key into the lock.

Inside the flat, it was bare bones. A few sticks of furniture, covered in dust. No mail was at the back, suggesting a hold had been put on it or else it was being diverted to somewhere else.

Watt went into the small kitchen and saw the fridge was empty.

'So, this is her address, but she wasn't living here. Not the place she gave as her address to her employer as Tamara Child,' Miller said. 'Her other place was a rental, probably just a place they could check on, but she'd only been there a month. Paddy, do you remember Faith Hope from back then?'

Gibb thought about it for a moment. 'I don't to be honest. It was Jack who was dealing with her. He would remember her, I'm sure.'

'I remember her. She was a friend of Amelia somebody. I can't recall her last name. Perry MacKinnon's girlfriend,' said Miller.

'We need to talk to him again. It seems whenever Miles Laing's name crops up, MacKinnon's isn't far behind.'

'Let's go and talk to him now,' Miller said.

'No disrespect, Frank, but Andy and I will talk to him. You'll have to sit in the car.'

'Like a good little boy?'

'Come on, Frank, the boss is right,' Watt said. 'You can't go in looking like that.'

'Right, fine, I'll sit in the car. Or the one I came in.'

They left the flat and locked the door. Miller got in the Renault and followed Gibb and Watt round the corner into Dean Terrace where

TRIAL AND ERROR

they parked in front of the clinic. Miller had the driver's side window open, staring at the hotel where he had gone with Carol.

'We won't be long,' Watt said, coming up to him.

'I'll be here.'

Watt and Gibb walked into the clinic. Miller remembered when it was an empty townhouse that MacKinnon had been about to convert into an extension of the clinic next door to it.

There were people milling about. Maybe that's why Miller didn't see anybody approaching until it was too late.

The passenger door opened and a man got in.

'I think the time is right for us to talk,' Miles Laing said.

CHAPTER 47

'Long time no see, Eric,' Mr Blue said, as Eric Smith pulled out a chair and sat opposite him. The afternoon crowd was thin, the lunchtime drinkers having gone back to their offices. Now, Logie Baird's bar was quiet.

'It certainly is. How did you know I was here?'

'I have my sources, let me just say. Sorry to hear about your little girl.'

'Thanks. You having another?'

'Let me get this. I'm just having the one.' Mr Blue went to the bar and ordered another pint of lager.

'Here's to old times,' he said, when he sat back down. They clinked glasses and Eric took a long pull of the cold liquid.

'Look, I'm not going to beat about the bush, old son. There's something being bandied about, and I owe you one from way back, so that's why I'm here.'

'Okay, I'm listening.'

Mr Blue fiddled with a beer mat before going on. 'They think Frank Miller is behind Emma going missing.'

'What? No. No way.'

'I'm just telling you what's being said. Apparently, when Emma went missing, Miller had left his flat and nobody knew where he was.'

'Why would he do that?'

'Word is, he doesn't want to marry Kim. Or even have a family with her. He said he regrets getting her pregnant, and maybe she would be better off out of his life. He's not right in the head, Eric.'

Eric took his phone out and called Kim's number but there was no answer. Then he called another number. 'Neil? It's Eric–'

He stopped mid-sentence as McGovern spoke to him.

'Well, where the hell is she?' He sat with a worried look on his face. 'Right. I'm in the pub across the road having a quiet beer with an old friend. I can go over and check now. Maybe he brought her home.' He nodded a few times.

'I'll go check and call you back.'

Eric stood up and looked at his friend. 'Miller picked up Kim from the hospital. He didn't tell anybody he was doing it, and he just picked her up and took her away. She wasn't supposed to leave the hospital, but she got a call from him and he picked her up in his car. They see her on CCTV getting into his car and they drive off.'

'I would normally say, fine, she's safe as she's with Miller, but good God, Eric, I don't think Miller's stable just now.'

'Christ, I hate to think he would do anything to her.'

'Me too, my friend, but I felt I would be doing you a disservice if I didn't give you a head-up.'

'Thanks, pal. I appreciate it. But I have to go.'

'No problem. Keep me in the loop.' *Call me on my burner phone, sucker.*

'I will.' Eric turned and left the pub. He crossed over South Bridge and walked up the High Street. He stopped opposite Cockburn Street, crossed over and walked down a bit. Saw the black Audi A6 parked in a permit holder's bay. He walked down. There were plenty of visitors walking down the street. When Eric got to the car, he looked in the driver's side window and didn't see anything out of place.

He tried the driver's door. It was unlocked. He opened it and had a look around inside. It was clean. Then he looked in the back and saw the blood on the seat.

He called Neil McGovern. 'It's me. I just wanted to call you and let you know that Frank Miller is a dead man.'

CHAPTER 48

'Why should I go anywhere with you?' Miller said. His voice was a bit nasally now. "I can have you lifted right now.'

'And yet you're not. Your two colleagues are just along the road in that clinic. You could keep me here and call for backup. But you aren't. And you know I'm not going to hurt you. I could have done that in my aunt's house, but instead, I saved your life by dragging you outside. After throwing your attacker over the banister, I may add.'

'Why should I trust you?'

'Because I'm asking you to. Because I want to get Emma back just as much as you do. And because I have a gun.' Laing was holding the pistol in his left hand, as if he wanted to keep it as far away from Miller as possible, and still have a chance of pulling the trigger if the detective made a sudden move. 'Just drive over to the park. I just want to talk and I promise you, if you want to take me in after that, I'll come quietly. I have the gun because I want you to listen first.'

Miller drove round to Inverleith Park. He got out of the car and watched as Laing got out of the passenger side.

'I'd like to have a walk, Frank. Up to the sundial garden. Where that poor woman was found.'

'That's fitting, I suppose.' They were parked in Portgower Place, the lane that led into Inverleith Park. Miller walked in front. Past the barrier that stopped the public from driving in. The sun was high overhead, making it feel hot. He was sweating, glad he'd kept his jacket off.

He entered through the gate into the sundial garden and they sat down on a bench.

'You have my undivided attention,' Miller said, wishing they were in the shade.

'Whoever fixed you up, did a good job.'

'Get on with it, Miles, for God's sake.'

'As I said, it was me who pulled you out of the fire. After I threw the biker over the banister. I have to admit, I thought he would land on his head, snapping his neck, but he's very fit, whoever he is.'

'You mean to say, you don't know?'

'I wish I did, but alas, no, I don't know his identity. Bruce and I followed you there. I gave you the clue. You had to solve this without me telling you exactly who to look for. That way, you'll put the pieces of the puzzle together and hopefully solve this, and save my life.'

'I don't understand.'

'You will. But before I start, I need you to promise me one thing.'

'You want me to leave you money in my will.'

'I want you to keep an open mind about what I'm going to tell you.'

Miller took a deep breath and let it out slowly. 'Okay.'

'It started thirty years ago….

'You're beautiful, you know that?' Sparky said to her.
'Oh, go on. I bet you say that to all the girls.'
'He does, actually,' Freckles said.
'Shut up. I'm paying the lovely lady a compliment. I mean it. You're the most gorgeous girl I've ever come across.'

'Well, you're not so bad yourself, handsome.' Rena giggled. Although she was eighteen, sometimes she felt like she was much older. Sometimes she forgot she had got pregnant at fifteen and had a little girl. These two boys were a couple of years younger but they were big and acted more adult than some of the guys she had been out with.

Especially the older one. Sparky. Everybody knew he was a bright spark, and the nickname had stuck. Handsome and intelligent. Freckles had a face full of them, but one boy had made the mistake of teasing him and had been given a kicking for it. Both boys made her feel good and she was glad she had bumped into them.

Her Saturday had started off boring as hell. Stuck with her daughter, her parents out doing God knows what, and she had been given the task of looking after not only Patricia but Leif, too. He wasn't so bad. Give him a fishing net and he would amuse himself for hours, but it was hardly fun for her. He was only ten and would be amused with anything.

John Carson

She had been excited, seeing the older boys coming.
'Really? Fishing with the little spaz?' Sparky said.
'Don't call him that!' she had said, but laughed anyway. 'He's only a little boy.'
'He knows I'm only kidding, eh boy?'
Leif ignored him and continued to sweep the fishing net along the banks of the shallow river.
'Haven't seen you down here before,' Freckles said.
'I come down here a lot. It's so peaceful. Gives me time to think.'
'Think about what?'
'This and that.'
'That's our names,' Sparky said. 'I'm this and he's that.'
She had laughed more than was necessary but her eyes were shining with excitement.
'How about going for a walk?'
Rena looked at her daughter. The little girl was sitting on the bank of the river, plucking at the grass, a little doll beside her.
'Sure. We won't go far?' she asked.
'Just somewhere more private,' Sparky said.
She knew the railway line was along the way but it was close enough for it to be safe to leave the kids. 'You'll keep your eye on Patricia, won't you, Leif?' she said. He looked at her and nodded, and went back to concentrating on the minnows in the water.
They walked along the pathway and up the embankment. There had been another railway line here but the tracks had been lifted years ago.
'We used to come up here and throw stones at the trains as they went under the bridge,' Freckles said, pointing ahead to where the bridge ran across the railway line.
Sparky looked at him and shook his head. 'Spaz.' Then to Rena, 'Years ago when we were daft teenagers.'
'Oh yeah? So, what are you now then? A couple of men?' She smiled at them.
'We're sixteen. Well, he will be at the end of the month, but I'm already sixteen. Men enough to deal with you, darlin'!' Sparky said, and squeezed her round the waist. She screamed and laughed, and then her arms were around him. He was kissing her passionately then.

TRIAL AND ERROR

The pathway was overgrown. Bushes and trees had grown on the bridge but not enough to give them the privacy they needed. They crossed it, an old iron girder affair, and on the other side, the bushes were deep.

'Keep a look out,' Sparky said.

'Why? What are you doing?'

Sparky tilted his head and raised his eyebrows. 'Spaz.' He laughed as he took Rena by the hand and led her further into the undergrowth. They found a bare patch which didn't look too dirty. Rena lay down and hoisted her skirt up while Sparky fumbled with the button on his jeans. Rena took her underwear off as Sparky got his shirt off. Soon, he had his jeans round his ankles.

A few minutes of fumbling and they were done. He stood up and put his shirt on and fixed his jeans.

'Send your friend in,' Rena said, far from satisfied.

'Really?'

'Yes. Tell him to hurry.'

'Fuck, yeah,' she heard Freckles say, and he came crashing through the bushes until he reached her. He stripped off and Rena was pleased with what she saw.

After they were done, they came out onto the pathway again.

'That was magic,' Sparky said, lighting up a cigarette.

'Can I have one?' Freckles said.

'Bugger off. They're too dear.'

'You nicked them anyway.'

'Fuck me, stop whining.' He gave his friend a cigarette and lit it for him.

'Oh God,' Rena said. 'I forgot the time. I'm meeting my friends after dinner. I have to go home and eat and then I'm going out.'

'Catch you around,' Sparky said, playing it cool, like going into the bushes with a woman was an everyday occurrence. They watched as Rena ran off. They sat and discussed in great detail each other's exploits in the bushes, embellishing their story.

Then they saw her. The little girl.

'Fuck me, you don't think she saw us, do you?' Freckles said.

'How would I know?' He looked at the little girl, holding the doll in her hand.

'Were you watching us?' Sparky said, anger welling up in him

John Carson

now.

The little girl started crying. 'I want my mummy.'

'Where's that little shit with the fishing pole?' Freckles said. 'I'll kick his head in.'

'He's fucked off as well.' Sparky was even more angry now. 'You think it's funny spying on us?'

'Maybe we should teach them both a lesson. That little fucker must be around here somewhere. Maybe he was spying on us as well and took off.'

Sparky grabbed hold of the little girl's hand and started dragging her towards the embankment at the side of the bridge. 'She likes playing with the big boys, so let's see how she likes our rope swing.'

Patricia was struggling, but no match for the two boys. Sparky dragged her down the side of the bridge to where the rope swing was tied to the girders. The knot in the end was always left tucked behind a girder. The railway tracks were down at the bottom.

Sparky grabbed the rope. 'Hold her, Freckles,' he said. After he got the end of the rope, he put it round the girl's right arm. She dropped her doll as she struggled and cried. Sparky tightened the thick rope as best he could.

'You want to play with the big boys? Let's play.'

Both boys loved playing on the rope swing, as the rope swung out, it took them right over the tracks. And because the solid stone bases were taller than they were, they couldn't see a train coming.

One boy would stand down the bottom of the embankment keeping a lookout though. They weren't stupid.

'Get down there, Freckles.'

Sparky waited until his friend was down and looking along the tracks. When Freckles nodded, Sparky pushed the little girl. Her feet scrabbled in the dirt and she tripped, falling, but just as she was about to hit the dirt, the rope swung out and up high.

Patricia let out an almighty scream. Freckles looked up just as she was coming towards him as he was coming back up the embankment and she collided with him, knocking him backwards. He landed on his back, the wind knocked out of him.

'Come on, you clot! Get up!' Sparky shouted, laughing. Patricia came back and then the momentum carried her back out

TRIAL AND ERROR

again. As she came back, Freckles tried to sit up but he couldn't even breathe. Sparky pushed Patricia again and she sailed out and then back in. Then once more. This time he wasn't even looking at Freckles.

Didn't see him waving.

Patricia sailed out at the same moment a train came under the bridge. Freckles couldn't scream, although he wanted to, as he saw the little girl being smacked off the front of the diesel engine.

Her body spun round, blood spraying everywhere as her head exploded, throwing her into the air, where the rope stopped her and brought her back down again where it hit the side of the freight cars.

The screaming of brakes filled the air.

Freckles ran up the slope, his breath coming back. Sparky stood looking, not believing what he saw. Freckles grabbed him and dragged him back up the embankment.

They turned and looked and saw Rena's cousin running towards them across the bridge. They ran in the opposite direction.

Leif froze as he saw his little cousin on the end of the rope, then all of a sudden, it was like his insides were given a jolt of electricity and he ran down the embankment.

Patricia's body was still on the rope but hanging against the side of the train. She was high up and he couldn't reach her. The train had stopped now and the driver was running along the tracks.

'You little bastard!' the man screamed. 'What have you done?'

Leif tried to jump up to get to Patricia but the man grabbed him by the shoulders and shook him.

'What did you do?' he shouted in Leif's face, but Leif couldn't answer.

He just kept staring at what used to be his little cousin.

CHAPTER 49

There were two police vans and a patrol car behind the Audi. Neil McGovern stood on the pavement next to Eric Smith.

'He's not home. I checked,' Eric said.

Percy Purcell, Bill Leach, and Harry McNeil were standing near the car. Sharon Hardy was on the phone, standing a short distance from everybody.

'What are we thinking here?' Leach said. 'Miller's gone off the deep end and he's done something to his girlfriend?'

'That's exactly what he's done,' Eric said.

'We can't jump to conclusions,' McGovern said.

'She's your daughter. He's taken her somewhere, obviously under duress as you can see from the blood on the back seat.'

'I'm having it impounded,' Purcell said. 'Has anybody searched it?'

'No, we were waiting for you lot,' Eric said.

Purcell pulled on a pair of gloves and opened the glove box. There was a phone in there. He took out his own phone and called Miller's number. The phone rang and Purcell's name came up on the screen.

'It's Miller's alright.' He popped the boot. 'Somebody have a look in there.' He took the phone over to Leach and Mc'Neil and he opened the text message page.

'There's the messages telling Kim he was picking her up and when he was at the hospital. So, he has got her,' Leach said.

'I've known Miller a long time, and I know he wouldn't do that,' Purcell said.

'Well, he obviously has. I want a warrant issued for his arrest. Abducting those little girls and his girlfriend. And murder.' He turned to Sharon. 'Get your boss onto it. Get a warrant from the sheriff.'

'Yes, sir.'

'What?' Purcell was aghast. 'Why would he take Emma? And kill the babysitter? All of this doesn't make sense.'

'He's been on edge lately,' McGovern said. 'I think he's

needing help now. We need to find him as soon as.'

'We need to find Kim as soon as,' Sharon said, coming across to McGovern. 'This stress isn't good for her baby.'

'What exactly do we have on Miller?' Purcell said.

Sharon came closer to him. 'He wasn't around when Emma went missing. He said he was going to Rena Joseph's house but then we get a call saying the house has been set on fire again. That's twice. Maybe he killed her and set the fire the first time. Then he sends a text message to Kim saying he'll pick her up at the hospital and take her home. Now we find blood in the car and they're both missing. And you don't think he was working with Miles Laing?'

'No, I bloody well don't,' Purcell said. 'There has to be some explanation for this.'

'Well, if there is, I'd love to hear it.'

Right then Purcell couldn't think of one, but he couldn't think of his friend as a murderer either.

Then his phone rang. 'Purcell.'

'Sir, it's DCI Gibb.'

'Go ahead, Paddy.'

'We think you might want to come and see this.'

'Where are you?'

'Down in Comely Bank.' He gave him the address.

'Have either you or Watt spoken to Miller?'

'He was with us a little while ago.'

Purcell saw Sharon studying him as he spoke so he moved over to stand at a shop window. 'Paddy, we need to know where he is. He took Kim and there's blood in his car. We think she's in real danger.'

'I don't know where he went. He was in an old Renault hatchback, and when we went in to speak to Perry MacKinnon, he was gone by the time we came out.'

'Did you speak with MacKinnon?'

'No. He hasn't been heard from in a little while. He left the clinic and was last seen getting into a black Audi.'

'Let me know if Miller contacts you. They're going to have a warrant issued for his arrest. Murder and abduction. I need him to call me. You hear me, Paddy?'

'Loud and clear.'

Purcell hung up. Looked at the car. MacKinnon was last seen

John Carson

getting into a black Audi.
> *Good God, Frank, what have you done?*

CHAPTER 50

Despite the heat, a shiver ran down Miller's back. A woman pushing a pram came into the gardens and sat on the bench opposite them.

Both men got up and walked away, looking like a pair of lovers who got disturbed before they had a chance to express their feelings for one another.

'Let's go down to the pond,' Laing said.

There were more people down there, feeding the ducks, playing with radio controlled boats and sitting enjoying the weather.

'I didn't see those boys again until a few days later. When I was coming home from school. They grabbed me and told me if I told on them, they would kill me.'

'And the police were still questioning you?'

'Oh yes. Every day. The sessions were getting longer and longer but I had a lawyer with me. Rena was a wreck. She pointed the finger at me, blaming me for what happened. She accused me of harming her daughter, because I was bored, she said. I told them there were two boys. I didn't know who they were or their names.'

'Didn't Rena say anything? Like who they were?'

'She even denied they were there. She said she asked me to bring Patricia home as she had to run home to use the bathroom. She thought I was right behind her, but got worried when I didn't come home.

'And they believed her. But those boys said they wouldn't just kill me, they would kill my family too. I was petrified.'

'Then you got charged with killing your little cousin.'

Laing looked at him and shook his head. 'No; Leif Torgerson got charged with murder. That was my name before they changed it to Miles Laing. I was put away in a young offender's institution until I was eighteen. The courts said the press weren't allowed to report my name or publish my photo. I was released on license. My parents were given a new name, just like me. We were given the hotel to run, sponsored by my grandfather. It was made to look like we owned it, but we never did. He did, my grandfather.'

They sat down on a bench, one that was furthest away from everybody else, in the shade of some trees.

'I was determined to have a decent life. I didn't have anything to do with Rena after that, of course, and everything I did had to be run past the parole officer. I wanted to go to medical school and become a surgeon. I was given permission.

'I became a good surgeon. I was chosen to work with Perry MacKinnon and Len Chatter. They were both good guys, especially Chatter who had more experience. I felt I was finally on the right track with my life, and then notice was given that the hospital was closing.

'Rena obviously still hated my guts made sure that I never worked as a surgeon again. She told Perry MacKinnon who I really was.'

'She did that to get back at you because she thought you killed her daughter.'

'No. She knew I didn't kill her. She just wanted to make sure that everybody still thought it was me.'

'Why would Perry MacKinnon believe her?' Miller asked.

'Because Perry MacKinnon used to go by the nickname Freckles.'

Miller sat up straight. 'MacKinnon was one of the killers?'

Laing nodded. 'Rena didn't say he was a killer, but she let slip he was one of the boys who had been with her that day. Me getting on the surgical team was just to keep an eye on me. Then when I was blamed for the mistake that Hugo Flynn had made while we were operating on that woman, they really did a number on me.

'I started drinking heavily, and taking drugs. I was a mess, Frank. I was having blackouts. I had a nervous breakdown and was put on meds. My parole officer said that I should just work in the hotel instead of going back to surgery. I agreed with him. My reputation was tarnished.'

Miller sat and looked at some swans gliding about on the still water of the huge pond. Their life was simple. He wished that his own life was simple.

'I have to admit, you tell a good story.'

'You don't believe me?'

'Listen, when I caught you eight years ago, you had cut women open and sewn them back up again.'

'That's what you were meant to believe.'

'You're telling me that wasn't you?' Miller looked at him in disbelief.

'That's exactly what I'm telling you. I want you to believe me.'

'Okay, let's just say for a second I believe you. Who was responsible?'

'MacKinnon. And his accomplice.'

'Let me guess; Sherri Hilton?'

'Correct. You knew she wasn't really American. No doubt Carol told you. She and MacKinnon came into the hotel one day. He made it clear that they knew who I was. They blamed Chatter for getting me emptied out the door. They said they would keep quiet about my real identity. They were giving me a subtle warning.'

'Like keeping you under control.'

'Exactly.'

'Why would MacKinnon kill Iris Napier, the first victim we found at St Bernard's Well?'

'He's a psycho. You know that he's a ladies' man. He would go out with any woman if she was gorgeous enough. But he couldn't have Iris Napier. She and I went out together. He saw her in the hotel bar one night. He wasn't happy, I could tell, but he didn't say anything to me.

'Well, Iris and I spent the night together. At her place. When I woke up in the morning, I couldn't even remember what we had done, I was so drunk the night before. I never heard from her again. Then she turned up murdered.'

'And you think it was MacKinnon?'

'I was suspicious. He came into the bar and asked me how I had enjoyed my night with her. I told him to mind his own business. Then she's found murdered. And MacKinnon is in the bar with a shocked look on his face. *What did you do to her, Miles*? he said to me. He made me think I'd murdered her.'

'You know something, when I came into the operating theatre, you had wrapped Perry McKinnon's head in cling film.'

'No, I didn't. He did that to himself. He killed Calvin Baxter. He never liked the man, and then Calvin was showing off his new girlfriend, who was gorgeous. MacKinnon was raging about that. I think they had given me something. I remember getting in the car with Sherri, and then I was at the hospital. She drove off and I saw Hugo hanging from the banister. In the operating theatre, MacKinnon told me to get dressed, we had work to do. I didn't know what he meant, until we went into the theatre.

'God, Marcie was dead on the table. He went out and then came back in with the others. He told them it was all over. It had to end. They looked confused, Len Chatter and Calvin Baxter. He showed them what he had done to Marcie. He said they had been summoned there and he thought he was going to catch the killer. I came in and that's when Len fell down. Clutching his chest. MacKinnon fought with Calvin. He overpowered him and wrapped his head, suffocating him.'

'And then we arrived.'

'Yes. He was mad at that. Time for Plan B, he said. I didn't know what he meant. Then he said, just remember what will happen to your family. Especially your grandfather. Then he left and came rushing back in. Then he wrapped his own head in the cling film. I was frozen to the spot. But when you and Andy Watt came in, I knew I had to act the part. For my family's sake. So, I acted like I had killed them.'

'You said that Len Chatter had bought your father's hotel, but it's owned by your grandfather's company, Thor Industries.'

'More fantasy. Len was dead when you got there, so he couldn't contradict me. It was all part of my story.'

'What about the others?'

'You know Sherri killed Ruby Maxwell, but again, they made me believe that I had had a blackout and murdered the others.'

'Sherri told Carol that she was your girlfriend and that you'd known her for ages.'

'That wasn't true. I hadn't known her for that long and she certainly wasn't my girlfriend. It was Faith Hope who was the mean one. She was a nurse but suddenly she had conned my dad into giving her a job behind the bar. She needed extra money, she told him.'

'She's the one who changed her name to Tamara Child and came into the hospital to get you out.'

'I know. I overheard her on the phone one night. She said, *It's me, Faith.* I thought I recognised her, but I couldn't place her. She'd had a little work done.'

'What about Sherri Hilton?'

'I've never seen her again.'

'I saw a nurse leave the floor that Carol was on, in the hospital. I looked out the window from Carol's room and it was raining and dark, so I didn't get a close look, but she turned and waved to me. I think that's her.'

'You could be right. But I haven't seen her.'

'Unless she too had a little work done. After all, MacKinnon is a plastic surgeon.'

Just then, the mobile phone that Miller had, rang.

'It's Andy Watt, boss. Listen, I'm not supposed to say anything, but there's a warrant out for your arrest. If you call me, I'm supposed to try and talk to you. So here I am talking to you. They'll arrest you on sight, for abducting Emma and Kim, and for murdering Lynn Sterling.'

'What do you mean, abducting Kim? What's happened to her?'

'He turned up in your car and took her away. She obviously thought it was you. The car is on CCTV and she got in the back. There's blood on the back seat. Oh, and her ex wants to kill you.'

'Jesus. Andy, let me know if they find Kim.'

'I will boss. Where will you be?'

'I'm not sure yet. But did you speak to Perry MacKinnon?'

'He's nowhere to be found. He wasn't at the clinic, or his new one.'

'Let me know if you trace him, Andy.'

'Will do, boss.' He hung up.

'That biker took Kim from the hospital in my car and now he has her. Have you any idea who that was?'

'No. It could be the one they called Sparky, I honestly don't know.' Laing looked at Miller. 'Do you believe what I told you?'

'I wouldn't have if you hadn't saved my life in your aunt's house.'

'They're going to try and kill me.'

'Why now, Miles? After eight years, why now?'

'Bruce Hagan. He was only in the hospital a few months. He and I hit it off right away. He was an outcast, being a copper. I told my story to him. Nobody on the outside knew I was talking to him. Except his wife. Amanda. She wanted him released into the Royal Scottish hospital, somewhere that didn't harbour killers. Bruce told her that he had been talking to me. She wanted an appeal made on his sentence, wanted him to see a new doctor. If he was on the outside, then he could tell somebody the real story of what happened to me and my cousin.'

'The next thing you know, there's a new female doctor, and you overhear her, calling herself by her real name; Faith Hope.'

'And then I knew they were there to kill me. But they had to do it slowly so as not to arouse suspicion. And let's face it, they had all the time in the world. Me and Bruce weren't going anywhere. So, we both knew we had to tell somebody. I knew they were planning on getting us out and then faking our deaths.'

'Then you called me.'

'I wanted you to keep me in your mind. I did say there was a first female you didn't know about. I meant my cousin, Patricia.'

'Oh, I did keep you in my mind alright.'

'You know something, Frank? Bruce just needs help. He isn't a killer.'

'I know that. And I think he'll get it. His wife seemed annoyed that he was out when we spoke to her.'

'I think she was just putting on an act. She's with him now.'

'Where have you both been staying?'

'In my grandfather's apartment. He has the penthouse in the ScotNet building on Lothian Road. He has people to look after him, but his health's failing now. He wants to see my name cleared.'

'You know something? I *do* believe you.'

'And just to convince you further.' He reached under his shirt into his waistband and, after making sure nobody saw him, slipped the gun to Miller. 'You can come with me to see Bruce, or shoot me, or whatever. I'm not running anymore, Frank.'

Miller stood up and put the gun in his own waistband. 'You might not be, but it seems that I'm on the run now. Let's go and finish this, Miles. I think I know who Sparky is.'

CHAPTER 51

Miller's face was still hurting. It felt worse now that the painkillers were wearing off.

He dialled the number he wanted. 'Andy. It's me. I'm coming in. This has to end. I want to get Emma back and I'm not going to be able to do this unless I come in. But I'm not coming to the station. It's too dangerous.'

'Where are you, Frank? I can come and get you.'

'I can't tell you that just now. Please understand. I want my little girl back safe and now I think they've taken Kim as well. I think they took Steffi Walker and Jane. They're going to punish us all, Andy.'

'Just tell me where you are. I promise you I'll be there in no time.'

'We don't have time. They're going to kill Miles Laing and Bruce Hagan. If something happens to me, I want you to look for the phone I'm using now. I recorded a conversation between me and Laing. He didn't kill any of those women. He's never killed anybody.'

'What are you talking about, Frank? He killed those women.'

'No, he didn't. It was somebody else. We don't know his identity just now, but I have a theory.'

'Tell me who it is.'

'We can't alert him. He's dangerous, Andy. I'm taking a leap of faith here, but I'm also putting your life on the line if I tell you.'

'Fuck it. Tell me anyway. At least I'll know who to look for if anything happens.'

Miller told him.

'Are you sure?'

'It's a guess, Andy, but not many people knew I was going to Rena Joseph's house, and he was one of them.'

'I'll kick him right in the fucking bollocks, the bastard.'

'Don't go near him, Andy. Miles Laing saved my life. Otherwise this guy was going to kill me. I've been in some fights, but this guy takes fighting to another level.'

'Street fighter.'

'No. I mean military. I want you to do some background checks. Get Neil McGovern to help you with that. He can get Ian Powers the computer guy onto it.'

'Where are you going now, Frank?'

'To look for Perry MacKinnon. He's the other one. They both killed a little girl a long time ago and Miles Laing got the blame and got locked up.'

'Jesus. I told you nobody knows where he is.'

'He's got to be somewhere. I want to find him. I need to have a personal conversation with him.'

'You and me both, boss. But if they're that dangerous, you can't do this alone.'

'I'll have Miles with me. He'll have my back so I won't be taken by surprise again.'

'You know if you get caught, you're both going away? Miles will get taken right back to the hospital. You'll go to maximum security. They won't believe you.' There was a pause on the end of the line before Watt carried on. 'Listen, boss, are you sure you can trust Laing? I mean, he did just escape from a lunatic asylum.'

'I know that, but I'm using my own judgement. He ran into a burning building and took on a man who was trying to kill me. He didn't have to do that. He didn't have to risk his own life, but he wants to clear his name.'

'After eight years?'

'It's a long story, but now I know why. Trust me, Andy, I've got this.'

'I know you're a rank above me and my boss, but I'm fucking telling you this right now; if you need me, you call me first. Okay? Laing's not the only one who's got your back. I don't care what the suits upstairs are saying, you need me, you call me, okay?'

'I hear you, mate. I appreciate it.'

'Keep me in the loop.'

'I will.' Miller hung up. Looked at Laing. 'We're going somewhere near here, but understand this; if we get caught, we're both fucked.'

'Let's not get caught then.'

They walked out of the park, two friends who were having a

lunch break together, not raising one eyebrow. Nobody would ever know that they were both on the run from the police, one a psychopath and one a rogue copper who was now armed with a handgun.

'Are you firearms trained?' Laing asked.

'I am.'

'Are you prepared to use that gun if push comes to shove?'

'Somebody's taken the woman I love most in the world and my little girl. I'll take his kneecaps off if it means him telling me where they are.'

'Glad to hear it. Where are we going?'

'Round the corner.'

They got back into the little car, which Miller was starting to like, and he drove out of Portgower Place and into Raeburn Place. Turned right then left, winding his way round to Dean Park Mews.

'Why are we here?' Miles asked.

'Because Perry the perv MacKinnon owns a mews house here. Or he did, but I don't think he would have sold it. These properties are investments and he seems to be doing well for himself.' He stopped outside one of the houses, which were once carriage houses.

'He owns this?'

'He did. We'll soon find out if he still does.' Miller brought out the little wallet he always carried in his pocket.

'You always carry a lock picking set?' Miles asked, surprised.

'You never know when you're going to need one.'

'I hope none of the neighbours are looking out.'

'That's why you're going to tell me if there is. Keep your eyes peeled, Miles.'

Miller got to work and soon the door was unlocked. He opened the door and they slipped inside. Miles picked up the mail and put it on a little table at the foot of the stairs.

'Keep your hands in your pockets so you don't leave fingerprints.'

Miller had been here before. Remembered the layout. MacKinnon had let his lover live here, before they broke up. Amelia. She had been young, her life ahead of her, until it had been cut short. By *The Surgeon*.

'He might be here, heard us coming in, so be on your guard,' Miller said.

John Carson

'I'm in the mood for smacking him now, after all he's put me through.'

They didn't split up. The house wasn't that big and they could take him if they both confronted him.

Perry MacKinnon wasn't there. There was evidence that a woman lived in the house, but no man. No men's razors in the bathroom, no man's clothes in the wardrobe. Just a female's. Maybe it was two women, for all they knew.

'Wherever he went, it wasn't here. God knows where he is.'

'I'm getting nervous, Frank. Let's get out of here. We can go to the apartment on Lothian Road.'

'That's exactly what we're doing. That way, Sparky will come to us. We won't need to hunt him down anymore. I just need to make a phone call first.'

CHAPTER 52

'Norma. I feel that I'm in your office more than I'm down in Holyrood these days,' Ewan Simmons said. 'This police station is becoming my second home.'

He walked into the conference room.

'Please sit down,' Norma said. 'Sharon, could you be a dear and pour us a coffee?'

'Of course.' Sharon went over to the dresser and poured two cups and brought them over to the conference table. She sat off to the side of Norma.

'The sheriff is signing the warrant for Miller's arrest. Then we'll pull out all the stops looking for him,' Norma said.

Simmons sat back in the chair. 'I'm so sorry that this has been a tremendous strain for you, Norma. I can't even imagine what you're going through. We'll do everything we can to bring Emma and your daughter back.'

'I appreciate that, Ewan. I can't even function properly here, but I would just be a basket case at home.'

He nodded at her. 'I heard through the grapevine that Frank Miller has been going off the rails for a while now.'

'I think my daughter should have seen the warning signs a long time ago, but I couldn't tell her. Now she's having his baby. And he's going to prison. Jesus.'

'I'm sure it will work out in the end. Keep the faith, Norma. As long as Kim is back with the children. Never mind Miller. Your daughter can do without somebody like that in her life.'

'I know you're right, but I can't help feeling that if she hadn't met him, then this wouldn't have happened.'

'By the same token, if she hadn't met her first husband, then she might be married to somebody else, her first husband wouldn't have cheated on her, she wouldn't have come back to Edinburgh and she wouldn't have met Frank Miller. It's life, Norma. We can't *if* and *but* our way through life. We have to deal with everything as we meet it.'

'I know, you're right. I just want them back, Ewan.'

'Keep the faith. You'll get them back. I'm convinced.'

'Miles Laing and that headcase Bruce Hagan certainly make a good team.'

'You mustn't think like that. But, tell me, what does Kim's ex think of everything?'

'He wants to have a word with Miller, but I told him not to be stupid.'

'Eric's not a man I'd like to mess with,' Simmons said.

'Frank Miller might be thinking that way before long.'

'I hope that there are as many patrols out looking for him as need be. I've already spoken to the chief constable, and he knows my view on this. He assures me every officer is at our disposal.'

'Being the Justice Minister has its perks.'

'It means I can leave the office without anybody wondering where I'm going. And trust me, my every movement is questioned. This case, however, takes precedence over everything else.'

'I appreciate your support.'

'What's the news on Miles Laing?' Simmons asked.

'Nothing yet.'

'The police have every resource known to man. The helicopter is available, teams of dog handlers. But I want to know if you can think of anywhere Miller would run to? Somewhere he could hide? I would be right on the phone to Jeni Bridge to make sure she can get teams to mobilise in a heartbeat.'

There was a knock at the door.

'Come in,' Norma shouted.

Percy Purcell came in. 'Ma'am, there's been some news about Frank Miller.'

'Oh God. Have you got him?'

'Yes. We found him in a mews lane in Comely Bank.'

'Are you going to bring him in?' said Norma.

'No. You see, we know that Miles Laing was armed with a handgun. Frank Miller and Bruce Hagan were shot dead.'

'Good God, no!'

'Miles Laing is dead, too. Stab wound. It seems that Miller was working with Laing, and somehow they must have got into a fight and Laing shot him, but not before Miller got lucky with a knife.' Percy

Purcell said.

'Oh my God, I knew it!' Norma said.

Everybody stood up from the conference table.

'I'm sorry that Miller was killed before you could have him interrogated. However, I'll call the chief and make sure this investigation is ramped up. We have to find the children,' said Simmons.

'Thank you, Ewan.'

Simmons walked out and went along the corridor and through the exit door to the stairs.

Neil McGovern came through a door at the opposite end and walked up to Purcell. 'Did you tell her?'

'Yes, I did.'

McGovern walked into the room, Norma got up and came round to her husband. Stood before him with tears streaming down her cheeks. She asked Sharon to excuse them and she left, closing the door behind her.

'Oh, Neil, Miller's dead. And now the chances of getting our daughter and granddaughter back are slim to none.'

McGovern smiled at her.

'Oh, I wouldn't say that,' he said, and led her to a seat.

CHAPTER 53

Fredrik Torgerson stood looking out of the floor to ceiling window of his living room. The whole wall was made up of them. *It will let in not just the views but as much daylight as you can handle. The back wall doesn't have any windows, so you will need the daylight.* He couldn't complain about the view; St John's church on the corner of Lothian Road, St Cuthbert's church over in the graveyard. The Castle sitting way across from him, this building and the barracks almost seeing eye to eye above the tenement opposite.

No, one thing the architect had got right, was his choice of windows for his view. And the light was superb. He didn't have a complaint. But today, it seemed as if the whole world was watching him.

Not for the first time, he was starting to feel his age. But at almost eighty, he was starting to think about being with his beloved Agneta, some fifteen years gone now. Gone too soon. Why would he want to live forever when his beloved was gone?

He turned away from the window. The sun was bright today but it was high in the sky. Still, his air conditioners were keeping the place cool. It never ceased to amaze him that Edinburgh residents could live without their air being chilled indoors. He could understand their houses, perhaps, but shopping centres? Especially the ones with the glass roofs? No.

Manfred knocked and entered. The man was a godsend. One of Fredrik's friends had once commented about how good Fredrik's butler was. The old man had almost burst a blood vessel. Manfred was his *assistant*. Butler indeed. Manfred had never let him down. Always made sure he got his meds on time. Drove him to where he needed to go.

A godsend.

'Yes, Manfred, what is it?'

'Your friend is here, sir.'

'My friend? I wasn't expecting anybody.'

'He says he just wanted to drop by for a visit. Shall I send him away?'

'No, no, send him in.' He walked slowly over to his comfortable chair and sat down.

Mr Black walked in and smiled. 'Fredrik! I hope you don't mind.'

'Not at all. Forgive me for not getting up. My sciatica is giving me hell.'

Mr Black laughed. 'Don't you worry about that, old boy.'

'Would you like a drink?' Manfred asked.

'A whisky would be nice.' Mr Black took a seat opposite the old man. Manfred poured a whisky from the drinks cabinet and handed it to him..

'You have a nice place here.'

'You told me that the last time you were here.'

'And it's still nice!' Mr Black laughed and put his glass on the little table beside his chair.

'You didn't come here to compliment me on my apartment.'

Mr Black's face became sombre. 'No, you're right. I came to offer my condolences about Miles.'

'Don't you mean Leif?'

'What?'

'You heard; he was called Leif back then. As you well know.'

'I don't know what you're talking about.'

'You came to me in the private club one night and struck up a conversation. It was the start of a friendship, or so I thought. But I was a fool. I usually spot people who are trying to get one over on me, but not this time. And why would I? This powerful man, making friends with me. I am a rich man, I have people who work for me, and plenty of people who want to be my friend. Not anybody like you though. So, I was glad to have a friend. A *true* friend.'

'I don't know what you're talking about. I'm really puzzled here.'

'Are you, Ewan?' Miles Laing said as he walked into the living room. Ewan Simmons looked between him and Fredrik.

'Good God, Fredrik, what's going on? I was told that he and Frank Miller were dead.'

'Did I kill you, Frank?' Miles said. Miller walked into the room.

John Carson

'No, I don't think you did. And I didn't stab you either. That's what you were told, Simmons. And let's not forget Bruce Hagan. We thought you would come here to finish off the old man. All neatly wrapped up.'

Bruce Hagan came in, and standing by his side was his wife, Amanda.

Simmons stood up. 'What the hell is going on here? There's a warrant out for your arrest. You'll never get away with this.'

'I was about to say the same to you. It's all over now. We got you and we'll get Perry MacKinnon. *Freckles* and *Sparky*. Wasn't that your nicknames, Sparky?'

The phone rang. Fredrik picked it up. 'I see. Hold on will you? I'll put it on speakerphone and you can repeat the message.'

This is the police, Ewan. We have the building surrounded. Come out now.

Ewan Simmons smiled and pulled out a gun. A Glock, Miller saw.

'Take the gun out, the one Laing stole from Faith in the ambulance,' said Simmons.

Miller reached round his back and drew the gun out. Simmons pointed his gun at him. 'Drop it. Kick it to me.'

When he picked the gun up, he had a look out of the window into Lothian Road. There was no traffic. It had been stopped, obviously. He could see flashing blue lights reflected in the shop windows opposite. The police were indeed down there.

'How did you know I was coming here?'

'I was puzzled how the biker turned up at Rena Joseph's house. Somebody knew I was going there and wanted to stop me.'

'It was Laing, obviously.'

'No. The only person I told was Percy Purcell, but then I remembered that you came out of the room. And that biker could fight. You're ex-SAS. That's when I put it together.'

'Very clever.'

'And nobody's going to suspect the Justice Minister, but nobody knows your background like we do. You're not going to get out of here, Simmons. Just tell me where Emma is,' Miller said.

'She's safe. For now.'

'Why did you take her in the first place? What did a little girl do to you?'

'Don't turn this on me, Miller! I took her because of you! Laing was talking to you. I couldn't have that.'

'Why? Because he had told Bruce Hagan who he really was? What had gone on all those years ago? You and Perry MacKinnon fooling around with Rena Joseph, and then you killed her little girl and let Miles take the blame.'

'Leif. He was Leif back then. And yes, we were larking about and we didn't mean to kill her. So what if he got the blame? His family were rich, he would get away with it. Or so we thought. But by the time they arrested him, it was too late. We made sure he knew what would happen if he told on us. Besides, they found *him* at the scene, not *us*. It was hard, but the three of us got on with our lives. Obviously Rena thought Miles had killed her daughter and hated him for it.'

Miller stared at him. 'Give me the gun. It's over.'

'Really? I just told you to give me your gun and then you think I'm going to roll over? We don't work that way.'

'You're not going to walk out of here.'

Simmons laughed. 'Of course I am. I'm going to kill you all and walk away. Starting with you Miller.'

Miller was standing in front of the tall window. Simmons was standing facing him, two windows over.

He watched Miles edge away slightly.

'One more fucking step and I'll shoot Miller in the guts and not in the head,' he said to Miles, who stopped.

'You had to take *his* side, didn't you? After he was dead, we were going to let the children go. We only wanted them as leverage. Now you've ruined everything. I'm going to have to kill them now. I have enough money to disappear, so don't think I won't just kill them. Starting with your stepdaughter.'

'Your right.'

'What?'

Miller wasn't looking at him but at a spot on the wall. 'Two right. Your right.'

'I know I'm right, Miller.'

Miller waited. Nothing. He turned and looked out the window. 'Two on your right.'

John Carson

Simmons turned to look out the window. His eyes went wide, realising at the last moment, but it was too late. The first bullet shot through the plate glass window, followed by a second.

The third bullet was so close behind the second one that Miller didn't even have time to throw himself to the floor before it struck Simmons in the chest, upper right, ripping part of his shoulder off.

He screamed and fell backwards. Miles ran over and kicked Simmons hard, but it was overkill since the gun had flown through the air to land on the other side of the room.

Miller went over to Simmons who was writhing in pain. 'Fuck. You're all dead, Miller.'

'Where's Emma?'

'Fuck you.'

Miller stomped on the wound. 'Where's Emma?'

Simmons screamed. 'MacKinnon has them.'

Miller stomped on the wound again, twisting his foot. 'Where?'

Simmons told him. Then he passed out.

Miller walked over to the window where the wind was rushing in now. He stood and looked towards the castle. He couldn't see the sniper, but knew that Eric Smith was one hell of a shot. He saluted and walked away.

'MacKinnon has them,' he said to Miles. 'I need to go and get my girls back.' He took out his phone. 'Percy? It's me. We need to go somewhere.'

CHAPTER 54

Eric Smith was still looking through the eyepiece when Miller walked up to the window and saluted.

'Go get our little girl, Frank,' he said under his breath.

'That was a good shot,' Brett Anders said.

Smith stood up and shook the American's hand. 'You taking out the window helped, believe me. Sunny day, no wind to speak of, 800 yards. And a torso shot. A newbie could have done it. But thanks again for the heads-up.'

'No problem my friend. I called a buddy of mine and he called London, who called Neil McGovern. It was the only way to draw out Simmons, making him believe that Miller, Laing, and Hagan were all dead. That only left the old man who knew the story. Luckily, Miller kept in touch with a colleague who told his boss. Purcell I think they said the name was. Miller said the only one who knew he was going to that woman's house was Simmons, apart from Purcell.'

They had pulled down two sash windows so now they closed them. 'The hospital will know that's not a close-up 9mm shot, but a .50,' Smith said. 'Neil will take care of that with a blackout order though.'

'You'd better get back down to the station. I hope they get your little girl back.'

'We will. I have every faith.'

'You could do a lot worse than have Frank Miller look after your little girl. He went above and beyond, told them to go fuck themselves when they suspended him. He didn't give up. Took a severe beating. There's not many men who would do that.'

'I know. I owe him a beer.'

They left the storage room and went downstairs and into the courtyard of the National War Museum in the castle, where an army Land Rover was waiting for them.

'Eric, I have to make a call,' Anders said.

He walked away and took out his mobile phone. Called a number. Left a message for Marie on her voicemail, feeling worried that she hadn't answered.

She had told him she wasn't going out anywhere. Maybe she was in the shower or something, he thought, joining Smith in the Land Rover.

Marie Anders wasn't in the shower. She was in a tunnel. When she and Brett had come down the other night, she had wanted to explore further, but they were at a T-junction and he had hesitated. He hadn't wanted to go any further.

She had teased him about being afraid of the dark and they had gone back to the house.

Now she wanted to see for herself where it led. Brett had been called away and said he would call her later. She didn't trust the man they were dealing with. Especially after they'd seen him creeping about the house where they were staying.

So now she was at the T-junction again, shining her flashlight left and right. To the right, the tunnel seemed to turn, so she couldn't see exactly where it was going. To the left, it was longer, before it too took a turn. She went left. It was big enough to walk in but not much more. Old, metal lamps hung from the ceiling, long dead.

She shone her light ahead and the tunnel curved round to the right. She followed it along and there was a fork. She went right this time, and a few feet in, there was an old staircase ahead of her, going down. She shone her light down, but there was a landing and then the stairs went down again, out of sight. She didn't go down it.

She went back and took the right fork. The tunnel veered round again and she walked along. More lamps on the ceiling and although the air was a bit stale, it didn't smell damp.

She came to a wrought iron gate set back into the wall. A passageway was beyond it. She pushed on the gate and it squealed as it opened. She winced and stood still for a moment. Heard nothing. She stepped past it, intrigued now. The passageway turned to the right and then there was a set of steps leading up to an old door.

She climbed them and reached out and grabbed the handle. This door opened without squealing. She stepped up into an old basement. It was cold down here and mostly empty except for a few odds and ends. There were more stone stairs and another door.

TRIAL AND ERROR

She climbed them and put her hand on the door handle, her light shining on it. She turned it carefully, slowly inching it round until she felt it give. Just a gentle push. She'd have a look at what was on the other side and then she'd–

The door was yanked open and the light from the room was blinding her. Then she saw the gun pointed at her.

'Glad you could join me,' Mr Blue said, and yanked her into the room by the hair.

CHAPTER 55

There was a lot of activity when Purcell pulled up behind the Land Rover. 'Isn't that your love rival?' he said, pointing to Eric Smith.

'Sod off, Percy,' Miller said.

'It's superintendent to you.'

'I'm not on the force anymore, remember?'

'Still, a bit of respect.'

'If my face didn't hurt so much, I'd try laughing.'

Purcell grinned. 'You had me worried for a bit there. I thought you'd gone over to the dark side.'

'No chance.'

'Welcome back, my friend.'

They got out of the car. Neil McGovern was standing next to Smith and a man Miller didn't recognise.

'This is a friend of mine,' McGovern said, taking Miller aside. 'He was the one who took out the window before Eric took the shot. He's American, but I can't tell you any more than that.'

'I don't want to know, Neil.'

'You looked fucked, me old son. But I'm proud of you. You haven't slowed down one little bit.'

Miller looked McGovern in the eyes. 'Let me ask you something though; did you really think I was working with Miles Laing? Before we found out he was innocent.'

'Of course not. And who would have thought it. He hadn't touched one person. They brainwashed the poor bastard, but Norma will get right onto sorting things out. He'll be a free man.'

'I hope she sorts Bruce out, too.'

'Of course she will. They're all with her now. She was shocked about Simmons though. But we'll get them all the help they need. And after Simmons comes out of surgery, he'll get what's coming to him, too.'

'Bruce is getting better, Neil. He'll never be back on the force, but he can live a semi-normal life.' Miller looked over to the tenement.

'Run me through it again.'

'Right. Percy was getting the team down here, getting the armed boys tooled up after you told us that Simmons tells you MacKinnon owns a flat here. Two over-zealous uniforms go up to the door instead of waiting. They were only to observe and report. When they turn up, they go inside and only one comes back out. However, he's got a demand from a guy calling himself Mr Blue, who said he knows where the kids are. He wants to give them back unharmed, but he will only show Hazel Carter.'

Another car was approaching from behind. 'Christ, this must be her now. I wish I'd emphasised more just how dangerous he is. Now he's taken a hostage. A police woman.'

McGovern was looking at the car approaching.

'You can't let her go in there,' Miller said.

'Listen, Frank, we have no choice. If he's serious, he'll give them to her.'

'This is all fucked up,' Miller said, not believing his eyes when he saw her get out of the car. 'Simmons said that Perry MacKinnon has the kids, not somebody called Mr Blue.'

'We checked his clinic, his home and even went through that mews house he has. Where you were. They stripped it apart. There's no sign of them. We have forensics going through everywhere he owns, to see if there's any sign of the kids.'

'What if he really does have them, Neil?'

'I'm open to suggestions. Right now, there's some nutter in there who says he can take Hazel to my granddaughter, and I want him to do it. I am not going to put Emma's life on the line.'

'That's exactly what you *are* doing, and not only hers, but Hazel's and everybody else's.'

'He just wants to talk, Frank,' Purcell said.

'Bullshit. Simmons was a pathological liar and he's been working with this guy, Mr Blue.' He turned to McGovern. 'Where the hell is MacKinnon?'

'None of the neighbours have seen any kids. In fact, they haven't seen anybody enter or leave.'

Hazel Carter came across to Miller. 'Good God, Frank, your face is a mess.'

'You should see the other guy.'

She smiled.

'You don't have to do this, Hazel. In fact, I'm not going to allow you to do it.'

'I feel tired, like I haven't slept in years, and I'm aching, and my heart feels like it weighs a ton, so if there's any chance that I might see my little girl again, I'm going to take it.'

'We have the back covered with marksmen,' Purcell said. 'There's patio doors leading out to the back garden and there's the front door down on the basement level. Or as the toffs like to say, *garden level*.'

'I'll be fine,' Hazel said.

'You're going to get wired up though, right?'

'Yes. I'll have an earpiece and a wire.'

Miller shook his head. 'I am not happy with this at all. You can't let her go in like this.'

'Nobody's happy about it,' Purcell said, 'but we have children to find and this bastard knows where they are.'

'Why don't we storm the place? Eric's used to doing that sort of stuff.'

'Time. He says if he doesn't have Hazel in the house in the next,' looking at his watch, 'five minutes, he'll kill the children.'

'I'm going in with her.'

'No, you're not.'

'Frank, listen,' Hazel said, 'I can take care of myself. I'll go toe-to-toe with that bastard. I need you out here in case it goes tits up. If I die, then I need you to find a good home for the kids.'

'Fuck me, Hazel, this is not about sexism, it's about you being a part of my team. And don't talk like that. That's a bloody order.'

'Let me do this.' She kissed him on the cheek and walked over to the tech van where they were going to wire her up.

'I'd like to put a fucking bullet in Simmons' head right now,' Miller said.

Purcell looked at Eric Smith. 'By Christ, I wish you boys were going in there.'

'Me too. Not enough time. Let's just hope he gives the kids to Hazel.'

'How many uniforms are in there?' Miller asked.

'One, now. There were two, but he threw the man out and kept the female. He said to the guy, make sure they're taking me seriously. He has a shotgun in there, and he said he'll kill anybody who tries to storm the place.'

The vehicles were acting as a shield for the personnel. Ballistic screens had been erected so anybody looking out of the window wouldn't get a clear shot. Miller knew it was overkill, as the windows were down at basement level, but everybody had to cover themselves from the *what if?* factor. The, *what if he got off a shot that ricocheted and hit someone between the eyes?*

The uniform was sitting inside a van. Miller stepped inside and sat down across from him.

'I want you to tell me about the gunman. What he looks like. What he said.'

The uniform looked at him. 'I've been in some fights, but I've never seen the look that this guy gave me. He just had this... *aura* about him, for want of a better word. You know how it is when you're in uniform; you get to size people up very quickly. When he took us into the house, I sized him up in a few seconds First, he acted like we were at the wrong address but the next thing we knew, he had pulled out a shotgun from behind the couch.'

'How many hostages does he have?'

'One of my colleagues. Female. There was a woman sitting on the couch, her hands tied. The man said, *Tell the American I have his wife. If he comes in here, she dies first.* That's all I saw. He sent me out to tell you he wasn't messing about.'

'What did he say to you about getting Hazel Carter?'

'He told me to get somebody to call Hazel Carter. He would only hand over the kids to her.'

'Did you see the kids?'

'No. I didn't hear any noise, either.'

'Was there anybody else in the flat that you could see?'

'No. We were only in the living room.'

'Give me a description of him.'

'You know, I wouldn't believe it if I hadn't seen it with my own eyes; he had a beard and a very badly-fitting wig. I mean, *really* bad. I gave my partner a look and we thought he was eccentric or something.'

'Anything else?'

John Carson

'Big, black glasses. That was it. But it was the wig that stood out.'

'Height?'

'Short. Not small short, but smaller than you and I.'

'It's safe to say that isn't Perry MacKinnon. He's taller than me.'

Purcell came over to Miller. 'Hazel's gone in.'

'Is she armed?'

'No.'

'Jesus. You better have an armed entry team ready to go at the drop of a hat.'

'We've got it sorted. Don't worry.'

Miller left the van, just in time to see the front door closing behind Hazel. Too late now.

CHAPTER 56

The shotgun blast was still ringing in her ears. Hazel couldn't take her eyes off the dead female officer. Turned sharply as two other figures entered the room. Two women.

'Who are you?' Hazel said.

The one behind was pushing the one in front, a gun prodded into her back.

'I'm Marie Anders.'

'Shut up,' the other woman said. Sherri Hilton.

'I remember you from before, but I would never have recognised you. Frank Miller was right; you didn't die.'

'I said, shut up.'

'Right, let's get a move on.'

Mr Blue threw the shotgun back behind the settee. Marie looked at it.

'It's empty and there are no more shells. So, unless you're going to try and use it like a club, I'd forget about it.'

'Maybe I don't need a gun.'

'Very admirable. In fact, if you don't want to come with us, then that's fine too.'

Marie looked at him, waiting for the catch.

'You either, Hazel. You can both wait here. They'll be booting the door down any minute. You can leave with them instead. But if either of you chooses to stay behind, I'll kill one of the girls. If you both stay, I'll–'

'Okay, we get it,' Marie said.

'I bet you wish now you'd taken out Fredrik Torgerson, like I wanted you to.'

'Not really, now that I see what you're capable off,' Marie said.

'How did you get in here?' Hazel asked her.

Mr Blue took out a handgun. 'We're going to show you.'

They led them through the kitchen, and opened a door. They went down into a basement, where another old door was. This was hidden, made to look like old shelves. Sherri led the way, the two women following, with Mr Blue bringing up the rear.

He closed the doors behind him and then he and Sherri brought out flashlights.

Down in the tunnel, they turned left, opposite to the way Marie had come. Mr Blue took the magazine out of the gun and put it in his pocket. Sherri shone the light on the two motorbikes that sat waiting.

'We're not going far, but this is quicker. Marie, get on behind Sherri. Hazel, on behind me. And for the last time, any monkey business and the children die. You see, somebody is waiting for us, and if we don't turn up, he knows to kill them.'

A look passed between Marie and Hazel. An understanding that neither of them would do anything stupid.

Then Mr Blue and Sherri got on the dirt bikes and started them up. The two women hopped on.

Hazel hated motorbikes and held on for dear life as Mr Blue followed Sherri, the buzzing noise of the bikes seeming to be a hundred times louder in the tunnel. The headlights bounced off the walls and more than once, Hazel thought she was going to fall off, but Mr Blue was an expert.

She held on tighter, thinking about her little girl.

Shortly after Hazel went through the door, they all clearly heard the sound of the shotgun going off.

'Shots fired! Lloyd Masters shouted. He was the firearms commander.

Miller and Purcell both ran over to the van where the firearms teams were piling out.

'Has anybody been hit?' Miller shouted.

'They're coming from inside.'

'Get the fucking door in, then!' Purcell shouted.

Eric and Brett Anders were standing close by. 'If he's shot my wife, I'll kill the bastard,' Ander said.

Purcell put a hand on his shoulder. 'You can't go in there.'

The entry team were down the stairs to the front door, covered by snipers, and the door was smashed in. The team were inside. They could hear shouts of *Clear!* Miller expected to hear more gunfire, and his stomach was turning upside down.

'If Hazel's dead, I swear to God, you can shove this fucking job up your arse, Percy. Then that bastard will know what it's like to fuck with me.'

'Don't you think you've had enough from him? Look at the state of your face.'

'It will be a different outcome this time.'

They watched as the team leader came back out of the basement flat, gesturing for Purcell to come and have a look.

Eric Smith and Brett Anders were standing at the side.

'Frank!' Purcell said, as he came back up the steps to street level. 'Come and have a look.'

Eric Smith and Brett Anders followed him.

'What's wrong? Don't tell me–'

'They're gone, Frank.'

'Oh, God, no.'

'No, I mean they're gone. Fucked off. There's no sign of them. The place is empty.'

'What? Gone where?'

'The tunnels,' he said.

'Marie must have been checking out the tunnels and he took her. That means the house they had rented for us connects to this one. And there was another tunnel leading away from this. What the hell are these tunnels anyway?'

'Running underneath here is the old Scotland Street tunnel, when trains used it to get up to Waverley Station. And there was a network of stations that ran from St Giles Cathedral, a station they called *Enlightenment.* Somehow these houses are connected to them.' He looked at Anders. 'Where's the house you were staying at?'

'Round the corner. I didn't realise it at first, but that makes sense.'

'Maybe a station master's house or something. There are so many places under Edinburgh, it's a wonder it hasn't crashed in on itself.'

'Percy, let me make a call. Get somebody into that tunnel though. They can't be that far ahead.' He took out the phone he'd been using and dialled a number.

John Carson

'Ian? Got a minute, my friend?' Ian Powers worked for Neil McGovern and was a computer genius. 'It's for the boss.'

'Sure, Frank. What do you need? I'm at my computer just now.'

'I need to know where the network of tunnels leads to from Scotland Street. I also need to know if there was any other place that Perry MacKinnon owns, somewhere that he could run to.' He told him where he was and what flat he was going into.

'Two minutes.'

Miller started walking towards the basement flat. Less than a minute later, Powers was back on the phone. 'Henderson Row and Henderson Row.'

'What?'

'The tunnels from Scotland Street lead up to Waverley but also on the old network. The trains ran along past the Henderson Row cable winding station. They're connected below ground. And guess what? The old cable winding station was pulled down, leaving the façade, and a small office block was constructed. They sold it to your friend, Mr MacKinnon. Planning permission was given to alter it into a series of offices and operating suites. He's going to turn it into a plastic surgery clinic. A work order was issued a few weeks ago for work to begin last week.'

'Thanks, Ian. I owe you one.' He hung up and looked at Smith. 'I think I know where Emma and Kim are.'

Smith grabbed a hold of his arm. 'Where.'

He told Purcell and Eric what he thought. 'Maybe Anders could go down with your team and show you where to connect with the Henderson Row line. Me and Eric will go to the old cable winding building.'

Back outside, Miller ran for the car they'd come in after Purcell had thrown him the keys.

CHAPTER 57

The motorbikes buzzed through the tunnel, the noise reverberating off the old bricks. Hazel held on for dear life as Mr Blue expertly weaved the bike round the bends. She leaned with him, feeling she had to duck her head. Then the machine started to slow down. The headlights picked out a black, steel wall with a door built into it.

'Get off,' Mr Blue said to her after they had stopped. 'Get that door open.'

She did, and thought about trying to overpower him but those thoughts were superseded by thoughts of getting her little girl back. She walked forward and pulled the large bolt on the door and pulled it open, the hinges grating.

'Go through it.'

She did and Sherri rode through it, followed by Mr Blue. Another part of the tunnel was blocked by another steel wall with a door in it. That door was open. They parked the bikes and Marie got off the back.

Hazel looked at the open door, which lead into a subterranean garage.

'This used to be a platform,' he said. Then looking at Hazel eyeing the doorway. 'Don't even think about it.'

Hazel and Marie looked around. 'Where are the children?'

'Good Lord, you are impatient. We have to go through this other door, into the cable winding area. You know, cable cars were pulled up and down Dundas Street by steel cables here, in the winding house–'

'Spare us the history lesson,' Marie said, and Sherri stepped forward and smacked her with a pistol she had taken out of her own waistband.

Marie fell down, but bounced back though was kept at bay by the pistol.

Mr Blue put the magazine back into the gun. 'Ladies, Sherri will take you to the children now.'

John Carson

'And then what?' Marie said.

'Our job is done here. We'll leave you alone now.' He smiled at Hazel Carter. 'This way, ladies. Since you don't appreciate history, I won't waste my breath on you.' There was a doorway off the old platform that had an old sign on it – *Staff Only*.

'We're not going through there yet. We need to go this way.'

They went through a door and along a series of corridors until they came to the rooms where the children, Kim, and Steffi were being kept.

'Jane!' Hazel said when she saw her daughter. 'Kim! Steffi! Thank God you're alright.'

'Oh my God, it is so good to see you,' Kim said.

'Everything's going to be okay now. You're safe.'

'Not quite. I lied. You see, we can't leave any witnesses,' Mr Blue said.

He and Sherri were both standing looking at the women and children and Hazel held her daughter tighter, knowing there was nothing they could say or do to convince Mr Blue not to shoot them.

She put Jane behind her just as the gun was pointed at her.

CHAPTER 58

'Give me the keys,' Eric Smith said as they ran. Miller knew he was a highly trained driver, having been taught how to get out of tricky situations when escaping. He gave him the keys to the Vauxhall.

They got in and started the car up. Miller winced as he got into the passenger seat. 'That bastard fucked one of my ribs,' he said.

'Did you get it checked out?'

'A friend of mine looked at it. She's a doctor.'

'You know something? I don't care if I die, as long as my little girl lives.'

'And you couldn't have told me that before I gave you the car keys?'

But Smith wasn't listening. He started the car and threw it into reverse, swinging the car round and then shoving it into first gear. 'Guide me, Frank. It's been a long time since I lived here.'

'Follow the road along to the end and then turn right into Dundas Street. We're only thirty seconds away. Or ten, since you're driving.'

Smith accelerated the car hard, punching through the gears, the tyres scrabbling to make a purchase on the cobblestones. Due to the parking on both sides of the street, the road was narrow. Smith carried on from Royal Crescent into Fettes Row, the lights and sirens blaring. A white parcel van turned in and saw the car coming towards him, headlights on full, blasting the horn.

The van pulled into the side, the driver gesticulating with one hand. Miller thought how lucky the driver was that he didn't want to get out for a bit of a road rage fight.

'Turn right here,' Miller said.

Smith pulled in front of a car causing the driver to slam on the brakes and lean on his own horn. They narrowly missed a Lothian Bus coming down Dundas Street. The traffic was stopped at the lights.

'Turn left then it's sharp left, when you get a chance.'

Smith had the car on the other side of the road, blasting the horn, and the drivers didn't move, waiting for him to go round.

Miller cut the siren, as Smith slowed down to make the turn into the narrow street.

'Right. There has to be an access for deliveries when this was an insurance building.'

Smith turned and they saw a steel, roller door for an underground parking garage.

'Duck,' he said, and floored the accelerator. The Vauxhall crashed through the door at high speed, then Smith slammed the brakes on, ducking down.

The windscreen exploded as the car ripped the door off its tracks and it clattered to the concrete floor. The car kept going and hit the back of a parked van. The airbags went off as the car came to a sudden stop. Dust lifted into the air.

'Jesus Christ,' Miller said, opening the car door. He looked over at Smith, who seemed unaffected by it.

'You alright, Frank?'

'I think I just broke another rib.'

They both got out of the car and Miller hunched over, the pain shooting through his side.

The car was wrecked, as was the back of the van.

They looked around the dimly lit garage that was harbour to building materials. Ian Powers had been right about work just getting started on renovations.

They saw a tunnel entrance that had been blocked off by a steel wall with a door in it. It was open and Miller could see a pair of motorbikes inside.

Miller was limping.

'You okay?' Smith asked him again.

'Next time, I'm driving the fucking car.'

Smith moved to one side of the door and waved Miller to the side. Miller was about to tell him he had breached property before, but probably not like Smith had, wearing a gas mask.

'You ready?'

Miller nodded.

'Right. I'll lead the way. You follow, but give me thirty seconds to make sure it's clear.'

'Okay. Go.'

Smith disappeared round the doorway.

CHAPTER 59

'What the hell was that?' Mr Blue asked as they all heard the crashing coming from outside.

'I'll go and see,' Sherri said.

She left the room and disappeared from sight.

'Right, you lot. Come with me, and if there's any monkey business, the kids get it first.'

'We're not going to do shit,' Hazel said.

'What did you say?'

'What, you going to take us out there and execute us one by one? Fuck you. We're done doing what you want.'

Mr Blue put the gun against her head. 'What if I just blow your brains out now?'

'Go ahead. You know what, I would expect nothing less of somebody like you.'

He took the gun away from her head. 'What do you mean, *like me*?'

'The sort who slaps women around. What, you go home to your wife and give her a good belting when she doesn't want to make you a sandwich?'

'I'm not married.'

'I'll bet you've hit a woman before.'

Mr Blue smiled and laughed. 'Of course I have. I've killed more people than you would believe. And got paid for it. Do you know what it's like to serve in Special Forces? No, of course you don't. You've never been in the army, I bet.'

'I have,' Steffi said, stepping closer. 'As a combat medic, I trained with Special Forces.'

'Well, good for you.' He smiled and pointed the gun at Hazel. 'Step back. I'm done talking to you, but you can bet the last pound coin in your purse that I'm not finished dealing with you.'

Steffi walked closer, putting herself between Mr Blue and the two kids. 'It was the same when you took me when I was walking from my flat. Overpowered me and put me in your stinking van. You couldn't stand up to me then. Fucking coward.'

He smiled, unfazed. 'I must say, you scrub up well. If the circumstances were different, I'm sure I could show you a good time.'

'Yeah, I'm sure you could. But I'm not the sort of girl who goes out with raging psychos.'

'But you don't know what you're missing. I can promise you if you went out with me, nobody would ever show you disrespect.'

'I don't need a tough guy to look after me.'

'Agreed. You're a tough, little ex-squaddie.'

'Let the children go,' Kim said. 'You're a tough soldier. Why would you want to hurt them? They can't identify you.'

'Why take the risk?'

'He's a liar,' Marie said. 'A conniving scumbag. He tried to get me and my husband to kill somebody for him.'

'I thought I told you to shut up?' Mr Blue said, gritting his teeth.

'You're a big man with a gun, aren't you?'

'Yeah, I am, so shut the fuck up.' He pointed the gun at her.

Steffi grabbed a hold of his gun and twisted his hand. He tried to headbutt her but only connected with the top of her head.

She shoved him hard, keeping herself close to him, controlling the gun arm. It was pointed away from the room.

'Move!' she shouted. Kim moved as fast as she could with the little girls, Hazel right behind her.

Mr Blue got his arm free and punched Steffi in the face. She punched him back, breaking his nose. Marie stepped forward and kicked him between the legs, then she grabbed hold of the gun and twisted it out of his hand, breaking two fingers. Then she shot Mr Blue in the knee. He fell down onto the floor, screaming.

'You should have known not to fuck with women when it comes to their children,' she said, pointing the gun at his head.

He screamed again just as they all heard a voice shout out to drop the weapon.

CHAPTER 60

Miller felt like he couldn't breathe for a moment. *What's Kim going to think when her ex turns up and saves the day? They'll think you chickened out and let him take all the risks.* He looked round the door and couldn't see anything. Further in was almost complete darkness.

Where the hell had he gone? Never mind, he owed it to Kim to get right in there with Smith. He was about to go through the door when it all happened at once. The motorbike roared into life and the headlight came on. Suddenly the bike was rushing towards him.

Instinct should have made him jump out of the way, but that wasn't his style. As the biker tried to run him down, he stepped to the side and then blindly reached out to the figure aiming the machine right at him.

His hand caught an arm and he held on tightly, being pulled off his feet and thrown across the concrete floor. The rider came off and the bike spun out of control on its side.

Miller landed on his back where he lay winded for a few moments.

The rider got up, took off the helmet and looked at him as he struggled to his knees.

'You always were a fool, Frank Miller,' Sherri said. He hadn't seen her in years and wouldn't have recognised her if he'd passed her in the street.

But he recognised who she had become.

'Sharon Hardy. Or do you still want me to call you Sherri?'

'I left Sherri behind a long time ago.'

'Nice touch, getting Ewan Simmons to put you forward to replace Kim while she was on leave.'

'It was a team effort.'

'I knew you were still alive all these years. That *was* you in Carol's room in the hospital that night, wasn't it? The nurse who waved at me from the roof of the car park.'

John Carson

'Of course it was. I came so close to killing her but then I had a change of heart. They all thought I was dead, so why not just leave it the way it was? It made my life easier. I got as far as her room, then I changed my mind. Just as well, as I saw you coming.'

'You just disappeared.'

'I was still around. I got a little plastic surgery, nothing drastic, just a little nip and tuck.'

'You were working for Perry MacKinnon.'

'And Ewan Simmons.'

'Those two were together that day, fooling around with Rena Joseph.'

'I heard the stories. They killed a little girl and then blamed Miles Laing. Or Leif as he was known then, before they changed his name to protect him.'

'You've been with MacKinnon a long time.'

'I love him, but I don't want to marry him. But I would do anything for him. Me and Faith Hope both adored him.'

'Even after he had that guy, the biker, execute her?'

'What? Shut up, you're lying.'

'Neither Miles Laing nor Bruce Hagan shot her. They tied her up and left her in the ambulance. That man you're working with killed her.'

'He calls himself Mr Blue. It's an old army thing apparently. Simmons was known as Mr Black.'

'Who is Mr Blue?'

'You don't have to know his real identity.'

Miller tried to get to his feet but the pain shot through his guts and he felt he would pass out if he stood up. He needed to get past her to get to the women and children.

'Was it you who attacked me in Rena Joseph's farmhouse? Dressed in your biker gear.'

'No, that was him.'

'I figured. He can fight like a machine.'

'He's ex-SAS. Like Simmons. They knew each other in the army. Served together.'

Then Miller knew who Mr Blue was. 'I know who he is. His name's–'

272

TRIAL AND ERROR

Miller didn't get to finish the sentence before the piece of two-by-four wood slammed into his side, breaking a couple of ribs. He fell onto his side, the pain searing through him like a branding iron.

'You should have fucking stayed out of this, Miller!' Perry MacKinnon screamed. 'You should have walked away.'

Miller struggled to look at him. 'You took my little girl. How could I walk away?' His breath was coming in rasps.

'She's not your little girl! She's not your child!'

'She is my little girl, you bastard!' Miller said, knowing he was about to die.

MacKinnon lifted the piece of wood above his head, ready to bring it down in a fierce, deadly blow.

'I'm going to kill you, Miller!'

CHAPTER 61

Kim was sweating but was holding her little girl's hand. Emma and Jane were crying, their mothers trying to keep them as calm as possible.

'The bad man's not coming,' Hazel said, as they heard the gunshot.

'Jesus Christ,' Kim said, trying to move faster. Round the hallways, which had old lights hanging from the ceiling, lit this time.

'I hope to God we don't get lost,' Kim said, but in truth, she didn't know where they were going. Then they were out on the old train station platform.

'Where to now?' she said.

The tracks had been lifted a long time ago, but it still looked like a railway station. Doors were open on each steel wall that blocked the tunnel, but only one had some kind of light coming through it. They walked down the ramp at the end, each woman holding on to her own child.

They saw the doorway ahead and walked towards the light coming in. They heard raised voices. Then they saw a figure from the shadows leave through the door. Then shouting and screaming.

'Oh my God!' Kim said. 'Was that Frank?'

'I honestly don't know, Kim. I can't make him out.'

'Maybe he's gone after Sherri Hilton.' She turned to Hazel. 'Or Sharon Hardy as we now know her.'

'The bitch. How in God's name did she get to stand in for you?'

'She came highly recommended by Ewan Simmons.'

'Figures. The bastard.'

There were no lights on in the tunnel but the light from the open door was enough to give them a semblance of illumination.

They had just got there when Kim looked and couldn't believe what she was seeing.

The man with the wood wasn't Frank. And now he was walking towards her.

TRIAL AND ERROR

Lloyd Masters shouted a warning as he and his men rounded the corner of the hallway, aiming their guns at Mr Blue.

'Hold your fire!' Purcell said.

'Marie!' Brett Anders shouted and he pushed past the firearms team.

Purcell walked forward. Looked down at the writhing figure of Mr Blue. 'Well, well, Michael Kelly. Not only Ewan Simmons' assistant, but his hired gun. No wonder your face was never shown in the paper or on TV.'

'You know this man?' Anders asked.

'Oh, yes, he's been a part of our Justice Minister's inner circle for quite some time now. Haven't you, Michael.'

They heard somebody approaching and Masters' team lifted their guns.

'It's me, Eric Smith,' he said, coming round the corner.

'Look who we have here,' Purcell said as the firearms team lowered their weapons.

'Michael Kelly,' Eric Smith said. 'I know him. He was one of us.'

'Well, now he's going to be one of them,' Masters said. 'A prisoner. I shouldn't be surprised if the judge orders a whole-life sentence.'

'Where's Kim and Emma?' Smith said.

'Didn't you see them? They left a few minutes ago with the kids.'

'No. There are a lot of corridors there. They must have gone out a different way.'

Marie was off and running.

Smith took off after Marie, followed by Anders.

'Get that bastard up,' Purcell said.

Some of the firearms team dragged Kelly to his feet. He started laughing. 'You won't be able to stop them, you know.'

'What are you talking about?' Purcell said.

Kelly looked him in the eyes. 'Frank Miller's already a dead man. Perry MacKinnon's going to kill him.'

275

CHAPTER 62

Kim put Emma behind her. They had all stepped through the door and were in the garage. Her eyes took in the scene before them; a woman getting on a motorbike; Perry MacKinnon walking towards them with a large piece of wood in his hand. Frank lying bleeding on the floor, unable to get up.

'Frank!' she screamed.

'You fucking meddling bitch!' MacKinnon said, and Kim took her eyes off Miller for a moment.

It was like the last seconds of her life were being played out in slow motion. Miller could hardly move, but he tried to get up anyway. He shouted *No!* at the top of his voice, putting a hand out before he fell back. She saw MacKinnon swing the wood back over his shoulder, his face full of rage. All Kim could think about was shielding her little girl.

Then somebody roughly pushed past her. Marie Anders brought the gun up and fired it while she was running. Once, twice, three times. The bullets were closely grouped into MacKinnon's heart.

The momentum of his back swing carried him right round so that he never got to bring the wood back round. He fell on his back, dead before he hit the concrete floor.

The motorbike shot out of the garage.

Sherri Hilton had escaped again.

Miller watched her go, unable to do anything about it.

The little girls were screaming.

Eric Smith and Brett Anders came running through the door from the tunnel, followed by Purcell. Lloyd Masters came out, his team members dragging Kelly.

'As much as it pains me, we need to get an ambulance for this guy,' he said. 'His lawyers will be having a field day otherwise.'

'You're right, Lloyd. But the first crew to arrive sees to Miller.' Purcell ran over to Miller and got down on his knees. 'Frank, stay with us,' he said, as he saw Miller's eyes flickering. Then Miller had a seizure.

TRIAL AND ERROR

Hazel was already shielding the girls from the sight, making for the door the bike had just left through. Steffi ran past Kim and fell onto her knees. Being an ex-army medic, she knew what she was doing. Smith joined her.

Kim stood and looked at the man who was going to be her husband. He had to live.

One of the firearms team, who was a trained medic, joined them.

They were all working on him when the ambulance crew arrived. Kim turned away and held onto Lloyd Masters.

She only turned back when she heard the words, *everybody clear*.

Then the paddles shocked his heart.

CHAPTER 63

The ward was quiet at this time of night. The last stragglers were gently reminded that visiting time was over for the day. The whole of the Western General was going into sleep mode. The patients on the head injuries ward were never any trouble for obvious reasons.

'Have you done much bank work?' the staff nurse asked the new girl. Bank work meant getting extra shifts through an agency.

'I've done a few.'

'Do you have a lot of experience?'

They were sitting in the nurses' station.

'Oh, yes, I've got plenty.'

'Thank God. The last girl didn't know what she was doing. You know, I'm surprised half of them even get employed, but seeing how short staffed we are, I see why they would take anybody on.'

Sherri Hilton smiled and thought she might just do two for the price of one if this stupid bitch didn't shut up.

Then she looked up as the blonde patient went back into her room, her baby bump still showing proudly. She'd make her pay.

How the fuck could Michael Kelly have screwed things up? Being charged with murder and abduction. Ewan Simmons' case was reported in the news of course, but they were being a bit more hush hush about it. Perry MacKinnon's death had hit her the hardest. She had loved the man. Faith Hope was careless. Sherri had liked her a lot, but she had let her guard down after getting those two morons out of the hospital.

She didn't know what had happened to Miles Laing or Bruce Hagan, but that was of little concern. Tonight, it was all about payback. Kim Smith was going to die, then she, Sherri, would disappear forever. She had enough money to get her face altered again. It had worked the first time, so why wouldn't it work again?

She had noticed that there weren't any guards on Kim's room. They probably thought that she, Sherri, was long gone and even if they didn't think that, they probably figured that she wouldn't come back again, like she had when Carol was here.

TRIAL AND ERROR

How wrong they were.

'Would you mind doing the rounds?' the nurse asked Sherri. Which meant going around and checking blood pressure or getting them a drink or just checking on them.

'Sure. I'll do it right now.' Sherri got up from the nurse's station and started at one end of the ward, going into the rooms and doing what she was expected to do.

Kim's room was just around the corner from the station. She couldn't be seen from there.

She opened the door and slipped inside. A little light was on behind the bed. Kim had slipped under the covers, she could see. She took out the syringe, and stood looking down at the bed. The bitch was sleeping and now she wouldn't ever wake up.

'Bye Kim. I hope you think that Frank Miller was worth it.' She stepped towards the bed and was about to go around to add the liquid to her drip when the bathroom door opened.

'Kim's not here,' Marie Anders said, bringing the gun out. She opened the dressing gown and the prosthetic training belly fell to the floor.

Sherri pulled the covers back and saw Steffi Walker wearing the wig. She turned towards Marie.

'Go ahead, honey, and I'll give you a taste of what Perry MacKinnon got.'

The door opened and Percy Purcell walked in. 'Now, that's not being very sociable,' he said to Sherri. 'You should have stayed away, just like the last time.' Uniforms rushed in and cuffed her, taking the scalpel from her hand.

'I'm saying nothing. You know that? Nothing! You lot think you're so smart.'

'Well, put it this way; you won't be waving from the roof of the car park this time. Take her away.'

Sherri relaxed for a moment and smiled at Purcell. 'This isn't over. You'll see. It isn't over.'

Marie Anders relaxed and handed the gun over to Percy. 'I wish it had been loaded.'

'Thanks for agreeing to help us out,' he said.

'No problem. Frank said she would turn up. How is he tonight, by the way?'

279

John Carson

'He's doing well. He'll need a wee while to recover, but he and Kim are going to have a break when he gets out of the hospital. They said they're going away for a long weekend, just them and Emma.'

'They deserve it. Hazel told me about what's going on. I hope it all works out for them.'

'They're meant for each other. He'll do the right thing now. He realises he doesn't want to lose her. He thought he was watching her about to be beaten to death. You saved her life.'

'Hey, I was just there at the right time.'

'Brett should be proud of you.'

'He is. He was worried about me doing this, but we've been through worse together.'

Purcell smiled. 'Come on, let's get you out of here and back to your husband.'

CHAPTER 64

Two weeks later

Miller knew he was lucky to be alive. The broken rib had almost gone through his heart and then it would have been all over.

He was using a walking stick to get about. It seemed that almost every inch of his body ached. He could have done without coming here, but Robert Molloy was insistent.

Miller climbed the steps to the entrance of *The Club*. The evening was cool but just as busy with tourists. It would hopefully calm down a bit soon.

He wished he had seen Sherri Hilton's face when Marie Anders had pulled out the gun, and Sherri had realised she had been duped. She had told Purcell that it wasn't over. Maybe she thought that one day shoe too would escape and come back at them. Bitter words from a sore loser.

The doormen were standing at the doors, a third man waiting for him.

'This way, Detective Miller, sir,' he said and walked in front of Miller. He was escorted through the back and then slowly up the stairs. He'd need a beer by the time he got to the top of Mount Everest.

The bouncer knocked on Molloy's door and waited for the answer.

'Detective Miller for you, sir.'

'Show him in.'

The man smiled and shut the door behind Miller, who was sweating with the exertion of climbing the stairs.

Robert Molloy was sitting behind his desk. A woman sat on the couch with a drink in her hand. She stood when he came in.

'Hello, Frank,' she said.

Miller paused for a second. 'Hello, Carol.'

'Sampson, get Detective Miller a drink. And show him to a seat. Can't you see he's walking with a stick? Ignoramus.'

John Carson

'I apologise, Inspector Miller. This way, sir.'

Miller followed him over to a comfortable leather chair, where he watched Carol sit down. The woman he'd been chasing. Was this a dream? Was he in a coma? Or worse, had he died and this was him meeting his wife again?'

No, this wasn't Carol.

Sampson handed Miller a bottle of beer and left the room.

'Frank, allow me to introduce my daughter, Venus Molloy.'

Miller held the cold bottle in his hand. Took a sip of the beer to lubricate his dry mouth before speaking. 'You're Carol's twin.'

'Yes, I am. I'm sorry about running away from you all the time, Frank. I wanted to talk to you, and to my dad, but I lost my bottle every time. Tonight, I was determined that I wasn't going to run any more. I came to see Dad, and I wanted him to get you here so I could talk to you both.'

'Mission accomplished.' Miller drank more beer, looking at the woman who was the exact image of his dead wife. She wasn't wearing jeans and a white shirt tonight, but a smart dark blue dress, with a dress blazer.

'You know what happened to Carol?'

'Yes, Dad told me. I haven't told him my story. I wanted to wait until you were here.'

'Go ahead and tell us,' Robert Molloy said.

Venus was holding a glass in her hand. Water. 'I don't drink,' she said, smiling and holding up the glass. She took a deep breath and blew it out.

'My mum was diagnosed with breast cancer a few years ago. She thought it was about time she told me my life story. That she was with Dad here, and she got pregnant. He couldn't marry her obviously. Dad wanted the baby to have a good home, so he arranged for a detective to adopt her. What he didn't know was, she had twins. She was worried that the detective wouldn't take the baby, and she would have to give both of us away, so she gave Carol away, and kept me. It was hard to split up twins, but though she was able to look after me, she couldn't have afforded to look after two.'

Miller listened intently, looking at her face, finding it hard to believe this wasn't Carol. 'I have to admit, I thought I was going off my head. I thought I was chasing a ghost.' He drank more beer, the walking stick still resting against his leg. 'It's a pity you didn't get to meet Carol. You would have liked her.'

She looked at Molloy before looking back at him. 'I did meet her. A few months before she died. It was fantastic. She told me all about you. You hadn't been married long, and I wanted to meet you so badly, but we had to take it easy. We were going to meet up after Christmas, in the new year, but she died on Guy Fawkes night. I was devastated. She showed me where you lived. I told her I wanted her to meet our mum. She wanted to, especially since she had cancer. But my mum passed away suddenly. Carol came to the funeral.'

'I remember her saying she was going to a friend's mother's funeral. That was your mum?'

'Yes. Carol was very supportive.'

'I wonder why she didn't tell me?'

'Because of her adopted family. She was planning to of course, but the time had to be right.'

'And now she's come back into my life,' Molloy said.

'How's Michael taking all of this?'

'Like somebody's playing with his favourite toy. But he'll come around.'

Venus stood up. 'As I said to Robert, I don't want anything. Mum left me the house, I have my job. I just wanted to meet my family, that's all. And you're family too, Frank. So now I'll be on my way. It was nice meeting you both.'

Miller struggled to his feet, leaning heavily on the walking stick. 'I don't know about Molloy there, but I would like you to meet my family. My fiancée and her little girl. She's pregnant. And my dad and his girlfriend.'

'Me too,' Molloy said. 'Michael will be happy to welcome you into the family. After he gets over the shock.'

'It's all a bit strange for me this.'

'Were you heading to Fife the night I saw you get off the train?' Miller asked.

'Yes. I live in a little mobile home park up from Hillend. It's not much, but it's home.'

'Will you please come and see me again?' Molloy said. 'We can have lunch on my boat. I can even send a car to pick you up.'

John Carson

Venus laughed. 'I live five minutes from the train station. But yes, alright, I'd like that.'

'You're welcome too, Miller,' Molloy said.

'I'd like to have a coffee with Venus one day, since I know I won't have to run after her. Then maybe later you could meet my fiancée.'

'I'd like that. If she could get over the fact I look exactly like your ex-wife.'

'Give her time.' Miller put the beer bottle down and went over to Venus and gave her a hug. It almost felt like he was hugging Carol again. He held on tightly. Closed his eyes. Went back in time for a few moments.

'Nice to meet you,' he said.

Aren't you going to stay and have a few drinks?' Molloy asked.

'Thanks, Robert, but I'm getting fitted for a suit in the morning.'

CHAPTER 65

A week later

'That's it, just a little bit closer,' the photographer said.

'Frank, I am so proud of you. I really mean that.' Norma Banks held onto Miller's arm.

He turned and winked at her. 'Don't cry again, Norma. We talked, and it's all water under the bridge.'

She smiled and held on even tighter.

'Will you two stop yapping?' Neil McGovern said, holding on more gently to his daughter's arm.

The photographer bounced around, taking photos.

Next were the parents of the groom.

'How are you feeling, Mrs Miller?' he whispered to her.

'I couldn't be better, Mr Miller.' She smiled at him.

Samantha Willis came up and slipped her arm through Miller's, while Jack took Kim's.

'I can't thank you enough, Sam,' Miller said.

'You've thanked us a thousand times. You're very welcome. My Scottish son-in-law. I love being part of your family.'

After it was their turn, they went inside. Emma had been outside and was now playing with Jane.

The hotel was on the banks of a loch in the Scottish Highlands. The sun had stayed out and the weather was warm.

'This is just perfect,' Kim said. 'I love you, Frank.'

'I love you too, honey.' He turned to kiss her, then winced.

'Is your leg sore?'

'Yes. But I'm okay. I'm healing more slowly than I thought.'

'Do you need your walking stick?'

'And have them think you've married a ninety-year-old? No thanks. I'm getting there.'

They stood looking out onto the loch in the distance, over the expanse of green lawn.

'This was so good of Sam and your dad,' she said.

'She is so good for him. I've never seen him so happy.'

She leaned in close. 'God, Frank, I keep replaying that day over and over in my mind. I thought you were–'

He put a finger on her lips. 'Don't say the word. All those people kept me alive until the paramedics got there. Then they did a brilliant job. Everybody did.'

'They gave me back to you.'

'And Marie Anders stepped in, let's not forget. Have you heard from them again?'

'They sent us a card. They're taking their little girls to live in New York. They're moving in a couple of weeks when they find a place. They want us to go over and visit.'

'I liked it when I went there with your dad. But that was business. Maybe we could visit at Christmas time when the lights are on.'

'That would be wonderful. But maybe next year when the little one is a year old.'

He smiled. Seeing Venus was the best remedy he'd had since Carol had died. Knowing that she had flesh and blood still living that he could talk to was the best medicine.

'There you are, you two!' a voice said from behind them. Percy Purcell.

'You know the term *Best Man* is just a figure of speech?' Miller said.

'Ha! You wish, Miller.' He walked up and put his arm around Miller. 'Wee bugger. Don't you ever do that to me again.'

'I hope you didn't give me mouth-to-mouth.'

'You'll never know. I swore the others to secrecy.'

'Well, I for one don't care if you did, Percy,' Kim said. 'He's my husband now, thanks to you all.'

Percy put his arm around her too and led them back inside. 'There are a lot of people waiting to have a word with you before the meal. And thanks again for inviting my old man.'

'We like Lou,' Kim said.

'I told him to be on his best behaviour. But all the gang's here; Hazel, Jane, Steffi, Julie. I believe Paddy Gibb is propping up the bar, along with Andy Watt.'

'Just like a boy's night out, then?'

TRIAL AND ERROR

'Exactly. But I get to dance with this lovely lady. Don't be hogging her all night.'

'You've never seen me trying to dance with a walking stick, have you?'

Steffi and Hazel came over when they saw Miller and his new bride coming into the room through the French doors.

'I am so happy for you,' Hazel said.

'Thank you.' He kissed her on the cheek.

'Me too, boss,' Steffi said.

'Thank you.' He gave her a kiss too. 'I heard that you were instrumental in saving my life. I can't thank you enough, Steffi.'

'Don't mention it.' She smiled but he could see her eyes glistening.

'And that was after you ladies took down Michael Kelly.'

'It was a team effort. But he said he was going to hurt the kids. It was game over for him then.'

'He and Simmons are going away for a long time, or they will be.'

'Hey, what's all this talking shop?' Lou Purcell said. 'That poor lassie's needing to put her feet up.'

'See? A couple of shandies and he's away with the fairies.'

'Well, I've news for you; I'm staying sober tonight. Elizabeth says I have to be on my best behaviour.' He gave Kim a kiss. 'You look beautiful.'

'Thank you, Lou.'

Miller walked through the groups of people, shaking hands, moving slowly, doling out a kiss to each cheek that was presented until he eventually got to the bar.

'Here he is,' Paddy Gibb said. 'Here's to you and Kim, son.' They passed Miller his own glass and they all toasted him.

'I wish Bruce was here,' Miller said.

'At least he didn't have to go back to the asylum,' Watt said. 'Now he's in the Royal Scottish in Morningside.'

'Aye, I think Hazel might have felt put out if he was here,' Gibb said. 'His new wife is by his side now.'

'They both saved my life, he and Miles. Christ, who would have thought my life would have been on the line twice within a week.'

287

'You should have been married to *my* missus,' Gibb said.
'I'll vouch for that,' Watt said. 'Right old boiler she was.'
'Hey, that's my wife you're talking about.'
'Ex-wife.'
They both laughed. 'And to the Lord we thank it.'
'I'll catch up with you later, ' Miller said.
'Save your energy, lad,' Gibb said. 'Don't be wasting it on dancing or anything.'

Miller walked back to his bride. Watching Perry MacKinnon about to kill her with a piece of wood would always send a shiver down his spine every time he thought of it. He owed so many people a debt of gratitude that he would never be able to repay.

Jeni Bridge caught him and gave him a kiss. 'Congratulations, Frank.'

'Thanks, ma'am.'

He made it back to Kim as people were starting to get seated at their tables.

'Shall we take our seats, Mrs Miller?'

'I'd be delighted to, Mr Miller.'

Miller heard a sudden commotion and then a scream. He looked over to the entrance to the hall and saw a man walk in. He was dressed scruffily, with unkempt hair.

He recognised him but couldn't place him.

But it wasn't the way the man was dressed that caught Miller's attention.

It was the gun he was holding.

He jumped in front of Kim as the first shots rang out.

TRIAL AND ERROR

AUTHOR'S NOTE

Thank you for reading the new Frank Miller. If you could please leave a review on Amazon, that would be great. Each and every one is appreciated.

I would like to thank, Julie Stott, Wendy Haines, Trace Hammond, Jeni Bridge, Fiona Jackson, Evelyn Bell, Louise Unsworth-Murphy and Barbara Bartley for sticking with Miller through thick and thin.

Thanks to my wife, who keeps me on the straight and narrow. And to my daughters, Stephanie and Samantha.

Thanks to Lothian Buses, for telling me how video is retrieved from a bus. Although I was a driver with LRT many moons ago, the buses didn't have cameras back then!

I have always been fascinated with the railway tunnels that run underneath Edinburgh, and wanted to use them in a book. I have used literary license and played around with the stations to suit the story, but the tunnels do exist. Maybe not in the way I describe them, but they're there.

I would like to thank a gentleman – who shall remain unnamed – who gave me his opinion on how warrants are executed in Scotland. Many thanks my friend.

And a very special thanks go to you, the reader, for accompanying me on this journey.

'Til next time!

John Carson
New York
December 31 2017

Printed in Great Britain
by Amazon